JUNO DAWSON

Margot & Me

HOT
KEY
BOOKS

First published in Great Britain in 2017 by
HOT KEY BOOKS
80–81 Wimpole St, London W1G 9RE
www.hotkeybooks.com

ISBN: 978-1-4714-0608-9
also available as an ebook

1

This book is typeset using Atomik ePublisher
Printed and bound by Clays Ltd, St Ives Plc

Hot Key Books is an imprint of Bonnier Zaffre Ltd,
a Bonnier Publishing company
www.bonnierpublishing.com

Supported using public funding by
ARTS COUNCIL
ENGLAND

LOTTERY FUNDED

Mum, Dad, Joanne, Jan, Grandma and Grandad,
thank you for your support over the last year.

'Life can only be understood backwards; but it must be lived forwards.'

Søren Kierkegaard, 1843

Chapter 1

'The problem with young people today,' Margot said about an hour ago, 'is that, from birth, every single one has been told they are somehow special.' We were at the Welcome Break motorway services, pacing back and forth on the grassy verge, stretching stiff legs.

'And what's wrong with that?' I asked, rising to the bait like a gormless goldfish.

'Well, Felicity, when the vast majority are then faced with their own mediocrity, those few *truly* extraordinary individuals are drowned out by their entitled whining.'

Like I have *no* doubt who *that* was aimed at. She hates me and always has.

When you think of grandmothers, you imagine cuddly old ladies with mohair cardigans, tissues up their sleeves and an endless supply of Werther's Originals. Kindly, peppermint-scented women knitting in rocking chairs, right? Maybe even a blue rinse and wrinkly cheeks you just want to squidge! My *other* grandma fits this description in every way, but not Margot. Nope. Margot is something else.

'What *is* that smell?' I pinch my nostrils shut, wind up the window and mouth-breathe. It *reeks*. Vomit and cheesy feet and wet garbage *at the same time*.

'Muck spreading,' Margot says curtly, not taking her eyes off the road. 'Country air: it's good for you. Take deep breaths.'

'Foul. I'm gonna puke,' I mutter, and put my headphones back on. I find it very hard to believe that Margot and me share any of the same genetic make-up.

Kill me now, I swear. Our conversation about manure is literally the first words we've shared since we crossed the Severn Bridge, and those were about whether or not Princess Diana's funeral was 'a bit much'. Mum is napping up front and I'm crunched into the corner of the back seat, pinned to the door by a sun, moon and stars duvet wrapped in a bin bag. I suppose it's my own fault for insisting on bringing *my* duvet, but I want as many knick-knacks from home as possible.

Margot, who will not tolerate Gran, Grandma, Granny or even Grandmother, drives like an android, the seat at ninety degrees and her arms locked at the elbow. Somewhere near the M25, I asked if we could have the radio on and was flatly told no, so I'm listening to my CD Walkman instead. I have to rotate the only two CDs I haven't packed.

About an hour back, we swapped the M4 for meandering country lanes and now we're truly in the middle of nowhere. Major bummer. So far, South Wales reminds me of camouflage: few buildings, just patchwork green fields stitched together by crumbly walls. Endless boring valleys peak and trough, the road twisting through the hills like an unravelled grey ribbon. I squish my face against the window and watch my breath steam up the glass.

My head is a gumball machine filled with questions. How can I be here? Why are we leaving London *now* when Mum's better? How can this be my life? Why am I like totally cursed? Am I being punished for sins in a past life? Unless I was literally Satan, this punishment seems way OTT. This must be how Dorothy felt when she woke up back in Kansas. No Yellow Brick Road; no Emerald City; no witches, good or otherwise. Just wall-to-wall suckitude.

In the condensation on the window, I draw a sad face with my finger. At least my nails are nice. Hard Candy – Iced Flamingo.

I close my eyes and imagine it's all a film: cosmopolitan city girl (with A+ fashion sense, natch) has to go live on a farm while her wicked grandmother cares for her recuperating mum. I'd be played by Jennifer Love Hewitt, Sarah Michelle Gellar or some other girl with three names, and Keanu Reeves would be the swarthy farmhand next door who takes me into the barn to deflower me.

The idea is dimly exciting and I wonder if I might be able to salvage the sorry situation. But when I open my eyes, all I see is bleak. Bleakety bleak, bleak. It's like a freaking Brontë novel out here. *Wuthering Valleys*. Six months, I tell myself, it's only six months. Mum *promised*.

But a lot can happen in six months. Back home, Xander and I weren't *exactly* together any more, but I can practically hear Tiggy sharpening her talons, ready to sink them into his flesh the second my back's turned. I reckon our 'never with exes' rule probably leapt out the window the second I left Zone 6.

The Land Rover shudders over a cattle grid and I realise Mum is craning around in her seat and waving at me. Her hair is slowly growing back after the chemo – fine baby-hair that just covers her scalp – but she still chooses to wear the wig: A 'sassy shag' not unlike Monica from *Friends*. It's real human hair and cost a lot of money. Still looks hella wiggy though. I haven't told her that, obviously. 'Fliss!'

I pull my headphones off. 'What?'

'We're here!'

'What?' I wipe the face off the window and take a look. Nooooooo. No. Nope. This cannot be it. It looks like a nuclear apocalypse happened. There's nothing to see.

'Welcome to Mari-Morgan Farm,' says Margot as we bounce along the dirt track. Drab structures sprout up as we pass over a bump and trundle downhill. Pressing my head to the window, I squint to get a look at my new – temporary – home.

'Is this it?' The words pop out before I can stop them. This is the first time I've clapped eyes on the farm. We were *supposed* to visit numerous times. If I'm remembering right, Mum had just recovered from the first bout of cancer when Margot moved here and we were all set to come up two summers ago – and then came Cancer: The Sequel so we stayed in London.

'Felicity!' Mum chides.

'Sorry! That's not what I meant . . . I just thought it was going to be bigger. I mean, when you hear farmhouse . . .'

'It's plenty big enough,' Margot says shortly. You really hear the full stops in her sentences.

The tyres crunch to a halt and I step out of the car, my Mary Janes narrowly avoiding a muddy puddle the colour of cappuccino. I'm greeted by a solemn, ivy-strangled block of a farmhouse. Stone grey as the sky, it's as final as a tombstone.

4

Like a child's drawing, it has a red front door, four evenly spaced sash windows and a chimney which will no doubt billow smoke. 'Oh, it's lovely,' Mum says. 'The views must be phenomenal.' She steadies herself against the car.

'Come along,' Margot says, going to her aid. 'Let's get you out of the cold.'

'Mother, relax! I can manage.'

'Rot. Inside at once. I'll put the kettle on while Felicity brings the cases in.'

'By myself? As if.' I gesture at my shoes and houndstooth miniskirt.

Margot's flint eyes cut me down like a scythe. 'I'm quite sure you'll cope. I suggest you hurry along. It's going to rain.'

No, I mean it: kill me now.

The inside of the farmhouse is as bogus as the outside. Once I've dragged cases, boxes, duvet and holdalls into the dim, narrow hall, with plenty of dramatic huffing and sighing, I investigate. There's trippy patterned wallpaper as far as the eye can see. God, it's enough to give you a migraine. While Margot and Mum talk in the lounge, I venture upstairs, taking care not to trip up on the tatty carpets.

My room is the smallest, with pink daisy wallpaper and room only for a single bed, a bookcase and a painfully slender wardrobe. Not so much a walk-in as a coffin. I estimate it'll take only about forty per cent of my *jackets*, never mind anything else.

The room, tomb, whatever, smells damp and earthy, like no one's breathed the air in a long time and it's gone stagnant. It's

5

freezing too. I note too late there's no central heating, only a sad, free-standing electric heater. Bonanza.

How is living in *actual history* going to help Mum feel better? I flop onto the bed, mattress springs protesting, and blink back tears. They burn and push behind my eyes. I fight the urge to stamp my feet. I told her this was a terrible idea, but she wouldn't listen.

Chemotherapy, as miraculous and wonderful as it is, cures you by almost killing you. After two years – on and off – of watching Mum waste away, lose her hair, including her eyelashes (they don't show that on TV), throw up all the time *and* not be able to do a single thing to help, I thought now was the time to get back to normal. I know it sounds a bit princess-like, but we did it – together . . . we got through it – together . . . and our reward is to come *here*. I love how Margot gets to swoop in like Supergran and be the hero *now* when I've been helping Mum in and out of the bath, cleaning the house and fetching all the groceries for like a year. How does that work?

A determined tear squeezes its way out. Good thing my mascara is waterproof.

'Felicity!' Margot calls up the stairs. 'Are you coming down for tea?'

'Just a minute.' It takes me all sixty seconds to breathe steadily and halt the tears.

I'm not finished exploring. There are five doors on the long upstairs landing. I have a little nosy around. I'm next to the bathroom, and I see Margot's room and the larger guest bedroom that Mum will have. I cross to the last door and press down on the handle. I push and pull but it's locked. All I can think is that it's an office or attic. I give it a jiggle to make sure. Oh, there's something *irresistible* about a locked attic door. I bet it's where Margot keeps the bodies.

'What are you doing?' Right on cue, Margot's shadow swings around the top of the stairs like she's frigging Nosferatu or something.

'What's in here?' I ask.

'It's just the attic, and you have no call to be up there.' And that's that, although I am of course now *twice* as keen to explore. I give the locked door one last look. Our time will come. 'The tea is stewing. Come along.'

I follow her to a murky lounge and am relieved to find there is at least a television. It's an antique, and there's no video machine, let alone a DVD player. I'm guessing cable is totally out of the question, but there *is* a TV. At this stage, I'll take whatever I can get. The rest of the furniture – all brown . . . *brown, why?* – is old but unfussy and functional. The mood perhaps wouldn't be so Prozac if it weren't for the thick net curtains barricading half of the light. It's like the decor is actively repelling happiness. At least a teapot in a knitted cosy waits on a low coffee table and the whole house smells of toast.

'Here we go.' Margot carries a tray through from the kitchen at the back of the house. 'There's nothing tea and toast won't remedy. Made the jam myself.'

It does look delicious – the bread thick and crusty, the jam purply-black with little seeds in.

'This is wonderful. Too much,' Mum says, already curled up on the sofa, covered in a colourful blanket – I suspect crocheted by Margot.

'Nonsense. I make the bread too. I don't have the luxury of a Waitrose on my doorstep, do I? Look at you – you need feeding up.'

A ghost of her former smile crosses Mum's lips. 'Like a Christmas turkey? Who'd have believed it?! My mother, in the middle of the wilderness, totally self-sufficient. If only Dad were alive to see it!'

Margot sits proudly in the armchair opposite. She wears jodhpurs and a cashmere claret jumper with a blouse underneath. She's grown her hair out. When I was little she always had a neat bob, but it's wild and wiry now and she's stopped dying it, the blonde now silvery white. I've seen old photos of her; she's always been striking, but more 'handsome' than pretty. She's taller than Mum or me, which only adds to her scariness. I suppose some would say she was statuesque, which works because, like a statue, she's cold as marble. Always has been. I know she held me when I was a baby because I've seen pictures, but I don't think I *remember* a single hug.

'I've got everything I need, thank you kindly. Eggs, veggies, meat, even goat's milk.'

I scrutinise the stripy little jug sitting next to the teapot. 'Is that from a goat? Gross.'

'No, that's from the farm down the road. Dewi Allen delivers me a pint a day. Not that there's anything wrong with goat's milk, mind.'

'I never in a million years thought this is where you'd end up. I always saw you retiring to the Med,' Mum says, taking a sip from a Welsh dragon mug.

That would have made more sense. Until a few years back, Margot lived in a très chic townhouse near Hampstead Heath.

8

Every morning, even on the coldest winter days, she would start the day with a bracing swim in the ladies' pond. When I was little, I remember big shoulder pads and big hair; electric blue stilettos and a briefcase. When we went to visit on a Sunday, I'd play with Grandad in the garden – they had a badminton net and a pond with bright orange koi carp – while Mum and Margot had coffee on the terrace. After Grandad died – cancer again – I was told to take my homework or a book to read so I didn't 'bother Margot'.

She's nothing like my Grandma Baker. She's *lovely*, and gives me a pound coin every time I see her, but since her hip replacement she's moved into my Uncle Simon's house near Margate. We've hardly seen her since Mum got sick.

Seemingly on a whim a couple of years ago, Margot took retirement from the newspaper she edited and announced she was giving it all up to live like some sort of hippy motorway-protester on a smallholding in Wales. We were like . . . OK . . . whatever. See ya, wouldn't wanna be ya.

Margot busies herself with building a fire in the fireplace. I've never lived anywhere with an open fire and find myself entranced, watching her place the kindling into the hearth and stacks logs up around it. 'Are you mad?' she says to Mum. 'I can't think of anything worse than slowly drying out like a raisin with all the other ex-pats. I've been looking forward to this for thirty years at that newspaper. Ha! Would you look at that!' She sets fire to a rolled-up sheet of the newspaper she dedicated her life to and touches it to the kindling. 'Poetic.'

I already know the answer, but I ask anyway. 'Do you have the Internet yet?'

'Pardon?'

When did she leave the paper? I guess they wouldn't have had even basic dial-up back then. 'Like the World Wide Web? It connects your computer to the telephone so you can send people messages.'

Margot laughs heartily. 'I know what it is, Felicity. I'm not senile. I don't have a computer. If I never see another one of those infernal things it'll be too soon.'

'I . . . I brought my laptop . . .'

'Fliss,' Mum says with finality, 'we'll sort all that stuff out later. Can we just get settled in, please?'

It's worrying how Mum still goes from awake to exhausted in a matter of minutes. Her face is suddenly grey. 'Sorry,' I say.

'You won't have long to be bored, Felicity. There's always plenty to do on the farm, and you start school on Monday.'

I look to Mum. Plenty to do on the farm? Do I *look* like Little Bo Peep? Also . . . Monday? I was told I could have some time to settle in. 'On Monday . . . ?'

Margot replies as abruptly as ever. 'Yes. What are you waiting for? You've already lost a week. Can't have you missing great chunks of your education – you did quite enough of that while your mother was in hospital.'

Panic flutters in my stomach. 'I just thought . . .'

'Fliss, it's for the best,' Mum puts in. 'We need to get you back into a routine.'

'But I don't even have a uniform yet.'

Margot sits back in her armchair and smiles a cruel smile. 'You can buy the uniform from the school. They've said you can go in civvies for the first day. All taken care of, my dear, all

10

taken care of. With your mother so sick, I imagine it's been a while since anyone told you no, Felicity Baker. Well, that stops now. Do you understand?'

'Yes.' In that moment, something red hot burns in my heart and what I understand is that I actually hate her. I guess, in this case, the farmhouse missed the Wicked Witch by a couple of inches.

Every night, before bed, I brush my hair with a sturdy tortoiseshell paddle. A hundred strokes. It was how I learned to count to a hundred. Oh, my hair is my thing, let it go. Naturally mahogany brown, it used to skim my bottom, but I had it taken midway down my back when that became a bit little-girlish. Also, Zoë Hinckley once told me I was dipping the ends in poop bacteria every time I sat on a toilet seat.

I spend the rest of the evening organising my new room into some semblance of a space I can exist in. For now, I don't suppose there's much I can do about the hideous wallpaper. It's like a hallucinogenic seventies Pucci nightmare, and it's a safe bet Margot hasn't redecorated since she bought the farm. As predicted, about half of my clothes will have to squat in Mum's wardrobe.

Edgar – Mum's handsome old bear – sits on my pillow. On my bedside table I've placed my framed photo of Dad. I know it sounds like totally awful, but I don't think I actually remember him. I don't think I ever remembered him. He was knocked off his bike outside Euston station and killed when I was three. Every once in a while I have a flash of something . . . his beard . . . a piggyback . . . but I honestly don't know if they're actual memories or memories of photographs I've grown up with. This photo shows us at London Zoo, me – all rosy red cheeks and gappy teeth – gleefully perched on Dad's shoulders, with a giraffe eating leaves in the background. How can I not remember that? I look so happy.

I've hung my portrait of the *other* Margot, Margot Fonteyn, over my bed. The best ballerina of all time ever. In the photograph, from the 1958 ballet *Ondine*, she's en pointe, skirts billowing behind her. Fingers outstretched and elegant. She's perfection. It also covers a chunk of the wallpaper. I'm not one for putting posters all over my walls though; I think that's cheap and nasty.

There's a brusque knock on my door and Margot barges in. She leaves a salmon-pink hot-water bottle at the foot of my bed and looks at the hairbrush in my hand with disdain. 'Vanity,' she says simply, and leaves. I close my eyes. So this is how it's going to be. Well, I'm certainly not going to give her a reaction, if that's what she's after.

I finish my hundred strokes and pop down the landing to wish Mum goodnight. I find her already sleeping, propped up by cushions. She's passed out while reading, the latest Jilly Cooper resting in her lap. She's so bony, I have no trouble laying her flat and she doesn't stir. I put the bookmark in her book so she doesn't lose her place, kiss her on the forehead and turn out the lamp. I've put her to bed like this a hundred times.

Downstairs, I hear Margot clattering pots and pans in the kitchen. Although it's still early, I'd rather stick a compass in my eye than hang out with her, so I decide to call it an early night. After my double bed back home, the bed is so small,

no room to roll around and get comfy. I'm scared I'll fall out.
I'm sure I once read about a girl who rolled out of bed in her
sleep and actually died. I lie awake for what feels like hours.
I hear Margot come to bed and switch the landing light off.
My heart is in my throat and I'm alert, hardly able to close my
eyes. It takes me a while to work out what's wrong.

It's *too* quiet. Way too quiet and way too dark.

The night is the thickest oil-slick black. I can't see *anything*
and I'm panicking. No amber glow from city street lights,
too cloudy for the moon. No wailing sirens or all-night pizza
delivery men zipping past my bedroom on scooters.

I don't like it.

Oh, this is ridiculous! I'm behaving like a two-year-old.
Scared of the dark! It's horrible though; I can't see past the end
of my nose. I can't take it. I get out of bed and fumble, arms
out, to where I think I put my CD player. I flick it on to the
radio and swivel the tuner. Eventually I come to a local station
and there's a phone-in called *Late-Night Love*. People can ring
up and dedicate a song to their wife or boyfriend or whatever.

'And the next request,' says a woman with a voice suitable
for only late-night radio or sex chat lines, 'comes from Ian in
Swansea. He'd like to dedicate this song to Candice. Sorry for
all the late nights, he says, I'll make it up to you in Benidorm.
It's "If You Leave Me Now" by Chicago . . .'

Perfect. The song starts and I turn the volume low, so only
I can hear it. I return to bed, focusing on the dim blue glow
coming from the display. I clutch Edgar to my chest and let
love-song lyrics fill my head, waiting for my eyelids to go heavy.

Chapter 2

I don't know why I'm surprised that the shower's rubbish, but the water pressure is about as effective as a thirsty kitten licking my head. Washing my hair is going to take hours. Worse still, the bathtub is hardly big enough to stretch out in. I suppose at least there *is* a bath.

My favourite indulgence is a piping hot bath with a cool flannel across my forehead. I don't know where I got the idea from, but there's nothing quite like it for making me feel like queen of the goddamn world. I can't imagine ever feeling very regal in here. Everything, and I mean everything, in the poky room is avocado green, right down to the furry toilet-seat cover.

My new mantra: *It's only six months*.

That said, I suspect I'll make peace with the scrambled eggs and bacon that greet me when I go downstairs. Mum is already at the rustic wooden table in the kitchen, Margot flitting around her like a hummingbird, pouring tea from the teapot. 'Come along, Felicity, you're not at a bed and breakfast. It'll go cold.'

'It's Sunday,' I say, taking my place at the table. 'And it took about an hour to get my hair wet.'

'Fliss . . .' Mum warns. She looks brighter today for a good night's sleep.

'Thanks for the eggs,' I say quickly.

'Fresh from the hens this morning. Tea?'

'Please.' Margot pours me a mug and I notice the spout of the teapot is chipped. None of the mugs match, but there's a jug for milk and a bowl of sugar cubes already laid out. While Mum's been sick, breakfast has been Pop-Tarts or a hasty Müller Rice. I could get used to this, although I won't give Margot the satisfaction of knowing I'm impressed with anything this farm has to offer.

Curiosity gets the better of me and, after I've helped Mum do the washing-up, I decide to explore. After all, I've never lived on a farm before – who has? – and you never know, Keanu Reeves might be waiting on his combine harvester.

I leave through the front door, past the Land Rover parked in the middle of a courtyard. The rain has stopped for now although there are some big, bad boss clouds rolling in over the hills. There's so much sky here, uninterrupted by tower blocks or aeroplane snail trails. The air smells squeaky clean, rinsed by the overnight downpour. London doesn't smell like this – mineral-water fresh. OK, I can learn to live a few months without black bogies, I guess.

On either side of the drive are stables – but Margot doesn't have any horses. I go over and poke my head through the door and find, quite literally, a pigsty. 'Oh wow,' I mutter. The pen is divided in two, I guess to keep the pigs apart. They are HUGE. The male, and he *has* to be a male, is a russet giant. The smell – wee and hay – isn't *quite* as gross as I would have expected.

15

At first I don't even see the piglets. They're so tiny, suckling on their mother, almost tucked out of sight. 'Oh my God! Too cute!' I say to myself.

'You can go in if you want.' I didn't even hear Margot approach; I'm going to have to get her a bell to wear around her neck. 'Just don't let them out.'

She's wearing a wax jacket and wellies, but I'm really not dressed for a pigsty, in my Mary Janes and pinafore dress. That said, I also *really* want to hold a tiny baby piggy. 'Can I hold one?'

'You may.' Margot unlatches the bottom half of the door and I enter, hand over my nose.

'How many piglets are there?'

'Four this time, I think.'

I count three feeding. 'There's only . . .' But then I see the smallest piglet I've ever seen, no bigger than a guinea pig, near the water trough, half covered by hay.

'Runt,' Margot says. 'He won't make it.'

'No!' I go to crouch at his side. He comes to as I stroke him. His little body is warm and covered in coarse hair, a lot like a puppy. 'He's not dead.'

'Not yet. They always make more than they need and then nature runs its course. Survival of the fittest and all that. The mother won't waste any energy on him.'

Refusing to give in, I lift the runt up and carry him to his brothers and sisters. He weighs almost nothing in my hands. 'Come on, little one. Breakfast time.' I nestle him up against his mother and will him to drink. He rubs his head sleepily against her, but doesn't latch on to her teat. He doesn't even open his eyes.

16

'I'm telling you, Felicity, there's nothing can be done. Stop wasting your time on silly things and help me out with your mother.'

I get to my feet and fix Margot with the steeliest look I can muster; I'm aiming for 'daytime soap-opera diva bitch'. How dare she . . . Does she have *any* idea what the last two years have been like? 'You know, while you've been out here playing Old MacDonald, I was the one cleaning up Mum's sick and holding her hand in the chemo lounge.' I say it to hurt her and she looks hurt – just for a second she wilts – but it's also the truth. 'She's better now; she doesn't need help,' I finish.

Margot rediscovers her composure, standing tall. 'It must have been very trying.' Not the apology I was hoping for.

I shrug, saying nothing. Yes, it was 'trying'. It redefined 'trying'. But now, thank God, it's over. I look sadly at the little pig. 'He's just a baby. Can't we help him?'

She shakes her head. 'Felicity . . . it's the way it goes.'

I can't bear to stay and watch a helpless piglet die. I rise and push past Margot. 'Whatever.' I'm not going to let her see me cry so try to pass it off as indifference. I take a deep breath and cross the courtyard to find the sheep pen and the goat, but there's nothing cute to look at over here. I suppose I'll get lambs in the spring.

What next? Following the weed-strewn path around the side of the house, I come to the back garden. There are vegetable patches on both sides, separated by a path. Each patch is meticulously labelled: carrots (planted 23/8); radishes; potatoes; cauliflower; parsnips. There are bamboo tepees for peas and beans next to the hen house – a little shed on stilts to protect the chickens, no doubt, from foxes.

It's so strange. My memories of Margot are hazy, but they're hazy because, for most of my childhood, she was working; always buzzing from meetings to lunches to parties. When we went up to Hampstead Heath on a weekend, Grandad would amuse me in the garden while inside Margot was screaming instructions down the phone at her minions back at the newspaper. How did she end up here with mud and manure under her once perfectly manicured fingernails? Grandad died in '88, almost ten years ago, so it's probably not a grief thing.

At the end of the garden there's a trellis arch, strangled by vines and rose stems. I pass under it and find a whole second garden. It's overgrown and wild, seemingly forgotten, but it's beautiful: a secret rose garden, secluded from the rest of the world. I feel very *Vogue* fashion spread all of a sudden. Thick, creamy roses with velvet petals are starting to die, crinkly brown at the edges, but it looks pretty cool and vintage-y. A broken swing dangles from the apple tree, the ropes as rotten as the apples scattered in the undergrowth. Still, it has potential – there's even a pretty wrought-iron bench where I could sit and read *Cosmo*. Midges swirl in the air and a cabbage-white butterfly flutters past my face.

Imagine if even Margot didn't know about this, it could be my own private retreat. In the distance I hear the faint chattering of a stream beyond the back wall.

Carefully, I trample through more weeds and rose bushes and find a rackety old gate. The catch is rusty, but I prise it and force the gate open, wary of nettles and pampas grass almost as tall as I am. The garden backs onto woodland, gently sloping downwards into thick forest. I take a look over my shoulder towards the farmhouse, almost checking it's not watching. If this were a horror film, I'd be screaming at myself to stay out of the woods, but it's noon on a Sunday – what's the worst that can happen?

I take a couple of steps towards the forest. The trees rustle and shiver. I shiver too. I strain to hear the stream.

Felicity . . .

It sounds nutso, but I swear I can hear my name, very gently, on the breeze.

Felicity . . .

I take another few steps down the path. Gnarly branches twist and coil around each other, forming a wooden mouth ready to swallow me into the woods. Within, the light is thick emerald green. I smell wild garlic (stinky) and honeysuckle (nice).

Felicity . . .

I hear it again. I *swear* I just heard my name. Goosebumps pop up all over my arms. The voice isn't menacing – more . . . enticing.

I enter the dark of the forest.

'Felicity!' OK, this time I really do hear my name. I whip my head back and see Margot filling the gateway at the bottom of the garden, hands on hips like a sergeant major. 'What on earth do you think you're doing?'

I shrug sheepishly. 'I just wanted to see the stream.'

She tuts. 'Dressed like that? Don't be absurd – you'll break your neck. Inside,' she commands, and I shuffle back up the footpath. Margot halts me at the gate. 'Don't ever go into

19

the forest by yourself. It isn't safe.' She steers me into the rose garden.

'What do you mean?' I ask, thinking about the breathless voice I *think* I heard.

'Just what I said. Stay out of the forest.' She says no more, but I'm intrigued. Scared, sure, but intrigued.

Chapter 3

I find a giant baby bottle under the sink in the kitchen while cleaning up after dinner. Immediately I think of the tiny piglet. 'What's this for?' I ask.

Margot peers at me over the top of her half-moon glasses. Her wrinkled hands are covered in grease, tinkering with part of a generator engine. 'Some of the lambs always need hand-rearing. Why?'

'Can I feed the little piglet?'

'Felicity, there's no point.' She rolls her eyes. 'Once the sow rejects a runt, it's as good as dead.'

'Please?'

'Oh, Margot, let her try,' Mum chips in from the dining table. Her wig is a little skew-whiff. I go over and straighten it up for her. 'What's the harm in trying?'

Margot looks like she's about to protest but bites her tongue. You can't argue with a cancer victim, even one in remission. 'Very well, but don't come crying when it dies.'

Why does she have to be so brutal all the time? What's her problem, seriously? 'I won't,' I say defiantly. I grab the bottle and unscrew the lid. 'OK. Do I just use milk from the fridge?'

Margot tuts loudly. 'If you want to bring about his death faster, yes.'

'Margot . . .' Mum warns.

She exhales through her nostrils as if weary and wipes her oily hands on a rag. 'Pigs can't digest cow's milk. You can either milk the sow or use some of the goat's milk. That'll do the trick. If you're serious about this, Felicity, you have to make sure he's kept warm with a heat lamp and feed him iron to help his immune system.'

OK, that's more work than I anticipated, but so what? If I prove my point, it'll be worth it. 'Fine. Do you have a heat lamp?'

While Margot grudgingly goes to find the lamp, I fill the bottle with goat's milk and head back to the pig pen. As I enter, I worry that the poor little thing will already be dead. Once again I find him shunned by the rest of the piglets, half buried under the sow's rear. 'Oh, poor little guy. What mean brothers and sisters you have.' I tread carefully through the pen to retrieve the sad creature. Ew, gross, my heel sinks into something I can't see and don't *want* to see.

Not quite sure what to do, I kneel down in the hay and scoop him into my lap. He stirs feebly, but it seems like the strength is leaving his body and he hardly bothers to struggle. I cradle him like a human baby and position the bottle to his mouth. 'Come on, you tiny weirdo. Eat something.' I'm not taking no for an answer. I force the bottle into his mouth and some milk trickles out. The piglet splutters and spits the milk onto my knees – man, this is grim. I try again, and this time it looks like he's swallowing. 'There you go! Good boy!'

22

Margot clatters in, carrying a big silver lamp. 'I can't believe I'm bothering with this.'

'Look, he's feeding!' I say triumphantly. 'What's he called?'

'I don't give them names.'

The piglet nuzzles against me. 'Well, that's stupid. I'll give them names.'

'Felicity, I really wouldn't, if I were you. You don't want to get too fond of them.'

I ignore Margot's advice. 'You,' I say directly to the pig in my arms, 'look like a Peanut to me. Peanut the Piglet!'

Margot mutters something under her breath and plugs the lamp in. I ignore her and continue to feed Peanut.

Who needs an alarm clock when there's a cockerel? The bloody thing starts crowing as the sun rises at about five. I stuff my head under the pillow but hear Margot rise and thud downstairs.

As soon as I'm awake, I'm awake. First day of school. I can't avoid it any longer and I can't deny I'm nervous. I wish I was still at St Agnes. I think about Tiggy and Marina and Booey and Livs greeting each other on the first day after the holidays and how excited they'll all be to see each other. I wonder if they'll talk about me. I've been going there since I was eleven and all the teachers liked me. Dr Greenaway once commented I was head-girl material. I hope someone else doesn't overtake me before I get back to London.

After I've showered, I take some time in selecting a perfect 'First Day Impression' outfit. I want something that demonstrates I'm from London, something that says I'm fashion-forward, something that *screams* I'm not from the Welsh Valleys. I select a simple black shift dress and wear it over a white blouse along with crisp white knee socks and the Mary Janes. I finish the look off with a black Alice band and a spritz of CK One. Cher Horowitz would be proud.

I imagine a new film. In this one I meet a group of tragic, downtrodden village girls and empower them through better fashion choices. I would totally watch that.

Feeling more than a little nauseous, but determined not to show it, I make my way downstairs. Once again there's an impressive spread on the kitchen table – well of course there is, Margot's been up since dawn. Strawberry jam, lemon curd, marmalade . . . all home-made in reused jars.

Mum, cradling a black coffee, looks tired, obviously having risen so early just to see me off on my first day. She hasn't bothered to put the wig on. Her scalp is still visible under the soft baby hair that's growing back. I don't like it when she's not in the wig; she looks like a cancer patient. With a bit of a shiver I have a flashback to the days when I'd find clumps of brown hair between the sofa cushions, matted in the carpets, clogging the plughole; everywhere. 'Mum, you should go back to bed. You look awful.'

'Charming. I wanted to wish you luck on your first day!'

'Thank you.' My tummy gurgles. I change the subject. 'Where's Margot?'

'Out collecting eggs.' Mum rests her mug. 'Fliss . . .'

'What?'

'You'll settle in, I promise. Don't make life hard for yourself.'

'I'm *not*.'

'OK . . .' She doesn't seem convinced. 'I had an idea. Margot and I are driving into Llanmarion today. Why don't I ask around about dance schools?'

I shake my head. 'No.'

'Oh, come on, Fliss. You haven't danced in years . . . not since . . . well, now seems like the right time to get back into it.'

'I don't want to.' I am aware how whiny I sound. Ballet feels like something a different girl used to do. The girl from The Time Before Mum Got Ill. I can't believe she was ever really me.

'It used to make you so happy.'

'So did My Little Ponies. I'm too old for ballet.'

Mum can evidently sense she's onto a losing battle. 'Fine. But what a waste of talent.'

'I don't think I could even do it any more. I'm also too fat for ballet.'

'Felicity Baker! What absolute shi—'

Margot bursts through the back door, casting a long shadow over the table. 'Righty-ho! Is it fried, poached or scrambled?'

'I'm not hungry,' I say.

'Nonsense! Breakfast is the most important meal of the day. Your brain can't work on an empty stomach.'

Mum joins in. 'Fliss, you're not going to school without breakfast.'

'OK, OK, I'll have some toast.' I pick a slice out of the rack and push myself away from the table. 'I need to go and feed Peanut before school.' As soon as I'm outside, I frisbee the toast into the trees.

25

Chapter 4

Peanut fed – and still alive – I refuse the offer of a lift. I need to learn my way around this wasteland, or I'll be stuck on the farm relying on Margot's highly questionable kindness until the end of time. Ysgol Maes-y-Coed – which I can barely say, let alone translate – is about twenty minutes away and Margot informed me there's a school service that trundles around the valley, picking stray children off the farms and hamlets.

I only recently learned that my education at St Agnes in London was courtesy of Margot and Grandad – I always assumed Mum had paid my fees, but she hasn't worked in a long time and I have no idea what TV producers actually earn. There is one private school in the area, but it'd be about an hour's drive each way and they have no boarding. I can't believe I'm even considering boarding school as preferable to staying at the farm. What decrepitude has my life become?

Boys cross my mind. I've never been to a school with boys before and I've been led to believe that, en masse, they're noisy, smelly, chimpanzee-like creatures. At St Agnes we were free to get on with learning without having to worry about them. That said, I hope there are some hot ones.

The bus, one of those sad green hoppers that delivers old

people to day centres, pulls up at the bus shelter. I check it's going to the correct school before I climb aboard. Gross, it smells of old-lady-cabbage-farts. When I try to pay with cash, the driver explains I need a pass from the school office. So much newness to deal with. The driver swerves off and I tumble down the aisle.

Luckily there's only one witness to my clumsiness. A giant sits on the back row and very nearly fills it. He's not fat, just huge, like a regular human blown up on a photocopier to 150 per cent. I get a first look at the Maes-y-Coed uniform – a navy blue sweatshirt with a white polo shirt. Hardly the blazer and kilt I had back home, which I always thought was pretty cute in a Malory Towers way.

I sit on the third row and smooth my skirt down. I open my satchel and take out this month's *Vogue*. Amber Valletta smiles from the cover, announcing 'Miniskirts are BACK!' I think this will send a very clear message to onlookers. I wonder if you can even get *Vogue* out here.

I'm so engrossed in 'The New Suit' I don't even notice the giant has moved into the row behind me. 'So then,' he says in a heavy Welsh accent. 'You m-m-must be M-Margot's granddaughter.'

Oh, I can't cope with stammers. I always feel so sorry for people with them. It's like when I see a blind person with either a white stick or a guide dog, I just totally want to cry for them. 'I am. I'm Felicity Baker. Fliss.' If nothing else, St Agnes taught me the value of good manners. I shake a bear-paw-sized hand.

'Dewi Allen. Nice to meet you.' He too is wearing CK One. Who isn't?

Why does that name ring a bell? 'The milk man?'

27

He smiles. There's a little gap between his front teeth. 'I'm Dewi Allen junior. M-my dad owns the dairy farm, isn't it. I help out, like, over the weekend.' I turn back to *Vogue*. 'What are you reading?'

'*Vogue*.'

'Mam sometimes read that. Dirty magazine, if you ask me, all those naked girls.'

I close the magazine and turn to face him. 'And how would you know?' He blushes and shrugs. I feel a little mean. 'Anyway, it's not pornographic, it's high fashion. There's a big difference.'

He smiles again. 'I didn't know there were different types of nipple.'

I can't help but laugh. For someone so huge, he has a harmlessness to him. I suspect a lot of it's in the lilting accent, to be honest. The bus stops to pick up more students – some younger, some older – and Dewi points out the local shops and unattractive attractions as we pass. As we roll through Llanmarion, there's a baker and a butcher, a bingo and pool hall, a town square and village hall, a very sad-looking leisure centre (I can smell the chlorine even as we pass) and, of course, the old colliery.

OK, it's early in the morning, but there's a ghost-town feeling about the place. It feels abandoned. Dandelions and dock leaves spring up through cracks in the pavements like nature's slowly reclaiming the streets after a war or something. Dewi explains that the mine used to be the heart of Llanmarion – nearly every man in town who wasn't a farmer worked there. Now, since it was closed, those too old to retrain spend the days drinking and smoking and waiting to die. Many were also waiting to hear if they'd get compensation for breathing difficulties they'd picked up down the mine. I had no idea. No wonder everything looks so grey and morose.

The school is as sad as the town. As the bus pulls into the car park I see miserable pebble-dash blocks with square black windows. In the sixties, this must have been cutting-edge design, but now it looks dirty and almost factory-like. I wonder if there's a conveyor belt.

I step off the bus, ready to report to the main reception. 'Do you want me to sh-sh . . .' He stops and blinks to compose his speech, 'show you where to go, like?'

'It's all right. I can find my way. Thank you though.'

'J-just go up those stairs and follow the path to th-the glass doors.' A couple of guys saunter over – Dewi's friends, I'm guessing. Clearly no one is taller than Dewi, but one is tall and thin like he's made out of pipe-cleaners while the other is a tubby little thing.

'*Bore da*, Dewi,' says the chunky one.

'Hiya, *butt*,' Dewi replies. 'Rhys and Matthew, this is . . . this is Fliss – Margot Hancock's granddaughter.' Another bus pulls in, a bigger one this time. The doors hiss open and a chatty gaggle of pupils pours out to fill the driveway.

'Ah, from Mari-Morgan Farm, no?' asks Rhys – the stringy one.

'That's me.'

'I'm well scared of that farm, I am,' the one called Matthew says. 'You know what they say about Mari-Morgan Farm, don't you?'

Dewi rolls his eyes. 'Matthew, don't be filling Fliss's head with your rubbish.'

29

'No!' I say. 'Go on, what do they say?'

'Oh, doesn't she talk posh, like?' Rhys chips in.

'You know what a mari-morgan is, don't you?' Matthew says, and I shake my head. 'It's like a water spirit. They got silver skin and black eyes. They live in water and, like, lure men to their death by drowning them.'

'It's just . . . just an old Welsh fairy tale,' Dewi says with a sneer. 'Don't p-pay any attention to him. And anyway, everyone knows they're green.'

'It's true, *butt*! That's why Margot changed the name of the farm, no? Everybody around here knows about the mari-morgans in the river.'

I know it's majorly ridiculous, but my heart whirrs faster. Water spirits? Sirens? As if! At the same time, I can't ignore the voices, the whispers I heard in the forest. That happened before I even knew what a mari-morgan was, before I knew Margot had renamed the farm.

'Are you OK, Fliss?' Dewi asks.

'I'm fine. Sorry, just a little spaced out. I should go find reception really.'

'Matthew, you dickhead, look what you done.'

'It's OK, really!' I fake a bright smile. 'I highly doubt there are water fairies living on my grandma's farm!'

I notice a trio of super-scary-looking girls loitering at Dewi's shoulder. They're all wearing their uniform in the same way – sleeves rolled up, collars upturned and very tight Lycra skirts with platform ankle boots. I doubt these are my new friends to rescue through fashion. One reaches up and taps Dewi on the shoulder. She has two blonde stripes dyed into the front of her hair and dark brown lip liner with pale lipstick. It's, let's just say, a bold choice. '*Bore da*, Dewi.'

'Oh, hi, M-Megan. How's it going?'

'I'm lush.' She peers at me through solid black eyeliner, seemingly applied with a marker pen. 'Who's this, then?'

'Hi,' I say, offering a hand. 'I'm Fliss Baker. I just moved to Mari-Morgan Farm.'

'Good morning!' she says in a pantomime English accent. 'Welcome to Wales, Your Royal Highness!' Behind her, her friends snigger into their hands. One of them is a bottle blonde with eyebrows that look like upside-down Nike ticks and the other is a hard-faced black girl with her hair spiked up like a pineapple.

Clearly I'm not going to let on if I'm bothered, which I'm not. These girls have just made it really easy to know who I'll be avoiding. 'Thanks. So far I'm having a lovely time. The farm is so beautiful.'

'And so is your outfit,' Megan says with a smirk.

'Megan . . .' Dewi says, although he doesn't sound too brave.

A little trick I learned when dealing with cattiness at St Agnes: the more horrid Megan gets, the nicer I'll be. She's not going to break me. 'Well! *So* nice to meet you, but I'd better go find out where I'm supposed to be! See you around!' I smile broadly, turn on my heel and set off up the path.

'What's she come dressed as?' the dark-skinned girl says, well within earshot.

'She looks like Wednesday Addams, yeah?' Megan says, and her sidekicks howl with laughter. *Not* the impression I was aiming for. I flinch but keep walking, head up high, and pretend I can't hear.

* * *

A nice lady called Yvonne from the school office shows me around. She has bushy burgundy hair and red-rimmed glasses. Once upon a time, she must have been very glamorous, but now the lingering cloud of Dior *Poison* that follows her is a bit of a hangover.

She tells me about the great rivalry with the Welsh-speaking school on the other side of town but I'm so overwhelmed that most of the tour goes in one ear and out the other. I'm clearly going to get very lost.

'Doll, your uniform's been paid for by your *naini*, so you can pick it up at the end of the day.'

'Could I change into it now?'

Yvonne looks a little taken aback. 'Well, of course. If you're keen! Come on round, doll and we'll find your size.'

I select a sweater, T-shirt and skirt and take them into the toilet to change. The uniform is shapeless, unflattering and there's nothing I can do to make it look less box-fresh. It screams 'new girl' just as much as my own clothes. I keep the knee socks and Mary Janes, obviously. I'm not changing my style simply because some hill-dwelling scrubbers don't like it. What do they know, anyway? Ginger Spice is *not* a fashion icon.

I leave my own clothes in a carrier bag behind the reception desk so I don't have to drag them around all day, and Yvonne prints me out a timetable. 'There you go, doll. Now hurry along or you'll be late for first period.' My first lesson is maths in E14. 'Up the stairs and don't forget we always walk clockwise in the E-Block.'

So many pointless rules to learn. It's a good thing my head is spinning or I might remember to feel nervous or lonely. I hurry upstairs just as a bell goes, signalling the end of what must be registration. Classroom doors open, students flood the hallways and suddenly I understand the clockwise rule. All I can do is join the current and see where it takes me. I manage to duck out of the stream and slip into E14. The teacher hasn't arrived yet and my new classmates run wild, chasing each other around and throwing missiles. This would *never* happen at St Agnes, where we have to queue in silence outside the classroom until a teacher lets us in.

At the back I see Megan and her skanky friends sitting on the desks and blowing bubbles with Hubba Bubba. Classy. I can't see Dewi anywhere, which is a shame as at least then I'd know someone to say hello to. I demurely seat myself underneath the window at the front, away from the chaos, and take *Vogue* out of my bag. I'm quite happily leafing through an accessories feature when I become aware of people staring. At the furthest end of the front row is a girl with copper-wire hair and freckles alongside a very beautiful Asian boy with swishy curtain hair.

I'm not sure why they're staring so intently, so I return to my magazine. Oh, what I wouldn't give for a pair of patent-leather Miu Miu sandals. In my peripheral vision I become aware of the Asian guy waving at me, pointing at the magazine. I don't get it – is he making fun of me? Or is he asking to see what I'm reading? I hold it up and point to the cover.

Across the room, he rolls his eyes and gestures, tucking his hands under the table. Now I'm really lost. I shrug just as the magazine is torn out of my hands. 'Oi!' I protest.

A stony-faced man with yellowed, nicotine-stained teeth stares down at me. 'Magazines aren't allowed in school. Books only.'

'But . . . I . . . It's my first day. I . . . didn't know.' There's a snigger from over my shoulder and I don't need to turn around to know it's Megan or her minions.

The teacher curls my *Vogue* into a baton and tucks it under his sweat-crusty armpit. 'You can have it back at the end of the lesson in that case.'

I now understand the pair at the other end of the row were trying to warn me. I look down the line and see them smile sympathetically. I half smile back.

The morning passes without incident, although I spend my break remedying the fact that they've put me down for music instead of theatre studies. As I'm essentially tone deaf, that won't do at all. By the time they've given me a whole new timetable, it's time for French.

At lunch I realise I've made another faux pas by bringing dinner money. The canteen is almost deserted and I soon learn why. Stainless-steel vats hold different kinds of brown sludge. One claims to be chilli, the other vegetable curry, both bubble like swamps with marsh gas. Almost everyone else has brought packed lunches, with only the obvious Free School Meals kids filling the cafeteria tables.

Luckily there's a cooler with sandwiches and drinks, so I grab a ham-and-cheese baguette and a bottle of water. God knows how, but I don't see Dewi until I walk into his chest, which my head barely clears. 'Oh wow, sorry!' I say.

34

'I'm sorry, like. I'm as clumsy as I look, I am. How are you getting on?'

'So far so good. Were you looking for me?'

Dewi shrugs. 'Oh no.' Oh, that's awkward. 'I'm supposed to be m-meeting Rhys in here, like.'

'Oh. Don't tell me you've come for the food.'

'Ha! No one eats that stuff. I mean, what is it even meant to be like?'

'Yeah, tomorrow I'll be bringing a sandwich!' And on that scintillating note I realise I have nothing else to say to Dewi Allen Jr. We stand a metre apart next to the salad bar.

'Yeah. Sandwich.'

'Gotta love a sandwich.' I don't even have an excuse to leave.

'Ah, look, there's Rhys!' Dewi seems as relieved as I am.

'Cool. Maybe I'll see you on the bus later.'

'Aye, that'd be lush. Catch you then.'

I don't know where I'm going, but I need to get away from the smell of brown liquid food products.

At the end of lunch I decide to brave the A-Block girls' toilets. I dread to think what they'll be like, and I am right to be worried. They're bus-station gross. The whole room stinks of smoke and pee, while the cubicles are covered in decades-old graffiti. Which would I rather – locking door, attached toilet seat or toilet paper? It seems all three is too much to ask for.

Finishing my hover-wee, I exit the stall to find Megan and her friends waiting at the sinks, a trio of gargoyles. They're blocking my exit and there are no other witnesses. Great. This day could only be improved by bursting into flames or catching rabies. 'Hi, Megan,' I say as sweet as candy.

'You think you're pretty hot shit, don't you?' Megan says, narrowing her eyes. With normal eyebrows and better make-up she could be quite pretty.

'No, I really don't.' I try to get to the sink, but the dark-skinned one blocks my path. 'Excuse me.'

'Let her wash her dainty hands, Rhiannon.' Megan is calling the shots. Rhiannon steps aside.

'Thank you.'

'You need to stay away from Dewi Allen,' says the blonde one. 'He's going with Megan.'

Really? I didn't get that impression at all. 'OK.'

Megan steps into my space and I'm forced to back into the corner furthest from the door. She smells strongly of menthol cigarettes and the Vanilla Kisses Impulse she's used to try to mask them. 'We saw you flirting with him in the canteen.'

I shouldn't argue, I'll only make things worse for myself, but I can't help it. 'I wasn't flirting, I was talking to him.'

'Come off it, hun. We saw it – you had your hands all over him.'

'Megan, I only met him this morning. There is nothing going on, I promise.'

'Good!' she says and backs off. 'Because you know what happens to snotty English bitches who come here and start touching people's boyfriends.'

I don't reply.

'Shall we show her?' Rhiannon says.

Megan smiles. 'Cerys, keep an eye on the door, yeah?'

I feel my heartbeat thumping in my skull. Every muscle feels electric, juiced, telling me to GET OUT, but I can't. 'Megan, what are you doing?' My voice is suddenly kitten small.

'You've got a lot of hair, haven't you?' I say nothing. 'Looks a bit dirty though. You think it needs a wash, Rhi?'

'Aye.'

And they're on me before I can move. They hit me like a wrecking ball, trying to force me back into the toilet cubicle. I cling to the sides of the frame but Megan karate-chops at my arms until I let go. Falling backwards, I feel my bum make contact with the toilet seat before they push me all the way to the floor.

I thought bogwashing was a myth, an urban legend to scare first years. Apparently not. 'Megan! Please!' I cry.

It's a small cubicle for three people and it's hard for them to manoeuvre me. I try to slither under the toilet . . . better than going into it head first, I figure. They try to turn me around. Rhiannon grabs hold of my hair and drags me up towards the bowl. The floor is damp, sticky and littered with stray squares of loo roll. It reeks and I see cigarette butts bobbing on yellow water. I grip the rim, bracing myself. 'Megan stop!'

'There's someone coming!' Cerys says, and Rhiannon lets go of me at once.

'Saved by the bell, yeah.' Megan looms over me. 'Maybe next time. Stay away from Dewi, yeah? And stay away from us, like.'

Saying no more, they sweep out of the bathroom. I blink back tears as I pick myself up off the floor. I will not cry, because if I cry they win. I clamp my back teeth together until the urge passes. I check myself over. I don't think anything actually went *in* the loo, thank God.

I'm *not* staying. I can't spend six months at this school. Can't deal with it, just can't. I dig my nails into my palms and stare my reflection dead in the eye. I'm going *home*.

* * *

That afternoon, after the bell has rung at three fifteen, I collect my clothes from Yvonne and make my way back to the minibus. Dewi sits on the back row as before. I don't know if Megan's all-seeing eye is watching me, but even as he smiles affably at me, I make a great show of sitting at the very front behind the driver.

Thankfully he doesn't try to talk to me on the ride home, and by the time I'm dropped off at the end of the lane I'm ready to sleep for a week. I ache all over with tiredness, even my hair. I can only hope my body adjusts to the new routine. As I drag my feet past the pigsty I remember I need to feed Peanut, when all I really want to do is collapse. Maybe Margot's right, and I'm not capable of looking after him.

I push through the front door and drop my satchel at the foot of the stairs. 'Fliss?' It's Mum, calling from the lounge. On hearing her voice, I have to fight a childish urge to run and throw myself into her arms. I want to plead, beg her to take us back to London.

'I'm home.' Utterly dejected, my limbs like limp noodles, I schlep through and find Mum on the sofa, reading a book in front of the fire. She's not wearing her wig and I'm reminded again of why we came to this hellhole in the first place.

'How was your first day, love?'

I can't. 'Yeah, good,' I lie.

'Did you make any new friends?'

'Yeah. There's a really nice girl called Megan.'

Chapter 5

September, October, November, December, January, February and then home. There are only six weeks until half-term – I mark that on my calendar – and then only seven after that until the Christmas holidays. I mark that on too. That all feels like a really long way away so I also make a note that I only have to get through four more days until Saturday.

With the day I've had, I don't know if I can hang on until February. What I need is a PLAN – a plan to show Mum that we can cope in London without Margot. We *have* coped for like two years. I don't see why we need Frosty the Ice Dragon sticking her forked tongue in now.

After dinner I feed Peanut out in the stable and already notice he's a bit livelier. This time when I pick him up, he bothers to wriggle a little bit. Good. He hungrily gobbles at the bottle and, as I leave him under the heat lamp, one of his brothers or sisters (I mean, who can tell the difference?) comes over to snuggle with him. OK, school was awful, but this sort of makes up for it. I feel porridgey warm in my tummy as I head back inside the farmhouse.

Mum and Margot are watching *Poirot* in the lounge. I hover in the doorway for a moment. 'Can I ring Tiggy?'

'Of course,' Mum says.

'Don't be on for hours. It's not you paying the bill, is it?' Margot adds because of course she does.

I ignore her and sit on the bottom step. The only phone in the house is on a little stand in the hallway by the front door. Obviously I know Tiggy's number off by heart.

She answers on the third ring. 'Hello?'

On hearing her voice, I almost burst into tears. I have to take a deep breath and pinch the bridge of my nose. 'Hi, Tigs. It's Fliss.'

'Oh my God! How are you? Is it awful?'

'I can't talk loud,' I pretty much whisper. 'But yes.'

'What is it like?'

'I don't know . . . just . . . nothing like home. At all.'

'What was school like?'

'Tigs . . .' I lower my voice further, 'they're basically savages. Seriously, the girls are like total Kappa Slappers.' I can't tell even her about what happened in the toilet. It's too shameful.

Tiggy giggles. I can so clearly see her lying back on her big double bed, fairy lights twisted around the bed frame. Her dead straight blonde hair is in its usual scruffy pigtails. 'Are there at least any cute guys?'

'No. Not even that.' Dewi *is* handsome in a mountainous way, but I'm trying to make a point.

'God, what's the point in going to a mixed school if there isn't even any totty!'

'I know, right? Tiggy, I want to come home.'

'Well, how's your mum?'

'She's fine.'

'Maybe she'll feel better and you can come home sooner?'

40

'God, I hope so. I'm going to go mental at this rate. How is everyone at St Agnes?' Tiggy gives me a lengthy update. Apparently Nicole Caruthers has had a really ill-advised perm and Carrie Button has gone to live in Jamaica with her dad, which is a huge mistake because everyone knows he's an alcoholic and serial philanderer. 'And what about Xander? Have you seen him?' Xander and I agreed that we'd stay friendly, but he hasn't been in touch yet, and I'll be damned if I'm gonna make the first move.

'I saw him on Saturday at the fair.' Pretty much everyone I know was at the fair on Clapham Common while I was trapped in Margot's car.

'Oh, OK,' I say, failing to keep wistfulness out of my voice. 'How is he?'

'I think he's fine.'

'Did he mention me?'

'Erm. Yeah, probably.'

'What did he say?'

'Oh. I don't know, I don't remember, but I'm sure he must have said something.'

'Great.' This doesn't exactly fill me with hope. I finish talking to Tiggy and somehow feel worse than before. I remain on the bottom step, head in hands. This isn't fair! I have to get back, back to my stolen life. Somehow I *have* to convince Mum to take us home.

Later that night, when Margot has driven to the pub in Llanmarion to meet with the vet or something, I'm unpacking the rest of my things. 'Why don't you sort your clothes?' Mum had suggested, turning off the TV. I had been slouched alongside her, bored out of my skull. 'You won't need your summer things for a while so you could put them in the attic for storage.'

I perk up at the mention of the Spooky Attic of Cursed Doom. 'It's locked.'

Mum smiles. 'And I know where she keeps the key.'

I sit up. 'Where?'

'Kitchen drawers, third one down.'

I get the key and hurry upstairs before Margot returns. She said she'd only be gone an hour or so. I just want to have a good nosy, knowing full-well Margot doesn't want me up there.

The key, a long rusty one, is stiff in the lock, but I tug on the handle and it grinds around. The door opens with a whine and I peer up a dark, narrow staircase that veers steeply to the right. I fumble along the wall for a light switch. A bare bulb flickers on with a low hum.

I swallow hard and edge up the steps. The air is cold and dank, danker with every step. It's freezing up here. Wind moans and howls through the eaves, rattling the bones of the farm. I wrap my arms around myself.

There's another bare bulb hanging from the centre beam of the sloped roof, and I have to stoop when I stand. Now that I'm up here, I regret my life choices. Again. With white dust sheets covering everything, it's like I'm surrounded by ghosts. Ghosts playing Grandmother's Footsteps when my back is turned. Although, on reflection, my actual grandmother is probably scarier than any ghost.

I peek under a sheet and see some stacked dining-room chairs. Another is draped over an old vanity unit. There are crates of trinkets I recognise from Margot's old Hampstead home.

42

I guess they don't really belong on the farm any more than I do. I find a box of glass trophies and awards: Young Journalist of the Year; Press Association Award; Lifetime Achievement. It's weird she'd dump them up here where no one can see them. I run my fingers over a burly mahogany armoire and immediately think of storing some of my excess clothes in it.

I'm about to head downstairs to fetch them when I see the trunk. No sheet, so it's smothered by a thick layer of dust, tucked out of the way in the corner of the chimney breast.

I should probably leave it. It looks old, even older than anything else up here, and cobwebs shroud it, but it's like a treasure chest, daring me to open it. There's a rusted clasp but no padlock. I check the coast is clear and kneel down in front of the trunk.

I blow on it, but that only shifts a fraction of the thick bluish dust. I prise the clasp apart and swing the lid open. My fingers come away filthy. I cough and splutter on the cloud I kick up. 'Oh gross.' I waft it away and look inside the trunk.

Oh. It's just books. Super-old books. The smell hits me like a slap. Musty old pages, almost sweet like almonds. They're a little brown and dog-eared, but they could be antiques. *The Swish of the Curtain* by Pamela Brown, *The Box of Delights* by John Masefield, Arthur Ransome's *Swallows and Amazons*. They could be worth something, I think. They all smell fusty, oaky and wise somehow. I flick through, looking at the gorgeous line engravings. It's so sad that books don't have illustrations in any more. I think about my own books – a mishmash of Point Horror, Sweet Valley High and Judy Blume, and think they look a bit immature next to these.

I pull out a judgemental leather-bound Bible and see there's something wedged underneath it. A slim tortoiseshell notebook. Unlike the other books, this one has no picture or title, it's just blank. I pull it free from the trunk. I open the cover. The lined pages are a little loose; a couple fall out and scatter over the bare floorboards. 'Damn.' I rush to collect them, worried they could slide through the gaps. There are a couple of stiff, glossy photographs among the fallen pages, both that lovely sepia yellow tone from the olden days.

The first is of a *gorgeous* man in army uniform. It's a portrait shot and he's smiling broadly with dimples to die for. The other is a classically pretty blonde girl wearing a dotty summer dress and cardigan while sitting on a wooden gate in front of a large paddock. She's laughing, maybe at something the photographer's saying. I gather the last couple of pages and turn the first one around to read it.

This book belongs to Margot Stanford. If lost, please return to Tan-Y-Pistyll Farm.

Oh my God. It can't be. I peep inside. It is though. It's Margot's diary. I look again at the girl on the gate. I squint my eyes . . . and gasp. It's *her*! She looks so, so different, but the high cheekbones and strong jaw are totally the same. She wants to try smiling more often; it suits her. I look again at the other photo. To be honest, I only remember Grandad as a balding old man, but I've seen old pictures and he didn't look anything like this guy.

I take a deep sniff of the notebook. It's gorgeous. I've only gone and found Margot's secret diary. I clutch it to my chest, hardly able to contain my glee. This is the find of the decade. I shut the trunk and hurry to the top of the attic stairs. If I strain I can still hear the TV downstairs. No one would ever know . . .

No! Reading someone else's diary must come with the worst karma in the world. I mustn't or I'll wake up with all of my own secrets tattooed on my face or something.

But . . .

This is *Margot*. She's *so* not the diary-keeping type. A quick look can't hurt, can it? I slot the loose pages and photos into the front of the book and turn to the first page. The entry is dated Wednesday 15th January, 1941. I do some maths. I'm pretty sure Mum said Margot was born in 1924 and her birthday is in March, so she was sixteen when she wrote this – just a year older than me.

Another – much naughtier – thought occurs to me, spreading through my mind like a toxic green cloud. If I can't convince Mum to take us back, perhaps there's some dirt in here I can use against Margot. Blackmail is a very strong word, but I don't want to be here and she doesn't exactly care for my presence either. So why don't I do her a favour? It'd be super-fun to take the old bat down a peg or two . . . but to have something, something juicy, over her could be my ticket back home.

Interesting. Evil, but interesting. I slink down the narrow stairs, still grasping the diary. I turn out the lights and lock the attic before walking to my bedroom and closing the door behind me.

OK, I *have* to look or I'll explode with curiosity. Margot at sixteen! I can hardly imagine it: some people just come out of the womb aged forty and she's one of them. I'll just read a *tiny* bit.

Wednesday 15th January, 1941

It all seems so unnecessary. I don't see what good leaving London is going to do at this stage – if I can survive the Blitz I rather suspect I can withstand any horrors Hitler has to offer.

What an endless and thoroughly testing day. I can scarcely believe today is the same day as when I left Paddington.

I was by far the eldest evacuee on the train and it fell to me to nanny the little ones in my carriage. I had bid farewell to Mother at home and made my own way to the station, hoping to avoid histrionics, but there were more than enough tears and white handkerchiefs on the platform. I was somewhat surprised there were that many children left in London. Perhaps the September campaign was finally enough to convince Londoners that war is truly afoot. Still, it wasn't quite the crammed cattle truck I had feared.

As we juddered and puffed out of the station, I introduced myself to my new companions. The first was Liddy, a roguish, ruddy-faced girl of eleven from Limehouse, and then two little brothers, John and William Pointer of Shoreditch, angelic until they opened their mouths and pure mudlark poured out.

Anticipating a long, tedious journey, I had brought a pack of cards and taught them Gin Rummy and Knockout Whist to pass the hours. Poor Liddy hadn't brought any lunch as instructed and so I split my spam roll and gave half to her.

By the time we chugged into the tumbling green valleys of Wales, the mournful sniffles had mercifully subsided and instead the train hummed with anticipation. Being that much older than the others I felt it was important to maintain my composure, just as Mother had in the months since Father went away, although I confess I too was nervous. Like everyone else, I was eager to learn where I would be living and with whom. Obviously I said nothing to the little ones, but rumours had reached London that all manner of horrors greeted some unfortunate evacuees. Some had even fled back to the cities.

As we drew near our destination, I ensured everyone had their cases and their billeting labels were clearly displayed. My own was attached to my collar and I felt faintly ridiculous. 'Margot Stanford – From Kensington, London, To Cardiff, Wales.' I was a misplaced trinket, lost and found.

The station was as charred and bustling as Paddington had been. Smoky, dirty chaos clogging my nostrils and catching on my tongue. The irony is that Cardiff had been badly hit of late. In fact, I was supposed to have made the journey a week earlier, but a New Year raid had left much of the city in ruins. Out of the frying pan . . . and all that. Fortunately, none of us was to be billeted in Cardiff itself – the surrounding rural environs waited. Male voice choirs and sheep, how blessed we are. I do so hope my sarcasm is apparent.

I shepherded the younger ones off the train to greet a billeting officer with a spiteful, puckered mouth like she was sucking on a particularly sour lemon. 'Line up! Line up!' she barked at us,

47

quite unnecessarily as everyone lined up most efficiently. By this stage in the war, we all knew it was provident to appear meek and well-mannered for prospective hosts.

I scanned the faces of the women who waited to receive us – most, I imagined, wives of the miners who were now part of the effort. Another billeting officer, a ham-faced, rotund man, joined Mrs Lemonface and they started to match us to our new families. Liddy, to my relief, was quickly packed off (I'd heard girls are preferable to rowdy little boys) with a kindly, maternal-looking woman. 'Margot Stanford?' the woman called and I stepped forward. 'How old are you?'

'Fourteen' I told her, lying through my teeth. Too old. Natural, I suppose, that Daddy would want his only daughter out of the city.

'You able?'

'And ready, ma'am.'

She eyed me up shrewdly. 'Go with Maggie Reed to Newport. You'll do for the factory.' I had expected as much, and I didn't mind being put to work. Mother is doing her bit and I will do mine.

I took my case, bid John and William goodbye and followed the billeting officer. Maggie Read wasn't much older than I, although I saw a ring on her finger. She was pretty, fresh-faced and I immediately decided she was a newlywed, a war bride with no children of her own. 'So nice to meet you,' I said. 'Thank you so much for welcoming me into your home.'

'Oh, it's not my home,' Maggie said with a shy smile and hunched shoulders. Good posture is so important and says so much about a person's character. 'It's Mam's.' I do so adore the accent, 'She's not been well, so I'm looking after her while my Huw's away.' So I was right!

'In challenging times, we all do as we must. I'm happy to lend a hand in any way I can.'

'That's very kind, miss . . . Mam can't manage the stairs at the minute, so you'll have her room all to yourself . . .'

There was a commotion back on the platform. I turned to see the porcine officer attempting to drag John away from William. The boys clung to each other, howling. I looked on, waiting for one of the teachers to step in and help them. I could only see one and she look utterly exhausted, two weeping girls clutching her skirt. I realised there was no one coming to the Pointers' aid, their mother hundreds of miles away in east London, their father even further. 'Excuse me, Maggie. Just one moment.' I dropped my case and hurried back down the platform. 'I say, what's going on here?'

'It's no concern of yours, miss.' The officer's face was now a most unappealing beetroot shade.

'I should think it is. I've travelled all the way from London with these little boys. Unhand him at once!'

He let go of John, who went and hid behind William. 'Margot, he's tryin' a split us up! I'm goin' wiv my bruvver!'

I look at the man's identification. 'Listen, Mr Ridwell, I understand you have a most trying job, but you can't separate brothers. That's simply beastly.'

He sighed impatiently. 'It's nothing to do with me, miss. Most houses are full now. We're squeezing little 'uns in wherever we have space.'

'Oh, there must be room for them both together somewhere. Look at them! They can't eat much more than a sparrow between them!'

I stopped. Darkness fell quite out of nowhere. His shadow engulfed the whole platform. I looked up and saw a lumbering giant of a man looming over me, appearing through the spiralling cloud of smog. His face was craggy and I'd optimistically describe his clenched fists as 'Strangler's Hands'. I didn't feel nearly so confident any more.

'What's going on here then?' His booming accent was the thickest I'd ever heard. 'Where's my boy?'

I puffed my chest out. 'Sir, are you hosting John Pointer?'

'Aye,' he growled.

My voice was suddenly thin as weak tea. 'I wonder if you might find it in your heart to take his little brother William also? It seems a shame to divide a family when they're already so far from their mother.'

The ogre shook his head. 'No. We already got a full house as it is.'

'I'm sure they wouldn't mind sharing a bed. They're so small.'

Mr Ridwell, with all the authority of a scared vole, turned to the huge man, wiping his sweaty palms on his overcoat. 'What do you say, Ivor? They could help on the farm?'

Ivor cast a contemptuous look over the boys. 'You promised me strapping young men, Rhodri. What am I meant to do with them? They couldn't lift a spade between 'em.'

Maggie hovered anxiously. Rhodri Ridwell fluttered ineffectually. It fell to me to take charge. 'Farm, you say? I could be of service on a farm if Maggie was happy to take the boys. What do you think?'

Ivor smiled a crooked smile. 'You? On a farm?'

'Why not? I'm both willing and able.'

Quite unexpectedly, Ivor grabbed my wrist. I noticed at once he was missing the last two fingers on his right hand, only stumps remaining. Well, that explained why he wasn't away fighting. 'Look at these nails,' he grumbled, inspecting my fingers. 'Never

50

done an honest day's work in your life.' He threw my arm down. 'I need a farm boy, Rhodri.'

'Listen!' I said, perhaps a little more forcefully than I intended. 'We don't have much call for farming in West Kensington, but I'm no better with a sewing machine than I am a spade! I'm eager to learn and the strongest here by some margin, I dare say. Now I don't know how you treat women in Wales, but in London we're a vital part of the war effort, which is, Mr Ivor, more than I can say for you.'

The whole platform went horribly silent and I wondered if he might strike me. I'd gone much too far with my impertinence and we all knew it. I held my breath.

Suddenly Mr Ivor let out a mighty, full-throated belly laugh. 'Oh, Rhodri! I have to take this one to meet my Glynis! Have you ever heard the like? Oh, girly, are you in for a surprise! Big talker, eh? You sure you fancy life on a farm?'

I rolled my shoulders back. 'I don't see why not.' I dearly hoped Glynis was his wife or daughter. I didn't relish the prospect of being stranded on a farm with him alone.

'Maggie,' said Rhodri, 'are you happy to take the boys?'

'Oh, I don't know. Mam was very particular . . . and she's not been well.'

'Oh, please, Maggie,' I said. 'You wouldn't see them split apart, would you?' I crouched to be on John and William's level. 'Now, boys, if you go with Miss Maggie, do you absolutely promise to be on your best behaviour?'

'Yes, miss,' they chorused.

'And you must do everything you can to help out . . . do chores to help Miss Maggie?'

They agreed at once and, after a little more pleading on my part, Maggie reluctantly accepted the pair of cockneys. They said their goodbyes and I was left with the hulking farmer. I looked up at him. 'Thank you, sir.'

'Let's see if you're still thanking me after a couple of days on the farm.'

He was certainly gravelly, but there wasn't any nastiness in his words, more bemusement. 'We shall see,' I said. 'I'm Margot Stanford.' I offered him my hand.

'Ivor Williams.' He held out his deformed hand and I shook it heartily.

By the time we arrived at Tan-Y-Pistyll Farm, night was sinking over the valley. What a doomy, desolate place this is: The windswept scenery brought Father Seycombe's spat sermons about purgatory to mind. The farmhouse and stables were steeped in shadow, a black spider in the corner of the hills.

It was the first time I've ridden in a truck – it was quite exciting to be so high up, even if Ivor's little lorry bumped and jolted along the dirt track to the farm. I came over quite peculiar and was glad when we pulled through the gate.

The farm was bitterly cold, my breath clouding even in the hallway, but it was presented well enough. I sensed a woman's touch – pink geraniums on the windowsill; some pretty watercolour paintings of the valley – and I was right. A farmer's wife with auburn hair secured in a loose plait emerged from the kitchen, wiping her hands on her apron. She looked me up and down and smiled. 'This the new farmhand? He's prettier than the last one.'

'Aye,' Ivor said, gruff as ever.

'What happened there then?' she asked. Ivor shrugged his overcoat off and hung it on the stair banister. 'Oh where are my manners? I'm Glynis. What's your name, pet?'

'I'm Margot Stanford. Pleased to meet you. It's my fault, I'm afraid, Mrs Williams. I volunteered to come here so that two little brothers could stay together.'

Glynis laughed, reaching up on tiptoes to kiss Ivor brazenly on the lips. 'Give us a cwtch, you big softheart!'

'Gerroff, woman!' he barked, but with a suggestion of a smile.

'I'll do whatever I can around the farm,' I told her.

'Aye, you will. Three extra mouths to feed now. I already put Peter and Jane to bed. It's not going to be easy, Margot. You should know that right now.'

There was something about this woman I rather liked. Grit in the oyster and all that. 'It never is, is it?' I replied.

She chuckled. 'Come on through. You must be starved. Rabbit stew?'

My stomach rumbled and I was reminded I should be ravenous. The stew was hearty and well-seasoned, served with hunks of warm brown bread. We ate at a well-worn kitchen table, handmade, I was informed, by Ivor. The craftsman himself ate in stony silence, washing down every bite with a glug of local ale, but Glynis was happy to talk. She asked umpteen questions about the Blitz and the state of London. I was surprised to see her supping the same ale and even more so when she offered me some too. I of course declined politely. Ladies do not drink ale.

Out here, the war had existed mostly on the wireless, no more real than a radio play. Having survived the bombardment I felt I spoke with suitable maturity and solemnity, an authority if you like, imparting what I'd heard Mother relay from Father.

'It must be terrible,' Glynis said, shaking her head. 'Weren't you scared, pet?'

'There's an awful minute,' I told her, 'after the air-raid siren has stopped but before you leave the shelter, when you just have no idea if your house is still standing. You're all huddled together in the dark, and everyone's trying to stay calm and jovial, but you can feel it. It's there, unsaid, but everyone is thinking the exact same thought: what if we're the only ones left? Someone opens the door, and you can only hold your breath and hope the world is still there.'

Glynis took Ivor's hand. 'Heavens! You poor thing. You're safe here now.'

'That you are,' Ivor said before leaving the table.

I might well be, but what about Mother and Daddy?

Presently, up in the box room I've been assigned, I am listening to the silence, if such a thing is possible. Here there are no bombs falling, no air-raid sirens wailing like infernal banshees, no fire engines racing through the wreckage of London. It's thickly silent, and I suspect that when the candle burns out the darkness will be all-consuming, more so than even the greyness of the so-called blackouts. I promised Mother I would document my life in Wales and so I have begun. Tomorrow is my first day of life on the farm and, as Dorothy herself would say, 'We're not in Kansas any more, Toto.'

Chapter 6

Too late I hear footsteps plod down the landing. There's a light rap on my door and I have just enough time to shove Margot's diary under my pillow as Mum pokes her head in. 'Are you all right up here?'

'Yeah, I'm fine!' I say, probably looking hugely guilty. One time Marina and I tried a Marlboro Light out of her bedroom window because we thought it'd be very sophisticated, and her mum smelled the smoke. She confronted us and, although we both denied it, I couldn't stop coughing. I reckon I probably look like Marina did on that occasion.

'What are you up to?'

I look around the room and see some CDs scattered on the carpet. 'You know, just listening to music and stuff.' I once read somewhere that lies are more believable if you make them vague. Only rubbish liars pepper their fibs with fine detail, and it's a dead giveaway.

'Fair enough, you OK though? You're very quiet.'

'Fine, I promise.'

Mum comes and leans over and kisses my crown. 'I'm off to bed then. You should get some sleep too – school tomorrow.'

'I can hardly wait.'

'Sleep tight.'

'Don't let the bedbugs bite,' I add. She leaves me alone and my first instinct is to read on. I have a million questions about the diary. I look at the clock and see I've somehow been reading for about an hour, sucked through a time tunnel to 1941. It's *so* strange. My head is like scrambled eggs. I just can't connect the girl in the book to the woman downstairs at *all*, and yet the logical part of my brain *knows* they're the same.

Margot renamed the farm. Interesting. Tan-Y-Pistyll Farm *must* be Mari-Morgan Farm, it just has to be – why else would the diary be here? Margot was evacuated *here* during the war? While my other grandmother, Dad's mum, is always regaling us with tedious war stories, I'm not sure I've ever heard Margot talk about that period in her life. Not once. She looks young for her age so I never really think of her as being old enough to have lived through it.

My mind boggles and I'm desperate to read more, but my eyes are also a little sore from deciphering Margot's finicky handwriting. Mum interrupted me at a good resting place, I suppose. I give the musty notebook another big sniff, still struggling to figure out how and why the diary is still in the farm's attic nearly sixty years on.

So far nothing incriminating or in any way blackmailable, but totally fascinating. The weirdest part of all is that, in the diary, I quite like Margot. She's pretty cool.

So Dewi and I are the only two people on the bus again. There's no way I can avoid him without being rude. 'Hiya!' he says brightly as I wobble down the aisle. From the driver's death-defying attitude to taking corners, I suspect he may be on day release from somewhere secure.

'Morning, Dewi.' I purposely sit opposite him instead of in the row in front. He just shuffles closer. I notice I've stood in a thick pink blob of bubblegum and groan.

'How was your first day?'

I scrape my shoe along the floor, but somehow make it worse. 'Fine, thanks.' I hope my clipped responses will cut the conversation short.

Dewi swings his long legs into the aisle. 'Listen, yeah. Th-the . . . the problem with sm-small towns is that you can't fart in the morning without everyone knowing about it by lunchtime.' I smile at that. 'I heard that Megan Jones was giving you shit yesterday.'

How is that even possible? We were the only people in the toilet! 'Oh God, it was nothing really. She just wanted me to know that, well, you were off limits. Not that you were . . . on limits. Oh . . . it was nothing.'

'For crying out loud!' Dewi rolls his head back. 'She really needs to chill out with that. There's nothing going on with me and Megan, like.'

'She seems to think there is.'

Dewi takes a deep breath. 'OK, look, we w-went together one time at Seren Lloyd's birthday b-barbecue. There was a bottle of Taboo and I was really drunk . . . But I've known M-M-M-Megan since primary school. I don't really see her like that . . . she's too full-on. Also she's been with half my mates, like, isn't it? That's just skanky.'

I say nothing, unwilling to pass comment. I don't care if Megan's working her way through all of Year 11 alphabetically;

that's her God-given right as a woman, but I'm not getting involved.

'I'll have a word with her, get her off your back.'

'No, please don't.' That would make things ten times worse. 'It's fine. I'll just stay out of her way and she'll forget all about it, I'm sure.'

Dewi looks a little hurt. He's huge, but he's still a puppy. A St Bernard puppy. 'I don't want you to think you have to avoid me though, yeah?'

His big hopeful eyes look into mine and I get awful dry mouth. Do I fancy Dewi Allen? The Gallagher eyebrows I could fix, for one. He's handsome in a hulkish way I suppose, the opposite of Xander, who is all cut-glass Calvin Klein cheekbones. Dewi was born in the wrong millennium: his thick brow and brick jaw would have been just what I needed if I were a cavewoman. We'd lie under a sabre-tooth-tiger fur next to an open fire and, yes, I'd snuggle in the nook of those mammoth-wrestling arms, but as it is, there's so much in my head right now. No room for a crush. I'll be thrilled if I can just survive until Saturday. 'Dewi . . . I won't avoid you . . . but you should know I was sort of seeing someone in London.' Not *strictly* a lie. I was *sort of* seeing Xander.

Apparently unable to mask his feelings, his face resembles a sad cartoon puppy for just a second before he recovers. 'Oh no! That's not what I meant, like! I just meant as friends.'

'Good. That's cool.' It'll have to be.

The minibus grinds to a halt and a load of Dewi's friends board, bringing the awkward to a welcome end. I have enough troubles with Margot and Megan without adding males to the mix, thank you very much. Although, I think to myself, it's nice to know that my appeal translates into Welsh.

First-period English is *Lord of the Flies*, a book I've already studied. I'm certainly not going to draw attention to this fact by volunteering answers. I scan the class, trying to find my people. A trio of girls kind of look like my old friends in London, shiny hair and nice manicures, but they regard me with suspicion as if I am a cuckoo planning to nudge eggs out of their nest. I try to make eye contact and smile at one of them and get called a lesbian for my efforts. Which is it? Boyfriend-stealing slut or lesbian? I can't win. I throw myself into the English questions to pass the time until the bell.

Break arrives and I try to think of ways to kill twenty minutes without looking like a loner. A shadow falls over my desk and I see it's the Asian guy and ginger girl who tried to save my *Vogue* from confiscation. 'Hi,' says the guy. 'I'm Danny. This is Bronwyn.'

People are talking to me. Progress. Danny is beautiful for a boy, but Bronwyn looks like a bit of a freak if I'm honest; she hovers shiftily behind Danny like she's ready to flee at a moment's notice. 'Hello. I'm Fliss.'

'Oh, we know,' Danny says. 'You're from London right? Is it amazing? Is it huge? Do you get lost?'

He's gay. I can tell at once.

'Outside, please!' the teacher yells. 'Come on, no one inside over break.'

I swing my satchel onto my shoulder. 'London is the *best*,' I tell Danny as we follow the procession out of the classroom and into the corridor, 'but you sort of make your own village. Like we live in Clapham so mainly stay south of the river. You don't get lost! Oh, well, I once got lost coming out of Stockwell tube. It's pretty hardcore round there.'

I see from his expression that's earned me some serious street cred with Danny. 'I cannot wait to get the hell out of here and move to London. Me and Bron are going to get a flat together in Camden, aren't we?'

Bronwyn makes agreeable noises. I stop at the water fountain and take a sip. 'You shouldn't drink that,' Bronwyn says, not making eye contact. 'If you, like, had the *first* idea what they add to it, you wouldn't go near that shit.'

'What?'

'Oh, ignore her.' Danny rolls his eyes. 'The government is trying to control us through fluoride or something. Last week it was GM crops.'

Bronwyn doesn't see the funny side. 'OK, Dan, whatever. You keep following the Pied Piper.'

Danny gives me a meaningful glance. '*Anyway*, we just wanted to say you shouldn't listen to anything Megan Jones says. She's a rancid psychobitch.'

'Thanks, I guess.'

'She's done her best to make my life miserable since Year 7, but her bark is worse than her bite, I promise. She once spread a rumour that my dad cooks stray cats. For real.'

'I'm just gonna stay out of her way.'

'Probably wise. On a lunchtime, we go to chess club in the library. You should come too. Megan Jones wouldn't be seen dead in there.'

And neither would I. 'Oh, I dunno. Thanks, but chess isn't really my thing.'

'Told you . . .' Bronwyn mutters.

Danny flicks his hair out of his eyes. 'We can teach you. Or you don't have to join in if you don't want to – it's just a cool place for the losers to hang out.'

'Believe it or not, I was pretty popular at my last school.' I don't even know why I said that. In my head it was a lot less conceited.

'Well, you won't be needing us then, will you?' Bronwyn scowls at me, puts big, squishy disco-looking headphones on and strides away.

'Oh. No! What I mean is—'

'Wow,' Danny says. 'Maybe you really are, and I quote Cerys Hughes, a "stuck-up English bitch". Gutted.'

He starts to sashay away, but I grab his rucksack strap. 'I'm sorry. I really didn't mean it like that. You're like the second person to talk to me since I got here.' I close my eyes and give my temples a massage. 'I haven't done anything. I don't get why everyone seems to hate me so much.'

'Duh! Because you're different.'

'Am I?'

'Yes. Welcome to Wales, hun. You wanna try being the only Chinese–Welsh kid in school.' The only *gay* Chinese–Welsh guy in school. That's got to suck.

'You know what? I would love to have lunch with you. Thank you for the invite.'

Danny's face lights up and I think I'm forgiven. 'Lush! I need to take a whizz, but at lunch you can tell me how you get your hair so freaking shiny! Meet you in the library, yeah?' He blows me a kiss and darts into the boys' toilet. I smile, giving my hair a congratulatory stroke. It was a near disaster, but I think I may have just salvaged my first new friendship.

The library is in the basement, which seems a little disrespectful somehow. I descend into the cellar like the idiot girl in a horror film, warily clinging to the handrail. A part of me wonders if this is all a wind-up and I'm about to get jumped by Megan and her cronies. To make matters worse, the canteen must be serving thrice-boiled sprouts today; the farty smell has drifted over from A-Block.

I reach the bottom of the stairs and see there is a sign pointing left to the library and right to the ICT suite. Heading left, I see closed double doors with an 'Abandon Hope All Ye Who Enter Here' poster in wizardy lettering. Oh, this is some geekfest, make no mistake. I hesitate for a moment. Do I really want to do this? If I go in here, I'm a certified freakazoid. That stigma is like herpes – once you've got it, it's there forever. Maybe if I wait it out a few more days, one of the pedigree girls will see I'm not a pariah and let me sit with them.

I'm being a snotty English bitch again. I doubt anyone even saw me come down here, and even if they did, I'm sure social mobility is possible. If nothing else, I have lovely hair. I enter the library with a resigned sigh.

Oh. I wasn't expecting this. The library isn't like any I've seen before. At St Agnes it was in part of a converted chapel, so it was high beams, stained-glass windows and a dried-up husk of a librarian who only ever said, 'Sshhhh!' This is something else. There are a few round tables at this end of the room, at which a few kids are eating their sandwiches, but most of the floor has been cleared and scattered with a Skittles rainbow of beanbags and throw cushions. It's more like a picnic area than a library. In the middle of the room is a tree. An actual tree. Its curling branches reach all the way to the ceiling. I look closer and see that while the branches are real, the leaves are paper, and on each leaf is the name of someone's favourite book.

The stacks are down the far end, rows and rows of books, while at this end there's a curving librarian's desk. The nearest walls are covered in graffiti, but not horrid squiggles under railway arches; this is a glorious mural. The painting depicts famous characters, manga-style, with quotes – 'Wherefore art thou Romeo?', 'Pass the damn ham, please', 'People always clap for the wrong things' and more.

'Pretty cool, right?' says a voice behind me.

I turn and essentially fall right into kind green eyes, flecked with brown like mint-choc-chip ice cream. They belong to a tall man with broad shoulders, strawberry blond hair and stubble. He is Hotty McHot Hot. 'Did you do them?' I ask, suddenly paranoid I might have bad breath.

'God, no – I can barely draw a stick man. Aled did them. He's allowed time out of class when he gets angry or frustrated, so we cooked up a plan to keep him out of bother.' It's such a strange relief to hear another English accent.

'You're English!'

He smiles. 'You got me. I'm Thom – well, Mr Deacon – but in here everyone calls me Thom.' I see from his name badge

63

he's Thom with an unnecessary *h*. Wearing a claret-coloured Fred Perry sweater and beige cords with Converse, he doesn't look much older than the sixth-formers, maybe twenty-four or twenty-five.

'Are you the librarian?'

'Guilty as charged.' He smiles and he has lovely white teeth. Thank God: bad teeth are a deal-breaker. 'You must be Felicity? I was told there was a new English girl.'

I look at my feet and tuck my hair behind my ear. 'That's me.'

'I believe Danny Chung is looking for you? He's on the bench in non-fiction . . . just follow the bookcases round to the back.'

'Thank you,' I say. I don't know why my mouth has turned doughy; *Cosmo* taught me how to Talk to Cute Guys with Confidence, but I can hardly string a sentence together.

'It's nice to meet you, Felicity,' Thom says, and offers me his hand to shake.

I gaze at the outstretched hand like I'm an alien who's never seen one before. Fricking idiot. I snap out of it and shake it. 'You too. Everyone calls me Fliss, unless I'm in trouble.'

'Better not be any trouble then!' He gives me a wink as he backs towards his desk. I feel a familiar hum in my tummy, a buzz I used to feel for Xander back home, but even stronger. I pray the glow doesn't travel to my face for all to see. Hottest. Librarian. Ever.

His hotness may go some way to explaining why the library is so popular, although it's a pretty niche crowd. One table hosts goths and moshers, two tables have chess matches in progress for nerdy types. Another table is set up for painting those little figurine things – the elves and dwarves and stuff. There seems to be a book group of sorts – a trio of girls all reading the same Terry Pratchett novel in silence. I stick out like a sore thumb, but I'm a gazillion miles away from St Agnes so set off to find Danny.

As directed, I follow the bookshelves all the way to the back of the library and find him and Bronwyn working at a PC. 'There you are!' Danny says. 'We thought you weren't gonna come. Well, I said you would, but Bronwyn thinks you hate us.'

Bronwyn's face doesn't register surprise. 'That's not *exactly* what I said.'

'I don't hate you,' I say, embarrassed. 'You're the only people in school who'll talk to me. Why would I hate you?'

'We're not very cool,' says Danny. 'If you hang around with us, everyone's gonna say you're a freak. It's social leprosy and we're highly contagious.'

I laugh way too loud for a library. 'Apparently I'm a freak already, so I'm already infected.'

'Grab a chair,' Bronwyn says, and I take that to mean I'm forgiven for earlier.

I drag one over and tuck myself in next to Danny. 'What are you doing?'

'You live at Mari-Morgan Farm, yeah?' Bronwyn asks.

'Yeah . . .' I reply uncertainly.

Danny's eyes light up. 'You've heard all the stories, right?'

I recall what Dewi's friends said yesterday morning. 'Oh, the terrifying water fairies? Yeah, I heard.'

'Those forests are like totally haunted.'

I do *not* plan on telling them I hallucinated a waterfall whispering my name. That really would promote me into a new and off-putting league of weird.

Bronwyn turns the monitor to face me. 'I don't know about haunted, but historically a lot of paranormal phenomena have been recorded in those woods.'

'*X-Files* fan?' I ask.

'Little bit,' Bronwyn replies with a nerdy half-smile. 'It's all recorded. Bodies found in the woods, suicides, dogs refusing to follow the paths or go near the stream, car engines suddenly cutting out.'

'Really?'

She means every word, I can tell. 'Check it out.' Sure enough there's a website page dedicated to spooky goings-on in the woods right behind the farm. Acid-green writing on a black background. 'This is my website,' Bronwyn adds, luckily before I slag off the migraine-inducing colour scheme. 'I just round up all the information. Thought you should see it. You know that whole valley is a convergence of ley lines.'

'Of what?'

'Ley lines . . . ancient pathways and water fords between points of archaeological interest.'

'Again . . . what?'

Bronwyn sighs. 'Ancient channels of mystical energy.'

'Oh. Right. I see.'

'I told you she'd think we're freaks.'

'I don't!' I argue. 'It's just a lot to take in.' I turn to Danny. 'Do you believe all this?'

Danny smiles. 'Llanmarion is so boring. Please don't take away the only thing that makes it interesting!'

I smile. 'I won't, I promise.'

'I also believe,' he adds, 'that we should definitely have a sleepover at yours! Imagine how scary that'd be – we could go for a midnight walk or camp in the woods!'

I agree, but there's no way I'm taking friends home to meet Margot. She's scarier than any water spirit could ever be.

Chapter 7

That evening, while feeding Peanut, I carry him in my arms into the back garden. Already I can feel him getting heavier. Under duress, Margot has been feeding him while I'm at school and I think within weeks he'll be a right little bloater. Apparently I only have to hand-rear him until he's on solids, which shouldn't take too long.

I carry him past the vegetable patch and into the 'secret garden', where I carefully perch on the old swing, not easy when both hands are taken up with a piglet guzzling milk out of a bottle. The branches complain and the ropes creak, but hold, as they take our combined weight.

I'll say this for the countryside: there's a lot more sky. I feel my shoulders sink as I unwind. School, although still horrific, is a little better with Danny and Bronwyn. I also spent much of the afternoon classes daydreaming about Thom the Lovely Librarian. I can't quite remember his face and can't wait to see him again tomorrow to remind myself.

It's twilight, the night is rapidly turning Dairy Milk purple and the woods are a shifting silhouette, rustling and bickering.

I think about what Bronwyn said. Dead bodies, suicides, cars cutting out . . . Really? It's just a bunch of trees. I inhale deeply and the air is as crisp and clean as an iceberg. The forest is still and, despite the ghost stories, so inviting. *Come on in* . . . the sentry trees seem to say, stepping aside to form an entrance. It's tempting to kick off my shoes and see where the path leads.

I look at Peanut. 'The woods are lovely, dark and deep,' I say quoting a Frost poem we learned at St Agnes. 'But I have promises to keep, and miles to go before I sleep.'

After dinner, I decide to make cupcakes for Danny and Bronwyn. And also – ulterior motive – Mr Thom Deacon. Like who doesn't love a girl bearing cake? It'll endear me to my new friends and, if I'm honest, my hope is that Thom will take one bite of my baking and want to marry me at once. Back at St Agnes my cupcakes were legendary and won first prize at the Winter Fayre last year. I flavoured them with cinnamon and orange peel for that Christmassy taste.

All wrong for this time of year of course. I don't know much about Danny, but I suspect he'll appreciate something cute, so I root around in the cupboards, pulling out a mixing bowl, icing sugar and some red and blue food colouring to make purple cakes. I even find some of those sugary silver balls for added kitsch.

I weigh out my ingredients, stopping to retune the radio on the window ledge to Radio 1, much to Margot's disapproval. 'What on earth is this racket?' she calls through from the lounge. The lounge and kitchen are separated by sliding concertina doors which usually remain open.

'Erm, Green Day.'

'More like white noise.'

'You're showing your age, Margot.' Mum smiles from the sofa, not looking up from the latest Danielle Steel.

Margot bulldozes on while replacing a blown fuse in a lamp plug. 'You ought to be listening to the news. You never know, Felicity, you might learn something worthwhile.'

I beat my eggs and flour, the bowl tucked under my arm. 'Ew, no, thank you. It's so depressing.'

Margot slams down her screwdriver. 'Margot . . .' Mum warns. 'Is this your influence, Julia?'

'Don't look at me. I'm her mother, not her warden.'

Margot looks right at me, her disdain cutting through from the lounge and into the kitchen like a steel arrow. She's made it very clear what she thinks of me: I'm fluff, worthless pink fluff. 'What sort of girl,' she says, a glint in her eye, 'wants to be a fool?'

I put my mixing bowl down on the counter. 'I'm not a fool,' I say, fighting to keep a sulky tone at bay. *Don't let her know she's getting to you.* 'I know enough.'

Margot scoffs.

'OK, maybe I don't know *exactly* what's happening in Sarajevo, but I know it's bad,' I argue. 'The news is horrible and ugly and bleak, so I'm going to do everything *I* can to make something pretty.' I point at the baking mess on the counter. 'I can't personally cook up world peace or whatever, but I can do mind-blowing fairy cakes and just maybe they'll make people that little bit happier so they won't want to go out and blow each other up.' I triumphantly lick a bit of batter off the wooden spoon.

That shuts her up. 'She's got you there, Mum.' Mum grins.

Margot pouts. 'Well, now I've truly heard it all. Saving the world, one cupcake at a time.' Maybe I'm seeing things, but I swear a tiny *suggestion* of a smile twitches in the corner of her mouth for like a second before it falls away again.

I watch *Crimewatch UK* with Mum and Margot, although Mum falls asleep halfway through. I'm not surprised – there were no good murders this month. Margot and I help her into bed and then I shut myself in my room.

What kind of girl wants to be a fool? What a witch. The diary is where I left it under my pillow. I know the *right* thing to do would be to return it to her at once and pretend I hadn't read any of it, but now I'm curious as to what happened after she arrived on the farm. Often, I think, the *right* thing to do is also the most boring. And there *has* to be something incriminating in here.

The irony that we both got uprooted from London against our will and transported to the very same farm is not lost on me – the mystery is why she'd come back to the dump, presumably out of choice, fifty years later. I tuck myself under the covers with the diary, leaving only the bedside lamp on.

I've already committed the cardinal girl sin of reading someone else's diary, so I don't see the point in stopping now.

Saturday 18th January, 1941

Well, a fine start my journal-keeping got off to. I was planning to write every day but, needless to say, as I've gone to my bed each night, I've been asleep the second my head touched the pillow. A combination of manure-ripe air and hard labour, I suspect. I have aches on top of aches.

My first two days on the farm have been punishing, which I suspect was Ivor's intention. I rather made a rod for my own back, didn't I?

The days start when the cockerel crows at dawn, for all of us. Even little Jane is expected to help out at breakfast. I met my fellow evacuees on the first morning. Jane is an adorable Botticelli-cherub-faced girl with moon eyes and chubby cheeks. She's from Liverpool and I do so adore the accent. Peter is a wiry, ruddy-faced boy of ten from Portsmouth.

Over Christmas, the schoolhouse in Llanmarion flooded when a pipe froze and burst. As such the children haven't yet returned. So while Jane helped Glynis in the kitchen and around the farmhouse, Peter and I were expected to help Ivor: letting the sheep out, mucking out the horses, collecting eggs (although Jane enjoys this task). Peter is already a dab hand at milking the cow and showed me what to do.

Oh, it's a ghastly process, rolling and pinching the fleshy teat, firing the milk into a steel bucket. It became painfully obvious on the first morning that the clothes I'd brought are woefully inadequate. I returned to my room after breakfast to find that Glynis had left some lumpen woollen trousers, jumpers and checked blouses for me to borrow. I pinned my hair back and wrapped a headscarf over it, every inch the land girl I've seen in the newsreels.

Now this is queer: not long after breakfast, a car arrived for Glynis and she was driven away without explanation. The same happened yesterday and again this morning. When I quizzed Ivor as to where she'd gone, he snapped she'd gone 'with the women'. I'm still none the wiser. How peculiar! I vow to get to the bottom of it.

It is clear to me that the farm is a lifeline to the village. Rations are every bit as tight, but out here borrowing from the land is far easier than in London.

From very early morning people come, often on foot, to trade for hardy winter vegetables – potatoes and parsnips. I was regarded with keen interest – word had travelled that there was a new evacuee girl on the farm. What a spectacle I must have been – covered in muck and milk and in Glynis's manly garb!

The rest of my first day was spent on the vegetable patch rather than on the fields. I suspect it's too early in the year for there to be much to harvest. Ivor isn't designed for stealth and I was aware of his constant supervision as I worked. I shan't lie, it was a hard drudge – scraping at the frozen soil on hands and knees, trying to unearth potatoes with a trowel – but I was damned if I was going to let Ivor know how cold and miserable I was. No, instead I whistled the jauntiest version of 'Oh When the Saints Go Marching In' that I could muster.

Exhausted and with every inch of my arms aching, I collapsed into bed after a mercifully hot bath. Already my hands felt calloused, Ivor would no doubt be thrilled to observe. He won't hear me complain however; I won't give him the satisfaction.

I'd only been in bed a moment when I heard a low, morose mumbling. A more foolish girl would think the room haunted. I sat up straight and listened intently. Someone was crying. Poor little Jane!

I'd brought my gown and slippers from home and put them on before venturing onto the landing. I could hear Glynis and Ivor talking downstairs, but the noise was coming from the next room. I popped my head around the door and saw Jane sitting on Peter's bed. Peter's head was buried in his pillow. 'Peter's sad,' Jane said.

'Peter? What's wrong?'

'I want to go home,' he said without looking up, his words muffled.

Now, I'm no nanny, but it was a fairly clear diagnosis of homesickness.

I sat on the edge of his bed and rubbed his back awkwardly. It's at times like this that I most notice I'm an only child: I simply don't know how to behave around children. 'There, there,' I said, improvising. 'Of course you do. We all do. We're all a very long way away from home.'

Peter turned to look at me, his eyes red. 'The man on the wireless said there'd been bombs over Portsmouth.'

'Oh, Peter, you mustn't worry. Your mother knows to get to a bomb shelter, doesn't she? She's no fool.'

'But what if—'

'Nonsense! Tomorrow we shall write to her. We'll tell her how brave you're being and make sure she's well. We'll tell her what fun you're having on the farm too so that she won't unduly worry.'

'Peter can't write, Miss Margot,' said little Jane.

I wondered what his life must have been like back home for him not to be able to write at his age. 'Very well, then you shall dictate, Peter, and I shall write.'

That seemed to perk him up somewhat. 'Can we? Do you promise?'

'Of course. But we must go to sleep now. We all have an exceedingly early start.'

'I can't sleep,' Jane said.

I gritted my teeth. I'm not sure I was ever destined to be a babysitter. I remembered my old nanny, Martha. What would she do? 'Jane, do you perhaps have a favourite book? You may have one story before bed as is customary.'

Jane dived off the bed and ran to the bookcase, returning with Peter Rabbit.

'That says Peter,' Peter said proudly.

'Yes, it certainly does. Now, are you both comfortable? Lie down and close your eyes so you can imagine the story better . . .'

Within minutes they were both sound asleep and I soon followed them to the land of Nod.

On Saturdays, there is a farmers' market in the town square. We helped Ivor and Glynis to load up the truck before squeezing onto the back, clinging to crates of veg as we bumped down the uneven roads.

It was my first look at Llanmarion beyond the farm and it was no less than breath-taking: The swooping valleys and snow-capped hills, a darling hump bridge over the rushing river. I resolved to take some photographs and send them to Mother with a letter at the first opportunity.

The market itself was set up on a village green based around a memorial to those lost in the last war. I couldn't help but think of those men like Daddy who had survived those horrors only to head into the mire once more, shoulders square, heads high but with a certain disquietude in the eyes.

This time, unlike last time, they knew what they were marching into. Last year I witnessed a conscription train leaving Victoria station – the songs, the masculine camaraderie, had a bit of a rictus grin, knowing, as they did, that many of them were boarding a one-way train.

I shuddered. Mother once told me if you dwell too much on what's really happening in the world you'd go quite insane, and I think she's right.

The market was bustling and we got to work on the stall. Glynis's home-made jams were especially popular, although how they make any money when she gives so many jars away for free is anyone's guess. After a couple of hours, Glynis suggested I go for a walk to get my bearings. 'Go on,' she said. 'You're not a slave, Margot. Go meet some people your own age.'

I was happy enough on the stall, but was also curious to see if there was anyone else from London in the village. I wandered aimlessly around the market, enjoying the freedom. People were jolly enough and made a little go a long way. There were slices of eggless cake and a tea urn steaming away. I chatted to some of the people I recognised from their visits to the farm.

The local postmistress, Myfanwy Jones, collared me at the tea stall and told me I must meet her daughter and niece. I took my tea and she frogmarched me to where the two girls were feeding pigeons with the crusts of a crab-paste sandwich.

Bess is a jolly little thing with an infectious giggle, while Doreen is a strikingly pretty girl of about my (real) age, who's come up from Southampton to be on the safe side. 'You must be Margot,' Bess said cheerfully, playing with her knitted mittens. She had chubby cheeks, rosy from the cold. 'We've heard all about you! What's it like up on the farm?'

'It's fine,' I replied, now feeling conspicuous in my Harrods coat. The smart tailoring and jade wool was in stark contrast to Bess's shapeless grey overcoat. I suddenly thought my attire ostentatious and made a note to not wear that coat in the future. 'Jolly hard work, but I can manage.'

'Why don't you girls get to know each other?' Mrs Jones said.

'We'll look after her, Mum!' Bess said. She waited until her mother was out of earshot. 'Come along, Margot,' she said gleefully. 'Let's see if we can find the boys!'

Together we went via a stall serving hot soup, where the chap was only too happy to serve three pretty girls with a wink and a smile. 'Oh, I could never work on a farm,' Doreen said, blowing on her broth to cool it. 'All that mud and hay. No chance!'

Bess scrunched her nose. 'It can't be much worse than working in the laundry at the hospital, can it?'

'Is that what you're doing?' I asked.

'Yes. Mam said we had to help. It was either the hospital or the infant school . . .'

'And we chose poor, wounded soldiers over little children!' Doreen said. 'I thought I'd meet a nice fella, but all we do is wash blood – and worse – out of sheets!' Bess collapsed into giggles as we wove our way across the green looking for somewhere to sit awhile.

A terrier had got loose from his leash and some younger children were chasing him through the crowd. I saw Peter taking control of the situation and felt a swell of pride – even after a few days I feel like he is the closest thing I've ever had to a little brother.

'Whereabouts is the hospital?' I asked, making polite conversation. I don't expect Bess and I would have been friends ordinarily, but I very much appreciated her company now.

'Oh, it's the old insane asylum,' Bess said with authority. 'It was closed for years, but now it's an auxiliary hospital for the troops coming in from Cardiff or London.'

'I wouldn't want to be there at night,' Doreen said, eyes wide. 'It gives me the willies during the day.'

Bess smiled. 'Well, if you really want a scare, we should go up to Margot's farm . . .'

'What do you mean?'

Before Bess could reply, a young man yelled at us from the war memorial. 'Oh look!' Doreen exclaimed. 'There they are!'

A group of boys were sat at the memorial's stone base, drinking homebrew ale from one of the stalls. They barely looked old enough. The first was all swagger and golden hair, parted dead centre like an oiled feather. 'Bore da, ladies! Who's this then, like?' On him, the accent wasn't as charming somehow, coarse as sandpaper.

At once Doreen flustered, hands flying to her head to revive her ebony ringlets. 'Hello, Bryn! This is Margot. She's staying at the farm.'

Bryn turned to his friends and smiled a wolfish smile. I'd met peacocks like him in London and remained unimpressed by their feathery displays. 'Nice to meet you, Margot. I'm Bryn Davies, Owen's lad.'

'Who, sorry?'

'Owen Davies,' Bess added quickly. 'The mayor.'

'Nice to meet you,' I said. I offered my hand to shake, but he scooped it up to his lips and kissed my gloved knuckles. I hope my grimace at least partially resembled a smile.

'What are you little ladies up to?'

'Nothing!' Doreen said too quickly.

'Why don't you join us?' He gestured to their makeshift bench.

'No, thank you,' I said politely but firmly. 'I have a sitting condition, as do all the women in my family, so I shall have to stand, or better yet, leave.'

The joke was completely lost on him. 'Aw, come on, ladies! Dad says we can drive into town for the pictures if you fancy it?'

'Oh yes, please!' Doreen and Bess chorused.

'What about you, Margot? I'll let you sit in the front.'

'Oh, I doubt there'd be room for all of us.'

I smiled again but had no desire to spend a minute more than was necessary in Bryn's company. Handsome, certainly, but too keen by far on his own flavour.

'The lads won't mind, will you, lads?' He turned to his companions, whom I confess I had more or less ignored, assuming they were cut from the same cloth as Bryn.

One was a tall, *rugged boy with a meat-pie face who looked a lot older than he was; the second was a rather beautiful, slightly younger boy with blond hair and freckles and the last was the first Negro I'd seen since I arrived in Wales. I assumed he was a fellow evacuee.*

'I don't mind. I'll just go home,' the freckled one said. I asked Bess later and learned he is called Andrew and his Negro friend is Reg.

'See?' Bryn grinned. My skin crawled. 'Plenty of room.'

Another thought occurred to me. 'If you're old enough to drive,' I asked, 'why aren't you enlisted?'

At once Bryn's face fell. 'I'm a reserve,' he said sulkily and the way he spoke made me instantly wonder what the real reason was. 'Anyway, you coming or not?'

'I should really get back to the farm. There's always so much to do.'

Bryn's sneer returned. 'You know Tan-Y-Pistyll Farm's haunted, don't you? Well, the forest is . . . You heard the voices yet?'

'What?' Doreen asked, horrified. I myself have never been prone to gullibility.

'It's true!' Bess said, giggling again. 'It really is! Everyone knows to stay out of the forest at night.'

'What nonsense!' I said, suddenly feeling the bite of the cold. 'I've never heard such tripe.'

'Never heard of the mari-morgans then?' Bryn postured, devouring the attention. 'They might look like beautiful girls – well, except for their pale blue skin and silver hair – and they sing oh-so sweetly, but once you've followed them into the water, they've got you forever.'

80

'What? Like sirens?' I couldn't help asking. Father has told me all the tales of the sea.

'Something like that,' Bryn went on. 'They live in the forest stream. There's a cave behind the waterfall, you see. People go in . . . and never come out.'

'My dad heard the voices once,' said the tall one, who I learned is called Bill Jones – no relation to Bess; half of Wales is called Jones.

'You must think me a fool!' I said, noting Doreen was spellbound by the story – or by the young man telling it.

Bryn looked to his friends. 'That's the thing with you city dwellers. You come to Wales thinking it's like England. But it isn't. We have our ways here, ways you don't understand.'

I smiled. 'I tell you what, Bryn – how about you stick to your ways, I'll stick to mine, and never the twain shall meet?'

'If you don't believe me, come into the forest with me. I'll show you.'

How impertinent! 'No, thank you!'

'Ah, come on! We'll all go.'

'We could take a picnic!' Bess said, clapping her hands.

'It's January!' I said. 'What kind of savage takes a picnic in the middle of winter? We'll catch our deaths.'

'We'll wrap up nice and warm! It'll be fun.' Bess looked a little hurt and I felt guilty at once. 'Oh, the forest is so beautiful, Margot. If we stay together and if we get home before dusk, it's quite safe, I promise.'

Oh, sweet, hopeful Bess. Such warmth of spirit is rare indeed and I didn't want to wound her feelings further. 'Well, perhaps. We shall have to see if the weather's dry.' I didn't suppose there

81

was anything improper about going into the woods with young men if we went as a troupe. I hoped Bryn might be deterred.

'Will you join us, Reg?' Bess asked, her voice suddenly squeaky.

Reg was hardly paying attention to the conversation, kicking a ball idly between himself and Bill. 'What? The forest? Yes, erm, I'll have to check with my family of course . . . but I'd like to.'

Bess smiled broadly. 'Wonderful. I do hope you can!'

I said nothing, but Bess couldn't have been more apparent in her affection.

So we have made vague plans for tomorrow, Bess excitedly planning what to bring and Doreen keen to ensure Bryn would accompany us. Hopefully, he'll turn his attention to her – she's certainly fairer than I.

Pleased to have made new acquaintances, I said my goodbyes. As I wove my way through the crowds to find Glynis and Ivor's stall, Andrew patted me on the shoulder. He was red-faced and out of breath from chasing me. 'You didn't believe all that nonsense, did you?' he said. 'What Bryn said. About the water spirits.'

'No! Of course not! Did you?'

'No! But listen,' he said gravely. 'I shouldn't be saying this really – he's been kind enough to show me around and all – but just be careful around Bryn. He's no gentleman.'

I couldn't help but admire his quiet chivalry. 'I didn't for one second think he was. But thank you, Andrew.' He bowed his head with a slight nod. 'Good day. Pleasure to meet you.'

'You too, Margot. Thank God there's a few of us now.' We shared a knowing smile and he headed off to rejoin the others.

I spent the rest of the afternoon helping Glynis at the stall. It was clear she was popular in the village, although she wasn't *nearly as prim or well groomed as most of the housewives. When I mentioned most people seemed very friendly, she retorted, 'Oh, I dread to think what they really say about us. Half of them say Ivor should have gone marching off even with his hand, but as long as we get them milk and butter I dare say they won't say anything to my face.'*

Just as we were shutting up, Reg came over with his host family – one of the surgeons from the infirmary and his wife. 'Hello,' I said. 'I see you've lost Bryn.' Reg smiled but said nothing. 'Although between you and me, I think Bess would like to get to know you better.'

'Bess is a really nice gal,' he said shyly. I couldn't tell if he was blushing with his dark skin.

'Londoner?' I asked.

'Battersea,' he told me.

'Oh. I'm just the other side of the river, in Kensington.' *There might only be a river separating us, but it means we live in different Londons, different worlds.*

'Very nice!' His smile was magnetic. 'Bit different out here, eh?'

'You're not wrong, Reg,' I said with a sigh. 'But we'll get by.'

'We ain't got much choice, do we?' He said it with a weariness older than his years.

'When did you get here? Has it been terribly difficult?'

'September. It ain't been easy, no. But I suppose it'll be a lot worse next year when I go off to serve our country, won't it, miss?'

'Crikey, just Margot, please.'

Dr Armistead concluded his business with Glynis. 'Come along, Reg. Don't bother the young lady.'

'He wasn't,' I snapped at once. 'Not in the slightest.'

'Nice to meet you, Margot.' He leaned over the stall and repeated what Andrew had said. 'It's good to have another Londoner in town.'

'Join us tomorrow if you can. I know Bess would love it if you could.' I smiled, gave his hand a firm shake and bid him farewell.

It started to snow as we arrived back at the farm. Soft, feathery flakes swirled and drifted up against the crumbling perimeter walls of the pastures. Soon the valley was white and pristine and I felt further than ever from London.

From my bedroom window I can see the forest, bare branches now silvered and frozen. I confess I opened the window earlier and listened a moment for the 'voices' Bryn spoke of. The night was as silent as the grave. Beautiful, but lonely. I cursed my nagging curiosity. Perhaps it was the conversation with Reg, but for the first time I can feel the bruise of homesickness under my ribs. I shall finish for tonight and write a letter to Mother, smother it with exclamation marks, tell her how happy I am and how wonderful everything is.

Chapter 8

Somehow it's gone midnight and I'm still awake. I'm desperate to read on, but if I don't get some beauty sleep, tomorrow I'm going to look heroin-chic in the worst possible way. No one wants that. Not even Kate Moss.

I think about doing what Margot did, opening the window and listening to the forest, but, if I'm honest, I'm scared I'd hear something I couldn't explain.

My alarm goes off at six thirty, half an hour earlier than I'd need to be up if I wasn't feeding Peanut, and pure spite for Margot powers me out of bed. I'm *so* not a morning person. After I've showered – not even bothering to wash my hair – I go downstairs to find that Margot is already fully dressed and preparing breakfast. 'You'll be late if you're not careful,' she says.

Doesn't the woman sleep? Perhaps she's a cyborg. That'd certainly explain why she's so dead inside. I imagine grabbing the frying pan off the hob, whacking her around the head and seeing cogs and wires spring out of her eyes.

'I have plenty of time.' I make a great show of getting Peanut's breakfast ready.

It's cold outside, the first real nip of winter, so I bundle Peanut into my arms and carry him back through into the kitchen.

He's getting wriggly; holding him while heating his bottle is a mission and a half. 'You should be able to feed him from a bowl after the weekend I would have thought,' Margot says, not even turning from the stove to face me.

'But still on the milk?' I sit at the table and Peanut hungrily takes the bottle.

'Yes. For the first month, and then he'll be on to feed and water.'

'You hear that, Peanut? You're gonna be fine! You're gonna grow up big and strong.'

Margot plonks the chipped teapot into the centre of the table and returns to her frying pan. 'And before long it'll be time to take him and the other piglets to the auction mart.'

I'm so intent on feeding the piglet, it takes me a second to process what she's just said. 'What?'

'To sell them,' she says matter-of-factly. 'For meat.'

'You sell them?'

Margot smiles and I swear there's cruelty in it, almost serial-killer-level glee. Oh, she's been working towards this grand reveal, I can tell. 'Of course. It's a farm, Felicity. I don't raise animals as pets! I take them to market and sell them! How do you think farms work? Where do you think the bacon you've guzzled for breakfast every morning has come from?'

Oh God, I've been eating Peanut's siblings. I feel like a cannibal.

'I did warn you,' she goes on. 'I told you not to give him a name, told you not to get attached, but you wouldn't listen, would you? Oh no, Felicity knows best.'

I look at the adorable baby in my arms and then to the sizzling pan of his relatives a metre away. I swear Peanut actually bats his lashes at me. 'You can't sell him.' My voice sounds bubblegum pink and babyish. Margot has cornered me into being the airhead she thinks I am.

'I have to. There's only room for two adult pigs. I'm not going to get into a discussion about it. I know how to run my farm, thank you very much.'

Peanut looks up at me with big, sad eyes. I know baby animals are designed this way to stop you from killing them, and boy is it working. 'Please, Margot, not Peanut.'

Another callous smile. 'Oh, is that how it works? So it's quite acceptable to kill and eat animals, just as long as they're not cute and helpless. What a glorious double standard!'

'Look!' I snap, too tired to even try being polite any more. 'What do you want me to say? That I'm a clueless little idiot who doesn't know anything about anything? OK, fine, I am! I admit it! But *please* don't kill Peanut!'

Mum pops her head around the door. 'What's going on?'

'Margot's going to kill Peanut!'

'Margot isn't doing anything of the sort,' Margot says. 'I'm explaining to Felicity how I run the farm and that all the livestock will be sold at auction in due course.'

'Oh, Mum,' my mum says wearily, supporting herself against the door frame. 'Just let her keep her sodding pig.'

Margot looks like she's going to bite her lip for a moment, but then lets rip regardless. 'Oh, well, that explains rather a lot. Clearly Felicity is a girl used to getting her own way in the pursuit of an easy life. I note she's been more than happy to eat my former piglets.'

'Well, what if I don't?' I offer quickly. 'What if I give up?'

'Fliss, don't be ridiculous.' Mum slides herself onto a chair at the table. She looks like she's hardly slept, eyes like a panda's.

'Well, why not? I don't even eat that much meat,' I lie. From nowhere, the image of a forlorn-looking Chicken McNugget waving me farewell pops into my head.

'You'd give up meat to save the life of one little runt?'

'Yes. If you promise I can keep him.'

Margot laughs. 'Very well. You have a deal. Now for the terms: it's all meat, not just pork.'

'Fine. What about milk and eggs?'

'That's up to your conscience.'

I can't give up cheese. I'd wither and die. 'I'll think about it,' I fib again.

'You'll cave,' Margot says with cat-and-cream smugness. 'A whiff of crispy bacon or roast chicken and you'll give in.'

'No, I won't,' I say, and I mean it. I'd rather starve than prove her right, the giant shit-witch. I'm beginning to think George had the right idea with the marvellous medicine.

'The second you do, "Peanut" will go to auction with the others.'

'What is *wrong* with you?' I snarl.

'Fliss!' Mum snaps.

I just don't get it. I spent all last night reading about a funny, smart girl who, if she went to my school, I'd want to be friends with. 'Like what happened to you? You weren't always such a cow!'

'Felicity. To your room, right now!' Mum slams her hand on the table, making the cups rattle. 'You do *not* talk to your elders that way!'

I stand and hand Peanut to Mum. Margot takes hold of my arm as I prepare to storm out of the kitchen. 'How on earth would you know what I used to be like?'

Damn. I try to remember what I said, but I can't. Did I give too much away about the diary? 'Well, I don't,' I back-pedal. 'I just mean I don't believe you've always been so mean – otherwise Grandad would never have married you, would he?'

She relaxes her grip on my arm. 'You know, Felicity, I could almost feel sorry for you. I remember, you know. Believe it or not, I remember what it's like to be your age, to think you know it all. How exhausting that is.'

'I don't think I know it all.'

'Yes, you do. You think I'm old and out of touch, and that you're the first person to ever feel the way you feel.' She makes a great show of serving the now frazzled bacon onto a plate. 'Schools give you knowledge and you mistake it for experience. Well, experience soon catches up and you'll realise you knew nothing at all. It makes stepping out into the world a much more intriguing concept. I'd embrace it, if I were you. I'm wise enough now to admit I know nothing at all. I'm making it up as I go along. We all are.'

If she thinks I'm going to mop up her phony soothsayer act like a sponge, she's got another thing coming, the pig-murderer. 'Whatever,' I say, and slope out of the kitchen.

By the time we arrive at school, my fury has somewhat subsided thanks to Dewi. We've been talking about *Party of Five*, which I love and he hates, and *My So-Called Life*, which we both agree was phenomenal. As we step off the bus he blocks my

89

path. 'What are you doing this weekend?' he says. 'Do you need anyone to show you around?'

Megan, Rhiannon and Cerys are loitering by the entrance to E-Block like those three witches from *Macbeth*. I take a step away from Dewi. 'I think Danny Chung is gonna give me a tour.'

'Danny Chung? You know he's a poofter, don't you?'

Did I just hear that right? The slur stops me dead in my tracks. Oh wow. And I thought Dewi was something more than an inbred hill-dweller. 'Are you kidding me?'

'What? He is, like. Everyone knows.'

'The word is "gay", and I don't care whether he is or not; apparently he's the only person around here with any style or brains.' I step around Dewi and the distaste on my face should send a pretty clear signal to both him and his townie girlfriend. They deserve each other.

I head straight for the library, its appeal now fully clear. It's an oasis in an arid, hostile desert. I'm angry. I'd really thought Dewi was one of the good guys. What a dick. As soon as I push through the library double doors, I'm hit by a wave of fresh coffee. Thom, Mr Deacon, is standing at the counter, percolator jug in hand. 'Morning!' he says brightly, 'Coffee? Decaf of course – I can't send you to period one twitching.' I hadn't remembered quite how handsome he was. This time I try to take a mental Polaroid to keep for later. Everything seems to go hazy, summery and soft-focus, just for a lovely moment.

Danny, Bronwyn and a couple of others are sat at the tables under the Book Tree. 'Sure!' I snap out of it. 'I made cupcakes!' I rest the Tupperware container on the front desk so Thom can see my culinary skills.

'You didn't!' Danny jumps up and runs over. 'Oh my God, you're the best.'

'They're a fairly unsubtle bribe, I'm afraid. I'm like totally buying your friendship.'

'Consider me bought. Can I have one?'

'Of course!'

I join the others while Thom pours me a coffee. Today he's wearing a marl long-sleeved T-shirt that shows off a muscular chest. Around his neck is a wooden bead necklace and I wonder if he's a surfer or an artist or something in his spare time. I bet he's in a band, something folksy.

Danny introduces me to a couple more of his friends. A boobalicious girl called Sophie and a gawky beanpole with braces called Robin, who frankly looks like he's being *attacked* by puberty. Robin doesn't say much but happily scoffs down two cupcakes, while Sophie is more cautious. 'Oh, I shouldn't really,' she says, picking at an edge. 'Mam keeps threatening to send me to a fat camp. Can you imagine, no? How awful would that be?'

'Your mum is a nightmare. You're not fat,' Danny says, face now covered in pink icing.

'Is she still on the cabbage soup diet?' Bronwyn asks, without a hint of irony.

'Oh, that was two diets ago. Since then she's done this Liz Hurley thing where you move around while you eat, and now she's not eating carbs or something.'

'She sounds fun!' I say, trying to become part of the conversation. Bronwyn still seems a little wary.

'You know Curl Up and Dye in town? That's her salon. She used to run the dance academy over my mum and dad's

91

shop,' Danny says. 'And yes, we have a Chinese takeaway. *The* Chinese takeaway. Could my life be any worse? No amount of Jean Paul Gaultier covers the odour of MSG.'

'She used to be a dancer on *Top of the Pops*,' Sophie adds. 'She's tampin' mad, I swear.'

'What do your mum and dad do?' Bronwyn asks me.

'My dad is dead,' I say, before quickly adding, 'Oh, but he died when I was tiny. I don't really remember him, to be honest.'

'I'm still sorry, babes,' Danny says. 'What about your mum?'

'Oh, she's fine. She works in TV.'

'No way!'

'Yep. She makes documentaries . . . Did you see that one about child assassins in Brazil on the BBC a couple of years back?'

'I remember that,' Bronwyn says, and for the first time I think I've earned an ounce of her respect. 'It was seriously powerful.'

'I'll tell her!' I say.

'Cool job!' Danny adds.

I decide not to tell them about the cancer. At my old school I got plenty of vicarious sickness benefits – time off, extra time in exams, attention and sympathy from teachers – and it was almost nice to begin with, but it got old pretty quickly. Too many sideways head tilts and understanding nods from people who didn't understand *at all*, all the cotton-wool conversations to buffer you should the worst happen. I couldn't bear being treated like I was made of bone china – I was fine; it was Mum who was sick.

It wasn't something I'd planned, a conscious decision, but I realise now that at this school I don't want to be Girl With Cancer Mum. I'd rather start afresh. Anyway, Mum is getting better, thank God. Once the drugs are out of her system, she'll go back to her job in London and everything will be the way it should be.

The bell sounds and we join the morbid procession to form rooms. 'Hey,' I say to Danny, 'what are you doing at the weekend? I thought, if you weren't busy, you could me show me around a bit?'

'Of course! God, where to start? So much to see! There's a derelict mine, some betting shops, the bench where the alcoholics sit . . .' He links his arm with mine and we laugh all the way to room E14. It's the first time I've laughed since I arrived in Wales and it feels like a thaw has begun.

Chapter 9

I'm so angry about Peanut that I don't read Margot's diary for the rest of the week. It's messing with my head too much. I started reading it to dig up dirt on Margot, not to like her, and if I read the diary that's in danger of happening. I haven't touched meat since Wednesday, even at school where I could totally get away with it. No. This is a war of wills, and I'm gonna win.

It's Saturday so, after the effing cockerel has finished crowing, I go back to sleep, ignoring Margot clattering around downstairs. I figure Peanut can wait for his breakfast. I pull the duvet over my head and for a few blissful hours pretend I'm back in London. I imagine meeting Tiggy and Marina in Starbucks for lattes and pains au chocolat before we head to Clapham Common or to Oxford Street Topshop.

When I finally rise at about ten, I pointedly ignore the pile of sausages and bacon in the centre of the kitchen table, instead selecting a fried egg and some toast. Margot observes me over her mug of tea but says nothing. For now, I think we've reached a stalemate.

I take a bath and I'm sorely tempted to read the diary while I soak, but resist and decide to reread *The Babysitter* instead. By the time I've rinsed the conditioner out of my hair (which feels like it takes about four hours) and fed Peanut, it's time to meet Danny in town.

The buses are so infrequent that when Margot offers to drive me part of the way I have little choice but to accept. 'Don't forget about your mother, will you? She still needs your help,' she says once we're zipping down the country lanes.

'I won't,' I say defensively. 'But she's getting better.'

'Still.'

'I've been looking after her for years. I know what I'm doing,' I add, leaving *while you abandoned her to live in the middle of nowhere* unsaid this time.

'I'm sorry,' Margot says, and I have to check if she's being sarcastic. She doesn't seem to be. 'That was unnecessary, you're right. It's nice you've made a new friend. And I hear the food at China Garden is very fair, not that I've ever cared for fast food. Too salty. Too many chemicals.'

I think there might have been something positive buried in that sentence somewhere, so I quit while I'm ahead. Margot drops me near Llanmarion bus station about ten miles away from the farm. She then goes off to run some errands but I only have to wait about five minutes for Danny's bus to arrive.

Llanmarion is even more poxy up close. There's a Wimpy and some pound shops, but there really are a lot of betting and charity shops – one no doubt facilitating the use of the other. 'Is this it?' I ask.

'Afraid so. If you want the proper shops we'll have to go into Swansea. It doesn't take too long on the train.'

'Well, this explains those suicides out in the forest,' I say with a sly smile.

Danny laughs. 'Come on, there's one good shop. Get this, it's a bookshop and it's got a café in it! Whatever next?!' He takes my hand and we set off past Boots.

As we pass the chemist there's a commotion. A burly security guard with a skinhead, steroid arms and ubiquitous Celtic-band tattoo drags a woman out of the store, and the security gates start pealing. 'Get off me!' she shrieks, adding some top-shelf expletives for good measure. She pushes the guard off her and staggers into the road, obviously wasted.

Danny steers me away. 'See her?' he breathes in my ear.

I look more closely. She has a haggard face, greasy hair scraped tightly back into a Croydon facelift. She's missing her front teeth, breasts spilling out of a boob tube under a soiled Adidas tracksuit. 'Yeah. God, what a mess.'

A pause. 'That's Megan Jones's mum.'

'What? She looks about fifty!'

'Nope. She's only in her thirties.'

She must, as my mum would say, have had a hard life. I feel a *smidgeon* of sympathy for Megan, although *my* mum's had issues too and *I* don't go around terrorising half the school. The security guard empties out her bags and sure enough finds a load of shoplifted baby clothes. Danny takes my hand again and pulls me away, although I'm oddly compelled to watch. 'Come on.'

We pass street drinkers and pramfaces and a crazy Bible ranter already worrying about the millennium. To be fair, all of these types inhabit Clapham High Street too, so I can't really blame this one on Wales. The apocalyptic cloud formations rolling off the hills I can however. In the car Margot commented the sky was 'black like someone's punched it' and she has a point.

96

Avid Bookshop is in an end terrace next to the postbox and a kebab shop. It's a weathered building made from warty granite and leaded glass. Upstairs the windows are steamed over from a hissing coffee machine. A bell tinkles as we enter and we head straight up the spiral staircase to the little mezzanine overlooking the bookshop. Danny was right; this is lovely – as lovely a bookshop as I'd have found anywhere in London.

And they do both lattes and pains au chocolat.

The tables are a Mad Hatter's Tea Party affair, with an assortment of mismatched Marie Antoinette chairs and antique crockery. For a second I can see this in a fashion spread, until I remember where I am. We order hot chocolates topped with gloopy whipped cream and marshmallows – the sort of calorie cocktail a true ballerina wouldn't even look at, let alone consume – and sit at the table nearest the window. I kiss my Fonteyn days farewell and take a big gulp of my drink.

Danny fills me in on essential Maes-y-Coed gossip: which teachers are having extra-marital affairs; which teachers smoke between lessons; which teacher *allegedly* murdered his wife. I'm not sure I believe that last one.

He gives me a bit of background on Bronwyn – apparently her dad is every bit as eccentric as she is, and her mum ran away to join a commune when Bronwyn was six. 'And what about you and Dewi Allen?' he asks finally, like he's been dying to the whole time. 'There are rumours . . .'

'They're not true,' I assure him. 'We just have to get the same bus. Anyway . . . he royally pissed me off the other day.'

'How?'

'It doesn't matter,' I tell him.

'Did you have a boyfriend back in London?' he asks, adding a third sachet of brown sugar to an already sickly-sweet drink.

'Sort of,' I say. 'There was a guy called Xander.'

'Was he cute?'

I smile. 'He was like totally dreamy. You know River Phoenix? Kinda like him. Before he died, obviously.'

'Did you break up?'

'Yeah . . .' I almost say, *I was too busy looking after my mum to have a boyfriend*, but stop myself. 'It didn't work out.'

'Did you have sex?' Typical! Boys are always *so* obsessed with doing it.

'Danny! No! I'm fifteen! And also I'm saving myself for Keanu Reeves.' Or Thom Deacon, whichever asks me out first.

'Not Dewi?' he asks with an impish grin. God, why are boys so immature?

'No. Absolutely not.'

'Shame. He's pretty hot.'

I decide it's safe to go for it. 'You think Dewi's hot? Does that mean . . . ?'

Danny rolls his eyes. 'Look. It's not a big deal, like. Yeah, I like guys, but you can't tell anyone, OK? I'm sure in Clapham guys can walk around holding hands and stuff, but here I'd get my head kicked in. Only Bronwyn and Sophie know.'

'I won't say anything, I promise.'

'I know everyone at school thinks I'm a giant flamer anyway, but if my dad finds out he might actually disown me.'

His tone is jovial, but I can tell he means it. What must that be like? To worry your dad might hate you for something you have no control over? OK, I'm not exactly flavour of the month with Margot, but this is much worse. 'Is it really that bad?'

'Ach, we've never got on. I don't think I was what he was expecting when the doctor said, "Mr Chung, you have a bouncing baby boy!" I'm a terrible disappointment.'

I take his hand over the table. 'I don't see why. Who wants a generic baby boy, when you could have a real-life Danny?'

'Aw, babes!' He smiles. 'It don't matter anyway, does it, like? I'll be heading straight to London when we finish Year 13. I wanna be in *Cats* or *Les Mis*.' He pouts. 'Yeah I'm a gaysian boy who lives in a Chinese takeaway and wants to be in musical theatre! I just collect those stereotypes like charms on a bracelet! What you gonna do about it?'

I return home and find a new addition in the living room. A video machine! I've never been so happy to see an old VHS player in my life. 'Where did you find it?' I ask, actually kneeling before it as though it were a religious icon. I feel I should leave an offering.

Margot swishes around in the kitchen with a feather duster. 'It was in Oxfam in town. Only ten pounds.'

This is the closest I will probably ever come to wanting to hug her. 'Thank you! Oh my God!' I turn to Mum. 'Can we watch a film tonight? *Pretty Woman? Dirty Dancing?*'

'Of course we can!' Mum smiles. 'But before we do that, look what Margot found in the attic . . .' She picks up the remote and presses play.

'What is it?'

'Watch.'

It's a grainy home movie. The date stamp in the bottom left-hand corner says 12/07/80 and a woman in a wedding dress is standing in front of a mirror. 'Is that you?' I ask, hand over my mouth.

'It is!'

A voice on the camera speaks. 'Turn around, darling, let's get a look at you.' It's my Grandad's voice and it's like hearing a ghost. I can just about see his reflection holding the camera in the mirror next to Mum.

Mum turns around to show him her dress. It's ivory lace with bell sleeves.

'Look at your giant Farrah Fawcett hair!'

'It was very fashionable!' Mum says, rubbing her crop. 'I bet you don't even remember me with hair . . .'

I roll my eyes at her. 'Duh, of course I do. You look pretty.'

We turn back to the video. There's a cut and now we see Mum getting into her wedding car with Grandad and Margot. 'Margot, I'm totally digging that hat!' I call to the kitchen. Margot comes through to have a look at the floppy wide-brimmed hat she's paired with a periwinkle bell-bottom trouser suit.

'It was truly the decade taste neglected,' she says with a wry smile.

The car leaves and there's another cut. This time, the church bells are ringing and, through a blizzard of confetti, stride my mother and father, hand in hand. 'Oh, it's Dad.' I cover my mouth with my hand and turn back to Mum on the sofa. She just watches in silence, misty-eyed.

He's so handsome. He had a neat beard and his brown suit has flares too. I cannot comprehend why he married in a brown

100

suit, but whatever. 'Give her a kiss, Paul!' someone shouts, and he kisses Mum. Everyone cheers. Mum and Dad laugh and laugh.

Behind me, Mum wraps her arms around my chest and gives me a backwards hug. I squeeze her hands back.

Later that evening I am settled in with Mum and Margot in front of the television, when halfway through my *Adventures in Babysitting* video there's a power cut.

'Oh, the bloody electrics out here are a joke!' Margot clatters around under the kitchen sink and produces a baton-sized flashlight. 'There's an old oil generator out back. I'll go see if I can get her fired up.'

The darkness is suffocating. 'Mum?' I say, unable to see her across the lounge.

'I'm here,' she replies, and that's all I need to know.

After ten minutes or so, Margot stomps back through the back door. 'It's no good. I can't get the back-up to start. We'll just have to wait.' She rounds up some candles – long and tapered, short and stout – and we play cards for a while. Margot teaches me Knockout Whist, and in return I teach her and Mum how to play Cheat. With nothing else to talk about except the games, we all relax. The candles on the coffee table give us a comfortable globe to play in, somehow more neutral than the whole farm, which is undisputed Margot territory. Thankfully the oven is gas, so we can at least make tea with water heated in a pan on the stove.

With no TV to watch we all go to bed early. I have two candles on my bedside table and, in the flickering light, Margot's diary seems to call to me. Oh what the hell. I push the duvet back to retrieve it from inside the pillowcase. Where was I? Farm. Spooky forest. Bryn is a tool.

Sunday 19th January, 1941

Well, today was MOST eventful. I'm writing wrapped in a blanket in front of the fire. Glynis is worried I might be hysterical and she could well be right. My thoughts are all hither and thither but I'll do my best to piece them together into some sort of logical tapestry.

Where to begin? I think today is the first day I didn't wake up disorientated, unsure of where I am. I rose early and helped Glynis in the kitchen. I still have no idea where it is she vanishes off to every day – even on a Sunday – but in the mornings it's all hands on deck, as Father would say. A farm never stops, there's always something to do: Ivor is in and out all day long, covered in oil and muck, and of course they have three extra mouths to feed.

I like Glynis an awful lot. She explained that while the barn and stables were built in the post-industrial boom, the old farmhouse had mostly been torn down and rebuilt by Ivor himself after the last war. It was an accident during construction that mangled his hand and arm.

I plucked up the courage to ask if they couldn't have children of their own. 'Well, that's what we tell people,' she replied with a slight smile as she sliced a bloomer loaf into generous slabs to serve with honey. 'Ivor and I are on the same page when it comes to wee ones. They're nice for a while, but even nicer to hand back.'

I didn't pry any further. Glynis seems happy with her choice, although I wonder how they've avoided falling pregnant. I do wish I knew where it is she goes each morning. I confess I've wondered if she's taking food to the black market, although that doesn't seem in character.

Busying myself with laundry and mending Peter's torn trousers, I didn't even notice the morning passing away until Doreen and Bess arrived at twelve on the dot. Neither had been out to the farm before and were keen to see the animals.

For Doreen it was quite the novelty. Interesting that after less than a week I consider myself to be an old hand, and expertly introduced her to the cow and chickens and horse.

The weather was winter crisp with pale, frosty sunshine. Pleasant certainly, but hardly picnic weather, so Glynis invited the girls to share a bowl of hearty vegetable soup with us before we set off into the woods for our hike. 'Just you be careful out in the forest,' Glynis warned me as I tucked my hair into my mohair hat. 'Stick to the paths, come back the way you go and stay out of the stream.'

'Because of the mari-morgans?' I asked with a smirk.

'No, because it's bloody freezing and you'll catch your death!' She wrapped a scarf around my neck.

I think my favourite part of the farm – and I haven't mentioned it yet – is the delightful rose garden beyond the chicken shed. Ivor built it for Glynis as somewhere to read on a summer's evening, so she says. Paving slabs lie in an intricate spiral, and there's a dainty wrought-iron bench under the shade of a handsome cooking-apple tree. At this time of year the rose bushes are thorny brown skeletons, but in the summer I can only imagine how sweet-smelling the blooms will be. I wonder if I'll still be here.

The three of us exited through the rose garden and were hardly two steps down the path when I heard Bryn calling after us the way Ivor rounds up the sheep. 'You didn't wait for us!' he shouted as he, Andrew and Bill followed us down the garden path.

'Who invited them?' I asked in a stage whisper.

'Doreen,' Bess said, her tone flat. 'I wonder why Reg didn't come.'

The boys caught up with us. 'You're not going into the woods alone, are you, ladies?' Bryn asked.

'Of course not,' I told him. 'I was just thinking how ghastly it would be to enjoy nature in the company of fellow women, or alone with my troublesome thoughts. Thank goodness you're here to save us from ourselves.'

Bryn was too thick-headed to pick up on my flagrant sarcasm, but Andrew suppressed a smile.

'Where's Reg?' Bess asked.

'We don't want him hanging around with us any more. People will get ideas.'

'What sort of ideas?' I asked firmly.

'My da doesn't want people thinking we're Negro-lovers. Everyone knows they're lazy good-for-nothings.'

'Oh for heaven's sake!' I exploded. 'What utter codswallop –'

But Bryn was already striding into the woods with Doreen trotting after him. Bess was crestfallen. I took her mitten-clad hand in mine and gave it a sisterly squeeze. I wanted to tell her how much trouble it would be for her and Reg in this godforsaken town, but a part of me realised I wouldn't be able to stop her heart's desires any more than I would the charging bull in the next field.

Bryn led the way into the woods, and suddenly it was a far less inviting prospect. Doreen clung to his arm like a damsel in distress although her act was more wooden than the surrounding trees. I managed to phase out his crowing and absorbed the forest. The air was a tonic, rinsing the last of the London smog from my lungs. With the exception of a few hardy evergreens, the trees were bare and the frozen ground hard-packed and silvery. It was like a Christmas card; I dearly wished I had brought my camera – I even saw a robin redbreast perched knowingly in a holly bush.

After a while I heard the waterfall and understood the tales of mysterious 'whispering'. The rushing water did sound like a trillion hushed conversations all at once. The air changed, becoming even fresher, as we neared.

'Here it is,' Bryn said as we zigzagged downhill towards the riverbed, the path becoming narrower, more treacherous. I had to cling to Bess a couple of times to stop myself slipping.

'I see what you mean,' I admitted. 'It does sound like voices.'

'Listen,' Andrew added and we all fell silent. The chatter of the stream was urgent, scandalised. The water was fast-flowing, much too quick to freeze, and would no doubt rage faster as the snow melted off the hills. The strangest part was, the water was so clear, so pure, I had the strangest urge to jump right in, to submerge myself entirely like a baptism. But Glynis was right of course; the shock of the cold would be deadly.

For a blissful moment, even Bryn stayed quiet, each of us happy to simply be. 'It's so beautiful,' Doreen said dreamily, stating the obvious.

'Follow me,' Bryn said, leading the way along the edge of the stream. Here the earth was slick and we had to take care,

helping each other from stepping stone to stepping stone. We formed a chain and it felt like an adventure – brave explorers trooping through the Amazon basin searching for rare orchids and the last dodo.

The rush of water grew louder as we neared the waterfall. Well, it wasn't much of a waterfall, more water running down over a craggy rock formation. 'This is it,' Bryn said. 'Where the mari-morgans live.'

'There's no such thing!' Bess said. 'It's just a story to scare children.'

'So go in the cave then.'

'No!' Bess said at once.

'What cave?' I asked.

'Just up there. Can you see?' Bryn pointed about halfway up the cliff face and I saw there was a jagged crevice, a slit between two boulders. 'That's where they take you.'

'Oh, what rot!'

'It's true. I've been in. And there were bones.'

'What kind of bones?' Doreen's pretty eyes were wide with fear and I wondered if her act might be for real. Perhaps she really is as feckless as she seems. How unfortunate.

'Human bones of course.'

'Bryn, stop it! You're scaring her,' Bess protested.

'But it's true. If you don't believe me, take a look for yourself.'

'Not a chance!' Doreen clutched Bess's hand.

'You'll do it, won't you, Andrew? Go on, be a man . . .'

'I'm not scared!' Andrew said quickly. 'Water pixies! I never heard anything so ridiculous.' Andrew's voice is clipped, well bred, like the men on the wireless.

'Go on then. We haven't got all day.' After a pause, Andrew hopped onto the lowest ledge of the rock face and hesitated again, seemingly uncertain. 'Come on, you great nancy!'

Poor Andrew. 'I'll come too,' I said suddenly, hitching up my skirt and striding onto Andrew's rock. 'We can help each other.'

'I can manage perfectly well by myself, thank you.' Andrew started to scrabble up the rocks toward the opening. The male ego bruises more readily than an overripe peach, I couldn't help thinking impatiently.

'Well, I want to see too, and I'm not going in by myself.' That seemed to mollify him. 'You're so brave,' I added, entirely for his benefit.

'Very well.' Andrew offered his hand and I took it, allowing him to pull me up. I turned back and saw Bryn's jaw clench. Good. I put on a little show of my own and grasped Andrew for support. He looked like the big matinee hero and it knocked Bryn down a peg or two as well.

I scraped my knee on the way up, but not so badly that it tore the wool of my stockings. Soon Andrew and I stood at the cave mouth, if you could call it that. 'Do you think you'll fit?' I asked, mentally measuring his shoulders.

'I might if I go in sideways.'

'Well, after you?' I offered with a small smile. Now that we were there, I didn't feel nearly so plucky. The air coming from within was dank and earthy, old somehow. Ancient and foreboding . . . sepulchral.

Andrew frowned and stuck his head close to the opening. 'Well, I can't back down now, can I? But suppose there's some sort of wild animal living in there.'

'Such as? We're in Wales!'

'I don't know. Wolves?'

'Do they have wolves in Wales? I thought they were extinct now.'

'How the jolly hell would I know?'

'We're waiting!' Bryn hollered from far below.

'Oh, have at it,' I said. 'I'm not giving him the satisfaction.'

'Me either. Oh well, tally-ho!' Andrew sat and stuck his feet in first, and then slid through the gap. 'Ow! It's awfully narrow.'

'Be careful. We don't want to get stuck.' More slender than Andrew, I was able to crawl through the gap. The rocks were slimy from the waterfall's splashing and soon I was soaked. The old duffel coat I'd borrowed from Glynis would be filthy – I'd have to wash it.

I slithered over the rock on my front. 'It's getting wider,' Andrew said, grunting as he went. 'Oh! There's a drop! Watch out.'

With every inch I crawled, darkness enveloped me. I recalled an old school lesson about light being unable to travel around corners, and suddenly I wished I had a lamp of some sort. I gasped as hands grabbed me, before realising it was Andrew trying to help me down. 'I've got you. Careful, it's a sheer drop. You'll be able to stand when you get down though.'

Fumbling in the blackness, my hands first took hold of Andrew's face before finding his shoulder to support myself. I felt his arms wrap around me and I dropped to the floor. It was pitch black, the blackest black I'd ever known. My eyes blinked uselessly, trying to scoop in light that wasn't there.

'Well, it could be brimming with water fairies – how would we ever know?' I said.

Andrew chuckled. 'Hang on. I think I have a book of matches in my pocket somewhere.'

'Always be prepared.'

'Well, quite. Here goes . . .' Andrew struck a match and a pathetic firefly of light erupted, illuminating little more than his own face. He held the match out for a few seconds in which we saw only rocks. 'Do you think it's safe in here?' he asked, as the match burned his fingers. He dropped it with a curse.

I reached out and felt the clammy cold of the cave wall. I gave it an experimental push. 'It feels solid enough.' The cave here was big enough to stand up in, but when I stretched my arms up, the tips of my fingers grazed the rocky ceiling.

'How deep do you think it goes?'

'Well, I don't think it's a gateway to Hades.'

Andrew struck another match and inched forward, his left hand groping into the dark. 'Oh, it smells,' he muttered.

'It is musty.' The damp smell was mixed with something rotten, almost sulphuric.

'Ow!' Andrew said again. 'I hit my head. It's getting lower.'

'This must be it,' I said. That meant the cave was only a few metres wide and long.

I stumbled over something, but something soft – and not bones or wolves. I held on to the wall with my left hand while my right unhooked my foot from whatever it was wedged under. I felt coarse material. 'Andrew, I've found something. Light another match. Over here . . .'

Andrew bumped into me. 'Here . . .' He struck another match and, as it briefly flared, we saw the body.

Chapter 10

What? I read the paragraph again. The *body?* There is NO WAY Margot found a dead body. I look at the clock on my bedside table. It's way after midnight and my candle has almost burned to a stump. I reach for my bedside lamp and find it comes on. The electricity is back.

I'm tired, but there's no way I can stop reading now. I sit up straight and continue.

We both let out a yell and recoiled, and Andrew dropped the match. 'What was that?' he cried.

'I don't know . . . It looked like . . . Quickly, light another match!'

'I don't want to!'

'Andrew, just do it!' I heard him crawl over. I reached out in the dark and poked warily at whatever it was. It was cold. There was a spark as the match ignited and, with trembling hands, Andrew held the flame nearer.

The boy could have been asleep if his skin weren't so grey and his lips so blue. He was younger than me, but older than Peter.

'Is it real? Is this a joke?' Andrew said shakily.

'No,' I said. I touched the boy's cold, stiff hand. 'He's dead.'

My first dead body. Even during the Blitz I never saw one at close quarters. He was so lifeless, so empty, so sad. I didn't know what to do or say. He made me feel empty and sad too.

'Margot, we have to get out of here right now! People might think we . . .'

'No, I think he's been dead for days. I mean, look at him . . .' The match stuttered out again and I grabbed Andrew by the shoulders. 'Come on, we have to get help.'

Naturally the others thought we had concocted an elaborate joke when we came screaming down the rocks. Bryn at once clambered up to get a look. Paying him no heed, we ran pell-mell through the forest until we tumbled out of the trees near the farm. Thankfully there's a telephone line there and, once we'd caught our breath and hurriedly told her what we saw, Glynis called the police. It seems I have earned her trust; not once did she question what I told her.

It was almost dusk when the constable arrived alone. I honestly think he thought it was a hoax until Bryn confirmed our story. As the mayor's son, I assume he had a certain authority. Indeed, the mayor himself – a portly man with a permanant self-satisfied smirk – arrived at the farm soon after, along with Bess's mother and Andrew's host. Everyone crowded around the kitchen table, clutching mugs of tea. Ivor went with the constable into the forest and, as much as we protested, we were made to stay at the farm. When they returned, they carried between them the body, wrapped in a tarpaulin. He was placed on a stretcher and taken away in an ambulance, although it was much too late for that.

Everyone swarmed on Ivor as soon as he set foot in the kitchen, demanding to know more of what he'd seen. 'It was the lad from

111

the Old Parsonage,' he muttered gravely. I saw it brought him no pride to bear such sad tidings.

Glynis's hand flew to her mouth. 'Oh, the poor thing. What happened?'

Ivor shrugged his Atlas shoulders. 'Who knows, like?'

With no further answers to be found and fresh snow falling, the farm emptied out and those of us living here ate a subdued supper of broiled rabbit and cabbage.

'Who was he?' I plucked up the courage to ask.

'I can't remember his name,' Glynis admitted, sorrowful. 'He was living with Geraint at the parsonage.'

'Is Geraint the vicar?'

'The organist.' There followed a pregnant pause. Glynis sipped on her ale. 'He's . . . Well, he's a funny sort.'

'Glynis . . .' Ivor said with a warning tone.

'What do you mean?' I asked.

'I shouldn't say. He's harmless, I'm sure, but he's a queer chap.'

'Glynis!' Ivor said more firmly, ending the conversation.

I settled Peter and Jane with a story – I'm trying to teach Peter to read – and then came to write about this extraordinary day. My hand is sore from gripping my pen, but I shan't sleep a wink tonight. Every time I close my eyes, I see the awful . . . absence in the boy's face, recall the unnatural wax of his skin. The poor, nameless stray. My heart breaks.

Tuesday 21st January, 1941

Is there any better way to wake up than to the smell of smoky bacon sizzling in the pan? I intended to write yesterday, but I was simply too exhausted. Another day of high drama in the village. I hardly know where to begin, but I do feel better after a good night's sleep. I write wrapped in my eiderdown, looking out of the frosted window over the snowy meadow. It's almost magically white. With every new day comes a clean page, ready to be written on.

Monday started with a fateful trip into town. The road was deemed too treacherous for Ivor to take out the truck, so Glynis asked if I'd mind awfully cycling into the village to collect our rations. She produced a trusty red pushbike from a shed and, although I thought the journey unwise, I felt unable to refuse. 'Just take the path slowly,' she told me, stating the obvious.

As it was, the forest had largely shielded the path from the worst of the snow, so the ride wasn't as deadly as I'd feared.

I went directly to the grocer's, ration books in hand. As we have our own supply of meat, butter and milk, I was to collect sugar, tinned fruit and cereals. I confess I was daydreaming as I waited in line and it took me a few minutes to tune into the hum of conversation. I gradually picked up on the salacious, outraged tone. 'Well, this is what happens, isn't it?' said Hilda Llewellyn, her hair still in plastic rollers, which I thought a touch uncouth.

'Aye, you can't trust them, that's what I've always said.' That came from Ted Morgan, the grocer himself.

'It's just basic science, isn't it, like? They're a primitive people.'

My ears pricked up. I hadn't heard talk of 'the colonials' since Grandfather died. 'Let's hope he swings for it.' Ted tutted.

'Excuse me,' I said, 'am I to take it someone's been arrested over the death of the little boy in the woods?'

'Aye,' said Morgan. 'That nigger staying with Pam and Lloyd.'

My stomach kicked violently, threatening to regurgitate my breakfast. 'You mean Reg?'

'Is that his name? Aye.'

I know that I had only met him once at the market, but, as a fellow-Londoner, I felt some sort of kinship with him. I mean, I grant you murderers don't go around advertising their homicidal tendencies, but all I had sensed from Reg was a quiet warmth. 'Oh my gosh,' I managed to say. 'Do you know what happened?'

Hilda was only too ready to share, her pop-eyed thirst for gossip bordering on frenzied. 'People are saying they saw them go into the woods together. Only poor Stanley never came out, did he?'

So Stanley was his name. 'That's hardly evidence though, is it?' The others weren't expecting such impertinence and stared in shock. 'Well, it isn't.' I collected our rations with as much haughtiness as I could muster and flounced out of the shop with indignation. As soon as I was clear, I shoved the rations into the basket and pedalled home like I'd never pedalled before.

I crashed into the kitchen half frozen and dishevelled like Scott of the Antarctic. 'Good heavens!' said Glynis. 'What on earth happened here? You look like you've returned from the front line.'

'Glynis,' I gasped, 'they've arrested Reg for the murder!'

'Pam and Lloyd's boy? What? Why?'

'Oh, why do you think?' I snapped. 'I'm sorry . . . It's just . . .'

'I see . . . Margot, I'll get to the bottom of it, I promise.' Glynis's face had taken on a determined air as she set out to make some enquiries, leaving me, Peter and Jane to help Ivor clear as much snow as possible from the farm and the road. The animals took care of themselves, huddling for warmth in the cosiest corners of the barns.

When Glynis returned some time later, it was with a deep frown. 'What's going on?' I asked, placing a steaming mug of tea before her.

'Peter, Jane,' she said, 'go and play upstairs, please.' They left the warm kitchen begrudgingly and as soon as they were out of earshot she continued. 'It's all true. Reg was seen going into the woods with Stanley, although he's denying it.'

There was something else, I could tell. Glynis's eyes were stormy.

'Glynis, sweetheart, what's wrong?' Ivor asked, shrugging off his filthy overcoat and hanging it on the stand.

Glynis shared a pointed look with her husband. 'Well, what about the other boy who was staying with Geraint Tibbet?'

Even Ivor, man of granite, flinched at that. 'He ran away.'

'What? Who? What boy?' I threw my hands up, exasperated.

Glynis stood and downed her tea in a single gulp. 'It doesn't matter.'

'But—'

115

'No, Margot, enough. There's enough rumour-mongering without me adding to it. I shouldn't have said anything at all.'

Maybe Glynis was satisfied, but I was not. There's more than one way to skin the proverbial cat and so I set off to Bess's house. By that time a meek sun was out and the worst of the snow was receding at the field's edges.

'Oh, Margot, it's terrible!' Bess wailed as soon as I walked through the door. Bess, her mother and Doreen lived in a humble but immaculately kept terrace in the heart of the village: no surface without a doily, no cup without a saucer. 'People are saying they'll hang him!'

'Not without a trial they won't.' I tried to calm her, offering to put the kettle on. 'What have you heard?'

'Only what Geraint Tibbet told the constables, and that's only because Gethin Williams told Mam at the post office. Stan went into the woods with Reg a couple of days ago and just never came home, so Geraint says.'

One heaped spoon of tea leaves would stretch to the three of us to save on rations and we split a slightly sad-looking scone between us. 'Well, I'm no Miss Marple, but that body seemed like it had been there for more than a couple of days.'

'Tell her what you told me, Bess,' Doreen said, her hair up in rags.

'Well! That Geraint Tibbet is a dirty old man and everyone knows it.'

This might explain Glynis and Ivor's meaningful glances. 'Really? What do people say?'

Bess shrugged inside her chunky cable-knit cardigan. 'You know, that he's a . . . pervert. I can't say it, Margot, it's too terrible!'

116

I didn't pursue it further. In my experience, every street has an oddball. If they're men they're perverts, and if they're women they're witches. I'm usually inclined to take it all with a pinch of salt, but this was something else when there was so much at stake. 'Did you know the other boy who lived with him? The one who ran away?'

'Yes!' Doreen exclaimed. 'We came on the same train! He was called Roger and he tried to get back to the south coast. Brighton, I think.'

'Why?'

'Lots of evacuees try to go home,' Bess said, pouring the tea. 'I suppose they're homesick, like.'

I arched a brow. 'Something of a coincidence, don't you think? One boy runs away, another dies in the forest.'

'You think Geraint killed him?'

'I don't rightly know. Maybe. Perhaps Stanley hid in the cave and died from the cold. After all, the nights are bitter. No one could survive that.'

Bess's eyes widened. 'You saw the body, Margot. Do you think he died of cold?'

'I'm not a physician, Bess, I have no idea, but there's no way they can blame Reg. I think it's purely because he's a Negro.' I took their silence to be agreement.

'What can we do?' Bess said glumly.

I'll be honest – did I trust the police in this backwards little town to give Reg a fair hearing? No, not for a second. I thought what Mother would do. Admittedly I suspect she'd look to Father to intervene first, but in his absence I think she'd stand up for what she believed to be right. And I would do the same. 'I think we need to voice our suspicions, however scurrilous they are. I

117

don't see them as being any less substantial than the evidence they have against Reg.'

And so that was what we did. We finished our tea and scone and marched right down to the constabulary – a thatched building not much bigger than a cottage next to the post office. Bess trundled alongside, her short legs struggling to match my stride. Doreen stayed at home, refusing to come out with her hair in rags.

Mother once told me that an illusion of confidence is often enough and so, with head high and shoulders square, I strode to the front desk and rang the bell with a firm hand.

A glass hatch slid open, from which the hollow-cheeked young constable who'd come to the farm emerged, and I wondered how he'd avoided being called up. Essential services, I suppose. 'Bore da, Bess . . . girls. What can I do for you?'

'Hello, Huw,' Bess said, blushing fuchsia.

'Good day, sir,' I said. 'We need to speak to someone about the wrongful arrest of Reg . . .' I had no idea what his surname was.

'Bawden,' finished Bess. 'Reg Bawden.'

At least Huw didn't laugh us out of the police station. Instead, he frowned deeply. 'What do you girls know about Reg Bawden?'

'Enough to know he didn't murder that boy in the forest.'

Apparently I said it loud enough to alert a more senior officer. A ruddy-faced man appeared behind Huw at the glass hatch. 'What's going on, Huw?'

'Dad . . . I mean Sergeant Thomas . . . this girl says she knows something about the murder.'

'And who might you be?'

'I'm Margot Stanford, sir, and I'd like to know on what grounds you're holding Reg Bawden.'

His face suggested he was far from impressed at having his detective work called into question. 'Oh, is that right, is it?'

'Yes, sir. Unless you have a witness, it's rather Reg's word against that of Mr Tebbit, isn't it?'

'Look here, missy, it's no business of yours. Go you on home.'

Sergeant Thomas went to close the hatch, but I reached out and blocked it with a gloved hand.

'Absolutely not. I'm not going anywhere until you tell me what evidence you have against Reg beyond the colour of his skin. Correct me if I'm wrong, but didn't another young man abscond from Mr Tebbit's care? Doesn't that pique your interest even slightly? Why two boys would invite such danger rather than remain in the house of a strange old man for a second longer?'

Red blotches began to spread from Thomas's collar towards his jowls. 'Oh, you want to be mighty careful with what you're saying, girly . . .'

I fixed him dead in the eye. 'He a friend of yours?'

The crimson mist reached his forehead. 'I'll say it again in case you're deaf. Go home.'

'No.' My tone left little room for debate. Sometimes progress is saying no and meaning it.

'How dare you, the flamin' cheek of it—'

'Now what's going on here?'

We all turned to see Ivor's bulk filling the doorway.

'What are you doing, Margot? Gethin said he saw you stormin' in here.'

I felt as if I'd been caught red-handed. 'Ivor. It's not right. They can't keep Reg without any evidence. They just can't.'

'Oh, is she yours, Ivor?' Thomas cut in. 'Take her home, will you?'

119

Ivor lumbered to the desk. 'See here, Dave, why are you holding this boy Reg?'

'Oh, don't you start, Ivor.'

'I mean it though. People in town are talking, Dave. Talking about Geraint Tebbit.'

'Aw, you're as bad as she is! Just keep your nose out!'

With Ivor at my side, I felt stronger. 'Have you actually spoken to the other boy who ran away?' I asked. 'I believe his name was Roger.'

Thomas said nothing, instead sighing like a steam train.

'It's a valid question, Dave,' Ivor agreed.

'No. No, we haven't.'

'I saw that body, Sergeant Thomas,' I said. 'He wasn't murdered; he died from cold, I'd venture. He ran away and froze to death. I'm right, aren't I?'

'Ivor,' Thomas said gravely, 'you need to take her home right now.'

'Come on, Margot. You've made your point. Dave . . . you can't try this boy without evidence. You better be sure before you do, you better be sure as eggs.'

Thomas glowered up at him. 'I'll thank you for your assistance when you come to me for advice on farming, how about that?'

Ivor's nostrils flared and the bull in the next field over from the farm was called to mind. 'Girls. Go wait in the van. Now.'

Too scared to disagree, Bess and I hurried out of the police station, Ivor taking over the battle. 'What now?' Bess asked.

I thought I was fresh out of ideas until it occurred to me, in such a small station, the cells were probably on the ground floor. 'Follow me,' I told her. Checking the coast was clear, we crept around the

120

perimeter of the police station. A narrow snicket led to a damp paved backyard. We had to clamber over some dustbins to get to them, but it was pretty simple to deduce the high, narrow windows covered by iron bars were probably the cells.

'Do you think he's in there?' said Bess hopefully.

'I suppose he must be. Say, help me with the bin.' Together we tipped a metal dustbin upside down, and I hitched my skirts and climbed atop it with Bess's help. I tapped ever so quietly on the glass through the bars. 'Reg? Reg, are you in there?'

I heard activity on the other side of the window – furniture shifting. The glass was frosted, but a distorted face soon appeared at the window. 'Who's that?'

'Reg, it's me, Margot Stanford.'

'Margot! What on earth you think you're doing?' His voice was muffled but I heard him well enough.

'I'm here with Bess. We came to see if you were all right?'

He paused. 'I've been better.'

'Are they looking after you? Are you warm and fed?' He assured us he was. 'Listen,' I said, 'tell me honestly – did you do what they're saying you did?'

'No! I done nothing. I only met Stanley once or twice for a kick-about. I wasn't nowhere near him when he went missing.'

I breathed a sigh of relief. I believed him with all my heart. 'Good. Tell them that. If they have no evidence, they can't do a thing.'

He looked over his shoulder. 'I better go. I'm standing on my bed and someone's gonna see.'

'Let me talk to him!' Bess tugged on my skirt.

'Bess wants a word,' I said, and clung to a drainpipe to help myself down.

121

I gave Bess a hand up and steadied the dustbin. 'Oh, Reg! I miss you!'

I heard Reg chuckle. 'Miss you too, Bess. I'll be out soon.'

I wished I was as confident. 'I'll wait for you!' Bess said tearfully, pressing a hand to the window. I stifled a smile at how melodramatic she sounded, positively cinematic in fact.

'Oi!' We both froze, Bess almost tumbling off her perch. I didn't dare look up. We'd been caught red-handed. 'Thought I told you to wait in the truck. What you doin'?' Ivor loomed at the end of the alleyway.

Bess hopped into my waiting arms. 'Nothing,' I said guiltily, quite clearly up to something.

'Think you should come with me right now before they put you on the other side of that wall.'

We shuffled past, shamefaced. 'Thank you for helping,' I muttered as I passed him.

'Hmmm.' And that was all he said on the matter.

By the afternoon, news had already spread. Word of a spirited English evacuee descending on the police station like a virago and giving Sergeant Thomas a piece of her mind was all anyone in town could speak of. I know because already Bess's mother and Hilda Llewellyn had stopped by the farm to truffle out further facts like hungry pigs.

By supper, word reached us that Geraint Tibbet had been taken in for questioning. That was the last I've heard, but I feel a swell of optimism. I don't claim full responsibility for the victory. I wonder if town gossip was tightening around the sergeant like finger screws until he had to act. I can only hope that they are in *the process of tracking down the other little boy and he'll confirm the dark and horrible truth I fear.*

I must push that ugliness aside. Proving Reg's innocence is a fight worth fighting. I think Mother would be proud.

Chapter 11

I sleep in until after eleven, blaming teenage hormones while I still have the chance. Margot and Mum chat downstairs as I drift in and out of indulgent Sunday-morning sleep, dreaming strange, BBC2-afternoon-movie black-and-white dreams of Reg and Bess and young Margot. Then Gregory Peck turned up and it all got very confusing.

As I stir properly, everything I read last night feels like fiction. It's just so . . . outlandish! Murder, well, not murder, but . . . paedophilia, I guess . . . and Margot somehow saving a man from death row. Except we never called it death row in this country, but still. How is it I've gone nearly sixteen years without ever hearing about this remarkable Atticus Finch moment? Neither Mum or Margot have mentioned it *once*.

I mean, how many times have I heard this story – valiant white saviour gallops in and rescues the downtrodden black guy, and everyone cheers for Kevin Costner or whatever. But then I think, this isn't a *story*, it's Margot's life . . . Margot's words, and I guess I'll never get to hear Reg's side of it, which is a shame, but what choice do I have? I can't exactly hop in the TARDIS to speak to him, and I can't ask Margot either without letting on I've nicked her diary.

It was a different time. I suppose, in 1941, Reg didn't have too many people – let alone white people – speaking up on his behalf, and I'm proud Margot did. I like to think I'd have done the same.

I hear Margot's Land Rover crunch away down the dirt track and take that as my cue to get up. Mum has fed Peanut, saving me the job. 'All done,' she says. 'Do you want brekkie? It's almost lunchtime, Fliss.'

'I'll just have this.' I take a banana out of the fruit bowl. 'Cup of tea?'

'Ooh, yes, please!' She eases herself onto the sofa.

'Where did Margot go?'

'She's taking the generator over to one of the houses in the hills – they didn't get their electric back or something. She'll be back in a while.'

I pour the tea and stir sugar into mine. 'Good. Let's make the most of it while she's gone.'

'Fliss,' Mum says wearily, putting her bookmark back into the latest Martina Cole, 'you promised me you'd give it a fair go.'

I carry the tea over and plonk it onto the coffee table. 'I *am* trying. It's her that's being a megabit—'

'Felicity . . .'

'She's a bully, Mum. She does it on purpose. She did it to *you* before you were sick.' I remember, on more than one occasion, Mum telling Margot to butt out of her work and stuff.

Mum sighs. 'Margot is old. She's set in stone. You're young and flexible. We might have to bend to fit around her a little.'

'There is no Pilates in the world that'd make us that flexible.' Mum smiles and it lights up her face. She is starting to look

125

better. I wonder if the last of the chemicals they pumped into her system are gone. Before long she'll be able to go back to work . . . and that means going back to London, unless she intends to make documentaries about sheep and hills.

I think about the triumphant Reg saga. 'What was Margot like when you were little?'

Mum shrugs. 'Not very mumsy. Dad did most of the parent stuff. You have to bear in mind Margot was already this famous award-winning journalist when I was born and those were the days before childminders and any concept of work–life balance. She was busy, I suppose. I didn't mind though; I was always very proud of her. She was right at the heart of the women's lib movement – not that she needed liberating from Dad, but even when I was little I thought that was a wonderful thing.'

I try to remember Grandad, but I was so young and he died so suddenly. I do recall him being kind, fuzzy and warm, always ready to swing me around their Hampstead garden. I had a choice of 'arms' (being swung by the arms), 'legs' or 'aeroplane' (which was one arm and one leg). That garden was something else: foxgloves and willows and the pond with the koi carp. He lived to defend those bloody fish from a dastardly heron. 'Was Margot alive during the war?' I ask innocently, not wanting to reveal I'm ransacking her private diary.

'Of course! She'd have been . . . a teenager. In fact . . .' Mum stands and walks to the sideboard. She slides it open and runs her finger along the spines of some dusty old volumes. She pulls one out and I see that they're photo albums. 'Let's see. This one is from . . . 1939, so just before the war.'

She sits alongside me on the settee and we leaf through gorgeous sepia images of Margot's life in London. In most of them she's pictured with her father, the admiral, and her mother. It's easy to see where Margot gets her looks from: she's got her father's statuesque height and, luckily for her, her mother's beautiful cheekbones and lips. My great-grandparents: perfect strangers to me, both long dead before I was born. We get to the end of the album and there's nothing from during the evacuation. 'Does she ever talk about the war?'

'Not really, actually,' Mum admits. 'Why don't you ask her yourself? Maybe that's what you need: to get to know each other better.'

I say nothing and Mum returns to *Sexy Mob Wives* or whatever it is she's reading. That's the problem ... I *am* getting to know Margot, and it doesn't make any sense whatsoever.

There's only one thing for it. After I've showered and gone way dizzy from hanging my head upside-down to blow-dry my hair, I dress in sensible shoes – some old violet Kickers – and finally venture into the forest. Eerie voices, mari-morgans, whatever, I have to know. If the cave behind the waterfall exists, I suppose that would go some way towards corroborating the diary. In history, the teachers are always telling us to question secondary sources, especially diaries, because of bias. Maybe Margot was so bored during her time at the farm she concocted a story about herself.

Outside, it's what Mum would call 'muggy', so I select a Miss Selfridge purple denim jacket and slip it over my Lipsy blouse. The ensemble vaguely matches, but who's going to

127

see it? I tell Mum that I'm going for a walk and exit through the rose garden.

I stand in the shade of the trees and remember Margot's warning to stay out of the woods and Bronwyn's ominous stories. I refuse to be deterred. A watery, diluted sun is trying to pierce the cloud, and chirping birds are in fine voice; it's really not scary.

But you can never be too careful. I find a flat piece of slate and every hundred metres or so I scratch an X into the bark of a tree so I can find my way back to the farm. If it's good enough for Hansel and Gretel, it's good enough for me.

I'm reminded of Center Parcs, the last time I was in a forest. It was BC – Before Cancer – and Mum took me and Tiggy for a long weekend. But the forest there felt very safe – the paths all clearly marked and signposted. It was like being in a forest theme park – artificial and sterile somehow, like every blue tit and squirrel had been hired to perform. This . . . this feels wild . . . wild and gnarly and angry and ancient. The branches overhead creak like old bones, as if the trees have stories to tell.

The paths wind and split with no logic, more like veins than anything man-made. After the rain last night, the air is rich with *that* soily, almost electric smell. Soon enough I hear the 'whisper' of the stream, and today she's not saying my name, because that's *crazy*.

The ground drops away without warning, splitting into a gorge. I almost career right over the edge and grab a branch to steady myself. A fast-flowing stream carves the forest, a fallen tree bridging the gap. Tempting though it is, I'm not so stupid as to try cross it in this outfit. Upstream, a rocky outcrop looms from which the water gushes, spills and tumbles. The waterfall is jagged, like a lightning scar on the hillside. There are glimmers of gold as weak sun bounces off the water.

I've never seen anything like it. It's honestly so beautiful I forget to breathe for a second, hand to my chest. This is way existential, but for a second I feel tiny, dwarfed by the power of the natural world. Or something . . . I know what I mean.

Getting down to the water's edge is more of an effort. If there is a safe and easy way, I can't see it. The slope is sheer and covered in brambles and weeds. All I can do is cling on to overhanging branches and sort of lower myself down the incline.

The rocks lining the stream are slick with moss and I continue to use branches to steady myself as I take them as stepping stones. If I fall and hit my head, no one is going to find my body for a long time.

I think about the corpse in the cave and shudder. Well, if he ever really existed.

I head upstream, and it's hard work. It's slow progress and my arms ache. A couple of times my foot slips into the stream and I'm soaked all the way through my socks to the skin. My Kickers squelch with every step.

I rest at the bottom of the waterfall. Water surges through a narrow gap between two mighty boulders at the top and then cascades down the cliff-face. Cool mist hits my face and I wonder just *how* frizzy my hair is gonna get. I scan the rocks, looking for the legendary cave. There's nothing obvious, but I do spot a crevice where two layers of rock don't quite sit together. That has to be it.

My feet are, I think, in very real danger of frostbite, but I've come this far. I set off over the rocks. This part is less treacherous than the mossy stepping stones – there are more footholds, and it's not too slippery if I avoid the splash zones.

Even so, I'm knackered by the time I get to the opening. Wow, I'm really out of shape. I vow to do Mum's old *Rosemary Conley: Legs, Bums and Tums* workout video as soon as I get home. Or tomorrow maybe.

Unless Margot neglected to mention it, the entrance to the 'cave' has since been covered in graffiti and there are a fair few crushed beer cans scattered around. This'd be prime real estate for winos and junkies, so I'd better be careful. Once a Girl Guide, always a Girl Guide, I pull the torch from my little Baby Spice backpack and shine it inside. I can't see anything much, but remember Margot's description of how the tight entrance opened out further in.

I dump the rucksack on the ledge. Carefully, and accepting I'm gonna make a total mess of the denim jacket, I lie on my front and wriggle through the gap like a snake. The torch beam is pretty weak – the batteries must be going – but I can see just ahead of myself. The dank cavern smells of wee and stale cigarette smoke. With my free hand, I feel for the drop Margot described. The tips of my fingers find a ledge and I pull myself along.

I'm in!

And I'm not alone.

There's a curse and a gasp and a scuffling of feet. My light clearly illuminates two pale, naked bums; two guys frantically pulling their pants up. And between them, on her knees, is Megan Jones.

Great. That's perfect.

Chapter 12

'Sorry!' I squeak and slither backwards out of the cave opening. I land awkwardly with a thud on my butt, but my desire to be as far away as possible overrides the pain. 'I didn't see anything, I swear!' I shout into the hole before seizing my backpack and clambering over the rocks, trying to get back onto the embankment. I throw a glance over my shoulder to see if they're chasing after me, but I don't see anyone.

Oh God, I could just *die*. I probably will.

This time, I don't climb down to the water's edge. Instead I follow the stream from the path running alongside the top of the gorge until I find the first of my marked trees. I break into a run, desperate to get back to the farm.

Maybe the stream *is* full of evil fairies. It certainly seems to be cursed. Dead bodies. Naked bodies. Of all the people in all the world it had to be Megan bloody Jones. Well, of course it was. Thanks for having my back, universe. The 'chatter' of the stream now sounds like mocking laughter.

I run from marker to marker, the forest spinning wildly around me like a giddy green carousel. I keep looking over my shoulder, sure Megan and her boyfriends are coming to kill me. I daren't stop. When the edge of the woods comes into sight

I allow myself a brief rest. I keel forward, hands on knees. My stomach lurches, but I'm not sick. For the first time, the farm feels like a safe haven.

As I stagger up the garden path, out of breath, Margot is feeding the chickens. She casts an eye over me, my jeans and jacket covered in mud, my sodden Kickers ruined forever. 'I did warn you about those woods, didn't I?' is all she says, before turning back to the chickens.

I don't reply. I just want to be in a bath.

Rainy percussion on the shed roofs has kept me up for most of the night and the spiteful weather shows no signs of stopping. Water gurgles and splatters from the broken guttering outside my window to the flagstones below and, to make this miserable Monday morning worse, today Bronwyn and Danny are on a geography field trip without me. How am I meant to face Megan without them? I think about feigning illness, but that requires effort and I always think to throw an effective sickie, you have to lay the groundwork the night before . . . making a great show of slinking off to bed early or pretending to have no appetite at dinner.

I kick the quilt off and cling to the faint glimmer of hope that Megan doesn't know it was my head that popped into the dark cave. Oh, who am I kidding? She's going to crucify me. I feel like I might actually hurl.

Margot, meanwhile, has invented a new torture treatment. I'm starting to suspect she stands at the bottom of the stairs actively wafting crispy bacon in the direction of my bedroom. Well, I'm not caving in. Over breakfast we say few words, but I pointedly smear butter and jam onto my toast, ignoring the flesh mountain of bacon and sausages in the middle of the table. I mean, who is she even cooking it all for? Mum eats like a sparrow. She might as well mount pigs' heads on pikes and just have done with it.

I decide, in the absence of any friends, to take Margot's diary to school. I'll find a spot in the library and continue to read it. I think about trying to tally up the dates with the local papers too, or matching it to the timeline of the war to see if everything adds up. I guess now that I know the cave exists, there's no real reason to doubt its contents, but I'm totally being pulled back in time like it's a magic portal or something. I want to know more; I want to see Margot's Wales; I need to know what happened next.

I read it on the bus into school, still pointedly avoiding Dewi. In the next instalment, Margot gives a brief update as to what happened with Reg: he was freed two days after Margot's outburst at the station. Apparently the police managed to track down the runaway boy, who'd been rehoused with a family in Swansea. He told them the reason he'd fled, confirming what both Margot and I had suspected. I'm grateful that Margot didn't include any gory details. Geraint Tibbet was arrested for 'indecency', and Reg released.

Worryingly, even Tibbet's arrest didn't stop speculation about the 'Negro' in Llanmarion. Poor Reg. Oh well, at least Bess was thrilled to have him out – and it was Margot who got much of the stick for being a 'darkie-lover'. To her credit, Margot didn't seem to care what the people of the village thought about her, and neither should I. I sat up a little straighter in my seat.

Dewi collars me as I step off the bus, hovering at my shoulder. 'Hey . . . Are y-you cross with me, Fliss? Is it about

D-D-D-Danny Chung? Look, I shouldn't have said what I said, OK? I wasn't thinking, like.'

My face can appear a little condescending at the best of times, but right now I'm actively switching it up. 'No. You really shouldn't. There's nothing big about being a bigot, Dewi.' I'm satisfied with my little play on words. Feisty.

For someone so towering, he suddenly looks like a shamefaced little boy. 'I know . . . I don't know why I said that, like. It was stupid. I was stupid. I actually really like Danny. He's a laugh.'

'Oh yeah? "Some of my best friends are gay"?'

'What?'

'Oh, never mind.' Haughty.

'I j-just thought that if you fancied him, you should know he's a gay.'

No way! He's jealous of Danny! It'd be cute if it weren't so sad. 'I don't fancy anyone right now,' I say, making myself very clear. He looks hurt and I feel bad for kicking the puppy. I soften my tone. 'Look, I'm just looking for some friends. People haven't been too welcoming if you hadn't noticed.'

Dewi perks up a little. 'If anyone gives you any hassle, you tell me, like. I'm soft as shit, but my size confuses people.' He gives me a wonky smile. 'I can . . . can always sit on them if all else fails.'

I laugh, forgiving him for now. There's a warmth about Dewi, not just his cuddly exterior, but something toasty from inside too. I think his heart's in the right place. What does that even mean? How can your heart be in the wrong place? You'd like totally die. Now that he's forgiven-ish, we walk to registration together.

First period is maths. At St Agnes, I was quite average at maths, but here I'm top of the class. I don't think my private-school teachers were any better; it's just that in my old classes there were only seventeen of us. Here there's thirty-two. It's a painfully slow double period of trigonometry before break and then I head for the library, Margot's diary in my arms.

I'm walking down the alleyway between blocks when there's a tug on my ponytail. Ow! It really, REALLY hurts like it's coming out at the roots. My head yanked back, I manage to twist around before my neck breaks to see Megan's shoes.

It's time then.

She drags me up against the wall and bangs the back of my head against the bricks. My brain rattles inside my skull painfully. My eyes flick left and right searching for a saviour. Why is there never a teacher around when you need one?

Megan gets right up in my face, her breath stinking of Wrigley's Juicy Fruit gum and Red Bull. 'Did you tell anyone?'

'No!' I squeal and she relaxes her grip on my hair. If nothing else, at least she's alone this time. Not that that would help in a fight. She'd pulverise me.

'Are you gonna tell anyone?'

'I didn't see anything, Megan.'

'Too fucking right you didn't, bitch,' she snarls. 'You know what'll happen if you say a word? Do people get bottled in London? Be a shame to mess up such a pretty face.'

My scalp scrapes against the wall again. 'I won't say anything. I promise.'

Megan takes a step back and I let out a shaky breath. 'Don't come near me, slut. I might fuck you up just for fun, yeah?' She

135

spits in my face, and I feel a thick globule of phlegm dribble off my nose. Scowling, she stalks away.

I can't stop shaking. It must be adrenaline left over in my veins, but my hands are vibrating and my legs feel rubbery. As soon as I step into the library, Thom Deacon stops what he's doing and comes out from behind his counter. 'Fliss? Are you OK? You look awful.'

'I'm fine,' I say, but my legs almost buckle under.

Thom steadies me and guides me to one of the tables. 'What's wrong?'

'It's nothing.' Tears fill my eyes, but I blink them back. I don't want to cry on him. Not hot.

'It's obviously something, Fliss.'

The library is pretty much empty, with half the year out on the field trip, but I still don't want to say anything. If he reports it and Megan finds out, I'm dead. I don't trust myself to speak so I just shake my head.

Thom Deacon moves in closer and I catch a hint of his aftershave. It's woody and mature, distinguished. I like it and wish I could rest my head on his broad shoulder. 'Listen, if someone's giving you a hard time, I can help. I'll be discreet.'

'Seriously, it's fine. I'll be fine.'

He sighs, frustrated. 'It makes me so mad. I don't get how you can be so horrible to each other. Can you imagine if adults carried on the way some of you lot do? I'm sure it's nothing you've done, Fliss. They're probably just jealous.'

Jealous? Of what? Is he saying he thinks I'm pretty? I look into his eyes, searching for the flecks of brown in the green.

136

Evergreen eyes, like the pines and firs in the forest. 'Jealous of what?'

He smiles warmly. 'You're new and different. You stand out. It'll get better when the novelty wears off, I promise, and in the meantime you've always got me. Where's Danny and the others today?'

I inhale deeply, pulling myself together. 'Geography trip.'

'Oh, of course. Well, let me make you a cup of tea. You look like you need it.'

I watch him go into his office.

In the meantime you've always got me. Some sort of inner volcano erupts in the pit of my stomach and toasty warm lava seeps all the way to my toes. *You've always got me.*

I think about Thom Deacon for the rest of the day at school, all the way home and I especially think about him when I'm in the bath.

I can't help it. My head is overflowing with fantasies about him, and not just the obvious sort. I imagine little, intimate moments of us together. I see him and me living in some sort of forest lodge, with an open fire and lots of exposed beams. There're probably some antlers over the fire. We sit together on a masculine reclaimed-leather sofa, a tartan rug cocooning us both. He brings me hot chocolate and I wear one of his chunky silver rings threaded through a chain around my neck so it's close to my heart.

He kisses my neck while we watch movies because he's let me choose and I've picked *Dirty Dancing* again. I lovingly tell him to knock it off even though I don't want him to.

He'd bring me breakfast in bed; we'd walk hand in hand through the forest and rub sun cream on each other's backs in the summer; he'd buy me that thing I saw one time and mentioned in passing that I liked. And, in return, I would *love* him more than he's ever been loved.

Oh God, my heart feels swollen.

It *hurts*. Actual aching in my chest. That's how much I want the dreams to come true. I blow some bubble bath off the palm of my hand. Am I crazy? Could Thom, no need for the Deacon any more, really be into me? He's not *that* much older than me – nine years tops, and that's nothing really. Like you wouldn't look at a thirty-year-old woman with a forty-year-old man and think that was weird, would you?

At St Agnes, a few years back, there was a huge scandal when Mr Parkinson, one of the physics teachers, moved in with a former pupil, Charlotte Istance-Tamblin. She was nineteen, and he was in his thirties and not a total moose to look at. They both *swore* the affair didn't start while she was still at school, but they made him resign anyway. As far as I know they're still together, so it *can* work.

Thom basically said he liked me. He said everyone was jealous of me and that he was there for me. We were so close in the library, almost touching. He totally rubbed my back. His hand grazed my bra strap. *What does it all mean?* I wonder, if those Year Eights hadn't been there, if something might have happened. My insides are all stirred up and murky. I plunge my head under the water to try snap myself out of it.

I wrap my hair in a towel turban and put on a plush dressing gown. I can't decide how worried I should be about Megan. I hate that she's even taking up room in my head when I'd much rather paper the inner walls of my brain with mental posters of Thom. Strange how going back to Margot's time feels like an escape: 1941 is about as far away as I can get from here.

My room is feeling more like mine and I light some magnolia-scented candles to settle in for the night with the diary.

Monday 3rd February, 1941

Yesterday Andrew taught me how to play chess. He thinks it hilarious that I didn't know how, although I pointed out that it was no less queer that he'd never played backgammon.

His host, Mrs Evelyn Pritchard, is a wealthy widow whose husband, so it is said, killed himself when the stock markets crashed in the Great Depression. The official version is that it was a heart attack. She sold their London property for a tidy sum and moved into their Welsh country retreat.

Andrew has rather landed on his feet. Mrs Pritchard's home is lovely. She calls it a cottage, but it's a handsome two-storey house set in expansive gardens and with a stunning view of the valley.

She fusses over Andrew as if he were a favourite nephew, wiping specks of dirt off his cheek and ferrying trays of biscuits to where we played in the conservatory. I didn't like to ask where so many digestive biscuits came from. They certainly weren't baked here, and Glynis has hinted at a black market. 'Can I get you anything else, Andrew dear?'

'No, thank you, Mrs Pritchard. This is all so generous.'

'Oh, get away,' she said. She is a rotund woman, with the air of a Pekinese dog weighed down by jewellery. 'After what you poor children went through in that cave. I don't know how you're coping.'

'Really, Mrs Pritchard,' I said, eating a third biscuit out of nothing but manners, 'we're fine. It's poor Stanley we should feel sorry for.'

She tutted. 'You know, I always said that Geraint Tibbet was a wrong 'un. You can just tell, can't you? If a man's not married by thirty, there's got to be something off, hasn't there? Inverts, the lot of them.'

Andrew and I shared an awkward glance.

'Right, I'll leave you children to your game. Give me a shout if you need anything and I'll have Marjorie whip something up.'

Andrew waited until the door was closed. 'Thank goodness for that.'

'Is she like that all the time?'

'It never ends. I feel positively suffocated. At this rate I'll return to London ten stone heavier.'

'Still, look at this place. It's nicer than most hotels, you jammy so-and-so.'

'Oh, I don't know. You seem to have done all right.'

I paused a moment. 'Yes, yes, I suppose it could have been a lot worse . . .' I stopped. He stopped. We were both thinking about Stanley, I could tell.

'Right then!' He changed the subject. 'Chess! It's painfully easy once you know how each piece moves! The aim of the game is to protect the king.'

'How typical.'

'Actually, tactically the queen is more useful: she can move any distance in any direction whereas the king can only go one square at a time.'

'Again typical – the woman doing twice as much work for half the recognition.'

Andrew laughed unguardedly and I felt more relaxed than I had done in an age. He ran through each piece, but, as with all things, I found it easiest to learn through doing, so we launched into a game. I soon got the hang of the basics.

'Do you know,' Andrew said as he moved a pawn one square forward, 'that Bryn is going about telling everyone that it was he who found Stanley?'

'I'd have expected nothing less.'

'He's a fathead,' Andrew remarked.

'Why isn't he enlisted?' I asked.

'Well, Bill told me that his dear father concocted some cock-and-bull story about his eyesight and got the doctor in the village to write a sick note. I suppose that's what you get when you're related to the mayor.'

'The cowardy custard! I knew it!'

'Of course, it could be scurrilous gossip.'

'That lump Bill Jones doesn't strike me as a gossip.'

Andrew only shrugged. 'It's your turn, Margot.'

'You know, Andrew, thank goodness you're here. You're like a little piece of home.'

He smiled broadly. 'You too, Margot.' He raised his china tea cup. 'To Londoners abroad.'

We toasted with a polite chink.

Chapter 13

Now hang on a cotton-picking minute. Hold up – is *cotton-picking minute* like totally racist? No time to stress about it now because a thought has just occurred to me and it's a biggy.

My Grandad was called Andrew.

How had that not popped into my head the first time Margot mentioned him? To me, Grandad's name *was* Grandad, so I've never thought of him as 'Andrew'.

I turn to the front of the diary and pull out the dog-eared photo of the hot soldier guy. I scrutinise it. It's absolutely, definitely not Grandad. I check my clock and it's not all that late. I listen out and hear Margot clattering around in her bedroom down the hall, getting ready for bed.

Stowing the diary under my pillow, I creep out onto the landing. The floorboards are mean and creaky. Obviously Margot doesn't miss a trick and her head snakes out of her bedroom door after about a second. 'What are you doing?' she asks.

'I'm just getting a glass of water, that's all,' I whisper so I don't wake Mum.

'Very well. Goodnight.' She closes her door and I tiptoe downstairs in near darkness.

Instead of the kitchen, I head into the living room and to the sideboard from which Mum showed me the photo album. I slide it open and pull out three or four leather-bound volumes. The first is super eighties and has loads of pictures of Mum with me as a baby. Indulging myself, I look to see if there are any of Dad. Sure enough there are – copies of ones we have, but they always give me a feeling a bit like Christmas in my chest. Probably because most of the pictures are us standing in front of Christmas trees.

He was a very handsome man, my dad. I wish I remembered him better.

I put the first album back and work my way left down the shelf, assuming someone as organised as Margot would file them chronologically. I pull another and see this one *has* to be the sixties. Mum is a little girl and most of them, unsurprisingly, are of her playing on various beaches. The page the book falls open on has a note reading *Julia in Monte Carlo, July '66* in handwriting I now recognise as Margot's.

Going back further, I find what I'm looking for. The wedding album. Everyone has a wedding album – well, all married people. Their wedding was on 11th July 1953, according to the front page. I leaf through the pictures. The wedding took place in a registry office in London, by the looks of things: a handsome building with imposing stone columns at the front.

Hand in hand, Margot and Grandad – as handsome as my old Ken doll – walk through swirling confetti, just like Mum and Dad did in the home movie. It looks like blossom. Both are laughing their heads off. It's weird to see Margot looking happy. She's wearing a smart, ankle-length white dress with capped sleeves and a belt at the waist. A cute little hat with a net veil is pinned into her hair. I'd totally wear that.

I do the sums. So they married in 1953, a whole twelve years after Margot arrived in Llanmarion. I suppose it *could* be the same Andrew, but then again, there are a *lot* of Andrews in the world. I think Grandad had freckles like the Andrew in the diary, but, again, so do lots of people.

I put the photo albums back in what I hope is the same order and slip upstairs, glass of water in hand in case old hawk-eyes is waiting for me on the landing.

I have a quite flick back through the diary, and so far she hasn't specified a surname. I guess there's only one way to find out. Who cares if I look like death in the morning?

Friday 14th February, 1941

Strange, isn't it, how quickly the unusual can become familiar? My life before the farm feels like a hundred lifetimes ago. Oh, of course I write to Mummy and she duly replies, assuring me she's well and safe and to pay no mind to the reports we hear of the bombardment. As ever, London keeps on.

I know I haven't written for days. I've been much too busy. You see, I finally learned where it is Glynis sneaks off to every day. Last Wednesday I had just dropped Peter and Jane off at the schoolhouse when I saw Glynis and a few of the other townswomen entering the Red Lion public house.

Now, not for a second did I think Glynis was creeping away from the farm for an early-morning tipple. Why, by supper time she'd be quite incapacitated. That said, a group of women slipping into a pub at such an hour was enough to arouse my suspicions.

The Red Lion, like many of the buildings in Llanmarion, is a drunk-looking stone building, painted patchy white. More uniquely, the pub still has its original thatched roof, black Tudor beams and stable doors. No place for a lady.

I couldn't think of any valid reason why I should have cause to knock on the door, but saw no harm in taking a peek through the window. Frustratingly, each of the windows had a wooden shutter over it, but I was able to prise one open an inch, enough to see Glynis and the other women disappearing through a door at the side of the bar, I assumed leading to a staircase, either upstairs or to the cellar.

'Can I help you, miss?' I whirled around to see a strikingly pretty woman. She had red lips and piled raven-black ringlets tumbling out underneath a teal-coloured hat with a peacock feather tucked into the brim.

'Gosh, I'm sorry,' I said. I decided that, in this case, honesty was the best policy. 'My name is Margot Stanford. I'm staying with Glynis Williams. I saw her go in and just wondered what on earth she was doing in a public house at this hour.'

'Ah,' the woman smiled. 'So you're Marvellous Margot. I should have guessed! Glynis has told us all about you. Listen, and think about your answer carefully . . . Can you keep a secret?'

'Yes,' I said without hesitation. 'I'm a sixteen-year-old girl. It's what we're best at.'

She laughed a husky laugh. 'Then you'd better come inside. I'm Agatha Moss, by the way.' I've learned by now the difference between a north and south Wales accent and hers was definitely northern.

With her own key, Agatha let us into the pub, which positively reeked of beer-soaked carpets and tobacco, and led me to the narrow door. She chivvied me up a flight of steep steps to a landing. 'Take the first door on your right,' Agatha told me.

I pushed it open and a group of women turned and stared in surprise.

'Margot!' Glynis exclaimed.

'Look who I found spying at the window,' said Agatha, taking off her trench coat and hanging it on a stand next to the door. The room, which must once have been living quarters, now appeared to be some sort of communications office. I'd never seen the like. Now, clearly I know nothing about telephone exchanges, but I was able to recognise radios and Bakelite telephones and other assorted machinery I could only guess at. Some of the operators already wore headsets with mouthpieces.

'Margot, what are you doing here?' Glynis continued. She didn't seem cross as such, more surprised.

'I'm sorry,' I said. 'I saw you coming into the pub and was, well, curious.'

A woman I wasn't familiar with chuckled. 'Well, you know what curiosity did to the cat, like, don't you?'

'Hush, Phyllis,' said Glynis. 'She meant no harm.'

'What is all this?' I gestured at the equipment.

'You realise we'll have to get her to sign the Secrets Act now.' Agatha poured herself a cup of tea from a refreshments table near the window. From the outside, to anyone looking in, this must look like a tea party and nothing more.

'I trust her,' said Glynis, 'and she's very bright. She'd be of more help here than she is on the farm, believe you me.' I could have chosen to be offended at that, but she was probably right.

'This is a listening post, isn't it?' I'd eavesdropped on enough of Daddy's hushed conversations to know there were tactical outposts outside of London. What good was putting all your eggs

148

in the basket most likely to be bombed? 'Don't worry, I shan't tell anyone.'

'No, you won't!' Agatha said. 'To answer your question, yes, we're an outpost. You see, Margot, it's not improbable that if the Luftwaffe should take Ireland, the Jerries could very well invade by sea, and if they should, the Welsh coast is where they'd land. We have to be especially vigilant out here.'

'Gosh, I had no idea.'

A couple of tired-looking women put their coats on and said farewell – the nightshift retiring for the day, I supposed. 'Well, now you're here, you can make yourself useful,' Agatha finished.

'I'd love to help!' How exciting! Cracking codes and deciphering, well, ciphers.

'Good. You can start by running out to fetch more milk for tea,' Agatha said with a sly smile. I liked her already, she reminded me of Mother – how I imagine she was when she was younger.

'Very well,' I replied, sensing I was being tested.

It's awfully exciting. I've been back every day since, helping out however I can, which is mostly making the tea, sweeping the floors and keeping the toilets spick and span. When I'm done with my chores, I'm allowed to assist Glynis. Granny taught me a little French on the Riviera and it's coming in very handy now. Oh, it's mostly a waiting game, listening out for radio conversations in and out of France and Germany; picking up on cockpit transmissions and identifying repeated phrases. It's all spaghetti, and the trick, I'm learning, is to find that needle in the haystack – picking out that tiny thread that's worth something.

Glynis has started to teach me Morse code. It's not as hard as I'd have imagined. Letters and numbers are made up of little tones, transmitted as 'dots' and 'dashes': a dash being three times the length of a dot. Each letter is divided by a silence the duration of a dot while words are separated by a silence equivalent to a dash. There's a different combination for each letter or number. Glynis says I'm a natural and soon she'll start teaching me the more complex and confidential codes.

I never thought when I was shipped out to Wales I'd end up as a codebreaker! A spy! It's funny, isn't it, where life takes you?

So that explains my lack of entries over the last week or so. Now let me tell you about tonight. Presently, it's the stillest hours of the night and only me and the stars are up. Sleep isn't anywhere in sight – my mind is much too busy, whirring like an engine.

Goodness! I'll start at the beginning. Each year, Bess's mother and some of the other local women organise a St Valentine's dance at the church hall. It has, I'm told, become an important date in the village calendar.

Bess was unable to contain her excitement, insisting that I join her and Doreen at their home to do our hair and make-up. I wore the prettiest dress I'd brought – still a fairly sensible polka-dot affair – with my jade-green kitten heels from Paris. I admit, getting ready was fun; we curled our hair in rollers and Doreen even drew seams up the back of our legs with an eye pencil. I didn't dare tell her I actually had some real stockings with seams back at the farm.

'Oh, I'm so excited!' Bess said. 'I just know my card was from Reg.' As is the custom, an anonymous heart-shaped card had been delivered to Bess's door that morning. I got one from Mummy, which was decidedly less interesting.

'Bess,' I said solemnly, 'you need to be very careful.'

'Oh, I know, but I don't care what people say.'

'You should,' Doreen muttered as she carefully applied lipstick.

'What's the worst people can do? Laugh at us? Spit at us as we walk down the street? Call me names? It all bounces off, like.'

I didn't like to tell her that people could, and might, do much worse than that. 'Reg is utterly charming,' I told her, 'but just be wary, Bess. Not everyone is as clever as we are.'

'This war is going to change the world, Margot,' wide-eyed Bess said with a mouthful of Kirby grips. She pinned a curl into a chignon. 'It's about the Allies standing up for what's right. Isn't that what the boys are fighting for? A world where people have the freedom to be whatever they want to be? To love whoever they want to love? To pray to whoever it is they believe in?'

Oh, poor, naive Bess. I'd heard, from the listening post and from Father, the most terrible rumours. Drifting across the Channel come dark tales of whole towns being flattened; of families fleeing their homes with nowhere to go; children without parents; Jews being rounded up and driven away on trucks like cattle. These are the things your nightmares would be scared of, and Glynis fears it'll only get worse.

Of course, I'm bound from telling Bess any of these things. 'Very well,' I told her. 'You have my full support, and should you marry, I shall be bridesmaid.'

'Maid of honour!' Bess smiled. Since his release, Bess and Reg had been stealing away into the woods for 'hikes', but so far Bess had told her mother she was helping me out on the farm. The villagers were still wary of Reg, however helpful and polite he was around town. It angers me, seeing him bow and scrape to people so clearly undeserving of his efforts.

Done up to the nines, we walked to the village hall and found it already thrumming when we arrived. The organisers had done a splendid job, stringing bunting and jam-jar lanterns from tree to tree. The hall itself, little more than a rickety wooden shed, is located between the church and graveyard. Still, with the band playing and a hum of chatter and laughter, it was positively enchanting.

'Goodness, look!' Doreen exclaimed as we tottered down the churchyard path, unsteady in our heels. 'Soldiers!' I suspect Doreen is wacky for khaki.

Sure enough, there was a huddle of men in uniform smoking outside the hall. 'What on earth are they doing here?' I asked.

'They're from the hospital,' explained Bess. 'Evening, Tommy!'

'Good evening, Miss Bess,' said a young man with his left arm in a sling. Bess told me they were invalids recuperating at the infirmary and those well enough had been brought to attend the dance.

Ivor, Glynis told me, would rather serve crumpets to Hitler than come to a dance, so while he stayed home with Peter and Jane, she was there helping out with the refreshments and had made a delicious fruit punch. I can't say for sure, but my light-headedness suggested it contained something a little stronger than mere apples.

As is so often the way, everyone clung to the walls nursing drinks, leaving a vast chasm in the middle of the hall until a couple of brave souls started to dance. As soon as a couple of bawdy Essex evacuees started something resembling a Lindy Hop, Bess grabbed my hand and we joined them. Dancing is NOT my forte, but I was having too much fun to feel self-conscious. Soon girls filled the dance floor, and where there are girls, boys will surely follow.

Bess paired with Reg, and I don't know where he had acquired such skill, but his dancing was phenomenal and Bess met his tempo admirably. Soon the rest of us cleared a space to let them showcase their jive. The room was divided. There were awed gasps and claps and cheers as they kicked and spun to the music; Reg even lifted Bess clean off her feet, swinging her left and right and over his head. But there were just as many disgusted tuts and sucked teeth. I distinctly heard a voice say, 'How can she stand to hold his hand?' I repaid the woman with a glare that could cut diamonds.

I danced and laughed until my make-up had run and my curls were falling loose. I can't remember the last time I'd felt so free and feather-light. It's so strange, but never once had I thought that being forced so far away from home would be, well, fun.

It was almost midnight when Glynis took me to one side. 'I'm sorry to spoil your fun, Margot, but just keep an eye on your friend Doreen. She's been drinking anything she can get her hands on, pet, and she doesn't look too steady on her feet.'

I scanned the hall. 'Where is she?'

'I'm not sure, love. Perhaps try the lav.'

I nodded. 'Of course.' I felt guilty. I'd been having so much fun dancing and watching Bess and Reg, I'd barely paid Doreen any attention, not that I'm her warden. I weaved my way through the crowd to the toilets, which were just by the side of a little stage at the end of the hall. The door was locked so I gave it a tap. 'Doreen? Is that you? It's Margot.'

'No, love! She's not in here!' came an embarrassed reply.

'Sorry!' I did another lap of the hall before leaving through the front doors. Once more there was a tight circle of soldiers smoking in the icy February night. 'Oh, hello there,' I said. 'I don't suppose any of you gentlemen have seen Doreen from the hospital, have you?'

"Ey up, lads, we've got a posh one,' a rugged Yorkshireman said with an affable grin.

One of his colleagues answered, ignoring him. The soldier stepped into the pool of light from the lamp and he was as handsome as any star of the silver screen. He had a square jaw and strong Roman nose; hair razor-short on the sides and slicked smartly back on top. 'Afraid not, ma'am, but we sure will keep an eye out now.' He had an accent – American or Canadian – as neat as a freshly trimmed lawn. His teeth were uniformly white and square and there was a most compelling dimple in his chin.

'Thank you.' I was unsure what else to say. I knew my mother, wherever she was, would frown upon my being with three gentlemen without a chaperone. By way of a farewell, I half nodded, half curtsied, unable to break the American's gaze.

Blushing, I expect, I set off towards the church, still wondering if Doreen had taken ill and come outside for air. It was possible she'd chipped off with a chap from the hospital . . . I can't say I'd have been surprised; she strikes me as a bit of a share crop.

The night was bitterly cold and I didn't savour being so close to the graveyard. A fog crept around the decaying headstones and mausoleums. I felt the same sensation I had done in the forest, the feeling of being watched, observed by the eyes of the night.

'Doreen?' I called, comforting myself more than expecting an answer. 'Are you out here?' I wrapped my arms around my body, cursing my foolishness at not fetching my coat.

'Didn't you see?' A familiar, cocksure voice cut through the murk. It was Bryn Davies. 'Doreen got so merry she had to go home with Myfanwy.' Bess's mum.

'Where are you?' I said, unnerved at the disembodied words.

'I'm right over here, pet.' I saw him sitting on a flat stone sarcophagus, smoking a cigar. He hopped off, lumbering towards me. He was drunk, I could tell.

'Ah, I see. Well, I'm glad she got home all right.' I started back towards the hall, but he caught my arm.

'Wait. Where are you going? Stay and chat to me, like, while I finish this. Do you like a man who smokes cigars?'

'Only marginally more than little boys who do so.'

He chuckled. 'Here, have my coat, Margot.'

'No, thank you.' I shrugged it off as he tried to swing it over my shoulders. 'Glynis knows I went to look for Doreen. I'd better get back inside before she sends a search party out for both of us.' I walked away, but he grabbed my arm again, pulling me back more forcefully this time.

'Bryn, let go of me.'

'Hush now – they won't miss you for a minute or two . . .' Hands on my shoulders, he steered me up against the side of the church, pressing my back into a stone alcove, away from prying eyes. I looked around, but I couldn't see anyone through the mist, and heard only the dim music coming from the hall.

Strange, isn't it, that sixth sense that somehow tells us when things turn rotten. I haven't liked Bryn from the moment I set eyes on him, but he'd never scared me. Now things were different. It was dark, we were alone, he was drunk. He did scare me now, but I was determined to hide it. 'Bryn, I mean it, I want to go back inside.'

'Margot, Margot, Margot . . . you don't have to play with me like this. I know you're a good girl – you don't have to lay it on so thick.'

I drew myself up as tall as I could. 'I'm doing no such thing.'

155

'I know what you girls are like. You all put on a show because you have to, but . . . it's all right, I won't tell anyone.'

I gave him a push. 'Bryn, there'll be nothing to tell. Now get off!'

But my anger only seemed to make him laugh. 'God, you're a live wire! Come on, you can trust me . . .'

'No!'

As I squirmed to get away he pushed me into the corner, bearing down on me, his lips pressing against mine. The back of my head scraped against the church wall painfully. My nails are short from the farm work, but nonetheless I dug them into the soft part of his cheek.

He recoiled, pressing his fingers to the scratch I'd made. 'Ow, you little—'

'Is there a problem here?' A broad silhouette emerged through the fog. An accent. American.

'Who's asking?' Bryn said.

'Lieutenant Rick Sawyer.' He pronounced it the American way – 'Lootenant'. 'You OK, ma'am?'

I pushed past Bryn, freeing myself. God bless America. 'I am now. Thank you very much.'

'No problem. Did he hurt you?'

I'm not a girl who wants to be weak, to be vulnerable, and I like to show it even less, but I was shivering and couldn't lie. 'Yes.'

'Oh, come off it, Margot! I didn't even do nothing, like!' He took a step towards us, but Rick pushed him back.

'I think you better leave her alone, kid.'

'Who are you callin' kid, Yank?' Bryn barged his chest into Rick's, at which with minimal effort Rick took a step back and swung for Bryn. It all happened in a blink. His fist shot out, hit

156

Bryn's nose with a thud that sounded like kneading bread, and the next thing I knew, Bryn was on his knees, cradling his face in his hands.

'Technically I'm Canadian,' said Rick, flexing his fingers. I had to laugh a little. It was so suave it didn't quite feel real.

'You wait till my dad hears about this!' Bryn yelped, blood running through his fingers. He sprang to his feet, retreating before Rick could floor him for good.

Rick simply laughed at his feeble threat. 'Miss, can I walk you back inside?' He offered me his arm.

'Yes, please.' I took it. He led me back to the path and my heartbeat returned to something like normal. With Rick I felt entirely safe. 'I'm so sorry about that. Is your hand all right?'

'Don't you worry about me, ma'am. Do you need a doctor?'

'Oh, goodness me, no. I'm more shaken than anything. I feel so foolish! I should have never come out here alone.'

'It's not your fault that guy's a jackass, but after you asked about your friend, I came to offer a hand.'

'It's much appreciated. Thank you again.' I felt faintly pathetic at needing to be rescued, but need I had. I dread to think what might have happened had Rick not come after me.

'May I ask your name?'

'Oh, where are my manners? I'm Margot Stanford. I'm staying at Ivor Williams's farm.'

'From London?'

'Indeed. How about you? You're from Canada? What on earth brings you here?'

'Canadian British. My mother is from Sussex. I came over a couple of years ago.'

'Just in time to fight!'

He smiled. 'Just in time to fight. I was wounded last May. Spinal injury – and not even in battle; a jack gave out at the airbase! They tell me I'm lucky to be walking.' Ah, so he was RAF, not Army.

'And how are you now?'

He winced slightly. 'I get by just fine, but there's still pain. I feel like a goddamn old man at twenty-two.' So that answered that question. 'And it's worse in the cold.'

I wanted to stroll with him for longer, but we came to a stop outside the hall. People were leaving now, wrapping scarves around their necks and buttoning up winter coats. I felt safe, the incident in the graveyard already seeming unreal. I wasn't sure how I'd deal with Bryn, but I was scared no longer.

Bess burst out of the door, Reg following behind. 'Goodness, Margot, there you are! We've been looking all over for you.' She saw who I was with. 'Lieutenant Sawyer. I didn't know you were here.' Bess used our pronunciation – 'Leftenant'.

'Good evening, Miss Jones,' he said with a tip of his cap, 'and, please, call me Rick.'

'Where have you been?'

I considered telling her about Bryn, but decided to do so later. 'I was looking for Doreen. Rick –' no, that felt too informal – 'Lieutenant Sawyer offered to help.'

'My pleasure, ma'am. Say, I'd better be getting back to the others, but it sure was nice to meet you, Miss Stanford.'

I fought to keep a fuchsia blush at bay. 'Not at all. Thank you again for your . . . assistance.'

He smiled a very handsome smile and bid us goodnight.

Now I can't seem to rid my mind of his face. I close my eyes, but all I see are his eyes, his dimples and those perfect teeth. I explore other avenues of thinking, but they all lead back to pictures of Rick Sawyer. Finally I understand.

This is how it begins, isn't it?

Chapter 14

I'm so angry about what Bryn did, I have to tell someone about it. With few other options, I opt for Danny and Bronwyn. We're having our regular second breakfast in the library. 'If I tell you a weird secret, will you keep it?'

'Of course!' Danny says with relish. 'You were born a boy, right?'

My hands fly to my face. 'No! Why? Do I look like a man?'

'Duh, I'm kidding, you loser!'

Bronwyn suppresses a grin because grinning isn't her style. 'Is it about the farm? Did a cow birth kittens or something?'

'Bron, let it go. The farm is not the Hellmouth,' says Danny.

I pull the diary out of my rucksack. 'I stole my grandma's diary.'

They both stare at me blankly for a second. 'OK, that is weird. Why would you do that?' Danny says.

'Is it all like "Today I went to bingo, got my blue rinse done"?' says Bronwyn.

I smile. 'It's not from now, and she's not exactly the bingo type. It's from World War Two.'

Bronwyn visibly perks up. 'Oh, OK, that actually borders on cool. Can I see?'

'Sure, just be careful. I'll have to return it at some point.' Bronwyn carefully leafs through with fingers that could use a manicure. She hands Danny the loose photos.

'Oh, she was gorgeous! She looks like a young Lauren Bacall!'

'Who?'

'Girl, do a Yahoo search.'

'It's kinda crazy. Like she was evacuated right here in 1941 to the farm. There were all these other evacuees. This ass-hat guy called Bryn Davies basically tried to rape her in the graveyard.'

Bronwyn and Danny share a loaded glance. 'No way!' says Bronwyn. 'Bryn Davies used to be the mayor.'

'Why am I not surprised? His dad was too.'

Danny raises an eyebrow. 'He was caught having it off with a prozzie in the town hall and had to resign.'

'Still not surprised.'

'He died, a couple of years back, I think.'

Bronwyn hands the diary back to me and I put it safely away. 'It's so weird. She was like hella cool – my grandma. In the diary she was like a codebreaker and just this badass . . . but now she's so . . . demon bitch from hell.'

Danny shrugs. 'Well, she's old. I wouldn't mess with my grandma either – she's a nipper. I mean that literally. If you do something wrong, she will physically nip you.'

I laugh but it bothers me. 'I guess so.'

'Have you read the whole thing?' Bronwyn asks. She runs a hand through her wild hair, a studded leather cuff around each wrist.

'I'm about a quarter in.'

'Well, maybe there's a twist in the last half.'

I shrug. 'I'll let you know.'

We're so lost in conversation I fail to see Thom emerge from his office with Sophie. 'What do you guys think?' he says. Today he's wearing a long-sleeved grey grandad shirt that gives further hints at how toned his body is. My stomach and chest do the weird flippity-floppity lurch they've started to do every time I think about him. Stupid, I know, but I suddenly worry he can telepathically know what I'm thinking.

'Think about what?' Danny asks.

'Shall we do *The Chess Club Presents* again this year?'

'No,' says Bronwyn.

'YES!' says Danny. 'We have to! Last year was THE BEST.'

'What's that?' I ask.

Sophie joins us at the table and takes a croissant. 'Don't tell my mam I had this, OK? It's like a talent-night thing we did last year at the church hall.'

'Oh, the talent show?' I'd seen posters up around the school.

'No,' Danny said with disgust, 'that's for the popular kids. All the pretty girls get together and do the Spice Girls and TLC and that. It's totally passé.'

'We are sort of an alternative,' Thom explains. 'So many people in the Chess Club are so talented but don't get a chance to perform, or don't want to get up in front of the whole school. This is on a smaller scale – and outside of school – just for friends and family. That said, there's no point in me organising it if there's no uptake.'

Danny claps excitedly. 'Well, I'm in. Last year I did "Memories" from *Cats* and it was a defining moment of my life to date.'

'The cat ears were certainly something,' Bronwyn adds with a slight smirk.

'Don't listen to her, Danny, Elaine Paige would have been proud. Fliss, will you do it?'

My swansong ballet performance comes flooding back. Painfully. I was thirteen years old, and my ballet school took part in a gala charity performance thing at the Albert Hall. A big deal, obviously – Princess Diana was there, God rest her soul. We did the 'Kingdom of the Shades' section from *La Bayadère*. Thirty girls, head to toe in pristine white, all en pointe in six rows of five – it should have been a sight no one would ever forget, and we'd nailed it in rehearsal, but the performance was all wrong, wobbly and ungraceful. I was no better than anyone else. We were a tutu-clad disaster. It was a sight no one would ever forget for all the wrong reasons.

I swear down I heard people in the audience actually tut.

Only afterwards did we learn that a scout from the Royal Ballet had been in the audience.

She came backstage to be polite but could hardly keep the disdain off her face. Madame Nyzda, our tutor, introduced me to the scout, who looked exactly as you'd imagine: retired ballerina, slightly reptilian-looking, who never quite made it big. She offered only the most fleeting, dismissive smile and wet lettuce handshake.

That was the night I gave up, to be honest. If it was going to happen, it would have happened there and then. That was my chance showing its face, and I was looking the other way. What was the point? What was the point in turning my feet into gnarled hoofs for nothing? Better to hang up the slippers and start on the cake.

'No. I don't think so,' I say.

'Didn't you used to do ballet?' Bronwyn asks.

'What? How do you know?'

'I searched for you online obviously.' Typical. She probably thought I was a spy so she'd spied on me.

'You do ballet?' Thom's eyes light up. 'That'd be perfect.'

As much as I want to impress him, I don't want it to be in a tutu. Ballet was part of my childhood, and I do *not* need him to see me as the Sugar Plum Fairy. 'Past tense,' I say, head down.

'Please!' Danny says. 'Don't make me do something by myself.'

'I'm gonna sing,' Sophie chips in.

I squirm. 'Maybe.' That meant no. But I do want to spend some time alone with Thom if I can. 'I'll definitely help out . . . like backstage and stuff.'

'Yeah, me too,' Bronwyn says, and I want to punch her.

The registration bell rings out and Thom stands to return to his work. 'Well, it's not until January so you have plenty of time to think about it.'

I walk in on something, an argument, when I get home. It's never a good sign when all conversation halts when you step through the front door. I hang my coat and bag on the banister and walk into the kitchen. 'What's going on?' I say. The chilly silence suggests they were talking about me.

Mum is sitting at the table, cradling a cup of camomile tea, while Margot is perched tersely against the work counter. 'Nothing,' Mum says. Margot purses her lips and, without a word, leaves the kitchen, slamming the door behind her.

'What was that about?' I ask.

'Oh, you know Margot,' Mum says, blowing her tea to take a sip. 'She's spent too long out here in isolation with the animals; she's forgotten how to talk to human beings.'

I smile. 'I'm not gonna argue with that.'

'Any homework?'

'No,' I lie. All I want to do is find out what happened next with Margot and Rick Sawyer. I make a cup of tea and head straight to my room.

Monday 17th February, 1941

*Today I saw him again under the strangest of circumstances.
Last night, just after we'd finished supper, young Sergeant Huw
Thomas from the constabulary came to the farm. I assumed the
worst, thinking he must have brought dire news about Mother
or Father, but not so, although he was here to see me. 'Could I
speak to Miss Stanford, please, Ivor?'*

*'Aye, Huw, come on in. Margot in trouble, is she?' he said with
a hint of sarcasm.*

*I stood up from the table. 'I've done nothing wrong,' I
protested.*

*Sergeant Thomas removed his hat and waddled into the
kitchen. 'No, miss. We believe you witnessed an assault.' Glynis
lifted Jane off her chair. 'Come on, children, let's go play upstairs,
eh?' She led Jane and Peter out of the kitchen, leaving us alone.*

*What happened in the graveyard didn't register in my mind
as assault, even then. 'Did I?'*

'The mayor has filed a complaint.'

*It still took me a moment to put the pieces together. 'Oh,
you mean Bryn?'*

'Margot, what's this all about?' Ivor said gravely.

Sergeant Thomas took out his notebook. 'Mayor Davies is alleging that a young RAF officer attacked Bryn at the Valentine's dance and that you were present, Miss Stanford.'

Well, there was absolutely no way I was letting Rick get in trouble over that weasel. There was simply no option but to tell the truth. 'Sir, the assault, if it could be called such a thing, was simply Lieutenant Sawyer protecting my honour.'

'Go on . . .'

'Bryn Davies was behaving in a most inappropriate fashion. Why, if Lieutenant Sawyer hadn't come along when he did, I dread to think what would have happened.'

'Margot . . . you never said . . .' Ivor looked deeply uncomfortable.

'I see,' Sergeant Thomas said. 'And you'd be prepared to say that under oath, would you, miss?'

'I swear on my eyes, Sergeant, and if Bryn Davies said anything to the contrary, I can assure you he's lying.'

Ivor stepped forward, towering over Thomas. 'And what has this pilot said, Huw?'

Thomas's face again turned the colour of raw bacon and I knew that I had confirmed what Rick must have told them.

'I'm not at liberty to say, Ivor. You know that.'

Ivor came to my side. 'Well, you tell Owen Davies that if his ruined little turd of a son comes anywhere near our Margot again, he'll have more than a fat lip to worry about. You hear me?'

I couldn't suppress a smile. 'Sergeant Thomas, I am more than willing to stand up in front of the whole town and testify that the mayor's son tried to attack a defenceless girl in a graveyard if

167

need be. In fact, perhaps I should press charges . . . He did hurt my head in the kerfuffle.'

Thomas backed towards the door. 'I'm sure that won't be necessary, Miss Stanford. Thank you for your time.' He made a sharp exit before I could bring charges against a local hero.

'Are you all right?' Ivor said, not looking me in the eye.

'Thanks to Lieutenant Sawyer I am.'

'Well, then I owe that man a pint. You let me know if Bryn Davies so much as looks your way.'

'I will. And thank you, Mr Williams.'

'My name's Ivor.' He lumbered out of the kitchen and I felt a great surge of warmth for the big man.

And then today there was another, rather more welcome, knock at the door. 'Margot!' Peter called down the hallway. 'It's for you!'

I dried my hands on a dishcloth and went to see who it was – I imagined it must be Bess. Imagine my surprise when I saw Rick Sawyer's broad silhouette in the doorway. In his hands was a bunch of freshly picked wildflowers: coltsfoot and glory-of-the-snow. So pretty and delicate, tied in a simple rose ribbon. I was taken aback, but my manners came to me promptly. 'Lieutenant Sawyer, what a nice surprise.' I swept a loose lock of hair off my forehead and tucked it behind my ear. And to think I wasn't wearing a scrap of make-up! How shameful!

'Oh, it's just Rick, ma'am.'

'Very well, I shall call you Rick if you stop calling me ma'am! I feel about sixty years old!' I suddenly remembered Peter was hovering between us. 'Peter, run along, please.'

With a smirk, he did as he was told, and Rick handed his makeshift bouquet to me. 'These are to thank you for getting me off the hook. And to say sorry . . . I hear you had a visit from the police.'

I accepted the flowers and instinctively took a sniff although they weren't especially fragrant. 'Not at all. It was the least I could do after you rescued me.'

'Aw, that guy had it coming if you ask me.'

'That he did. Won't you come inside? I could make us some tea.'

'I spend so much time inside at the hospital I wondered if you might want to accompany me on a walk in the woods? The sun is out and I could use the fresh air.'

My last walk through the woods had ended with finding a dead body in a cave, but I could overlook that fact to be at Rick's side. Even so, it wasn't entirely appropriate for a young woman to vanish off into a forest with a gentleman. 'I'd better ask Glynis . . . she might need me around the farm.'

As it was, Glynis found it highly amusing that I would even ask her permission and sent us off with her blessing. I changed into a smarter skirt and blouse, putting on some lipstick and blush as quickly as I could.

The sun was out and the air promised the first of spring. Buds were ripe on the trees and bluebells sprouted up among the long grasses. As we weaved in and out of shards of meek winter sunshine, Rick told me about life in the RAF. He described his childhood on a sprawling wheat farm outside of Banff, about bears plucking salmon from the river, wolves running wild and proud Mounties in red. It all sounded wonderfully exotic to me, but he assured me it wasn't so different to Wales, only instead of sheep there were bears. He walked with a pronounced limp that I hadn't noticed before, but if he was in pain he didn't wear it on his face.

'What about you?' he said. 'London, huh? I can't imagine living anywhere so noisy.'

'I think London's in my blood. I was born there. I don't even notice the noise. I love it; it's so colourful, so fast, so vibrant. All different types of people living their lives and no one bats an eyelid. Although I'm very lucky, I suppose: they say there's one London for the rich and another for the poor.'

'Is your father a rich man?' he asked.

'Not so much rich as powerful, although arguably they are one and the same. He works very hard so the navy looks after us. I've never wanted for anything.'

'Look!' he said suddenly in a hushed voice. 'A robin!' He took my hand and steered me to follow his gaze. His hand in mine felt so natural a fit.

Its red breast flickered at the centre of a holly bush. 'Oh, how sweet!' We watched it together until it took flight. He didn't let go of my hand and I didn't try to pull away.

'Only child?' he asked.

'Yes. Mother wanted to be a mother but isn't altogether keen on babies, it has to be said. And with Father away so often . . . What about you?'

'I'm one of six boys.'

'Six boys! Goodness!'

'Yeah, you didn't let food go cold at our table!'

'Five brothers? Gosh, I can hardly imagine.'

170

'I like having a big family. Christmas back on the farm is something to behold.'

'I bet it is.'

'Family is very important to me. Sure we fought and scrapped when we were kids . . . See this scar?' He pointed to a fine line running through his left eyebrow. 'That's from where Ennis shot me with a BB gun.'

'That's a good thing?'

'No! But you know what I mean. It doesn't matter that there's an ocean between us; I know they're out there and that feels good. Wherever they are is home.'

I looked down at the footpath. 'I'd have liked brothers or sisters, I think. I care deeply for Mummy and Daddy, but they've always been so much older than I, sort of distant. We don't talk about the things that really matter. We'd never talk about love or family.'

'That's a damned shame.'

'Is it? One can't miss what one's never had.'

We came to a rest in a broad clearing not far from the stream. I could hear the rapturous applause of the waterfall over the next hill. There was a fallen log, just the right size to serve as a bench. Rick sat and I perched next to him, smoothing my skirt – a heavy wool number in a burnt-orange shade. 'My mom –' I loved how he said 'mom' – 'always let us know it was OK to cry, you know? Being all the way out there on the farm, away from prying eyes, meant it was just us. We didn't have to do anything or be anybody we didn't want to be.'

'Where was your father?'

'He died.'

'Oh, I'm sorry.'

'No, it's OK. He got tuberculosis in '29. There wasn't anything we could do. It crept up on him pretty fast so he didn't suffer for too long. Died the way he lived – on the back of a tractor!'

'And he left quite the legacy . . . six little Sawyers!'

Rick smiled and it felt like there were coals glowing in my chest. I tingled all the way down to my toes. He was achingly handsome, and next to him I felt positively square. I don't know how best to describe it; it was like standing on a very high, very precarious ledge. 'Margot?'

'Yes?'

'I think you're quite the lady. Might I call on you again?'

I found myself slap-bang in the middle of a dreadful romance paperback and I didn't mind one little bit. 'I'd like that very much,' I said, and his face lit up once more.

Hand in hand, we walked alongside the stream, talking about everything and nothing, until it became clear his back was causing him pain. He accompanied me back to the farm, ever the perfect gent, and we said our farewell at the kitchen door.

I wasn't sure quite what the etiquette was in that situation, but Rick made it easy by simply kissing the back of my hand and retreating with a warm smile. 'I'll see you on Friday night,' he said, giving an absent-minded salute as he left through the gate.

'I can't wait.' I think at that point I experienced my first swoon, dear diary, a breathless, light-headed rush of anticipation. I was so high it felt a lot like vertigo.

The rest of the week is going to be a turgid countdown to Friday, I can already tell. It's funny, isn't it? You never think you're going to be that kind of girl until you are.

Chapter 15

I tuck the diary under my pillow, a little envious of the heart-coals Margot wrote about. I don't think I've ever felt like that, but it's the kind of movie love everybody wants – Cher and Josh in *Clueless*, Ross and Rachel, Meg Ryan and any man in a Meg Ryan movie. God, I hope that's the ending I get with Thom.

It's weird though, thinking of Margot having hornyteengirlsexythoughts. Like gross or what? She's practically a corpse. I remind myself she used to be pretty foxy, even if it was the olden days. I guess part of me thought sex didn't really exist before colour TVs, as if babies used to be knitted instead of born.

Something else is apparent too. My grandad was not called Rick, so Margot evidently erm . . . dated . . . people before him.

The next morning I burn the toast – annoying – and quiz Mum. 'When did Margot meet Grandad?'

'Fliss, that toast is going to burn again. Will you please keep an eye on it?'

'Damn.' I yank out the grill, because, unlike the rest of the civilised world, Margot doesn't own a toaster.

'And I have no idea. I think they got married in '53 though.'

'And you were born in . . . ?'

'1957. Thanks for the reminder.'

'But where did she meet Grandad?' I vigorously scrape the black layer off the top of the toast into the sink, which never really works – it still tastes burned.

'Fliss, I have no idea, and there's a much more efficient way of finding out.' She nods towards the garden.

Man, I wish I weren't so nosy. I take my charcoal toast into the garden, the paving flags freezing cold under my bare feet. 'Margot?'

She's scattering feed for the chickens and they're happily pecking it up. 'Is the kitchen on fire? I can smell burning.'

'Oh, that was just the toast. Margot, where did you meet Grandad?'

She stops throwing the feed and looks at me, frowning slightly. 'Just after the war,' she says after a pause.

'Not when, where.'

Another pause. 'London.'

I wait for more information, but she offers nothing further. 'Oh, OK.'

'Why the sudden interest in your grandfather?'

I want to know everything: I want to know about Rick, about the farm, about Ivor and Glynis who I love. I have about a trillion questions and I can't ask any of them. 'No reason. I just realised I had no idea how you two met.'

Margot shrugs and continues to feed the chickens. 'It was the early fifties . . . 1950 or '51, I expect. We courted, we married, we had your mother. Things back then were delightfully linear. The done thing was done without exception.'

'How romantic,' I mutter.

'Romance,' Margot guffaws, 'is the hallmark of truly uncreative souls. Any fool can do hearts and flowers, Felicity. Real love is both silent and invisible, in my experience.'

It angers me. She's lying. How can she have forgotten how it felt to get those flowers from Rick? I want to pull the daisies up out of the rockery and slap her around the head with them. 'I don't think that's true,' I say. 'Who doesn't love flowers?'

She rolls her eyes. 'Strange gesture, I always thought. Pulling something up by their roots and then displaying them as they wither and die. They'd be better off left in the earth.'

'Wasn't Grandad romantic?'

'He knew better, and that's why I loved him.' She stops as if she's said too much. Her words knock me back a little. Yeah, she was always honest, brutally so, but that statement felt a little less stony than usual. It was weird.

I don't know what to say so I retreat with, 'I'd better get ready for school.'

'Yes, you better had.'

About halfway through chemistry, I become aware of a mean giggle behind me. I look around and immediately Megan and Rhiannon duck below their Bunsen burner. I turn to Bronwyn. 'What are they sniggering at? Do I have something on my back?'

Bronwyn checks. 'Oh, shit. Don't move.'

Of course I move immediately, my hands reaching up behind me. 'What? What did they do?'

The giggles get louder. 'They've thrown little balls of chewing gum into your hair. Sit still. I'll sort it.'

Those bitches. You don't mess with the do. 'Is it coming out?'

'Some of it's tangled.'

'Oh, for God's sake!'

'Keep your head still. You're making it worse.' Bronwyn pulls on my hair and I feel it tug.

'Ow!'

'Sorry. We might have to cut it out.'

'No way! I need a mirror.' I ask to use the bathroom and scowl at Megan on my way past. I head to the nearest girls' toilets and crane my neck to assess the damage. I can see little hairy clumps where the gum has matted it. This isn't going to be easy. I'm in front of the mirror for a good ten minutes, carefully prising my hair out, strand by strand, and, even when I'm done, I don't feel sure it's entirely gum-free. I give it a brush with my Body Shop pop-out, and it more or less runs through. As a precautionary measure, I then quickly braid it into a plait.

The second I leave the toilet, I see Megan heading my way. She tries to push me back into the bathroom, but I grip the door frame. I don't want to be alone with her in there. 'Get off, Megan. I mean it.'

'Or what?'

'Just get off me!' I shove her back but she grabs my new plait and yanks my head down.

'You better not grass on us, or the next time I'll just cut it all off, yeah?'

'Ow! I won't!'

'What *is* going on?' There's something unique about the way a teacher's voice can boom down a corridor. I recognise

176

the voice as Thom's. He's struggling down the hall with a trolley full of books. 'I said, *what is going on?* Megan Jones, get off her right now.'

She lets go of my hair. 'Sorry, sir, I was just messin', like.'

'Fliss? What's going on?'

I say nothing. Nothing at all. I won't grass, but I won't lie either.

'Megan, I think you should get back to class.'

'Sir, I need to use—'

'Now, Megan. Get back to class right NOW.' The last word is barked.

Megan skulks back towards the lab, muttering, 'Ginger faggot,' under her breath. 'Fliss?' says Thom. 'Are you OK?'

'I'm fine.'

'What was all that about?'

'It was nothing.' I press my back against the door frame, just wanting to get away before I burst into tears. If he says or does one more nice thing, that's very likely to happen.

'Fliss, I'm not stupid and I know what I just saw. Listen, I'm not supposed to say things like this, but Megan Jones is only hanging on at this school by a thread.'

It sounds almost too good to be true, a school without Megan. But what would happen at three twenty? Would she be waiting for me every day a hundred metres beyond the school gates? She knows where I live.

I just can't. I shake my head.

'Fliss, all you have to do is tell the truth. We'll make sure you're looked after.' That's the *one more nice thing* I can't hear. Tears erupt in the ugliest way along with a high-pitched sob.

177

I don't want to cry and I especially don't want to cry in front of Thom. I cover my face with my hands. 'Fliss, come here.'

He wraps an arm around my shoulder and pulls me into his chest. He's warm and his cashmere jumper is so soft. I rest my head on his shoulder as he pats my back. It's like I'm a sad blob of butter melting on him and his strong arms are holding me up.

Now I've started, I can't stop. All the sadness and frustration I've been bottling up since I arrived in Wales is now pouring, unfiltered, onto his sweater.

'This is so embarrassing,' I say between sobs.

'Don't be silly!'

'Please don't look at me. I must look so awful.' My mascara is *not* waterproof.

'Come with me,' he says. 'Let's go back to the library. I'll tell your teacher I borrowed you to do a job.'

I wipe my eyes, which must look full-on Marilyn Manson, and follow him towards the library. That's when I feel it. I feel it. I feel the same blazing warmth in my chest that Margot did with Rick.

Oh my God. This is so much more than just a random crush. I am in love with him.

Friday 21st February, 1941

*I'm tired and blissfully happy, but I wanted to write about tonight
before I fall asleep, as I believe some of the magic will have worn
off in the light of morning.*

*It occurred to me after my last meeting with Rick that there
was precious little for us to do in Llanmarion. There's a war on
after all, and there are no restaurants or dances – if he even can
dance with his bad back – to attend. I wondered, perhaps, if he
might drive us into Cardiff or Swansea to the pictures, but I know
from the listening post that Cardiff is under constant threat of air
raids and I'd rather not spend my night out with Rick in a shelter.*

*Once more I asked Glynis's permission to go out with Rick.
In the absence of Mother and Father it only seemed appropriate,
although again Glynis seemed to find my formality amusing.*

*At six o'clock on the dot Rick arrived at the farm gate, in a
car he'd borrowed from a soldier friend for the evening. He was
out of uniform, but dressed smartly in a blueish-grey suit and
matching trilby. I had also brought some of my finer clothes out of
retirement: my jade-green coat paired with a peacock-blue beret
Father bought me in Paris.*

'Good evening, Miss Stanford,' he said, standing on the front step.

'Lieutenant Sawyer, how do you do?'

He smiled again and I melted a little; I'd forgotten how crushingly handsome he is. 'I wondered if you'd like to accompany me on a picnic?'

'A picnic? It's dark already!'

'Trust me, ma'am, it's all under control.'

I took his arm and he led me to the car. From their bedroom window, Peter and Jane spied on us as we left, giggling behind their hands.

He drove us up into the hills, the car chugging along the winding roads, brushing against wild hedgerows that spilled over. It was frightfully dark away from the town, but I felt safe with Rick. He seemed to know where he was going and eventually he pulled into a lay-by and told me to wait while he unpacked the boot. 'You think you can manage a short walk in those heels, miss?'

'I'm quite sure,' I said, stepping out as he held the car door open and offered a supportive hand.

'It's not far, I promise.' He helped me over a wooden style and we stuck to a well-trodden path that led further into the hills. My shoes were woefully inadequate, but I didn't complain. Eventually it became clear where we were headed: the lake; the source, I supposed, of the stream that runs past the farm. 'Have you been up here before?'

'No,' I admitted, 'I can't say I'd thought about it.'

'It's quite something.' And it was. We arrived after walking for about fifteen minutes. The still, black water was surrounded by dramatic cliffs, the pearly moon reflected on the surface. 'It's called the Devil's Cup,' Rick said. 'You can see why.'

'Yes, it's very apt.' The rocks made it rather like a vast stone bowl. On this lip, however, there was a shallow rocky bay of sorts, where one could wade into the water if one so desired. There were large, flat boulders on which to rest also, and on one of these was set up a bonfire. 'What's all this?'

'I came up this afternoon to set up,' he said, and I was touched he'd gone to so much effort. In no time at all, an impressive fire was crackling and snapping. Still, he wrapped a tartan blanket around both of our shoulders and we huddled together. 'Are you hungry?' he asked, revealing a picnic basket full of crusty fresh bread, cooked meats and cheese. I have no idea if he has his own ration book or not, but he'd obviously found a way.

'Oh, Rick, this is just lovely. Thank you so much.'

'Not at all. I figured there had to be something we could do in this Podunk town.'

I didn't know precisely what that meant, but I got the picture. 'This is perfect. Just perfect,' I told him.

'Next time there's a dance, I'm hoping you'll agree to be my date,' he said.

'Oh, I don't know, I'm not much of a dancer. In fact I have two left feet.'

'I don't believe that for a second!'

'It's true!'

'Well, then maybe I'll just have to give you a couple of lessons, if you'd permit it.'

I smiled up at him. 'You can dance? Even with your back?'

'I sure can. Mom always said, "Boys, how you gonna get a pretty girl to dance with you if you can't even dance yourself?" and so she taught all of us in the kitchen at the farm.'

'Well, aren't you just full of surprises! In that case, I'd absolutely love a dance lesson.'

'Deal!'

He'd brought along a bottle of port too. I had often had a tipple at Mummy's dinner parties and I thought a little couldn't hurt. I can't deny it warmed my throat as it went down too.

For a time we were content to watch the hypnotic flames and the column of silver smoke billow aloft. The night sky was vast and I felt there were a great many more stars here than there were over London. Being pressed together like sardines felt so right, not wicked in the slightest. I let myself lean against him, head resting on his shoulder. The fire rippled on the surface of the lake and we were entirely ensconced in its glow. A little bubble filled with love.

I think there was love there. I could feel it between us – the air was thicker and richer than it had any right to be.

We talked and talked. I told him all about Mummy and Daddy, about my schooling. He asked what I wanted to do after the war. 'I honestly don't know,' I said. 'Everything's going to change, isn't it, whether we win or lose.'

'Oh, we'll win,' he said with certainty. I think the alternative is too simply terrible to dignify. 'You want a family or are you one of those career girls?'

'I want both,' I said, and the prompt nature of the answer took me by surprise. 'I'm so enjoying working with Glynis and the girls. It's keeping my brain busy. I think it's good to keep a busy brain, don't you?'

'Yes, ma'am.' He gave my gloved hand a squeeze. 'All I can see is this war, you know? Get better and get back to the base so I can do my part. If there's a future beyond that, I don't know what it is.'

'It's not such a terrible thing, I think, to invest oneself only in the present. It means you won't miss anything.'

'I couldn't agree more, Margot. Right now, you, me and this fire are the whole world.' How I've balked in the past at the mere idea of 'love at first sight', but I had no concept of how fast these things can seed and put down roots. 'Margot Stanford, I find you fascinating.'

I laughed. 'I think that's a compliment.'

'It is! It is. I think about you a lot, you know.'

It was everything I wanted to hear. I'm sure there are rules about these sorts of things, but in the moment I couldn't remember any of them. 'I think about you too. All the time, in fact. Rick, you'll think me awfully naive, but I've never felt like this before. I'm scared of it.'

'I know what you mean . . . When I came to Llanmarion I wasn't expecting to . . . Don't worry, it's all going to be OK.' He pulled me close, enveloping me, and I believed him. As long as we are together, I can keep this golden feeling alive.

I wonder if it's about belonging.

I want to be his. I want him to be mine.

Chapter 16

I honestly consider throwing a sicky ('milching' as Danny calls it) to stay home and read more of the diary. Margot is a big fat liar if she says she doesn't believe in love – well, romance at least. I can feel the love radiating from every written word. I don't pretend to be ill though, because if I do I won't be allowed to go to Danny's sleepover. His mum and dad are going to Dublin for the weekend for their anniversary, so we have a free house.

Danny lives next door but one to his family's Chinese takeaway, the China Garden. It's open even with his parents away. They serve Chinese cuisine and, oddly, fish and chips. A neon sign flickers in the window and there's a fish tank in the waiting area, alongside posters for a travelling fair and a dubious-looking 'Puppies for Sale' sign. Above the shop is the now derelict dance studio: a sign above the side door saying 'STEPZ – CONTEMPORARY DANCE, JAZZ AND TAP'. Box-step hell. I can only imagine the sequinned Lycra horrors that must haunt that space.

Danny beckons me in and Bronwyn is already in the lounge. I think if I had free access to a Chinese takeaway I'd weigh about three tonnes, but Danny assures me that the novelty wears off. Nonetheless I order chicken and cashew nuts with egg fried rice. Prawn crackers come with everything, even the fish and chips.

We sit around the coffee table with *I Know What You Did Last Summer* playing in the background. I'm not a big fan of horror films, but this one is pretty mild and has both Ryan Phillippe and Freddie Prinze Jr to look at. 'This film sucks,' Bronwyn says through mouthfuls of bean curd. 'I mean, she's literally running *towards* the killer.'

'Girl,' Danny says in all seriousness, 'don't be talking shit about Buffy.'

'Can we watch the Sandra Bullock one after this?' I ask.

'Sure,' Danny says. 'So. I have news.' He pauses for dramatic effect.

'Go on . . .' I say.

'I've met someone!'

'What?' Bronwyn explodes. 'Who? In Llanmarion?'

'No, are you mad? He lives in Newcastle. I met him in a chat room.'

I rest my chopsticks. Danny was very impressed with my chopstick skills – Bronwyn had to ask for a fork. 'Dan – he could be anyone. He could be a hundred years old.'

'She's right,' Bronwyn added. 'It's probably that guy.' She points her fork at the guy with the hook presently killing Sarah Michelle Gellar.

'It's not! He showed me pictures! And he's gorgeous.'

'Oh, come on. I could show you pictures of a hot guy and I'd still be a weird Welsh ginger girl.'

'We spoke on the phone too.' I dreaded to think how those conversations went. 'And I'd know if he was a dirty old man.

He's called James and he's at sixth-form college.' He looks a little hurt that we aren't taking him seriously.

I relent. 'Well, if you're happy, I'm happy. And I want to see the pictures. But don't do anything crazy like booking train tickets to Newcastle just yet.'

'I won't. Although we're both desperate to see *Les Mis* in London so maybe . . .'

'Danny, be careful.'

'I will, I promise. Your concern is touching.'

I smile and feel very peaceful. Perhaps the most peaceful I'd felt since I moved. There's a definite unclenching in my jaw and shoulders, like I've found my niche. 'I don't want to get all mushy, but I just want to say thank you both for adopting me.'

'Any time!' Danny says with a grin. 'I know we're not your fancy London friends with Louis and Gucci . . .'

I had plenty of sleepovers back home, but none quite like this. They were always oddly political, like if Dee came, Aria wouldn't, but then if we invited Aria but not Dee, Marina wouldn't come in support of Dee. Even if we could agree a guest list, they usually ended in tears, with someone smuggling in illicit vodka or some terrible secret coming to light. It's refreshing to just sit around a coffee table with Chinese food and a horror film. I haven't even bothered to put make-up on. 'This is better without the Gucci and Louis, believe me.'

After the film finishes, Danny suggests Truth or Dare. Bronwyn and I protest, but I'm learning that Danny usually gets his own way. 'OK, I'll go first,' I say. 'If you had to make out with someone from school, who would it be?'

'Oh, gross,' Danny says. 'They're all mutants.'

'Well, you know who I'd pick,' Bronwyn says, forlorn.

'Who?' I ask.

Danny rolls his eyes. 'Bronwyn has a major thing for Robin.'

'Robin in the chess club?' He's there every day, mostly reading comic books or *Doctor Who Magazine*. I had no idea Bronwyn was into him.

'I've loved him since we were about three,' she admits sadly. 'I don't think he even knows I exist.'

'We wondered if he was gay for a while, but he has the biggest crush on Seven of Nine in *Voyager*.'

'He seems pretty shy,' I offer. 'I think you'd have to make the first move.'

'No way! Every time I talk to him, this noise just comes out: "Flobadobadobadob!"'

We laugh. 'What about you, Fliss? Who would you snog?' Danny asks.

'I don't have to answer; it was my question.'

'That's not the Wales rules, hon.'

'Well, I do have a teeny little crush.' Understatement.

'Dewi Allen?'

'No!'

'I'd cwtch Dewi,' Danny says. 'You've seen his hands, and you know what they say about men with big hands . . .'

'Big gloves,' Bronwyn and I say in perfect unison.

'Dewi's cute. He is adorable, but I'm not sure I see him like *that*, you know what I mean?'

'So who's your "teeny little crush" on?' Bronwyn asks.

'If I tell you, you can't say a word. Swear.'

'We swear.'

I take a deep breath. 'OK. I like Thom. Mr Deacon.'

Bronwyn and Danny share a meaningful glance. 'I knew it!' Danny exclaims with glee.

'Oh God, was it that obvious?'

'No. But we're intuitive like that,' Bronwyn says.

'You can't tell anyone.'

'We won't.'

'And I think he likes me back . . .'

This elicits another meaningful glance. 'Are you sure? Did something happen?' Danny says, his tone low and gossip-thirsty.

I don't know why, but I fib before I can stop myself. 'Yeah. Kind of.'

'Oh my God! What?'

'We sort of . . . hugged a little in the library. And he told me I was beautiful.' This is a total lie, but the scandal in their eyes is surprisingly addictive. I can't stop.

'Does he have a wife, or a girlfriend?' Bronwyn asks, and I realise I haven't even thought of that.

'No,' I say defensively. 'He doesn't wear a wedding ring, does he?'

'I did a little snooping once,' Danny says. 'I mean, he is hot in a weird ginger way, so I wondered if he was gay. I asked if he had a girlfriend and he just said that teachers don't have private lives and sleep in Tupperware tubs in their stock cupboards.'

'There's nothing weird about being a hot ginger,' Bronwyn adds.

'I'm sure he's single,' I say, and it's a wish as much as anything. 'He must be. I think he really likes me.'

'This is the most exciting thing that has ever happened ever,' Danny says. 'What are you going to do? If he does anything, he'll lose his job.'

'Will he? He's not actually a teacher, is he? But this is exactly why you can't breathe a word. We should take a blood oath or something.'

'No, thank you,' Bronwyn says. 'I'm not willing to swear on hepatitis.'

'But you have to promise. This is serious.' I've said too much already. If rumours start drifting around the corridors at school, Thom will run a mile.

'Babes, who else do you think even talks to us at school?'

'Excellent point.' I smile. 'OK, whose turn is it?'

'Danny,' Bronwyn says, 'truth or dare?'

'Dare!'

Exactly two minutes later, Danny calls down to the takeaway and, in a strange Chinese accent, orders a portion of Cream of Sum Yung Gy.

Wednesday 26th February, 1941

Once more my correspondence has been inconsistent. I suppose that's testament to how much fun I've been having, too busy living life to write about it. Good writing comes from pain, and happy people have none. I wonder if, in generations to come, we'll all look back at our tear-soaked, heartbroken diaries and doubt we were ever happy at all.

It seems insipid when written down, but I've spent every day since my last entry with Rick. He'll get better, and we both know it's only a matter of time until he's fit enough to return to duty. With a sand timer emptying over us, it feels like there isn't a second to waste.

Yesterday morning I received an invitation from him. It was most mysterious – a handwritten card asking if I'd be able to meet him at the hospital today. I telephoned the hospital at once and left a message to accept.

This morning I cycled out to the old asylum and saw what Doreen meant. It is an imposing redbrick building, hidden from the road by weeping willows and a high, spiked fence. I imagine it's quite nightmarish after dark. I left my bicycle outside and hurried up the stone stairs to the grand front door.

190

Inside was bustling, overcrowded by soldiers, doctors and nurses. Every room and corridor was in use. Some men looked to be in bad way, lying on stretchers, their faces burned and bandaged.

I felt terrible. I almost forget there was a war on. Now I was reminded – and for every man wounded, there were sure to be more dead.

Not wanting to be a nuisance, I asked the receptionist where I could find Rick. She told me to take the grand staircase, go all the way along the corridor and find the old ballroom. I did as instructed, weaving through soldiers on crutches and officious, starched nurses with bedpans and clipboards.

Before it was a hospital, and before it was an asylum, it must have been an opulent home, but now it has fallen into disrepair. The paint is peeling and whole chunks are missing out of the cornices.

I found the old ballroom and slipped in through the double doors. Once upon a time the room must have been quite breathtaking, but the chandeliers and drapes have long-since been replaced with beams and benches and exercise bikes. At the centre of it all was Rick, lifting some weights under a doctor's supervision. 'Oh, I'm sorry for bursting in,' I said.

'We were just finishing up,' Rick said.

The doctor handed him a towel to mop his brow. 'Ah, this must be the Margot we've been hearing about incessantly.' He was a moley little man with thick, round jam-jar glasses.

'I haven't been that bad,' Rick said with a grin. 'Come on in.'

'I'll leave you young lovebirds to it,' the doctor said, exiting the way I'd just come in. That remark left us both shy.

'Look at this room,' I said, making small talk. 'That light . . .' Radiant yellow sunlight positively poured through the three vast windows spaced along the back wall, as thick as custard.

'It's something, isn't it?' He looked splendid, even in his plain white T-shirt, shorts and plimsolls.

'Is this what you wanted to show me?'

'No,' he said with a grin. 'I thought it was time for that dance lesson, what with the St David's Day fair next week.' He bounded to the corner of the room, where there was a record player.

'Rick, I'm not sure I'm dressed for dancing . . .'

'You can dance in your pyjamas if the mood takes you!' He lifted the arm and placed the needle on a record. There was a hiss and a crackle before 'Jeepers Creepers' by Louis starts to play.

Rick returned to me and I'm not so backward that I didn't know where my hands were meant to go. I gave him my left hand and placed the right loosely on his shoulder. One shouldn't have to grip for dear life. 'Mom always said that when you're dancing, you listen to two things: the first is the music and the second is your partner's body. Just follow the mood and see where it takes you.'

We started to dance. Rick was light on his feet and I just followed, letting him do all the thinking. He smiled. 'Ready for a spin?'

'I think I can manage that.' He gave me a gentle turn and I spun too fast, colliding with his chest. 'See, I told you I was clumsy.'

'Don't look at your feet, look in my eyes. There you go.' He twirled me out again, and this time I coiled back into his arms perfectly. 'We'll make a dancer of you yet.' It sounds barmy, but I

192

felt more girlish than I think I ever have before – as carefree and light as a feather on a breeze.

We laughed and spun until 'Jeepers Creepers' ended. Rick flipped the record and a slower song followed it. He returned and held me closer. 'Just listen to the music.' I felt his breath on my forehead.

All of a sudden I couldn't swallow. I knew what would happen if I looked into his eyes. I didn't know if I was ready – kissing, like dancing, is something else I didn't know how to do – but I listened to the music, and I listened to Rick and I knew it was the right thing to do. I tilted my head up and Rick caught my eye. He seemed to pause for a moment before leaning in.

Just as his lips were to touch mine, there was a commotion from the hallway as a soldier on crutches clattered into the ballroom. 'Oh sorry, Rick old chum. I didn't realise there was anyone in here.'

We pulled apart at once. Rick cleared his throat. 'Hey, that's OK, Clive. Come on in.' He went to help his friend, and I took that to be the end of our lesson. I absent-mindedly touched my fingertips to my lips.

Sitting here now in the rose garden, I'm still gaily humming the tune we danced to, and I still feel as light as a feather.

Underneath this entry, there's line after line of the same three words, written time and time again in different ways . . .

Margot Sawyer
Mrs Richard Sawyer
Mrs Sawyer
Mrs Margot Stanford-Sawyer

Mrs Margot Sawyer-Stanford
Mrs M. Stanford-Sawyer

I smile to myself and shake my head. The girl had it *bad*.

Although, now you mention it, *Mrs Felicity Deacon* doesn't sound too shabby.

Thursday 27th February, 1941

Oh poor, sweet Bess. I'm so angry my hand is shaking and I can hardly hold the pen. I feel red and hot all over, like a boiling pot of lobsters. Oh, I could spit! Heavens to Betsy, where to start? Everything is such a mess.

As spring arrives in Llanmarion, I have cast off the scarves and gloves and many of my inhibitions. Rick is gregarious, although never coarse, and it's difficult to be uptight around him. The village seems to have accepted us a pair, which is what makes what happened to Bess even crueller. More on that shortly.

Our courtship has lost its formality. There's no time for ceremony. There's a war on. Wartime rules apply. Our time together is now smudged at the edges like a Monet or Van Gogh: springtime yellows and greens, blossoms and buds and, of course, daffodils in abundance.

By his own admission, Rick is not much of a reader, but loves stories. Today we walked through the village, bought iced buns from the bakery and took them down to the pond near the village green, to read. We've already ploughed through Jane Eyre *so we* started Treasure Island. *I rested my head in his lap and shaded my eyes with the paperback as he stroked my hair.*

'Look!' he said. 'Ducklings!'

'You are incapable of concentration!' I derided him with a smile, sitting up to look at the baby ducks. They were, of course, quite adorable.

And that was when it happened. 'May I kiss you?' he said, nudging me with his shoulder.

Now the moment was here, I felt as still as the pond in front of us. 'I think you ought. I was about to send a written invitation.'

Used to my needling, he tilted my chin up with a thumb and pressed his lips to mine. I didn't dare breathe. I don't know how I'd imagined it would be, but it was even better than that; so soft, so warm, as intimate as a secret.

For a moment I was completely paralysed. 'Are you all right?'

'Just to check, you'd better do that again,' I said.

He smiled and kissed me again, longer and deeper this time. I knew showing such affection in public was scandalous, but I found I didn't care one jot. For a moment we were one being. I felt his lips on mine and all my thoughts, all my worries, seeped out of me, soaked up like rain into the grass. Eyes shut, colourful speckles swam through my vision. I don't know how long we kissed for, minutes or hours, but I'm quite sure I could feel the turn of the earth.

There's every possibility we'd still be kissing if Bess hadn't come tearing across the village green like a harpy in full flight. 'Oh, Margot, there you are! I've been looking everywhere.'

I gathered myself and stood as she nearly collapsed in my arms, red-faced and out of puff. 'Bess, what on earth's the matter?'

She started to cry, and I could tell by her raw eyes that she'd already cried a bucket. 'It's Reg . . . Margot, he's gone.'

'What? Gone where?'

Rick stood too, brushing down his trousers. 'Gee, Miss Jones, are you all right?'

'No! He's gone and I don't know where.' She dissolved into uncontrollable sobs and I hugged her tight.

I sat her down on the bench at the very edge of the pond. People were looking over – a prissy, shrew-like mother gathered up her two children and moved them away. I stroked her hand. 'It will be all right, Bess. Take your time and tell us what happened.'

'He's gone,' she repeated once she'd caught her breathe. 'Da found out and said he'd kill him with his bare hands when he got back. Mam talked to Rhodri Ridwell and had him sent away.'

'No! That's beastly!'

'No one will tell me where he is.' Her bottom lip trembled again.

'He's left Llanmarion?' Rick put in.

'Yes. I don't even know if he's in Wales.'

I sprang to my feet, indignant. 'Well, this isn't fair at all. Reg has done absolutely nothing wrong. Let me speak to Rhodri. If his host family are willing to have him back, then . . .'

Rick took my elbow and gently steered me away from Bess. He spoke softly but firmly. 'Listen, Margot, this might not be the worst thing—'

'What?' I exploded. 'How can you say that?'

'This isn't London. What if Bess's pop does get his hands on Reg? Being moved isn't the worst thing that could have happened to him. Hell, we don't even know if he's really been sent away . . .'

'You don't seriously think . . . ?' He shrugged and I felt like I could very well vomit. 'Surely not?'

'Not everyone is as open-minded as us. There's been talk at the hospital . . . When Reg was arrested, good men, good soldiers, were talking about taking justice into their own hands.'

'Well, first of all, let's clarify that that is not the attitude of good men or good soldiers, and secondly, whatever you do, don't say that to Bess. She's inconsolable as it is.' I looked back and saw her blowing her nose on a handkerchief. I pictured Reg lying in a ditch somewhere, battered and bruised, and sincerely hoped he really had just been sent packing. 'I wonder if I can get Ivor to discover where he's been sent. I think he knows Rhodri well. If it's a lie, I can find out.'

'I swear on my life, Margot,' Bess announced, 'I'm going to find him and go after him. I love him and he loves me and that's all there is to it.'

I tried to smile for her, but both Rick and I knew that that was not all there was to it. Not in a town like Llanmarion.

In the end Bess stayed the night at the farm. She was so cross with her mother that she couldn't bear to be in the house. Glynis was more than happy to have her stay.

There was no other choice than to sleep top and tail. At least it removed the need for a hot-water bottle. We went upstairs with mugs of Ovaltine and some fruit cake I'd made with dried raisins. It was a little dry, but I've never claimed to be the best baker in the world.

'Oh, Margot,' Bess said, filling her face with cake, 'there's no way he's run away. He'd never leave me. He said so himself.'

'When did you see him last?'

She leaned in conspiratorially. 'Have you heard of the old Whaddon farm?' I said I had not. 'Last winter, old Alun Whaddon basically drank himself into an early grave – oh, don't tell anyone I told you that, but everyone knows – and he didn't have no sons to take over the farm so it's just still standing there while they sort it all out. Anyway, like, Reg and I have been going to his old hay barn to—'

'Yes, Bess, I more than get the picture, thank you.'

Bess nodded. 'We were there last weekend. Margot, he told me he loved me. We're not stupid. I know that next year he'll be called up, but we made plans. We were going to get a house in Greenwich. The way he described it made it sound magical, like.'

I didn't have the heart to tell her otherwise. 'Bess, I don't know what to say.'

'You think I'm soft in the head, don't you?'

'I think no such thing! I think you're phenomenally brave to follow your heart. Usually that's the least sensible path to take so it needs twice the gumption.'

She shook her head, bob bouncing around her face. 'I know what boys are like. I know they tell you tales to get their way, but Reg was different. I believe every word he's ever said to me.'

I took hold of her hand. 'Then I'm sure, if he can find a way back, he will.'

She crumbled into tears and I could do nothing more than hold her tight until she was all cried out.

Poor Bess has been miserable all day. True to my word, I sent Ivor to talk to Rhodri and, although he was reluctant to get involved, he dutifully reported that Reg had been rebilleted on Anglesey in *the north. Glynis assured me Holyhead is positively cosmopolitan compared to Llanmarion and he should be safe enough if he doesn't go looking for trouble. On Rick's advice, I have kept this knowledge to myself, fearing Bess will indeed flee the village if she gets wind of his location. She's only fifteen. I would feel dreadful if something were to happen to her.*

I have been busying her with preparations for the St David's Day celebration. The Welsh take it very seriously indeed and I feel we can all benefit from some cheer. The whole town gets involved. Bunting zigzags down the streets and red dragons billow from almost every window.

I understand their national pride – people in such a small country with so few voices have to shout extra loud to keep traditions alive, I believe. Why, the Welsh language is all but dying out in the south, so I'm told, and that would be a crying shame.

I'm excited for the parade and the fete. It'll be just the tonic for Bess, I'm sure.

Saturday 1st March, 1941

The war has arrived in Llanmarion. Even hearing the things I hear at the listening post, the war has always felt like something distant, something across the Channel. Tonight we were all reminded that truly the world is at war. We are all fighting. People, not numbers, are dying.

My ears are ringing and my hands won't stop shaking. I won't sleep a wink tonight. I believe the worst is over, but I daren't close my eyes. So I shall write. I shall write until the sun comes up. At this very moment, it feels like it might not.

Today was the day of the village fete. Ivor loaned the back pasture and there were fairground rides – a carousel and a big wheel – donkey rides, skittles, and I suggested croquet, to much derision.

Agatha Moss was in charge of the cider stall with some of the other ladies from the outpost, while Bess and I were to make candyfloss. There were daffodils for sale and, just for a day, it seemed everyone was willing to forget rationing and repairing and absent sons and husbands.

Of course it was Christmas come very early for the children of Llanmarion – those born here and those sent against their will. Children came from all over – I recognised some from the train. Jane attached herself to the donkey man, an unusual Irish fellow with very few teeth, and declared herself his helper. I asked if she was in his way, but he humoured her presence, letting her brush the donkeys' manes and feed them carrots.

Oh, what a gay day it would have been. Children ran around freely as bands played on a makeshift stage made from bales of hay. I don't know how it had escaped me that Ivor played the drums, but play he did, comically enormous behind a drum kit with a trio of bearded musicians I recognised from around town – one with a tin whistle, one a banjo, one a hurdy-gurdy. 'I had no idea Ivor could play,' I said to Glynis.

'Oh aye,' she said, admiring him with glazed eyes. 'Still waters run deep with that one.'

There was a tap on my shoulder. I turned to find Rick standing with a hand out. 'Miss Stanford? May I have this dance?'

I cringed. 'Ready as I'll ever be.'

'You're better than you think you are.'

I smiled as he led me to where other couples were dancing. Bess looked on glumly, no doubt recalling her night two weeks ago at the dance. It hardly seems possible that I've only known Rick for fourteen short days. It feels like a lifetime. He took me in his arms and we swayed to the music. I didn't know what I was doing, but it was enough to be close. All of a sudden I understood the appeal of dancing. It's about the closeness, an excuse to touch.

Next to us, Andrew danced with Doreen. He was quite the Fred Astaire and Doreen made a perfect Ginger. Next to them *we must have looked so painfully clumsy, but I didn't care. Not one little bit.*

A football match broke out late in the afternoon, evacuees versus townsmen. It was friendly enough, although I noted Bryn steered well clear of Rick, who played for a while for the evacuees – against doctor's orders, I would hazard.

Perhaps it was our own fault really.

Perhaps it was what we deserved for leaving the listening post unattended.

The first bombs fell at dusk.

There was no time, no warning, no sirens, only the blast. No one saw the big black shapes soaring over the horizon until it was much too late – we were all too busy watching the football.

We would later learn that German planes heading for Cardiff suddenly veered off course. It's likely the payload was dumped too soon en route to Swansea, although some think the outpost was the target.

In the moment it didn't matter. We just ran.

I don't know how to describe it. The first bomb fell in the hills. I felt a whoosh of hot wind in my hair about a second before a hungry, ear-splitting roar tore through the valley. Rick stopped running and looked me squarely in the eye. The colour ran out of his cheeks.

The ground shook and there was a terrible, terrible pause. Everything stopped. There was shocked silence for a second before frantic birds poured out of the trees.

We came to our senses. All at once, the people of Llanmarion understood we were under fire. We were exposed, out in the open. We were going to die. I didn't want to die.

The screaming began. People scattered, rolling off in all directions like marbles.

'Sound the alarm!' someone cried. My mouth went dry and I'm ashamed to say my feet froze. I didn't dare look up in case there was something falling towards me. If I was to die I didn't want to fear it; I just wanted to go out quickly and silently.

A hand grabbed my hand. 'Rick –'

'Run!' he urged, dragging me towards the farm. It was noisy, jagged chaos. Mothers grabbed tearful children, some yelling to find theirs, but the nearest shelters were in the town centre. There was nowhere to hide.

There were children everywhere, children miles from home. Some just stood and wept. I didn't know how to help them. I was useless.

More thunder. The earth shook. I smelled smoke.

Rick pulled me so hard I felt my arm straining in its socket and my feet struggled to keep up, pummelling the dirt track. 'Rick, slow down!' I begged. He careered forward, barrelling past anyone who got in our way. Some people ran towards the farm, others headed for their vehicles parked in the lane. Others just milled around, dumbstruck.

Black towers of smoke now loomed over Llanmarion village, as tall as Big Ben.

'The cellar! The farm has a cellar, right?'

'Yes!'

We tumbled onto the front drive down the side of the stables, Glynis already at the door with Peter. As soon as she saw me, her eyes widened. 'Margot, where's Jane?'

I could hardly breathe for running. 'I don't know! I thought she was with you!'

'No!' She pushed Peter through the door. 'Quickly, the cellar!' She ran down the drive. 'Jane!' she screamed at the top of her lungs.

And suddenly I knew where she was. The donkeys. She wouldn't leave the donkeys. 'I'll get her.' Wrenching my hand free of Rick's, I ran back towards the fete. I hurtled past the barn and on into the fields. From here I could see the rides and the stage, but I couldn't see Jane. 'Jane!' I called in desperation.

'Margot! Come back!' It was Rick, hot on my heels. The ground shook again and we both fell. This time I felt the full punch of the blast. That one must have been close. The air was thick with smoke, the smell of bonfire night. It was coming from the church, the church had been hit.

My knees were skinned and bleeding through my stockings. As I scrambled back to my feet, I saw the donkeys. More precisely, I saw Jane trying to drag all three into one of the little steel shelters where Ivor kept the hay. It leans drunkenly at the best of times and was certainly no bomb shelter. 'Jane!' I shrieked, setting off in the direction of the structure. 'Jane, come here at once!'

'He ran off and left them!' she cried.

'Well, of course he did!' I took hold of her arm, but she snatched it back. Rick caught up with us and, in one movement, scooped the little girl into his arms and set off back towards the farm.

I tethered the donkeys to the hay stall and wished them well. Another bomb fell. Another explosion. I felt the hot sting on my face. Singed my nostrils, brows. Now a thick, acrid fog blanketed the pasture. I could hardly see past the tip of my nose.

205

I became aware of a high-pitched whistling, like a kettle singing. Something close, something hurtling towards us. 'Margot, run!' Rick yelled. He and Jane were up ahead of me, and my heels sank into the soil as I tried to run up the slope.

I still refused to look up. I didn't want to see.

'Margot!' he cried again.

I reached the edge of the field, and Rick dragged me over the wall. With Jane in one arm and my hand in his other, we ran as the shriek grew deafening. Glynis waited at the door. 'Quickly!' She grabbed Jane and we tumbled through the front door.

The bomb hit. We all fell into an untidy pile in the hallway. The front windows shattered. The whole farmhouse seemed to shake. I clung to Rick and waited for the walls and ceiling to bury us alive.

After a second, I realised that wasn't going to happen, at least not immediately. That last blast had felt close. Too close. 'Quickly, the cellar.' Glynis limped towards the door under the stairs. 'The roof might collapse.'

'Are you all right?' I asked Rick.

'Yes, are you?'

I nodded. Dust and dirt swirled through the broken windows and I could hardly see in front of my face. There was another deafening crash. The ground rumbled. I ducked down and Rick wrapped himself across me. Something was coming down . . . the barn perhaps?

Rick guided me to the door and we hurried down the stone cellar steps to find Ivor, Peter and some other villagers who'd fled in this direction. Their faces were covered in grime, only white eyes staring expectantly up at us as we came down the stairs. Ivor pulled Glynis into an embrace and held her tight.

After that all we could do was wait for the siren to stop, which it did about forty minutes later. An awful, awful forty minutes in which we said little, each imagining only the worst about what was happening above ground. Eyes wide in the gloom, we huddled together for warmth. I think I was in shock, I couldn't stop shaking. Jane clung to me and, in turn, I clung to Rick. The pain in my knees was now a warm, dull ache.

I feared that if the farm crumbled around our ears we'd be trapped down here, to die slowly as we ran out of air, but I thought it wise to keep such thoughts to myself.

I thought about Bess and Doreen and Andrew. Where were they and had they reached a bunker? I tried to remember where I'd last seen any of them, but only remembered the first blast and the ensuing chaos.

When the sirens stopped wailing, I wondered for a second if I'd gone deaf. Ivor stood cautiously, stooping to avoid hitting his head on the ceiling. 'I'll go see what the damage is. Wait here.'

'For the love of God be careful,' Glynis urged.

He returned a only few minutes later but it felt like an age. 'It's safe enough.'

We emerged together. The farm was thick with choking dust and smoke. I placed a handkerchief over my nose and mouth and trod gingerly through the hall.

'The barn is down,' Ivor said flatly. 'I need to go out and look for any unexploded bombs.'

'Oh no, you bloody don't, Ivor Williams,' Glynis said, pulling him back with more strength than I'd have credited her with. 'That's what the army is for.'

Rick, feeling some residual guilt at his inaction, went immediately to see where he could be of aid. 'I need to go,' he said to me. 'I've got to help where I can.'

I decided my place was at the farm. 'Please be safe.' I gave him a long kiss and didn't care who saw.

Without prompting, I found a broom and got to work.

Luckily the farmhouse itself wasn't too badly damaged, just filthy. Ivor boarded up the shattered windows while Glynis, the children and I cleaned in sombre quiet.

Glynis forbade me from going over to the post office to check on Bess, and the telephone lines were down.

And so at about one in the morning, with no word from Rick, I came to bed and started to write. I can't sleep. I close my heavy eyelids and the memory of the sirens rings in my ears again. I don't want to die, not now that I have something so precious to live for.

Sunday 2nd March, 1941

Agatha Moss died when a tree came down on her car. Sergeant Huw Thomas from the police station died putting out the fire at the church. Betty and Rodney Houghton, two children evacuated here for their safety, died when the attic collapsed in on their bedroom, burying them alive.

Llanmarion is in mourning today. Silence shrouds the whole town. You could reach out and sink your fingers into the sadness. This war is real to us now. Any delusion that this was all a jaunty holiday to the Welsh countryside is forgotten.

Rick held my hand as we lay flowers outside the ruined church. It's quite understandably become a totem for the grief, its blackened bones reaching into the white sky. Bess, Doreen and Andrew stood alongside us. Even Bryn was respectfully silent. We all wore black.

Oh, it's just too awful for words, so I shan't write any more.

Chapter 17

Oh wow. In my head it's like a movie. I can't imagine really, truly being there as bombs rained down on Llanmarion . . . rained down on *this house*. My other grandma, Dad's mum, always used to say what kids today needed was a good war, but I think I've always thought of war as fictional.

In my mind, if I'm honest, Hitler is no more real a villain than Darth Vader. Reading the diary, I *still* can't properly feel the *true* horror of death camps and gas chambers – because how can anyone unless you were there – but I am beginning to appreciate that there was a whole other war for people right here.

People really died. Not just soldiers in tanks and aeroplanes. Not just unfathomably huge numbers of Jews, and gay people, and gypsies, and disabled kids and stuff. Not just evil demon Nazis with red skin and horns. People like Agatha. I liked Agatha. She was badass. Like it totally sucks! I wanted more stories about Agatha – a spin-off where she cracks codes and becomes a feisty pilot or something – but she wasn't a character in a book, was she? She was someone Margot knew. And she died.

I lie in bed and, for the first time this autumn, feel cold. I pull the blanket at the foot of the bed over the duvet. I feel a weird mix of grateful that wars now happen miles from home and at the push of buttons, but I also feel differently about Margot. About anyone who survived the war. I can see why they think we're all so trivial.

Maybe I am trivial. Maybe we're all trivial. Funny how the dark brings dark thinkings. Maybe I'll feel differently when the sun comes up.

And I do. Dawn brings the first frost of the year and the pale fields outside my window look like they're sprinkled in glitter. The day feels fresh and so do I, even after only a few hours' sleep.

Once a year, a girl must make a ground-breaking decision: today I will bring my winter coat out for the first time. It's a dark purple wool with a big tawny fur collar. I wonder if I should wear my suede knee boots too. Oh, why not? Yep, it's winter fashion time. I love winter clothes.

I trot downstairs for breakfast, the coat resting over my arm. Margot, at the kitchen table, glances at my boots over her mug. 'Are you wearing those for school or to stand on a street corner?' she says.

I roll my eyes. 'Lots of girls wear them.'

'Lots of working girls, yes.'

I decide to take the high road. 'You know what, Margot? It's a lovely morning and I don't want to start the day with an argument. I'll wear the clothes I like and you do your homeless chic.' OK, maybe the road wasn't *that* high.

She laughs, genuinely. It's odd to hear. 'You're quite right. That's what we historically fought for, I suppose. The vote,

211

equal pay and the right to dress as ludicrously as we like, free from judgement.'

I think that's as close to a compliment as I'm going to get so let it drop. 'Where's Mum?'

Margot doesn't answer at first, then gets up and empties the last bit of her tea into the sink. 'She's not feeling very well so I told her to go back to bed.'

My heart beats a little higher in my chest. It's a flashback to the worst days of her treatment – the days when she'd go for results or the day after a fresh bout of chemo. 'What's wrong with her?'

Margot runs the taps to wash up. 'Oh, nothing serious. Just a bit of a cold, I expect, but as she has no need to be up, she might as well be in bed.'

I scrutinise Margot as she busies herself at the sink. She doesn't seem overly worried, so I tuck into some toast, but I can't shake a weird feeling. Mum is fine now. She's in remission and has been for weeks, this is a fact, but I still feel a chill, and it's nothing to do with the weather. When Mum was really sick, it was like a dull, constant ache pressing into the side of my brain. It didn't matter how busy I was or what I was doing, the *dread* was always there, even in my dreams. It took me ages to lose it; I often caught myself thinking I'd forgotten something, when all it was was the fact I had nothing to stress about.

Just for a second that ache is back in my head.

I make myself shake it off. Everything's fine. And I'm wearing my furry coat today.

As I leave the farm, I squeeze behind the stables and trample through unkempt grass until I find what I'm looking for. Sure

212

enough, when I flatten down the grass I find the stumps of the old barn. Fragments of the walls remain, sticking up out of the earth. The ruins remind me of Tetris blocks.

I shiver a bit. I try to imagine the sirens, the smoke, the panic. I try to imagine squatting down in the cellar. I'm standing in history, right now. I guess we always are.

At lunchtime I help Thom catalogue some new library stock. All I'm doing is sticking a label in the front of each book and putting it on the trolley, but he seems grateful for the helping hand. I use it as an opportunity to grill him about his life. We know there's no wedding ring, but that doesn't necessarily mean anything. 'Do you live in Llanmarion?' I ask as innocently as possible.

'No,' he says, scanning a new book onto the system. 'It's never good to live too near to the school you're working at.' I want to ask where he does live, but that seems too nosy. 'Why did *you* move here?' he asks.

'To live with my grandma.'

'Everything all right at home?'

'Yeah, everything's fine.' It's sort of true. 'We'll probably go back to London next year.' I wish I hadn't said that. What if he thinks I'm desperate to get away? For the first time, I wonder if I even want to leave Llanmarion if it means losing him. 'Or maybe not, I don't know. Llanmarion isn't so bad.'

He smiles and I feel a little buzz between us. I want to move closer, to hold his hand. 'Tell me more about your ballet past. There's still time to sign up for *The Chess Club Presents*.'

Uh. Embarrassing. 'It's a really long time since I last danced. I don't even know if I could do it any more.'

213

'It must be like riding a bike, no? I once went to see the Royal Ballet in London and I thought it was out of this world. I mean, how the hell do they jump so high? Are they on wires?'

Well! This little development changes everything. 'Hmm. I dunno. Maybe I could dig out some old ballet slippers.'

'You should. That'd be awesome.'

I want to impress him, but I honestly don't know if I could any more. I'm so out of shape, so un-supple. 'We'll see.'

'Would you wear a big pink tutu?' Thom says with a broad grin. He's flirting. He is *definitely* flirting.

'No! Like people don't take the piss enough!'

He laughs and scans another book. My heart is hammering and I go a bit dizzy. Every inch of my body is buzzy. I want him so bad. The want is a big lump I can't swallow. I've never wanted anything like I want him.

Sunday 30th March, 1941

So where were we? Life slowly returned to normal following the air raid. Plentiful stiff upper lip and Blitz spirit as everyone chipped in to rebuild Llanmarion.

We do not complain. We do not cry in public. This is a war.

Since St David's Day no further bombs have fallen on the village, although Cardiff and Swansea continue to be targeted. Rick helped Ivor clear the fallen barn until his back became so bad he had to take to his bed for a week. There's now a skeleton structure on the edge of the field. Ivor says he won't bother to rebuild it until the war is over in case it gets blown up again, which I thought very pragmatic.

Bess continues to pine over Reg, although seems to have switched her attention to Andrew, who has been a most reliable shoulder to cry on. With so many of the men away fighting, Andrew, Bryn, Bill and some other local boys have taken it upon themselves to secure the church until such time as it can be repaired. The whole spire came down so it'll take some fixing.

Rick's recovery took a knock-back after his exertions during the raid and the clean-up, but he is up and about again, thank goodness. During his convalescence I took him bunches of hyacinths for his bedside and read him Wuthering Heights, which he enjoyed, but I could sense cabin fever setting in. Among the poor souls with lost limbs and missing eyes, I think Rick feels as if he's wasting a bed.

It sits heavy in my heart, but I know a part of him longs to return to service. The male ego is a soft-boiled thing and I think languishing here emasculates him. Of course no one openly criticises the injured soldiers at the infirmary, but there is some unspoken urgency for them all to get out and resume their manly destiny of dying over a field in France.

Yesterday, as a late celebration for my birthday, we drove up to the Devil's Cup again. It was positively spring-like and I wore no coat, only a cardigan the same hue as the meek sunshine. I tied my hair back with a royal blue ribbon and felt truly light in spirits for the first time since that night.

We drank brandy wine and kissed as the sun shimmered on the lake. Since the night of the bombing our kisses have taken on new urgency. Quite suddenly he stopped and stroked my cheek. 'Margot, I love you,' he said.

I knew of our love the first time I met him, but this is the first time he has said it aloud. 'I love you too,' I replied simply.

We kissed a while longer. I probably shouldn't commit this to the page, but I let his hands explore my body and it was exhilarating. When they started to wander too far, I gently reminded him that I'm a lady. 'Richard Sawyer, behave yourself.'

He did as he was told. 'I don't wanna lose you.'

I cupped his handsome jaw in my hand. 'Whatever makes you think you will?'

The sun shone in his eyes, giving them an amber glow. 'We don't know how long this war's going to go on. We don't know if I'll survive it. If any of us will. I don't want to . . . I can't wait for it to be over for us to be together.'

I knew what he meant. Since St David's Day I no longer assume I have the forevers I thought I had. I dare myself to imagine the day down the road when we will be able to marry, but it seems so far away. 'We have time,' I said feebly.

Rick shook his head. 'Margot, if this war's taught me anything it's that we've got now. All we ever have is now.'

He was right. We have this moment and our love, and what else really matters?

Chapter 18

Ew. Is Margot about to have sex? I don't know if I'm ready for my grandma to go full Judy Blume on me. This diary should come with one of those little aeroplane sick bags if that's the case.

I'm in the library waiting for Danny to finish his overdue maths homework so we can go back to his and watch *Neighbours* and *Home and Away*. 'Why don't we ever go back to yours?' he asks. 'It's gotta be bigger than mine.'

'Yeah, but our TV is tiny and Margot doesn't even have a video,' I lie. Also I just don't want to explain Mum's wig or baldness. 'Anyway, hurry up, Helen Daniels isn't going to live any longer just because you forgot your maths.'

'OK, I'll be like ten minutes.'

'Oi, Fliss.' It's Rhys, Dewi's friend. He and Dewi are doing their homework on the next table over.

'What?' I say.

'No shouting,' Thom says from the front desk. 'It *is* still a library.'

Rhys beckons me over, although Dewi is suddenly beetroot-faced. 'What's up?' I say more quietly, heading over.

'Dewi drew you,' Rhys says excitedly. 'Show her, you tit.'

Dewi looks like he'd rather do anything but. 'Rhys, you're s-such a dong.'

'You drew me?' I ask with apprehension.

'He's really good,' Rhys says.

'Am I clothed?' I ask.

'Y-yes!'

I smile and shake my head. 'You don't have to show me if you don't want.'

Dewi sighs and reaches into a Fido Dido ringbinder. 'I like draw comics and stuff. You know, like Spider-Man and X-Men.'

I take a look. It's a proper comic strip – well, I think, as if I know *anything* about comic books. Although I did like that Batman film that had Michelle Pfeiffer as Catwoman. In the ink illustrations, I see a cute, big-eyed me – with accurate headband and shift dress – holding books to my chest.

To the rest of the world, it reads, *Fliss Baker was just the new girl. But what Llanmarion doesn't know is that, by night, Fliss becomes BRITANNIA, defender of London.* The next illustration shows me in a skintight scarlet catsuit, thigh-high boots, gold crown and Union Jack shield. My hair is billowing behind me and I have a pet lion cub who looks a bit like Simba.

A huge smile splits my face. 'Dewi, this is like totally amazing!'

'You . . . You think?'

'You're so good! Is this like what you wanna do for a job?'

'Oh, I dunno . . . I'm glad you like it.'

'Well, you've dramatically overestimated my bra size, but this is so cool!'

Dewi blushes again, unable to look me in the eye. I see Thom looking over at us. I *really* don't want him to think I'm with Dewi. 'I'd better get back to Danny,' I say, stepping away. 'But let me know what happens next for Britannia!'

He grins shyly and I head back to our table. 'Are you done?' I ask Danny.

He rolls his eyes. 'I didn't realise there were questions on the back. Sorry. I'll be quick as I can.'

That gives me time to read the next journal entry. With some trepidation I turn to the page and read on.

Wednesday 9th April, 1941

I wonder, when writing diary entries such as this one, if we in some way hope they'll be found. There's something decidedly Catholic about confession. I'm certainly taking my chances, and I shall have to start hiding this diary, but I don't think I can process everything in my head holus-bolus unless I sort the noise into words.

I blame the rain.

We were out for a bike ride and the skies were cuckoo-shell blue one second and the next doomy clouds like black ink seeped across the heavens. I wonder, if I'd read them like Rorschach blots, I'd have foreseen what was to come. 'We should think about heading back,' I said a breath before the first heavy dollops of water fell.

The clouds erupted and a punishing, freezing torrent battered us. 'Good golly, run!' Rick said.

Laughing and whooping, we took off down the track, pushing our bikes, but we were equidistant to the village and the farm and long before we reached either we'd be drowned rats.

'Have you ever seen the like?' I called over the downpour. There was a dirt track leading off the main path that seemed

to lead to a big wooden barn. I don't know who it belonged to, but it was still standing after the bombs. Better than nothing. 'Quick! Look! That barn!'

Rick didn't argue. We left our bikes leaning against the gate and climbed over. Running to the barn, I saw the doors were closed, but the padlock had been smashed off. Grateful for someone else's act of vandalism, I threw open the doors and tumbled inside.

There was no machinery to be seen, only a few sad bales of hay and an old watering trough.

'What is this place?' I asked.

'It's the old Whaddon farm,' Rick said and it took me a moment to realise where I'd heard of it. This was where Reg and Bess had their secret liasions. 'Old man Whaddon died last year and—'

'Ah yes, I'm familiar,' I said, my cheeks rosy pink.

Rain hammered against the corrugated iron roof. There was a greedy rumble of thunder and I clung to Rick, remembering the bombardment.

'It's just thunder,' he reassured me. 'Looks as if we're gonna be here a while.' There was another flicker of lightning and a crash as if the sky was splitting. Daddy always said, the closer together the thunder and lightning, the closer the eye of the storm. The storm was upon us.

Even the short run had left me soaked to the skin. I wrapped my arms around myself and shivered. Rick slid out of his blazer and draped it over my shoulders. 'I'm frozen,' I said, a fat raindrop running off my nose. He held me close, rubbing my back. He was as wet as I was so I'm not sure it helped either of us.

'Maybe . . .' He stopped.

222

'What?'

'No. I . . . I was gonna say we should get out of these wet clothes before we catch a chill.'

I looked up into his eyes and bit my lip to hide a smile. 'Richard P. Sawyer . . .'

He smiled back. 'I'm serious! I don't want you to get hypothermia or something. Look . . . go up there.' There was a sturdy ladder leading to an upper level overlooking the barn. A hay store, I supposed. 'There's even a blanket.'

I'm not sure I'd have called it a blanket, but there was a hessian curtain hanging along the edge of the top level. I was so cold my teeth were clattering together. 'Very well. You wait here.'

I climbed the ladder and went behind the curtain. I peeled my flimsy dress from my skin and let it fall to the floor. I was wet to my underwear. I hesitated a moment and then took those off too. I wondered if Rick was watching my silhouette from below so I peeked my head around the curtain. Like a perfect gent, his back was turned. His shirt was stuck to his back. Oh, it just wasn't fair. 'Lieutenant Sawyer?'

'Yes, ma'am?'

'There's plenty of curtain for two . . .'

He grinned and started up the ladder. I pulled it down and wrapped the edge of the material around my chest. 'Are you going to avert your gaze while I strip?' he asked with a wicked glint in his eye.

'Of course. What kind of wanton hussy do you think I am?' I winked and turned on my heel. The barn was musty and cobweb-strewn, but otherwise clean. It merely smelled of dry hay, not an unpleasant odour in the slightest.

My back was still turned when I felt his arms wrap around me from behind, his body pressed against my back. He kissed the groove between my neck and shoulder, brushing my wet hair aside. He was so warm and his kisses were silky soft. My whole body hummed.

I turned to face him and closed my eyes. He wrapped the blanket around the both of us and we embraced, skin to skin. Oh, it felt divine. He ran his fingers through my hair and we kissed.

What we did came so naturally I cannot pretend it felt immoral. Quite the contrary, it seemed like the exact right thing to do. I couldn't stop myself and I can't say I was inclined to do so. I felt so safe, so special in Rick's arms.

In the warmth of the little barn, covered by a rough cloth, Rick and I made love on a bed of hay.

I blame the rain.

Chapter 19

Oh, gross. Well, that's put me right off my dinner.

Chapter 20

The next night I go to Bronwyn's for supper. I'm a little nervous because I haven't really spent much time with Bronwyn alone as Danny's always around to dilute her a little bit. If I'm honest, I don't think we have a single thing in common. God, if Tiggy and Marina and the St Agnes girls could see us together, they'd totally wet themselves.

We walk home from school together, heading out of town in the opposite direction to the farm, towards the old mine. I realise Bronwyn must live on the Coedwigoedd estate – the grotsky council estate built after the war for miners and their families.

The houses are a nightmare in pebble-dash. The nicer ones have manicured gardens with terracotta pots, the worst are burnt out and boarded up with steel panels. 'The estate thought a paedophile lived there –' Bronwyn points to a charred ruin – 'so they chased him out of town and set fire to his house.'

She's under a leopard-print umbrella and mine is Burberry. There's a mist of drizzle wetter than it looks. 'Oh, wow. Was he a Charlie Chester Child Molester?'

Bronwyn shrugs. 'Probably not. He just had a glass eye and kept himself to himself. I hope he's OK, wherever he is. It was pretty scary. The people on the estate might as well have chased him down with burning torches. It was like Frankenstein or something.'

'I suppose that's one of the good things about living in the city – no one really pays you any attention until they run you down by accident.'

Bronwyn smiles. 'If I can trust Dad to look after himself, I'll move away for uni.'

'Where?'

'Maybe London. Mr Deacon thinks I should apply for Oxbridge, but I don't know if I could stomach all the weird ceremonies and braying Etonians.'

I don't let on that half of my school end up there. 'God, I haven't even started to think about it. It feels like it's years away.'

'You don't know what you'll study?'

'Not really. I always thought I'd go to a ballet school,' I confess, 'but now I'll need a plan B. How do you become a personal shopper? I think I'd be good at that.'

Bronwyn cuts me down with a glare. 'There's more to you than shopping, Fliss, whatever you say.'

I give her a smirk. 'How awful. I'll have to work on being shallower.'

'You want people to think you're a pink wafer biscuit, but you're not. You're more of a Jammy Dodger.'

'Ha! Is that a good thing?'

'More substance. What biscuit would I be?'

'Definitely a Hobnob. Nutty.'

'They're oats, but I'll take that.'

Bronwyn stops at a rickety wooden gate. Her garden is a bit of a state – a privet hedge bulges through the fence, swallowing half the pavement, and overgrown grass has almost entirely reclaimed the flagstone path leading to the front door.

Bronwyn shoulders the door open, sweeping aside a mountain of ignored circulars, menus and bills. The house smells. I can't identify what of, but it's an almost-sweet, toffee odour.

The frayed brown carpets are thick with cat hair. Someone has stripped the wallpaper in the hallway and never bothered to repaper or paint. 'Ignore the mess,' Bronwyn says, but it's easier said than done. She guides me into a lounge where two mismatched seventies sofas are gathered around a grand wooden coffee table covered in ashtrays and discarded Rizlas.

My face has never been very good at hiding disgust. I force the muscles in my mouth to go slack, to avoid curling down at the edges. It looks like a crack den. I'm in a Prodigy video. 'How many cats do you have?' I can see at least three: a fat black one, a tabby and a fluffy little kitten.

'Four, I think. Esmeralda had kittens before we could get her spayed.'

The kitten is certainly cute. Bronwyn scoops it up and hands it to me. I'm fairly sure she'll be infested with fleas but I give her a cuddle anyway and she mewls appreciatively. 'Where's your dad?'

'Oh, he's away all week setting up a sculpture park in Nottingham.'

'You're by yourself all week?'

'Sure. He works away a lot.'

I clear aside an issue of the *Guardian* from two weeks ago and perch on the edge of the nearest settee.

'We didn't pay the TV licence so we can only watch videos,' Bronwyn explains. 'I hope that's OK.'

'You don't have a TV?' I fail to disguise the horror. 'What do you do in the evening?'

'Surf the net mostly. You hungry?' Although I worry about the hygiene rating their kitchen would get, I sit at a Formica folding table as Bronwyn prepares some pasta in a tomato-and-basil sauce. She manoeuvres her way around the kitchen like an expert chef, flourishing salt and pepper, adding a slosh of red wine to the sauce. It's pretty clear she is used to fending for herself.

There's a photo pinned to the fridge. 'Is that your mum?' It has to be, they're almost identical.

'Yeah. I haven't seen her since she visited in '95. I think she's somewhere on the West Bank now.' She can't quite hide a soft resignation in her voice.

'Do you miss her?'

'She's been in and out my whole life.' I say nothing. 'She's like Rafferty . . .' She points at the fat black cat that slips out through a flap in the back door. 'He vanishes for days on end. Some other families must be feeding him somewhere – look how fat he is. I guess some people just can't stay still.'

She serves the pasta and brings a dish to me. She explains her dad is vegan but she loves cheese too much to give it up. I sprinkle some grated cheddar on top of the pasta. It's funny, I've stopped missing meat really. In fact, thinking about it now leaves a slightly metallic taste in my mouth.

After we've eaten, Bronwyn dumps the dirty plates onto a towering pile of dishes lurching out of the sink and we head upstairs to play on the net. I feel so cut off at the farm that I'm looking forward to just checking in to MSN and seeing who's online.

Cats line the staircase, along with old Yellow Pages. I spot Bronwyn's room immediately because there's a battered 'KEEP OUT – AREA 51' metal sign on her door. 'Come on in,' she says.

Her room, thankfully, is slightly tidier than the rest of the house. She flicks on a lamp with a red bulb and it's a little like being in a photographer's darkroom. In this light, no wonder it always looks like she's put her eye make-up on with a paint roller.

The walls are a shrine to grungy bands. Kurt Cobain's mournful eyes peer down at me, heavily ringed with kohl, while Richey Manic smiles coyly, displaying the 4 REAL he's carved into his arm. I recognise Björk and Shirley Manson and that's about it.

Above her computer, predictably, is the I WANT TO BELIEVE poster. 'Can I just see if my old friends are online?' I ask. 'I promise I'm not using you for your Internet connection. It'd just be cool to say hi.'

'Sure. Although I want to trade you.'

I log in and swivel around in the chair to face her. 'What do you mean?'

'Well . . .' She sits on her bed. 'You know I like Robin . . .' Her eyes are fixed on her hands.

'I do.'

'Well, I want him to notice me. I'm so tired of being "one of the guys". I can't stand Sophie – all she ever talks about is calories – and every time Danny gives me a makeover I end up looking like a drag-queen porn star.'

I blink dumbly and wonder if I'm dreaming this. 'Bronwyn, are you asking me for a makeover?'

'I dunno. I guess. You know I want to be a feminist and everything, but I would also like to kiss a boy before I turn thirty.'

'OK . . . you can do both! But you don't *need* a makeover.'

'Oh, come on, Fliss – I've seen how Dewi and half of the Year 11 boys stare at you. How do you do it?'

'Really?' I laugh. 'I don't know! It's not like I do it on purpose! Although maybe it's something to do with the hair.'

Bronwyn runs a hand through her Fraggle Rock curls. 'Like that's gonna happen!'

I briefly look at my MSN. Xander and Marina are online, but Bronwyn needs my attention more. 'I don't think it's really got anything to do with what you look like, Bronwyn. I just think Robin is super-shy. Like I said, you're gonna have to make the first move.'

'I don't want to make the first move. I want it to be like a movie or something, where he chases after me in the rain and we kiss.' I can't help but laugh. 'What's so funny?'

'Nothing. Just something I read in Margot's diary. I would have said that never really happens, but it did to her.'

'So can you help me?'

I shrug. 'I don't see the point in changing your hair and clothes and stuff unless you want to change them forever. It sounds Sweet Valley High, I know, but if he doesn't like you

231

for you there's no hope. Maybe it's about letting him know you want to be more than just friends.'

'And how do I do that?'

'Turn up the flirting a little.'

'Oh, that's so cringin'.'

'It doesn't have to be crap chat-up lines and stuff.' I join her on the bed. 'Look. I'm gonna flirt with you now, but I'm pretending to be a boy, so this isn't a lesbian thing, OK?'

She rolls her eyes. 'Thanks for the disclaimer.'

'It's all about finding a way to get into his space. Like, "Hi, Robin, I like this coat. Where did you get it?"' I rub the sleeve of her school jumper. 'Like see how I'm so close you can like totally smell my perfume? Or, "Robin you have an eyelash on your cheek."' I gently brush an imaginary lash away.

She bats my hand away. 'OK, I get the picture.'

'I know it's totally fromage, but everyone knows the signs. It's a way of saying, "I'm flirting with you, dummy," without actually saying it.'

With a deep sigh, Bronwyn's shoulders sag. 'I guess. But what if it doesn't work?'

'You can't make him like you, but you know he's not the only boy in the world. In fact, if anything, you're out of his league. You could do better. Oxbridge will be teeming with tall nerdy guys who like the Manic Street Preachers!'

She smiles broadly. 'OK. But will you do one thing for me?'

'Go on.'

'Will you show me how you get your eyebrows so perfect?'

I giggle. 'That I can do. I will require a pair of tweezers and a forty-watt light bulb.'

It sounds majorly dorky, but I've started to really look forward to getting into bed with my hot-water bottle and settling down with the diary. I tell Mum I'm reading *Of Mice and Men*, which I *should* be reading for English, and she beams with pride at my swottiness. 'Are you feeling better?' I ask when I get back from Bronwyn's.

'Not too bad, thanks,' Mum says, although she still looks a bit washed-out. 'Probably getting a virus or something.'

'Nothing serious?'

Across the lounge, Margot is reading in her armchair. She seems to freeze for second, pausing mid-page-turn. 'I just needed a lie-in,' Mum says.

'You're sure?'

'Yes.'

'Good. I'd better get on with this reading then. Goodnight!'

'Goodnight, Felicity,' Margot says, returning to her book as I go back to the one she wrote. I just hope that's the end of the Lady Chatterley barn action. I need the edited-for-TV version. Or a therapist.

Monday 21st April, 1941

Heavens above. I don't know what to do. I worry by committing these words to ink I'm making them flesh, and some secrets should stay invisible. Too much information can feel like a hex. It's human nature to absolve oneself of responsibility, and by passing the secret on I'm locking the curse within the page. I have to get it out or I'll pop.

Where did we get to? Ah yes, the barn! I wish I could say I felt even a trace of guilt, but I don't. My only regret is that I want to be that close to Rick every night. I want to fall asleep listening to him breathe and wake up warm in his arms. As it is, we've only been able to sneak off back to the barn a couple of times since.

The oddest part is how much I want to talk to Mother about it. I feel like a woman now. I am ready for the war to be over so I can officially start my life. I often daydream about a cottage by the sea, perhaps in St Ives, of long walks on a windswept beach. Other times I imagine a smart townhouse in Marylebone with colourful window boxes, and a red front door with a gleaming brass knocker.

The strangest thing is, not only do I feel different, but I suspect I must look different too. Glynis saw it at once. We were at the listening post, working on a particularly devilish code. Four of us pored over it, trying to crack it faster than the people down at Bletchley. We are still keenly aware of Agatha's absence. The office feels very different without her.

Glynis peeled off her headphones and took a sip of tea. 'Margot,' she said quite unexpectedly, 'do me a favour.'

'Of course.'

'Just be a little bit careful with Rick, yes?'

My first reaction was to want to slap her face. Ridiculous, yes, but she had touched a very raw nerve. 'Whatever do you mean?'

She tilted her head almost sympathetically. I did not care for her patronising tone. 'This war, Margot – none of us knows where it'll take us, where it'll leave us.'

I paused to select my words. I didn't want to sound like a silly schoolgirl. 'I'm not a child. I know he'll have to leave eventually.'

She paused for a moment. 'It's not whether he leaves. It's whether he comes back.'

'No.' I shook my head. 'We mustn't think like that. If we start to think like that, we may as well admit defeat right now. It might take some time, but we won't be at war forever, and then we'll be together.'

Glynis took my hand over the table. 'I hope so, Margot. Honestly I do. I really, really hope so.'

As the weather improved, so did Rick's condition, a fact we both blithely ignored. As he was a little bit better, I agreed to teach him how to ride a horse. Bess and Andrew came with us too.

There's only one horse on the farm and he isn't broken in to ride, so one day last week we cycled to the next village, where there is a riding stables.

Andrew had clearly ridden before, but Bess and Rick were both nervous. Rick's horse, to match his height, had to be a good eighteen hands, and I couldn't help but laugh as the colour drained out of his face.

In the end we rode two horses between the four of us and took turns to ride or to guide. With Rick on Bainbridge, I led the handsome chestnut beast gently by a guide rope. Luckily he was a docile creature and needed only the lightest encouragement.

We followed the towpath and had a picnic in a clearing in the woods. After a couple of hours, Rick relaxed enough to feed Bainbridge the apples I'd brought from home. He caught my eye as Bainbridge gobbled them from out of his palm and I was almost knocked clean off my feet by how much love sailed between us. I feel tipsy on it, merry like Grammama when she's been on the sherry!

In short, the happiness I feel far outweighs the worries I have about Rick leaving Llanmarion. It's worth it. All and any love is worth it.

But incident never feels very far away, and that brings me on to what happened this afternoon. Deep breath. It was an uncommonly warm day for springtime and I was quite overdressed in a woollen skirt and stockings. As soon as I finished my shift at the office, I rode straight over to the hospital to meet Rick.

We strolled, swinging our joined hands gaily, through canary-yellow fields of rapeseed towards our barn. Of course I don't relish that we have to sneak off to a derelict barn – it makes it all feel sordid and illicit – but what other choice do we have? We cannot legitimately lie with one another until we are man and wife.

Only, as it turns out, it is far from being 'our barn'. So far off the road, Rick and I assumed the place was forgotten. We waltzed in, as carefree as daisies. It was only when we heard a loud curse and hay came fluttering down through the gaps in the planks that I was made aware we weren't alone.

'Who's there?' Rick demanded. 'Come out at once! This is private property.' I didn't like to tell him people in glass houses shouldn't throw stones.

Amid a rustle of trouser legs being hastily hauled up and a clatter of belt buckles, two ashamed little faces popped over the side of the top floor. My hand flew to my mouth. It was none other than Andrew and Bill Jones.

They knew what we were doing in the barn, and, by golly, we knew what they were doing too.

Chapter 21

Holy gay love tryst, Batman! This diary is the gift that just keeps on giving. My mouth is actually hanging open. Who knew people in the forties were so randy? I guess this is what happens when you don't have MTV. Or maybe it was because they were all aware that they could snuff it at any given moment, so they all threw caution to the wind.

I recover from the SCANDAL but start to worry. If Andrew from the diary is my Grandad Andrew, that is, again, icky. Why do my grandparents keep getting it on? At this rate I'm going to have to shower with a scouring pad just to feel clean. My brain starts to do sex maths. Number one: if this Andrew *is* my Grandad, maybe he was bi. Loads of people are bi. Kurt Cobain was bi. Brian Molko is bi. I don't wanna think about Grandad having sex EVER, but I don't really care if it's with men or women.

But what are the odds? There must be a trillion Andrews in the world. It seems unlikely that Diary Andrew is Grandad Andrew.

There's only one way to find out. I glance at the clock to make sure it's not too late, and carry on reading.

'Margot!' Andrew said, his mouth a surprised little circle.

'What are you doing?' I said, although I knew full well; the question was more a reflex than a request for information.

Andrew scrambled down the ladder. 'Look, Margot, it isn't what it looks like . . .' My expression must have been deeply sceptical. 'You can't tell anyone. Do you understand what would happen?'

'Shut your mouth, you idiot.' Bill, coming down the ladder, thumped Andrew in the back.

'Bill, she saw us.'

'Shut your mouth!' Bill raised his fist to silence Andrew, but Rick stepped in between them.

'Cool it!' he commanded, holding Bill back.

I held up a hand. 'Calm down. I won't say anything, and neither will Rick.' Bill's shoulders went down an inch. 'Why do you think we were sneaking out here? We can keep a secret if you can.'

I gave Andrew a subtle smile, and although he was too scared to smile back, he did look bashfully to the floor. Andrew, perhaps not a surprise, but Bill Jones! I say!

Father always tuts and sneers when people mutter about pansies, but I can't imagine it's something a man, if so inclined, can avoid. Mother's eldest brother, Edmund, who fled Berlin just before Hitler came to power, is a confirmed bachelor and I have always found him to be utterly delightful.

'If you say anything, I'll say you made it all up,' Bill added huffily.

'What two guys do on their own time is their business,' Rick said with a shrug.

'It was nothin'.' Bill buttoned his shirt and skulked out of the barn.

I looked to Andrew. 'Are you going to be all right?'

'I'll be lucky if he speaks to me again.'

'Would that be so terrible?' I asked.

Andrew blushed a rosy pink shade. 'I like him rather more than I'm supposed to.' He shook his head. 'And almost certainly more than he likes me.'

'Oh, my poor, sweet Andrew.' I took his hand in mine. 'I don't think Llanmarion is where your great love affair is meant to take place.'

'It's working out all right for you,' he said without missing a beat.

I swapped a quick glance with Rick, reminded of that invisible shawl I feel wrapped in. Sometimes I wonder what fates conspired to steer us both to such a hidden pocket of the universe at the same time. It seems so lucky, so fortuitous, I hardly dare sneeze lest I blow our chance away.

Of course I won't say anything about what we saw in the barn. It's Andrew's business, and I'd sooner die than make life any harder for him. I can't imagine it's easy as it is. It's tempting to tell Bess, but I don't trust her to be discreet.

Now that I am in love, it makes me angrier that Bess and Reg, and Andrew and Bill can't be. It seems so fundamental. Stern words from a pulpit won't turn back a tide.

Forgive me, diary, I must now go and help Glynis with vegetables for dinner. The new mundane beckons again.

Chapter 22

I wake up and make it as far as the shower, but I quickly realise I'm not well. There's a shiver inside my bones, and muscles I didn't know I had ache. I wonder if I've caught whatever virus it is Mum has. Even Margot notices. 'Are you all right?' she asks as I sit at the breakfast table. Mum isn't up again.

'I feel pretty gross.'

Margot frowns and holds the back of her hand to my forehead. With a 'hmm', she dashes upstairs, to return a moment later with a thermometer. 'Here, pop this under your tongue.' I do as I'm told and a minute later she whips it out of my mouth without warning. 'Goodness. No, you're not well. Back to bed with you, young lady.'

I don't even have the strength to argue. I practically have to drag my hollow limbs up the stairs back to my room.

I toss and turn, one minute burning up and fighting off sheet tentacles, freezing cold and rattling the next. Crazy fever dreams about Margot and Andrew and Rick and Dewi and Bronwyn and Thom filter in and out of my head. I keep waking up in a panic, thinking I have to be somewhere.

In the worst, Mum has been rushed to hospital while I'm lying here. 'Mum!' I yell out at one point.

'What?' She pokes her head around the door.

'Mum?'

'I'm here.' She sits at the foot of the bed. 'Are you feeling any better?'

I don't. It feels like there's broken glass in my throat. 'I had a dream about you. Are you real?'

A gentle smile. She looks very beautiful, like a painting from the Louvre or something. The sun hits her pale face and it's way Renaissance. I can never pronounce Renaissance. 'Yes, I'm real. You poor thing. Let me get you some paracetamol.'

I grab for her arm. 'No, don't go.'

She sits back down. 'It's all right, Fliss. I'm here.'

I scoot over and she lies down next to me. I hold her close and drift off into a shallow sleep.

The rest of Thursday is a write-off and, let's face it, if you've had Thursday off you're hardly going to go back to school on Friday. The teachers barely bother to hide their hangovers on a Friday. Lots of 'Quiet Reading Time'.

I do feel a bit better though. The burning throat and shivers seem to have morphed into a stinking cold, which I can deal with, even if I do look like a gooey plague victim. Mum and Margot let me sleep until about nine thirty and then I feel well enough to head downstairs. I want out of the bed. it's sweaty and smells like ill person.

I have some toast before sinking into a hot bath. Well, if you're gonna be ill, do it right, I think. I daren't read the diary in the bath in case I drop it, so I take a Nancy Drew Case Files paperback I already read a few years back and soak until the water goes tepid and Nancy figures out who's leaving the sorority spooky messages.

Because I'm off school, I tie my hair into a messy bun and put my dressing gown on. Mum has changed my bedding while I was in the bath and, truth be told, I'm probably well enough to have gone to school.

Ah, well. As it is, it's another day with Margot's diary. I get under the covers (the farm is only getting more Baltic as we head into autumn) and turn to the next entry.

Thursday 1st May, 1941

May Day! And what a glorious spring day it was – warm enough to wear a light cotton dress and sandals.

Llanmarion was determined to plough ahead with the May Day fair despite what happened on St David's Day. The maypole was erected and the children from the primary had been practising for weeks. There were some tightly clenched nervous jaws, but the celebration would go ahead as planned.

We took along a picnic – all of us: myself, Rick, Bess, Andrew and Doreen. Bill Jones was there too, but notably wouldn't even acknowledge poor Andrew. Still, we brought a wonderful spread: pork pies and cucumber sandwiches and honey on crusty bread. It was all wonderful until we realised we'd set out our blanket right on top of an ant's nest! Oh, you should have heard Doreen squeal as they crawled over her legs!

Peter's class was involved in the dance so, after we'd eaten, we gathered around to watch. Rick wrapped his arms around my waist and I snuggled close. He'd been sullen all day. 'Are you quite all right? You're very quiet today.'

'I'm fine and dandy.'

He gave me a kiss and I turned to return one. Some of the wizened old hags from the village looked across at us with scorn on their faces, but I cared little. They were young once, and you're not telling me they weren't partial to kissing. 'You seem sad.'

He shook his head. 'I'm not sad, I'm in love.'

'Well, that's a good thing!'

'I love you so much, Margot, it almost hurts.'

It seems so silly to write it down, but I did start to panic. 'In a good way, I hope?'

He paused for a moment and it was simply awful. Then, thank goodness, he smiled. 'It's like an ache,' he said. 'A big, warm ache . . . right here.' He took my hand and held it to his breastbone. I could feel his heart, thumping away.

'I'm glad to be in your heart.'

He held my face in his hands, as if he wanted to get a good look at me. 'God, you're beautiful. And brilliant.' He kissed me again.

I smiled. 'Don't take the Lord's name in vain.'

He laughed and kissed me again as the music started.

Oh, Peter was sweet in his short trousers. The dance began well enough, but soon descended into wonderful chaos as one clumsy oaf went the wrong way and a tangle of red ribbon ensued, which soon turned into and a scrappy fist fight between two little boys. Poor Miss Dipping, the school-mistress, had to step in to split them up and untangle them.

We laughed so much we cried. It was the best thing I've seen all year!

I turn the page for the next entry.

Only there isn't one.

It's just a blank page. I turn again and this time there's an envelope, pressed as fine as a leaf, between the pages – jammed firmly into the spine. I prise it out. The envelope has been opened with precision – the reader has used a paper knife. It's addressed only to 'Margot'.

Somehow I know it's a love letter from Rick, and that feels even worse than reading her diary, more intimate. Is that going to stop me?

No.

I'm a terrible person.

I slide the letter out, a single silky sheet. Rick's handwriting is instantly male.

My beloved Margot

I have fought in wars, been prepared to die for king and a country I didn't always call home, but it turns out love makes us all cowards. By the time you read this, I will have gone. Call me a coward if you want, but I can't stand to see your face as I break both our hearts.

I write this letter and curse the fates. Time is so cruel. It seems so stupid that much of love is at the mercy of timing. A week here, an hour there, a minute later or a second earlier and we might have never met and no one's heart would have to get hurt.

I was never meant to be in Llanmarion, and neither were you. We were never supposed to meet, but I can't regret this love. Know it was love, my dear. It is love. When I'm with you I feel like I'm glowing. I felt it the first night we met and I still feel it now. I wonder if I'll always feel it.

But, and it pains me to write this, my heart belongs to another. I know I should have told you from the start, but you intrigued me, and before I knew what was happening

I was on your doorstep with flowers. I had to know you. I wasn't to know we'd both fall so deeply so fast.

I was promised to another girl right out of school in Canada. Childhood sweethearts. We came to England together, and we were to marry, until the war broke out and delayed our plans. She's not like you, Margot. She's a sweet, simple girl. A gentle soul who deserves better. As passionately as I feel for you and as much as I've imagined a future for us beyond the war, I do not believe she could survive my betrayal. She is waiting for me in Ontario, waiting for my return after the war.

You, you my beloved, are strong enough to weather any storm. Of that I am certain. I don't know if I'll recover from this agony, but I know you will.

What we have was this village. You, me and Llanmarion, like one of those snow globes at the Christmas market. Imagine that, and try to trap the love we have in a glass bubble, something you can keep and treasure forever. Something that was perfect. Maybe it's better I leave and let it be perfect in perpetuity. Just think, we'll be young and beautiful and happy forever in that snow globe. We'll never get old, never fall out of love, never remind each other of how we're decaying. Maybe this is for the best.

Please don't hate me, Margot, I don't think I could stand it. I don't know where they're sending me and perhaps it's best if you don't try to find out. Pretend I died some gallant, Nazi-fighting death and you loved and lost a war hero.

My cowardice doesn't darken that light in my heart. That will always be there. I will always love you, Margot Stanford. I am so very sorry.

Farewell, my beloved,

Rick Sawyer

Chapter 23

Nooooooo!

At some point while reading the letter, my hand has absent-mindedly flown to my chest like I'm stopping my mashed-up heart from spilling onto my clean duvet cover.

Jesus, Mary and that other one, this is AWFUL. Because I went into it expecting a love letter, I read again, my heart sinking further into my stomach with every line.

He left her?

He just left?

He had a girlfriend?

What?

Again, noooooo! No, no, no. This isn't what was meant to happen at *all*. Poor, poor Margot.

I carefully fold the letter back into the envelope and tuck it back in. I have to know what happened next. I turn the page, and thank God there's more.

Friday 9th May, 1941

I don't know what to write. I've been staring at an empty page for days. What is there to say?

He left me here.

It feels like I am rotting from the heart out. My arms and legs and mouth continue to soldier on, but my insides are festering and mouldy, writhing with maggots. How I wish I could cry. How I wish I could scream and shout, but those are pastimes of the living.

I got the letter two days ago. It was waiting on the doorstep when I got home with Glynis. We were positively exuberant as we'd managed, between us, to break that devilish cipher. And there it was.

It's all so clear now. I last saw Rick on Sunday. It was a bright and sunny day and so we went up to the lake. I fell asleep on our picnic blanket, Du Maurier open on my chest. I awoke and found him gone. I looked up and saw him at the water's edge, skimming pebbles across the surface. Circles rippled, and I sensed he was brooding, perhaps aware we'd both have to acknowledge his improving health soon.

251

Now I know his thoughts weren't nearly so noble. I watched him awhile. I wonder if that was when he knew. When he decided to leave me here. I suppose that ache he felt in his chest wasn't love after all. It was guilt. Guilt: cold, black and greasy.

He calls me his beloved, but how could he love me and be so ruthless? I could have no more left Rick Sawyer than I could leave my own body, and yet he managed it. I read his letter once, and thought it must be some horrific nightmare. I read it twice and it felt like I was in a novel. Only on the third read did it truly sink in.

He has gone.

And with him went my spirit.

Saturday 10th May, 1941

I couldn't avoid it any longer. I had to tell Glynis why Rick hadn't called on me this week. 'Margot, is Rick well?' she asked me as we tidied up after supper tonight. The lambs are getting a bit bigger now. The children were out helping Ivor with them, so it was just the two of us.

I retrieved the letter from my pocket. I don't know why I've been carrying the cursed thing around with me, but it's all I have of him now. Without a sound I handed it to her. She read it quickly and her eyes dimmed with pity. 'Oh, Margot, sweetheart. I'm so sorry, like.'

'Thank you,' I said in the absence of any original thoughts.

Glynis sat me down at the kitchen table. 'You poor thing. This is absolutely awful. And to tell you in a letter – what sort of a man does that?'

I said nothing.

'Ah, Margot. I thought he was one of the good ones too.' She took my hand. 'It feels awful, doesn't it? This won't make you feel any better just now, but we've all had our hearts broken at some point, you know? For me it was Gryff Owen. We were twelve and

253

I thought he was the most spiffin' chap in all of Wales. Only he said I was big as a heifer. Can you imagine? Although I was a bit podgier back then, mind you.' I must have glazed over. 'Margot? I know it feels like a catastrophe, but it will get better, I promise. Hearts heal, just like broken bones, so they do.'

I looked inside myself before looking up at her. I dug around in search of an ember in the ashes, some glimmer of warmth. 'I think it's beyond healing,' I whispered.

'Aw, sweet girl, don't say that, pet. I just know some other man is going to sweep you off your feet, and on that day you won't even remember Rick Sawyer's name.'

I did not believe her. I still don't. I am so cold and so numb like I'm pumped full of morphine. I have to think out and orchestrate every laboured moment and force my body to comply. Left to its own devices, I think it would find a dark, hollowed tree trunk in which to lay down and die.

Monday 12th May, 1941

Having slept for much of the weekend, I'm now mildly embarrassed to read my last entry. Such doleful histrionics are beneath any of us. I sound like some thinly sketched Brontë heroine, struggling across a metaphorically windswept moor.

It's with shame I'm reminded of the people who are actually dying both at home and overseas. Those vast, faceless legions of soldiers and civilians. And here I am, wallowing in my trivial misery. Well, it just won't do at all.

I went into work today. Since Agatha died we have been rudderless and we need all hands on deck, as it were. Truth be told, I welcomed the distraction. There was so much to do I honestly haven't thought about Rick all day.

Even writing his name is painful though. I'm so bruised, but I am now feeling the stab of pain, which I hope means I may one day heal. Just like Glynis said I would.

My friends are being very sweet, indulging my little bereavement. Yesterday Andrew, Doreen and Bess came around with a freshly baked batch of scones and some blackberry jam. I had little appetite but they'd pooled their rations and I forced myself to pick at one out of gratitude.

Bess is angry on my behalf, almost as angry as when Reg was exiled. Andrew seemed sad. Doreen exuded a hint of smugness that her suspicions about soldiers being a bad sort had been proved right. It seemed the only person without an opinion was me.

I wish I was angry. I wish I was sad. Instead I feel entirely flat, like someone's been over my insides with a rolling pin.

I am no doctor or scientist, but I have often wondered if there's a delicate chain connecting the head and heart. Some link that enables matters of the head to be warmed with feeling and our heart's desires to be tempered by reason. Just at present I'm starting to question if the chain has been severed.

Chapter 24

I read the next couple of entries in the library. Poor Margot. She writes about work at the listening station, and Bess's attempts to track Reg down and Andrew and Bill's secret tryst, but you can tell her heart's just not in it. Her writing is flat and, for the first time, a little boring. She's keeping the diary up, but there's no mistaking what she really *wants* to be writing about. Rick is there, plastered in the gaps between the words and the space between the lines.

I watch Thom go about his business, seething with white-hot jealousy when other pretty girls come in. I'm lucky, to be honest, in that most of the girls who come in here would rather shag a book than they would a human, and that suits me fine.

The library is packed today. It's teeming down with rain outside, properly bouncing off the pavements, so everyone is looking for something to do inside. It smells slightly of damp BO – that bin-bag-full-of-grass odour. Thom looks torn between being thrilled to have actual kids borrowing books and horrified at having them trash his library.

I don't wanna be *that* girl, the one who is all about boys and nothing else, but the fact of the matter is I don't feel for anyone else the way I feel about Thom. Love is like a box of Cadbury's Roses – there's all different types. The love I have for Mum comes from just below my heart and it's warm and orange. My love for Danny and Bronwyn and my friends back home comes from my throat, from laughter, and that love is magenta pink. What I feel for Thom, however, comes from a cavern below my tummy and it's darkest blood red. It feels thicker in my veins than the other types.

If that's what Margot felt for Rick, I totally get it. What are you meant to do with that once they've gone? I'm guessing it clogs and clots in your body, breaking down slowly. She must have felt so awful. My old science teacher once showed us a smoker's lungs in formaldehyde – all black and tarred and shrivelled. I wonder if that's what a broken heart looks like.

I'm so angry at Rick. I wonder if he's still alive so I can track him down and kill him. I searched for him on the library computer – under both 'Rick' and 'Richard' – but I can't find him.

'What's up?' Danny asks. He's giddily flicking through the Argos catalogue because his mum and dad are letting him get a mobile phone for Christmas. He wants one with snap-on covers. I'm, like, what's the point? Who's he gonna ring when no one else has one?

'This diary is like totally scrambling my brain.'

'Man, you're a slow reader.'

'I'm savouring it, philistine.'

'What's going on?'

'She fell madly in love with a sexy pilot.'

Danny's eyes light up. 'Is it like steamy and stuff?'

258

'No!' I say. 'Well, maybe a tiny bit, but that's not the point. He ran off and left her. He already had a girlfriend.'

'Ooh, love rat.'

'Totally. And now she's heartbroken and I think my grandad might be gay. Or bi.'

'Keep your voice down!' Danny hushes me. 'What do you mean?'

'There's a guy called Andrew, which was my grandad's name. They met in Llanmarion when he was an evacuee too, but I don't know if it's the same Andrew or not.'

He shakes his head. 'Oh, as if! How many Andrews must there be in the world?'

'I know. That's what I thought too. I'm still sad for her though. She was head over heels. He left her a letter. Here.' I slide the envelope out and hand it to Danny. 'Be careful. That thing is like fifty years old.'

Danny sets about reading it and I flick to where I've left my bookmark. I turn the page and find it blank. I flick ahead and find the last quarter of the diary is empty. My heart skips and I start to panic. How can it be over?

I turn back and see there's one entry left. Just one. What? 'Oh my God!' I say.

'What?'

'There's only one entry left.' There's only one thing to do.

Friday 30th May, 1941

Oh, diary. For a week I've avoided writing, because once it's in ink, it's sealed as truth. I write with a trembling hand, more scared than I have ever been, but I can avoid it no longer. It's not a question of if, but when.

I don't know what to do, and as much as a comfort as you have been, you're only a book. I need help and have no idea which way to turn.

You see, it seems I am with child. Oh there's no 'seems' about it . . . I am carrying Rick's baby.

And thus, in black and white, now it is truth.

Chapter 25

I gasp and drop the diary. Danny looks up, still reading the letter. 'Dramatic much?'

'Oh my God.' I read the last entry again to check I'm not daydreaming. Nope, I read it right the first time. Some of the girls on the next table look over with disdain.

'Fliss? Are you OK? You look like you're throwing a whitey.'

The library lurches forward, like that bit in *Titanic* where it rears up out of the sea. I grip the table for support. Wow, I feel drunk, like the time we stole a bottle of Tia Maria from Marina's sister and drank it on Clapham Common. The cogs in my head clank around, trying to process the information. If Margot was pregnant in 1941 . . . Mum wasn't born until '57. What the . . . ?

I turn the pages, flicking through them frantically. There's nothing else. Not a prologue or addendum or note or anything. Not a single further word is written in the book. *That's all, folks*.

'Fliss, you're freaking me out. What's going on?'

I close the book. 'Nothing,' I lie. 'It just ends.'

'What?'

'There's, like, no more.'

'OK, slight overreaction there. I thought you were having an embolism or something.' He rolls his eyes.

'Sorry. It's just so abrupt. Now we'll never know what happened.'

Danny laughs kindly through a mouthful of Jelly Tots. He's segregated the green ones and made a little pile of them on the table. 'But, Fliss, we do! She became a bitter old crone who lives on a farm and everyone except her lived happily ever after.'

I can't deal with the news and Danny at the same time. The drunk feeling has much too quickly become like the hangover I had the day *after* the Tia Maria. 'I need the loo. I'll see you in English, yeah?'

'Sure.' He hands me back the letter.

I go to the girls' toilet and let freezing cold water run over my hands at the sink. I'm actually *mourning* the diary. I didn't realise I was so close to the end, and I wasn't ready. It feels like it's been torn away from me. How can it be over? As crazy as it sounds, I haven't had a chance to say goodbye – to Bess, to Glynis and Ivor. I've come to . . . well . . . love them.

From out of nowhere, a fat tear runs down my cheek. It's hot and salty as it hits my lip. I bat it away with the back of my hand. Margot was pregnant? Mum has a brother or sister? Was abortion even around in 1941? I so should have paid more attention in history lessons.

I *know* I went into the diary with the aim of finding ammunition I could use against Margot somehow, but that's not where it ended up. It's probably the best book I've ever read, including *Are You There, God? It's Me, Margaret*, and that's *really* saying something.

I go to my afternoon lessons, but I can't concentrate at all. There's a huge splinter in my brain and I can think of nothing else. I feel twitchy, unable to sit still for a second, writhing in my seat. When Miss Tunney calls on me to answer a question, I just stare at her blankly and she makes a snide remark, suggesting I should spend as much time on the reading as I do my nails. Maybe if she spent more time on *her* nails she wouldn't be a 'Miss' at forty-six. I keep that thought to myself.

The rain is still coming down when I get home, and it feels like the sun didn't bother to come up at all today, one long daynight. The long driveway to the farm is a minefield of vast, murky puddles I have to skirt around. I hang my dripping coat and umbrella at the foot of the stairs and head upstairs to change. I'm soaked all the way to my underwear so I change into my Little Miss Naughty pyjamas. 'Mum?' I hear sounds coming from her bedroom.

'It's me,' says Margot. 'Your mum's downstairs.'

It's now or never. It feels like the universe has given me an opportunity and I have to grab it. Urgh, I might vom. Green Jelly Tots and Diet Cherry Coke churn in my tummy. Can I really do this?

I have to know.

I take the diary out of my school bag. I kept it safe from the rain in a Miss Selfridge plastic bag. I lurk in the doorway of Mum's bedroom, where Margot's stripping the bed.

She doesn't look up. 'Your mum's making dinner tonight. Sausage casserole for us. I imagine vegetarian sausage casserole for you. I don't know how you stomach that Linda McCartney muck – it tastes like something that's been scraped out of a vacuum bag.'

It feels like the words are being strangled. 'Margot?'

'What is it?' She slips a pillow into a pillowcase.

Just do it. 'Please don't be cross, but I read this.' I hold out the diary and Margot stops what she's doing. At first she frowns, and then realisation spreads over her face: a wave from her eyes, spreading south until her mouth goes slack, lips parting in surprise. 'I know I shouldn't have done. I found it in my room,' I fib, 'and I wondered what it was, so I looked. Then I just couldn't stop . . . It was so . . . interesting.' I falter.

Margot says nothing. She's frozen, staring dumb at the diary. Her jaw clenches but she doesn't even blink.

'I . . . I need to know what happens.' My voice is wafer thin. I whisper, 'What happened to the baby?'

I'm not expecting the slap. Margot's hand whips out and strikes my face. My teeth rattle in my skull before a red-hot sting burns my left cheek. She snatches the book from me and I press my hand to my face. I exhale, too shocked to speak.

'How dare you?' Margot's eyes blaze through the dim amber lamplight of the bedroom. A gust of wind throws rain against the window. 'How *dare* you?' she says again.

'I . . . I just—'

'You will not breathe one word of this to your mother, is that understood?'

'But—'

'Is. That. Understood?' Her eyes widen to manic proportions and her nostrils flare.

264

I dip my gaze, so weak, so compressed by her glare. 'Yes,' I say feebly.

'This is the end of the discussion.' She sweeps past me, the diary in her arms. 'Finish making your mother's bed and come downstairs for dinner.'

I wait until she's gone before I start to cry. I curl up on Mum's bed and sob silently, too scared to make any noise.

Chapter 26

Margot's slap didn't actually leave a mark on my face, but the next day I wore *Sleeping with the Enemy* levels of blusher to try make her feel bad. If she did, she didn't show it. I scowled at her over breakfast as she thumped plates and mugs down with fire-and-brimstone intensity.

Worst part? I felt guilty. Whatever else, I had no business reading her diary. Fact. I probably deserved the slap.

Somehow, for the last week before autumn half-term, we manage to avoid each other. When she enters a room, I make an excuse and leave. If Mum notices the frostiness, she doesn't comment on it.

Second worst part? I miss the diary. I'd so looked forward to curling up in bed with it every night. It was as comforting as Horlicks and Hobnobs. I miss Past Margot. I hear her clipped voice in my head, passing barbed comments on stupid things teachers say.

I guess *that* Margot died when the diary finished.

'What shall we do today?' Mum says quite unexpectedly. Now it's Tuesday in the half-term holidays and I'm bored already. It's Halloween this Friday and we're watching *Halloween* at Danny's, but that's AGES away.

'I dunno,' I say. 'I'm supposed to write an essay on *The Woman in Black*.'

'No!' Mum rises off the sofa with purpose. 'Let's go shopping.'

'What?'

'Let's go into Swansea and do some proper shopping. I think, just this once, we can relax our "we do not speak of Christmas until November" rule.'

I cast an eye over her familiar old towelling robe. That ugly thing is practically a second skin. 'Are you feeling well enough?'

She rolls her eyes. 'Yes, Fliss, I am fine. I am so bored of being a sick person. Some days it feels like I'm a walking, talking illness. I swear I used to do something other than sleep. I look at that BAFTA and wonder how I ever got it.' She gestures meekly at the bronze mask on the mantelpiece. 'Can we just have a nice, normal, mother–daughter shopping day?'

'Absolutely!' I gulp down the last of my tea excitedly. 'Can we go to Miss Sixty?'

'We can go wherever you like. My treat.' Wow. Usually I have to save up for stuff.

'Does Margot have to come?' I can't keep a sullen top note out of my voice.

'Today is just you and me.'

It feels like shards of sunlight bursting through months and months of cloud. This is it. This is where real life starts up again. Me and Mum, back to London. 'This is gonna be so cool. I'll get in the shower.'

By the time we're both ready, Margot still hasn't returned from the auction mart. 'I'm sure she won't mind if we take the Land Rover,' Mum says, grabbing the keys off the hook in the kitchen. On the drive, I see Margot must have taken the truck – and with it some of Peanut's brothers and sisters. 'Oh, it feels so good to be out of the house.' Mum turns her face to the sun.

She still looks a little gaunt and pale, but at least she doesn't need to wig it up any more. Her hair now resembles Winona's new pixie crop and it kinda works on her. I like it.

All the way to Swansea we listen to Take That at full volume and sing along at the top of our lungs, the way we used to BC. Swansea high street isn't exactly Oxford Street, but it has actual, recognisable chains with real-life fashion in.

First stop is Virgin Megastore to stock up on CDs. I get the latest from the Backstreet Boys, but also the new Prodigy and No Doubt. I think the Spice Girls might be deeply uncool already, but I might ask 'Santa' for their new one as a stocking filler, then I can blame him if I get any flak. Who am I kidding? I can totally just tape it off Danny – I *suspect* he'll have it.

After that, Mum treats us to a 'nice' lunch at the Conservatory. It's a gorgeous restaurant, unsurprisingly featuring a big glasshouse on one side. We're seated next to an ornamental indoor pond filled with huge white-and-orange koi. It reminds me of our 'Girls' Days' BC. Sometimes when Mum got back from filming abroad, she'd treat me to a spa day, or a manicure, or a West End show or a fancy lunch. This is as lovely as anywhere I've eaten in London, even if the menu is a little, erm, shall we say 'provincial'. There's a lot of jacket potatoes and steak sandwiches on offer. I play it safe and go for minestrone soup.

'Shall we have dessert?' Mum says as the waiter hovers over us. His much too small white shirt can barely contain his pecs. It's all a bit Peter Andre for my liking.

'I will if you will . . .'

'Why don't we share a sticky toffee pudding?'

'Hang on,' I say. 'Does it have dates in?' I've never understood why you'd put fruit in a cake. Way to ruin cake, guys.

'I don't think so,' he says in a thick French accent. 'But I will check.'

He returns a moment later and confirms there aren't, so we order sticky toffee pudding and custard and it's immense. I won't need to eat again until Christmas.

'OK,' Mum says, 'what's the plan? Do we look for Christmas presents or shall we just look at clothes?'

I figure in October there's still plenty of time to get gifts so suggest I *may* need some winter clothes. I whip through Topshop like Taz of Tasmania before heading to Miss Selfridge, where I try on every party dress I can get my little hands on. 'What do you think of this one?' I say, modelling an A-line shift dress in softest pink suede. 'It'd look cute with my purple platform boots, don't you think?'

Mum sighs. 'But where on earth would you wear it in Llanmarion?'

I pout. 'I don't know. Like parties and stuff?' I realise this year there won't be a St Agnes Christmas party and I won't get an invite to Bethany Monroe's cocktail night or the charity carol gala.

Mum inhales deeply through her nostrils and closes her eyes.

'Are you OK?' I ask.

'I'm fine. I might need a coffee in a bit.'

'Sure.'

We get Mum a cappuccino and head to Miss Sixty, where I buy a somewhat risky denim miniskirt. After that we take a look in Schuh and finally Etam. I try on a pale purple leather biker jacket. I can't decide if it looks amazing or a bit cheap and nasty. 'What do you think?' I leave the mirror and turn to Mum.

She's not just leaning on a clothes rail, she's gripping it.

'Mum? Are you OK?' Her eyes are glassy, fixed on the floor. Suddenly I feel like I'm falling. That feeling when a lift goes down too fast. 'Mum?'

Her lips are milk white. 'Just give me a second, Fliss.'

She staggers forward and I try to steady her. Even I'm surprised at how light, how fragile, she feels. 'Mum!' I sink to my knees, trying to lower her gently to the matted carpet. 'Please, help!'

People are already staring and I look up into their eyes, begging them to do something, *anything*. Why are they just bloody standing there? I beg. 'Please help! It's my mum! She's not well!'

A shop assistant not much older than me ditches an armful of jumpers on the floor. 'Erm . . . I'll call an ambulance.'

Mum's eyes roll back into her skull. 'Mum? Mum, can you hear me?'

'Fliss . . .' she mutters, like she's dreaming me.

'Mum . . . stay awake!' I pat her cheek with my palm because that's what people do on TV. 'Mum?'

Her eyes close and I look up at the onlookers. They stand there gormless, virtually indistinguishable from the mannequins. 'Mum,' I whisper in her ear. 'Please don't die.'

You can't, I think. You can't die in Tammy Girl.

Chapter 27

By the time the ambulance arrives, she's come round a bit. She's able to answer the paramedic's questions, but to me, because I know her, she's still pretty out of it. 'I just felt faint,' she says, but she still can't stand without support. They put her on a stretcher and wheel her out of Etam's stockroom and into the waiting ambulance. 'Can we not make a big fuss?'

'She had cancer. Ovarian cancer,' I tell the lady paramedic on the curb. She scribbles down notes. 'She finished chemo in, like, July.'

'OK, thanks, lovey. Hop in and we'll get her to A&E.'

I always thought it'd be exciting to ride in an ambulance, but it was just awful. Mum drifts in and out of sleep all the way to the hospital, but she grips my hand tight. Or maybe it's me gripping hers, I can't tell. Over and over, I repeat the same phrase in my head: *Don't die don't die don't die don't die don't die don't die* . . . What else are you meant to think? We've come so far. Five years and five hundred miles to escape Death. We've beaten him. Me and Mum together. He can't have followed us to Llanmarion; I don't remember leaving a forwarding address. Even if we had, I never thought he'd be arsed to come to this shithole.

An owl-like doctor and a nurse greet us on arrival. The paramedics babble away in medical jargon and I don't understand a word they're saying. 'What's going on?' I ask.

The doctor looks at me over his horn-rimmed glasses, although he continues to walk briskly alongside the trolley. 'We don't know just yet. Are you her daughter?'

'Yes.'

'What's your name?'

'Felicity. Fliss.'

'Well, Fliss, your mum's in safe hands now and we don't think she's in any immediate danger, she seems to be stabilising nicely. You just sit tight out here and I'll be back with more information as soon as I have it.' And with that, all three vanish through a plastic curtain like they're going into the car wash.

I'm alone in a sad, minty green corridor that smells of disinfectant. There are brown signs pointing left and right in English and Welsh and I don't even see a chair to sit on. I hover, about an inch away from lying flat down on the floor and crying.

A nurse with simply enormous boobs and poorly dyed carrot-coloured hair takes pity on me. 'You all right, love?'

'They just took my mum in there.'

She tilts her head. 'Oh, bless. Come with me. There's a family room. Is there anyone I can call?'

'Can you ring my grandma?'

Strangely, the thought of Margot arriving is hugely comforting. I think of the girl who kept her head as bombs fell and when Reg was arrested: good in a crisis. She rocks up about an hour after the nurse calls her. The double doors burst open and she sweeps in on a gale-force wind, thunder on her face. She's still in her wellies and wax jacket. 'What's going on?' she barks.

I rise from the armchair and put last January's *Elle* to one side. 'They won't tell me,' I say. 'She's been in with them for about an hour now and no one is telling me anything.' My voice gets higher and higher with every word.

'All right. Calm down. I'll find out what's happening.'

'They just keep telling me to wait.'

Margot purses her lips. 'We'll see. Come with me.' I leave all my shopping bags stuffed in the corner and follow her into the corridor. 'Where did they take her?'

'Through there.' I point.

Without a word, Margot just pushes her way through the plastic curtain and I go after her. We don't get far before a nurse stops us. 'Excuse me, what do you think you're doing?'

'Where's Julia Baker?'

Margot tries to step around him, but he blocks her path. 'Madam, please! She's under observation.'

'Don't "madam" me, young man. This isn't a prison. I want to see her. I'm her mother.'

He sighs. 'Wait here.'

A moment later he returns with Dr Owl. 'Hello there. I understand you're Julia's family.'

I feel totally rinsed out, heart beating in my ears. 'That's right,' Margot says. 'How is she?'

'She's stable and conscious. She's tired, but you can go through now. We've just moved her onto the oncology ward.'

I'm not a doctor, but I've heard that word plenty of times. Oncology equals cancer. 'Margot, what's—'

'Come along, Felicity,' she says, cutting me off.

We follow the nurse, Gary according to his name badge, into a lift to the fourth floor. More toothpaste-coloured corridors, on and on like in *Labyrinth*, until we finally reach the cancer ward. There are about twenty beds, each partitioned with fabric screens. Mum is in the fifth bay. She's been propped up and is awake. She already looks a million times better.

I throw myself at her like a two-year-old. 'Mum!' I bury my face in her chest.

'My God, Fliss, I'm so sorry,' she says. 'You must have been terrified.'

'It's OK,' I say, wiping back a tear of pure relief.

Margot looms over the foot of the bed. Her face is ashen, but her arms are folded. 'Julia, what on earth were you thinking? Taking the car? You're nowhere near well enough! Felicity, was this your idea?'

'Oh, Mum, stop bloody getting at her!' Mum snaps. 'It was all my idea. I was bored, all right?'

Margot seems to soften. 'Felicity,' she says, 'you'd better sit down.' She gestures to the blue visitor chair next to the bedside cabinet.

I don't want to leave Mum's side. I perch on the edge of the bed. Mum holds my hand. I can see where the silver needle sits in her vein, stuck down with a bit of surgical tape. 'Why? What is it?'

'She has to know, Julia. It's gone on long enough. It's not fair.' Margot's voice is quiet and firm.

'Mum . . .' my mum starts, but then just stops and squeezes my hand more tightly.

274

I look between them. 'OK, like now I'm wigging out. Will someone *please* tell me what's going on?'

They share a highly loaded glance. 'Fliss,' Mum begins, 'you have to understand that we both just want what's best for you.'

I don't know where this is going, but my gut is screaming that the destination isn't exactly Disneyland Paris. A fresh tear sneaks out of the corner of my eye. 'Mum, are you ill again?'

'Yes,' she admits, and a tear rolls down her face too. She quickly wipes it away, pulling herself together. 'Well, no, that's not right either . . . Fliss . . . I was never better.'

'What?'

She takes a deep breath. 'In July, Dr Palmer told me the cancer had spread to my bones and that it wasn't responding to the chemotherapy. There's nothing else they can do, love. It's terminal.'

My hand covers my mouth although there's no sound coming out. It feels like I've been punched in the stomach.

'I had two choices. I could either keep having more chemo and radiotherapy, even though the chances of it working were slim-to-none, or they could make me comfortable for the last few months with painkillers. Fliss, you know more than anyone how sick the chemo made me, and they don't think it'll make the slightest bit of difference. I don't want to spend my last days with you off my face on drugs. I want to enjoy my time with my family. That's why we came to Llanmarion.'

Last days. I'm suddenly very aware of time. I can practically feel the seconds floating up like bubbles and then popping, gone. 'How . . . long?' I ask, my voice hardly there.

'They said six months, perhaps a year, but that was in July.' She can't look me in the eye. A suffocating silence fills the cubicle. Margot is still stood like a tombstone over the bed. I look between them.

'You lied to me! You told me you were getting better!' Six months? Six months is all that I have left with Mum? No! Six months from July . . . which leaves me with, like, three.

'Felicity, this is not the time or the place—' Margot interrupts warningly.

'No!' I snap. 'You lied!' I pull my hand back from Mum's.

'Felicity!' This time Margot shouts.

'Stop it right now, both of you!' Mum says. 'Fliss, you can either throw a tantrum about how I don't treat you like an adult, or you can actually behave like one. Which is it to be?'

Well, I can't say *anything* now, can I? I hide under my hair and bite my tongue.

Mum goes on. 'I didn't want you to know until you absolutely had to, Fliss. I hoped they were wrong. I got a second opinion when we got here. I wanted to be sure. What good would knowing have done you? Who wants to hear they've got six months left to live? I just wanted things to be as normal as possible – for us.'

'How could they be?' My voice trembles.

Mum looks me dead in the eye. 'I had to bring you here first. To be with Margot. I think the universe is sending me a pretty clear message that it wants me dead.'

I must visibly flinch.

'We've got to accept that now, Fliss. We haven't got time to faff around with *wishing* when there's so much to do in so

276

little time. Fliss, I'm not going to leave you alone in the world. I have to know that you're gonna be OK with Margot.' Now she turns to Margot. 'And you – shut away in the middle of nowhere – it's not healthy, Mum. You're just going to get worse and worse until you're the mad recluse that kids tell scary stories about. That's why I *need* you two to get along. I don't want to . . . go . . . worrying about what's going to happen to either of you. I want to go in peace.'

That shuts us both up. Now it's not just me staring at Mum open-mouthed, but Margot too.

'So now you know, Fliss. *This* was the time to tell you.'

I guiltily track back through all the stupid stuff I've said and done since July. Every time I've whined, every time I've asked for money, every time I've wittered on about something on the TV. 'I . . . I could have helped.'

'You have, Fliss. You've done enough these last few years, more than most girls your age have to do. I want to see you *live*.'

My brain starts to process what I'm being told. I thought Mum was getting better. After all this time it turns out she's not. It's the bit at the end of the horror movie when the dead monster gets back on his feet.

My mum is going to die.

In a matter of weeks.

I start to panic.

I want a do-over.

I want the last five years back so I can make every moment golden for her. I want to scrub clean the times I refused to do my chores or stayed out late or played my music too loud.

'Mum, I don't want you to go.' It sounds pathetic, but it's all I want to say.

'I don't want to go either,' Mum says, holding me close.

They might discharge her tonight, we're told, so me and Margot are sent to the family room to wait. The heating is on too high. My eyes feel dry. Hot Dettol and machine coffee acid sting my nostrils. I sit, but Margot stands, loitering by the door. She looks me over. 'Are you all right?'

Is she serious? 'No. My mum is dying.' The room bulges with the silence that follows. 'Did you know?'

'Yes,' she admits.

'The whole time?'

She considers her next words for a second. 'We thought it best to give you a chance to settle into Llanmarion before you knew the truth.'

The anger is the only thing keeping me afloat, so I cling to it like a life raft. 'You should have told me. It's not fair.'

Margot doesn't take her eyes off me as she lowers herself into one of the stiff armchairs opposite. As elegantly as you possibly can in Hunter wellies, she crosses one long leg over the other. 'I bet you don't remember Lewis, do you?'

The sudden change of topic throws me. 'What?'

'Lewis. Your mum went out with him about a year and a half after your father died. Tall man, long blond-ish hair.'

I tuck my hair behind my ear with great purpose. 'Is this going somewhere?'

'He was absolutely charming. Very talented visual artist, if I remember rightly. Started a charity to get young offenders into the arts. Handsome, intelligent and sweet. Knew your mum was still grieving, waited like a perfect gentleman.'

I throw my hands up. 'So what, Margot?'

'The reason you don't remember him, Felicity, is because your mum broke it off with him. For you. She thought it was too soon. She didn't want you to feel as if she'd replaced your father with a new one.' Her eyes drill into my skull. 'She could have been really, really happy with Lewis. And she gave it all up for you.'

I can't take it any more. Why is she doing this to me? 'Oh my God! What do you want me to do? Feel worse? I don't think I possibly could!' I blub.

'Don't ever question why your mother does the things she does. One day you'll understand.'

Through snot and tears I stare her down. 'What? When I'm a mother? I guess I'm not much younger than you were.' She recoils slightly, only a fraction, but enough for me to notice. At once I feel bad for hitting so far below the belt. 'I'm sorry.'

Margot doesn't retaliate, although she'd be well within her rights to. Instead she sighs like she's never been more disappointed in anything.

Chapter 28

Here's the science bit. Concentrate.

At some point since her last bout of chemo, malignant cancer cells spread to my mum's hip bone and her spinal cord. Her bones are crumbling, she has too much calcium in her bloodstream and she's in constant pain. She's constipated and losing bladder control. In short, Mum's forty-year-old body has completely turned against her.

She is dying.

How could I have not seen this? I'm so stupid! Am I that self-centred? It had struck me as a *little* odd that she was still looking so pale and skinny, but I allowed myself to believe it was just another cold, that it was all totally normal for her to be so frail. I pushed it under a mental rug. I didn't *want* to see it. I pretended.

The hospital kept her in on the Tuesday night, but Margot brought her home the next day. She spent the rest of half-term week in bed or hobbling around with a crutch. Her hips are breaking up. It's too awful to think about for long.

I throw myself into being a perfect little nurse. I pull up carrots and parsnips and cabbages from the vegetable patch to make broth. I get Margot to kill and pluck the chicken. You have to draw a line somewhere, right? I read to her and help her to the bathroom. At least now I know the truth I can help, reverting back into nurse mode. It's babyish, but I suppose a part of me thinks if I take good enough care of her she might not . . . well, die.

Margot and I . . . cooperate, I guess. For Mum's sake. We're finally on the same page. I can play nice if she can. All the days roll into one. I make up an excuse to skip Danny's *Halloween* night, and, before I know it, it's Sunday and I haven't even started my holiday assignments. 'I'll get Margot to write you a note,' Mum says from under a blanket on the sofa. 'Christ, Fliss, I've written you excuse letters for less. You once had a period every week for a month so you didn't have to do swimming.'

'No. I don't want people feeling sorry for me.'

'Your classmates won't see the letter, will they?'

'Yeah, but if don't hand in any homework, they'll ask why.'

Mum shrugs. 'Fine, better get on with it then.'

I hate having to go back to school. I'm terrified to leave Mum with Margot in case something happens while I'm away. It seems so *pointless* being at school when I should be spending as much time as possible with Mum. Every time I think about what's going to happen, a different physical reaction hits me: sometimes I can't breathe; I get stabbing pains in my chest; my palms sweat; I feel nauseous. If I cling on to her, with all ten fingers, she can't go.

I can't imagine her not being here. It makes as much sense as trying to imagine what it'd be like to be a stapler or something. At the moment it feels a lot like trying to breathe underwater. I can only hold my breath for so long. I don't know what'll happen when I can't any more.

'How was your holiday?' Danny asks as we sit on a bench near the water fountain before registration. 'Sucks you were ill.' I momentarily forget I told him I was sick last Friday.

'It wasn't too bad,' I lie. 'How was yours? Did you meet James Off The Internet?'

'No,' he says with a pout. 'He couldn't afford the train fare to Leeds.' Danny spent some of the holidays with his family up north while Bronwyn was on a silent retreat with her father.

'Oh, that sucks.'

'I know. I'd got myself all fired up. We've spoken since, but if I wanted a pen pal I'd write to a prisoner, you know what I mean?' I give his arm a friendly rub. 'Oh, I don't wanna talk about it,' he says, turning to Bronwyn. 'How was the retreat?'

'We retreated from the retreat,' Bronwyn says with a smile while devouring a banana. 'Dad lasted a day and a half. I knew there was no way he could stay silent for five days!'

'So where did you end up?' Danny asks.

'We went to a caravan park in Tenby. It was pretty cool. We played Monopoly and Trivial Pursuit all week. And talked. A lot.'

I almost tell them about Mum. It's right on the tip of my tongue, but I know that if I open a floodgate I won't be able to shoulder it shut. It's some relief just to be with them again. I try to take strength from that.

I try to focus in first-period textiles but I hardly hear a word Mrs Blackwood is saying. We're supposed to be designing accessories based on the work of existing artists. I opted for a range of Lichtenstein cushions, thinking it'd be easy, but looking around, I see half the class has had exactly the same idea. I knew I should have picked Dali.

Instead I stare out of the window, watching a fat spider with almost tiger-like markings in her web. A daddy-long-longs is tangled up, struggling to fly free. *Give it up*, I think. *The struggle only makes it worse*. Sure enough, the spider just watches and waits for her prey to tire before she moves in for the kill. I think of Mum and her five years of fighting. Would it be easier if she had just lain down and let death take her?

I don't even realise I'm crying until a tear plops onto my coursework and the ink turns into a black cloud. I screw my eyes shut. I can't break down in class.

'Fliss.' Mrs Blackwood looms over my desk. I wonder how long she's been standing there. She's a tall, angular woman with a badger stripe in her hair and dresses straight out of the eighties – all shoulder pads and elastic belts. 'Can I see your homework, please?'

'Oh. Sure.'

I open up my A3 portfolio folder and display my Lichtenstein mood board. I made a special trip to the library to photocopy images of pop art as inspiration. 'Is this it?' she asks. That phrase is never good. No one ever looked at something amazing and said, *Is this it?*

'Erm . . . yes.'

'Fliss, you had a whole week and this is what you managed to produce?'

'I'm sorry . . . I –' I can't think of a good lie quickly and I don't want to tell her the truth.

She interrupts. 'Where are the fabric samples? The market research? Initial sketches? Fliss, this coursework counts towards your final grade.'

'I know, it's just that—'

'This is an embarrassment. I don't know how you dare hand this in, to be honest.'

'Because I don't care!' The words are out of my mouth before my brain filter kicks in. 'I just don't care!'

Her mouth hangs open. The rest of the class falls gravely silent. I grab the coursework out of her hands, scrunch it up and slam-dunk it in the bin as I flee from the classroom. I don't wait for whatever token punishment she has to dole out; I just need to be out of there before I erupt and everyone sees. No one follows me – because I have no friends, I think, full of misery.

My feet guide me in the direction of the library, like I'm on autopilot. There's still about half of the lesson left and I have nowhere else to go. I race down the stairs and punch through the doors. Sometimes there are English or drama lessons in here, but it seems deserted now, thank God. I flop down onto a beanbag in the corner, draw my knees under my chin and breathe for the first time in about three minutes.

What the hell did I just do? I screamed at a teacher. Total exorcist moment. Jesus. I cover my mouth with my hands and try to force the room to stop spinning. I can feel the adrenaline zooming through my veins. I need everything to freeze-frame, just for a second, while I reboot.

'Fliss?' Thom emerges from his little office. He's the only thing making being at school even slightly worthwhile. 'Are you OK?' He leaves his pile of books on his desk and heads over.

I don't trust myself to speak, so I just shake my head.

'What's wrong? It's not Megan Jones again, is it?'

'No. No, it's not her.'

284

He pulls another beanbag over and sits next to me. 'Then what is it? Why aren't you in class?'

I look into his eyes and feel better already. 'I screamed at Mrs Blackwood and threw my coursework in the bin.'

'You did what?' He's shocked but can't keep a little smirk off his lips.

I somehow manage to laugh and cry at the same time. I sound like a dolphin.

'Fliss, what's up? I won't tell anyone, I promise.'

This time the words do make the dive. 'My mum,' I say. 'My mum's dying.' His eyes widen and I break properly. It all pours out in a gross gush. I hide my face with my hands, trying to make the sobbing as silent as possible.

'Oh my God, Fliss. How long has this been going on?'

'Five years.'

He wraps a strong arm around my shoulder and pulls me in. I wish I could be absorbed into him. 'Jesus, why didn't you say something?'

I wipe my eyes on a sleeve. 'Because I didn't want anyone to see me like this, that's why.'

He reaches into his pocket and produces a tissue. 'It's clean.' As daintily as I can I wipe my nose. 'Fliss, this is a huge thing. Is it cancer?' I nod. 'And it's terminal?' I nod again. 'Man, I'm so sorry. You're insane if you think you can go through this by yourself. Do Danny and Bronwyn know?'

'No. No one does. It turns out that's why we came here. So I can get to know my grandma before my mum dies.'

'Oh, Fliss. Awful question, I know, but how long does she have?'

I shrug and swallow back more tears. 'I don't know. Six months. Maybe less.'

'Fliss, you need help. No one, none of us, could cope with this alone.' I nod again. 'All this time and you never said.'

It doesn't matter that I've only just been told. I should have known. She's my mum. These thoughts are skittering madly round my head. 'If you say something out loud it makes it real,' I say, but it sounds so airheaded.

'Hoping something will go away if you ignore it for long enough never works . . .' He reaches over and wipes a tear from my cheekbone.

Is he talking about us? Does he mean his feelings for me? He's *touching my face* for God's sake. I knew it. He's in love with me too.

I know what will make everything better. I lean in and kiss him on the lips. His jaw is rough like sandpaper, but his mouth is warm and soft. I cup his face with my hand and it feels like I'm floating.

I get all of that in the split second before he recoils in horror. 'Fliss! What are you doing?' He springs up off his beanbag.

My mouth opens but nothing comes out.

He pulls out a regular seat and sits on it, rubbing his face with his palms. 'Fliss, I'm so sorry, but you've got the wrong end of the stick . . . I'm engaged to Miss Crabtree . . . and you're . . . you're a pupil.'

The word 'pupil' makes me feel about ten. Also *Miss Crabtree*? Really? She's so *plain*.

'I was just . . . trying to be nice, Fliss. I want to help, I really do, but I can't do . . . that. It's . . . well, illegal.'

Oh God, no. What have I done? New tears burn my eyeballs. My mouth is dry. 'I . . . I . . .' Everything I touch turns to crap.

'I'm sorry, Fliss. I'm sorry if I've in any way made you think—'

'No,' I say finally. 'It's my fault.'

I get to my feet and grab my bag.

'Fliss, wait. I'll make you a nice cup of tea.'

'I have to go,' I say, and walk away, eyes fixed on the floor. I don't look back. I can never look back. I can't be here any more. I have to be far, far away. Out of this fucking town – and I *never* say that word because it's common. I'm leaving. I'm leaving right now.

Chapter 29

The good thing about being in Llanmarion is that there's nothing to spend money on but my allowance has been going into my account every month. I have a Solo card and I know how to use it.

I head for the station, stopping only to withdraw enough money to buy a train ticket and some food for the journey. Llanmarion isn't on a train line, so I take the bus to the next town and wait. The station is a squat, sandstone building, blackened with soot or whatever. It's all very *Railway Children*.

I don't know exactly where I'm heading, but London feels like a good start. I'll either go to Tiggy's or Marina's or change at Victoria for my uncle's house in Kent.

As long as it's not here, I don't care. How can I possibly go back after what just happened in the library. It replays in my mind's eye and my skin crawls all over again. *You stupid little idiot*. I'm angry that he didn't tell me he had a girlfriend (and Miss Crabtree . . . *really*?) but mostly just mortified. I can't ever go back.

'Where are you going, pet?' says the woman in the ticket office.

'London, please.'

'Return?'

'One-way.' I hand her the money and she slides just one orange card under the window. I realise I have no clothes, but Tiggy and I are about the same size and, although she's weirdly protective of her stuff, I'm sure she'll understand I'm in dire need.

I walk through onto Platform 1 and see there's a Cardiff service in eleven minutes. I sit on a peeling red metal bench and wait. It's a weirdly still day, hardly any breeze at all. I can just slip away. No one will even know I'm gone. There's a couple of other people waiting for the train, but they totally ignore me, even though I'm in uniform.

The train arrives with a sweaty hiss and it's a sad local service, more like a bus on rails than a proper train. I take a quick look back over my shoulder and, oddly calm, I get on.

One stop later, I get off.

What the hell was I thinking? That I'm going to run away and live in Tiggy's spare room? As if! That's almost as embarrassing as snogging a librarian. I stand on the platform, scowling and letting the crazy seep out through my feet. I shake it off.

I'm not leaving Mum. I won't. Running away would be the easy option. I could hide from everything. But that wouldn't make it stop.

I cross the railway bridge to the opposite platform and wait for the next train back.

I go into the forest like I'm Maria von Trapp or something. Oh no, wait, that was the hills. Same difference. I don't know what else to do.

I can't face home. I can't face school. So I wander in the woods.

I keep my head down, avoiding the gaze of dog walkers. My coat doesn't entirely cover my uniform, so it's pretty obvious that I should be at school, but no one says anything.

It's a proper winter day: cold and crisp, but with white linen sunshine. Luckily I've got my scarf and gloves. I follow the path alongside the stream. The urge to jump into the icy water and let it rinse all the toxic crap away is strong. It'd probably kill me in the process, but right now I'd almost welcome a big black nothingness. It sounds pretty peaceful.

I find a narrow section of the stream and start to build a little dam with pebbles. I don't know how long it takes, but it goes some way to blocking out the voices in my head. One voice, a chirpier version of my own, keeps telling me that Mum will be FINE. That sometimes good things happen to good people and she might undergo a miraculous recovery, astounding doctors and experts alike. Mum could go on Oprah, who'd give us (and the entire audience) a free car.

Another black, murky voice – a demonic cross between Margot and Megan Jones – tells me to get real, that she'll be dead in a matter of weeks and I might as well deal with it.

In a way, they're equally horrible. One offers hope, the other reminds me hope is the cruellest taunt of them all.

I'm going to be an orphan. *An orphan*. Like Oliver or Annie. How? As if that actually happens in real life.

I can't live without Mum. I never have done. I don't ever want to. It's always been me and her. We never did the church thing; she never tried to make me believe in a god, so I don't think she's off to hang out on a cloud with Elvis and Marilyn Monroe, and neither does she.

I wonder what death is like. Like, when you're asleep, I think on some level you *know* you're asleep, even if you don't remember your dreams. For a minute I try to imagine death, but trying to be aware of a total lack of awareness messes with my head, so I focus on blocking the stream.

A pool starts to fill on the other side. My dam is working.

I pull the whole thing down and the water gushes through, flowing as normal.

Fliss . . .

I look over my shoulder. Once again the stream sounds like it's whispering my name. I swear I'm not imagining it. I screw my eyes shut and try to block out the wind rustling through the trees and the birds twittering.

Felicityfelicityfelicity . . .

I'm suddenly freezing cold. The waterfall is just uphill, it's just the water, but it sounds so like my name.

Fliss . . .

This time, it's clearer. Stranger still, the voice reminds me of Mum. It reminds me of the time I went to see her in hospital after her hysterectomy. She was so woozy, but opened her eyes just long enough to smile dreamily, take my hand and say my name. At the time I had a feeling that she could have died, but came back especially for me. I was the reason to fight.

'Mum?'

Fliss . . .

I spring to my feet.

I shouldn't be here.

I should be with her.

She's calling to me.

I know these woods now; their subtle differences; the weird tree faces and log landmarks and chaotic paths. In no time at all, I'm at the back gate to the rose garden.

I can't believe the sun is dipping into the hills already. It's the colour of pink grapefruit, and very pretty, but it has got so late so fast. Those woods are a time zone of their own, I swear. I shoot up the garden path and tumble into the kitchen.

Both Margot and Mum, on her crutch, rush through to greet me from the lounge and hallway respectively. 'Fliss! Where on earth have you been?' Mum says, eyes wild. 'School called hours ago to say you'd gone missing! We've been worried sick.'

Margot says nothing, but looks pale-lipped.

I rush over to Mum and hug her. 'I'm sorry. I'm so sorry. I just needed some time. I'm here now and I'm not leaving you ever again.'

I press my head into her bony collar and she strokes my hair. 'I know,' she whispers.

Nothing more is said over dinner. I watch Mum fall asleep on the sofa in front of *Prime Suspect*.

Oh God, I don't want her to die. I'm going to miss her so much. It's going to hurt so bad. I'm not even aware of Margot watching me. 'Felicity? Are you all right?'

'I'm fine,' I say.

I excuse myself and run upstairs to the bathroom like I'm going to vomit. That's what it feels like. I don't, instead I cry.

It's like that dam: it all comes gushing out at once. My mouth is open like there's a howl, but no sound comes out. I tuck myself into the space underneath the sink and sit on the avocado pedestal mat, arms wrapped around my legs.

It passes. I feel better, like I've done a massive poo or something, unclogged.

Mum is going to die. I get it now. It's going to be awful, but she's going to go. I can't stop it.

I wash my face, although it does nothing to improve my bloaty red eyes and puffy cheeks. I dry myself and step outside the bathroom to find Margot emerging from my little box room. We mirror each other at opposite ends of the landing.

'Good girl,' she says.

I blink at her. I don't get it. For once she doesn't sound sarcastic. 'What?'

'Let it all out. My advice, for what it's worth, is to just *feel* it,' she says. 'While you still can.'

None the wiser. 'I don't get it.'

Her eyes are sad. 'Over time, we teach ourselves to stop feeling. It's the only way we survive.' She taps her breastbone with her index finger. 'It all becomes scar tissue and gristle. It's such a shame. So just let yourself feel it, truthfully and wholly, because one day you won't any more.'

'But I don't want to feel like this. It really hurts.' My voice crackles.

'It's better than nothing at all. Believe you me.' She turns the corner of the landing and heads downstairs.

I watch her go before heading to my room, wondering what Margot was doing in there. Perhaps they think I'm shoplifting or doing drugs or something. Nothing seems to have been moved around; the room is exactly as I left it this morning, except for one tiny detail.

The diary is on my pillow.

Chapter 30

I hold my breath in case I accidentally blow it away. I'm not hallucinating. The diary is on my pillow and clearly Margot put it there. I approach it with extreme caution and sit gingerly on the edge of my bed. I pick the book up and inhale deeply, reminding myself of its antiquey aroma.

I hardly dare hope, but flick through to where the story ran out.

I gasp.

There are *new* entries.

I check I'm not mistaken. Nope, they're definitely new. The handwriting is the same although a little scrawlier, less regimented. It's also now in blue biro instead of black ink.

My eyes sting again but I blink back tears. I'm so bored of crying I like actually feel a bit soggy. What's Margot doing? She's finished her story. For me? I take a moment to let that sink in. She wants me to know – she must do. She's sharing the rest of the story.

And she's right, I can feel it. My heart feels like it's swelling. I guess she must trust me, even if it's just a little bit. I'm gobsmacked but weirdly touched.

It's something. From Margot, I'll take anything I can get.

I turn to the first new entry.

For Felicity

A note on memory: some memories, even from my childhood, are crystal clear. I remember the jaguars at London Zoo in the snow and the night the bombs rained down on Llanmarion, the smoke at the back of my throat. I remember Glynis's blackberry jam for goodness sake, but others, even my wedding day, are as faded as the photographs in the albums.

I took my memories of that time and locked them very firmly away. As such, I honestly can't say what is a real memory and what's a narrative I've since constructed. It's true that we take what's real and turn it into a story.

And now a note on stories: I think storytelling is a vital part of human communication – we share and trade our stories. So many languages but we all speak 'story'. From those first cave paintings all the way up to your Internet journals we're all reaching out for anyone who'll listen: telling our stories, exchanging little pieces of ourselves. Perhaps this diary can help you and I to understand each other better.

I'll do my best, but I'm not promising anything. As you would expect, precise dates elude me, but I'll write it as I remember it.

These chapters of my life are painful, but your mother is right, Felicity. If it's to be just you and me, we have to know each other. You already know more than most.

I've looked back over what I wrote with great amusement at times. I remember the period well, but scarcely recall keeping a diary. How readily I left it behind. What a pompous young woman I was! Pompous, but spirited, certainly. In fact, I rather remind myself of you.

I can't decide if that's a an insult or not. I guess as I like 1940s Margot, I'll take it as a compliment.

So, Felicity, for you, I will try to tell you the rest of the story. I suppose I shall start back where I left off. Let's see, shall we?

Summer, 1941

When I could conceal my pregnancy no longer – and bear in mind our clothes were honestly made from parachutes – I told Glynis one evening as she pruned the rose bushes. I showed her my bump and she dropped her secateurs.

I tearfully begged her not to tell my mother and father, but that was too great an ask. 'Oh, Margot,' she said, 'I can't keep this to myself, you know I can't.'

'Why not? I'm offering to give you the baby. You and Ivor can raise it as yours.'

I remember her sad, pitying eyes. 'I would do anything for you and Peter and Jane, but this isn't right,' she told me. 'You'll feel very differently when there's a little baby in your arms.'

'I won't,' I told her defiantly. 'I tell you I won't.' You see, I was so angry at Rick by that point. Angry he'd gone away and left me with this unwanted souvenir. Angry that he was blissfully unaware, somewhere far away from Llanmarion with his real girlfriend. I went to sleep each night haunted by their imagined laughter; Rick Sawyer and the 'sweet, simple' girl living the life that should have been mine. I never told him about the

child – how could I? I had no way of reaching him.

Let's get one thing clear right from the onset. I never saw Rick Sawyer ever again. If you're hoping for the heartfelt reunion in the pouring rain, you'll be bitterly disappointed. Join the club, as they say. That's not to say I didn't think of him. Some loves leave permanent marks across the heart, and he was certainly one of those. To this day, if I see yellow rapeseed or a copy of Wuthering Heights, I wonder if he's still alive and, more keenly, if he still sometimes thinks about me.

'Margot. I'm sorry, but we must tell your mother,' Glynis said, and that was what we did. Together we drafted a carefully worded letter explaining what had happened. I remember never once feeling judged by Glynis. My predicament didn't discolour me in the least, not in her eyes.

The letter was sent and precisely five days later, a stern black car, not unlike a hearse, bumped and rocked down the track to the farm. I'd been warned it was coming of course.

With the same sad suitcase I'd arrived with, I left the farm. Bess, Andrew and Doreen came to see me off. If they knew the real reason for my exile, they were polite enough to keep it among themselves. The official line – preparing me wonderfully for an illustrious career in the press – was that my mother was sick and I was returning to London to care for her.

'I'm going to write to you every single day,' Bess said, hugging me tight. 'Llanmarion simply won't be the same without you.'

I noticed how she'd started to sound like me. 'Well, not every day,' I replied with a smile. 'But once a week at least. Keep me abreast of all the village news.' On the spur of the moment I leaned in more closely and whispered through her hair, 'Reg is on Anglesey. Rhodri has an address. There isn't time to explain how I know.'

If she was cross I'd kept it from her, she didn't let on. She just hugged me even tighter. 'Oh, Margot, thank you. I love you and I'll miss you.'

'I'll miss you too. Terribly.'

I hugged Doreen before Andrew stepped in. His eyes were watery. 'I can't believe you're going back to civilisation and leaving me here.'

'Oh, it isn't so very awful, is it? And what's the alternative?' We both knew that there was every possibility he'd be off to fight if the war was still going in two years' time.

'Thank you, Margot. For everything.' No further words were required. I knew exactly what he meant.

I crouched to say goodbye to Jane and Peter. 'Now, you two will behave for Ivor and Glynis, won't you? And, Peter, there's no reason on earth that you can't read Jane a bedtime story.'

'But I want you to do it,' Jane protested.

'Peter will do a wonderful job, won't you?'

'I promise.'

'Good boy.'

I rose to embrace Glynis. 'We're always here,' she breathed into my ear. 'Always. If you need us . . .'

'I know.'

Ivor pulled me into a bear hug. He let me go and gave me a wink. 'Shame, ain't it? Best farmhand I ever had.'

It was with great sadness that I climbed into the back of that car. As we rolled down the drive, I closed my eyes so I couldn't see their faces in the mirror.

* * *

I arrived back in Kensington by dead of night and this was no coincidence. Mrs Watson, the fussy little housekeeper, met me at the car and bundled me inside with great haste. Mother waited in the hall. Everything was almost as I remembered it, except darker, more claustrophobic: the mosaic tiles, the wood panels, the foreboding oil paintings. The grandfather clock tutted out Mother's disapproving silence.

'We shall talk in the morning when your father is here,' she said, pointedly avoiding my gaze. Her hair was pulled back in a severe chignon, her lips berry red. See what I mean about the strange details your memory retains?

'Father's coming home?' I asked, my heart sinking. Apparently a pregnant seventeen year-old daughter out of wedlock was deemed of more pressing concern than a world at war.

'Go to bed, Margot.'

As I passed her, suitcase in hand, she made no move to kiss my cheek. I climbed the stairs feeling very alone and very scared for whatever the morning would bring.

The next morning I was shown to my prison. I was moved into the back bedroom, overlooking the garden, where neighbours and people from the street wouldn't see the scarlet letter. It could not have been made clearer that I was casting a terrible cloud of shame over the Stanford name, although very few words were spoken.

That first morning back home, Dr MacDonald came to examine me. I'd never liked that man – thin and bald like a boiled ferret. He had spidery little fingers and I hated feeling them on my skin.

'I'd say she's about four months along,' he said, telling me nothing I didn't already know.

Mother, apparently unwilling to believe it until a doctor confirmed the diagnosis, clutched a handkerchief and wept silently. Father simply glared. 'No one is to know. Is that understood?'

'Of course, Admiral Stanford. Our discretion is guaranteed. I shall have to brief a nurse and midwife. No one need know beyond that.'

'You see, Margot,' said Mother, 'it'll be all right. We shall all move on and soon forget all about it.'

No one seemed to be able to say the word 'baby', so I thought I better had. 'What will happen to the baby?'

'It's all taken care of,' said Dr MacDonald, snapping his case shut. He said no more. I couldn't help but imagine him tossing the infant into the Thames as they had done in Victorian times.

Like something from an H. G. Wells story, I could feel the life inside me growing, taking shape every day. But I couldn't think of it as a child, only as what Rick had done to me. All that love, that sweet nectar, had turned to glass and nails in my abdomen. I knew I was monstrous, but I wanted rid of it. Nowadays, of course, that wouldn't have been an issue; I would have had a choice.

I was permitted to walk down the landing to the bathroom, but that bedroom, those four ivory walls, a ceiling and a bay window, became my entire world. Of the house staff, only Mrs Watson knew of my condition and ferried three meals a day to the bedroom on a tray. It was August, but I wasn't even allowed in the back garden in case someone were to see over the wall through the willows. I was allowed to read and knit and embroider. The back room had a window seat that captured the sun between two in the afternoon

302

and about six at night, so I would spend the afternoons reading or just staring out at the world beyond.

I watched as the sycamore leaves turned yellow and their keys spiralled to the ground. The leaf litter turned brown and the branches bare. At the same time I ripened, bigger and bigger every day. The body can do the most incredible things. I was so lonely up in that room. Father went back to Dover, and Mother could hardly stand to look at me.

In the absence of company, I started to talk to the bump. I knew instinctively that the baby was a boy. I sensed it. I gave him a running commentary of the lives of the foxes that lived in the shrubs at the bottom of the garden and the heron who troubled the fish pond. I read to him. Just because his father was a despicable rogue didn't mean he deserved to be deprived of good literature.

But it so reminded me of reading to Rick by the lake. I was so sad, waterlogged by it.

Christmas came and went, demarcated only with some turkey and a piece of figgy pudding. The lawn became silver and frozen and it was too cold to sit by the window without a blanket around my shoulders.

I spent many hours wondering if I was being punished. The isolation, the starvation of conversation soon turned inwards. It wasn't that my parents were being cruel; it was that I deserved it because of what I had done with Rick. I know now that that's not true, but at the time I convinced myself it was.

By the time January came, I firmly believed I was a sinner who had given into the devil's desires and was now reaping my just deserts.

January, 1942

It's quite clear to me now that, had it not been for the baby, I would have gone stark-raving mad up in my Rapunzel tower. Of course, without the baby I wouldn't have been in there in the first place, but I've never been a fan of circular logic.

The baby was due any day, by Dr MacDonald's estimations. I'd grown used to the sensations coming from within. Perhaps the beating of his little heart compensated for my broken one. I knew he would be taken from me, but as the weeks ticked by I started to wonder if I could keep him. If need be, perhaps we could pass him off as my little brother until I could move away with him.

I was bigger than an elephant, too hefty to lower myself onto my window seat any longer. Instead I took to a rocking chair, watching fat flakes fall from grey skies.

It was now a year since I'd made the train journey to Llanmarion. During my exile I came to think things would not ping back to normal as soon as the baby came, whatever Mother said. How could they? What's more, I wasn't sure I wanted them to. The war rumbled on, my old friends were scattered around the country and my new ones were in Wales. Perhaps I would return to the farm after all. I doubted anyone in Llanmarion would care one jot if I returned with a baby in tow.

I awoke in the early hours of January 18th, a terrible cramp seizing my whole body. I knew at once I was in labour. The contractions weren't painful at first; rather it felt like my spine and stomach were in spasm.

I called Mrs Watson and she alerted Mother and Dr MacDonald. The midwife was called Trudy Mayhew, a pretty platinum blonde, not too many years older than I. She arrived in a starched uniform. 'Hello, Margot,' she said. 'Let's have a look at you.'

She lifted my nightdress and I felt her poking around. There's nothing like birthing live young to put you on an equal playing field with farm animals, it has to be said. Any delusions of humans being more somehow more evolved or refined went smartly out of the window once the pain kicked in. 'Oh, I don't think we'll be waiting all that long,' she said with perhaps too much cheer. 'Off we go!'

It was long, painful and difficult. At first I panicked. I felt an almighty burst of adrenaline surge through my body and it took me back to the night the bombs fell – the desperation, the urge to fight. Suddenly I couldn't get him out of my body fast enough, I truly thought I would die if I didn't. And then the pain kicked in. Truthfully it felt as if my torso was being ripped in two. It was all I could think about – I no longer cared what I sounded like, what I looked like: I was panting and naked and screaming, writhing on the bed like an animal. Mother left the room.

Only then did I sink into it. Either the pain eased or I went numb, because my body and my baby seemed to find a rhythm. I worked with the contractions to push him free.

He was real! Such a silly thing to think, but all of a sudden he was a real, live baby and not just a shameful secret. So very real. I heard a gooey gurgle followed by a gasp and a squeal. He was alive and so was I. All the fight went out of me and I fell back into my own blood and filth.

Trudy held him in her bloody hands. He was tiny and curled up, gleaming and pink. He howled and howled, apparently dissatisfied at his arrival. 'There you go, Margot. Well done. It's all over. Would you like to hold him?'

God help me, but I did. The thing that had been growing inside me was flesh and blood and so, so small. We'd got through the ordeal together and now it seemed like the most obvious thing in the world to hold him. I reached out for him.

'I don't think that's a good idea.' Mother reappeared at my bedside.

'We have a wet nurse waiting.' Dr MacDonald reached out to take the baby.

'Please . . .' I said, exhausted, hardly able to hold my head up.

'Margot, darling,' Mother said. 'It's not your baby. It'll be easier this way.'

Dr MacDonald swaddled him in terrycloth blankets. 'He seems to be in fine health. All is well.'

'Wonderful . . .' Mother escorted him, and my child, out of the room.

Trudy silently began to clean me up. She carried a washbowl and flannels to my bedside and diligently worked. 'You poor little girl,' she whispered. 'But don't you worry. He's going to a good home, I promise. Nice folks with money.'

I couldn't speak, but nodded. I think I must have been crying, because Trudy wiped my tears away.

'Did you have a name for him?' she asked.

The strangest thing is, I did. Some subconscious part of my brain been telling me stories, stories of some parallel existence where Rick and I had raised him as our son.

I would have called him Christopher.

Chapter 31

I think I'm all cried out. I now feel barren, hollowed out like a Halloween pumpkin. Oh God . . . that's . . . *horrific*. Poor Margot. I obviously don't want a baby until I'm at least thirty-six, or maybe *ever* after reading *that*, but I can't even *imagine* what it'd be like to see only a glimpse of your own child before it was swept away.

Wow. My great-grandmother was a piece of work. And I thought Margot was hardcore.

I glance at my clock. It's ten thirty-five and I should be asleep really. That's where the writing finishes, although Margot has left a note at the end:

So there you have it. That's what happened after I left Llanmarion. I never saw Christopher again. I don't even know what they called him. I shall answer your questions, Felicity. I suppose once you start unravelling a ball of wool, there's no point in stopping.

I am happy – for want of a better word – to talk about Christopher, but please respect that your mother doesn't know she ever had a half-brother and I don't think now is the time to tell her. Alternatively, if you would rather communicate through the diary, you can list your questions here and leave the book somewhere I shall find it.

M x

Oooh, a kiss! Wonders never cease! Without hesitation, I spring off my bed and grab the nearest pen – an old ballpoint with a pink-haired troll on the end. I brush it on my cheek for a second, thinking about what I want to know.

Thank you, I start, for letting me know about Christopher. I'm so sorry about what your parents did. I think that was an awful thing to do.

 I do have some questions if that's OK.

1. What happened to Bess? Did she find Reg?
2. Is Andrew – the one from the diary – my grandad?
3. What happened after you gave birth? Did you go back to Llanmarion?
4. Did you see Glynis and Ivor again?

I chew the troll's arm for a second before I think that's all I want to know for now. I poke my head out of my bedroom and hear the television downstairs. Margot seems to be watching *Newsnight*, so I creep down the landing to her bedroom and leave the diary on her pillow in the same position I found it on mine. Margot's room, unsurprisingly, is unfussy but kind of elegant: the walls and quilt are a muted, clean blue-grey. The only flare of colour is a mason jar of cabbage roses on the windowsill.

I then go to say goodnight to Mum and hurry to bed, excited for what Margot will write next. As I drift off, I realise it's the first time all week I haven't gone to sleep thinking about what's happening to Mum.

I figure that if Margot can get on with life after having her baby snatched away, I can probably face Thom after all. Every time I think about the botched kiss, my insides shrivel up and die like a salted slug, but the horror of what happened will only follow me if I flee town, so I trudge to the bus stop.

Over a breakfast of eggs and soldiers, I asked Mum if she wanted me to stay home from school, but she was adamant it should be business as usual. 'No,' she said with certainty. 'You are going to school and that's the end of it. What you need is routine, Fliss.'

I can't argue with that. I board the bus and within seconds Dewi comes to sit on the seat behind me. It takes him a couple of tries to start his sentence, but I don't feel so awkward any more. '. . . H-hello, Fliss. You OK?'

'Yeah, I'm fine.'

'Oh, OK. It's j-j-just everyone was saying you'd r-run away.'

I cringe. 'Oh, God. Really?'

'Yeah. Or some people said you'd been . . . been k-kidnapped.'

'It's nothing like that.' I pause, wondering what to tell him. Dewi's eyes are as big and kind as chocolate buttons, but I don't really know him at all. 'Just some stuff going on at home, that's all.'

'Oh? What is it, like?' he asks expectantly.

'It's nothing.' I shake my head and he seems to get the hint.

'OK. Well, I hope . . . I hope it's not too b-bad.'

'Thanks, Dewi. It'll be fine.' I say the words automatically, without even realising it's a lie. Things won't be fine. They won't be fine at all.

When I arrive at school I'm immediately intercepted by Mr Treadwell, my registration tutor. 'Good of you to join us, Miss Baker,' he says. 'This way, please.'

We go to his classroom, where we're joined by Thom and Mrs Evans, head of Year 11. She takes us for drama sometimes and I like her. She's about seventy per cent dangly earring and pashmina. I don't know how much Thom has told them, and he won't look me in the eye. If he's told them the truth – that I'm a teacher molester – I'm as good as expelled. I feel a bit sick. 'Morning, Felicity,' Mrs Evans begins. 'You know why we're here, don't you?'

'Because I ran off?' I'm not mentioning the non-kiss unless he does.

'Because you left school without permission.' She goes on to give me an extended club remix of the in-loco-parentis speech. 'Mr Deacon told us you're having some problems at home . . . ?'

'My mum is ill.'

'Yes, I know. She came in to see us right at the start of term, but asked us not to tell you.'

Oh. 'Oh.' So *everyone* knew but me. Great.

'Mr Treadwell has been keeping an eye on you for me.' Excuse me while I laugh for like twenty minutes. Mr Treadwell has done precisely nothing beyond confiscate my September *Vogue*. Mrs Evans continues. 'I am aware that you don't want special treatment, Felicity, but we are all here to help you. If

311

you need time out, take time out. If you need extra time for homework, you can have it, but you absolutely *have* to let us know. You can't just abscond like you did yesterday.'

'I know. And I'm sorry.' I look to Thom. I don't think he's told them about the kiss, thank Christ. I wonder if he's worried about getting fired or something. What was I thinking? It was so majorly boneheaded. I try to psychically tell him I'm sorry.

'If you need anything, we're always here to listen. I understand you spend a lot of time in the library?'

I look guiltily to Thom. 'I do.'

'We're so lucky to have Mr Deacon, aren't we?'

'Fliss –' Thom finally speaks – 'I've spoken to your teachers and they've all agreed that you can bring your work to the library any time you want. I . . . we . . . we all want to help.'

He does not love me like I love him. He never loved me. He thinks I am a little girl. It breaks my heart, but if he's still going to let me in the library after my kamikaze kiss, I have to move the hell on. 'Thank you. And I'm sorry.' I look right at him. 'Yesterday . . . it just all got too much.' I look sheepishly at my hands. 'I didn't know what I was doing.'

'Well, of course, dear,' Mrs Evans cuts in. 'Now, I hope you don't mind, but yesterday afternoon I took Danny Chung and Bronwyn Parry out of class to try to establish where you were, and it was necessary for me to tell them what was going on.'

Oh wow. Well, I guess that saves me a pretty gnarly job. Thom goes to the classroom door and I realise my friends are hovering just outside and probably have been the whole time.

Danny and Bronwyn rush in and I stand to greet them. 'Fliss! Why didn't you say something?' Danny hugs me tightly,

312

knocking the breath out of me. 'Oh, we're not cross . . . but we could have helped.' He lets me go.

'I don't see how, unless you can cure cancer,' I say sadly.

'Well . . . well, I don't know! But we can talk about it. If you want to, obviously.'

'Dan, chill pill. You don't have to do anything,' Bronwyn adds to me. 'If you want us to pretend everything's normal, we can do that.'

'Yes! Whatever you need,' Danny says earnestly.

The teachers leave us to it. There's still about ten minutes until the first bell. The three of us stand in a wonky, awkward triangle, arms folded. 'I'm sorry I didn't say anything,' I say.

'Fliss, there's nothing to be sorry about,' says Bronwyn.

'What did they tell you?' I shrug, wrapping my arms around myself.

They exchange a look. Danny breaks the ice. 'Mrs Evans said your mum was really ill, like.'

I am not going to cry. 'My mum is going to die,' I say, voice flat, and it makes it all real. They both do the 'head tilt' before we mash up into a three-way hug.

I rush home after school, eager to see if Margot's had time to answer my questions. As I practically skip down the drive, feeling weirdly light for having offloaded a tonne of emotional baggage onto Danny and Bronwyn, I see Margot mucking out the pigsty. 'Hello,' she says. 'How was school?'

We stand a few metres apart. It feels like a truce is in place. 'It was OK. Everyone knows about Mum now.' Margot nods but says nothing. 'How is Mum? Is she all right?'

'She seems a bit perkier today. We went for a walk, just down to the stream. She seems to like it down there.'

My heart sinks a little. 'It feels like I'm missing stuff.'

Margot rests her pitchfork against the wall. 'Your mother wants you in school.'

That's all she needs to say. 'Do you need a hand?'

She pauses. 'Yes. That would be useful. Go and change out of your uniform first.'

Mum is having a little nap on the sofa, but I wake her to ask if she had a nice walk (and, to be honest, check she's not dead). She's OK. I make her a cup of Gold Blend before hurrying upstairs. Hardly daring to breathe, I open my bedroom door.

The diary is back on my pillow. I quietly clap my hands together. I'm dying to read what she's written, but first I have to go help clean up pig poop. I figure it's the least I can do.

1942, London

The first question is answered easily enough. Bess and I corresponded on a regular basis all throughout the war. Alas I did not return to Llanmarion at that time.

Birth is a most gruesome affair and it took me some time, a few stitches and many sitz baths to recover. Mother was worried people would guess what was really behind my strange quarantine if they saw I was still carrying baby weight and was decidedly buxom so I was held hostage for a few weeks more.

I distinctly remember, just a few days after Christopher was taken away, I was rather formally invited to join Mother for breakfast in the dining room. While I bathed, the housekeeper laid out a starched dress and crinoline slip. For the first time in months, I tidied my hair with a pair of ivory combs and went downstairs with great trepidation.

'Oh, Margot dear,' Mother said, standing to greet me with a kiss on each cheek. 'Don't you look lovely. That cornflower blue is wonderful for your complexion. Sit! Sit!'

I did as I was told. Mrs Watson poured the tea. 'Now Margot dear, we need to talk about what you'll do now. I don't think it's wise for you to return to Llanmarion, do you?'

I looked at my hands, folded in my lap. 'Well, I don't know.' I did want to go back. I missed the farm, Bess, Andrew, Glynis and Ivor . . . and, if I'm honest, Rick most of all. Despite everything. I knew he wasn't there, but that place was full of memories of him and I longed to submerge myself in them.

'What you need is a new start. You can finish your studies and I'm sure we can think of something to do to keep you busy. There is still a war on, you know?'

'I know.' I couldn't lift my teacup off the saucer, my hands were trembling so badly. 'What happened to the baby?' I asked in a threadbare voice. 'Is he with a new family?'

Mother reached over the table and took my hands. She smiled a red-lipped smile. 'What baby, dear?' She gripped my hands so tightly it hurt. 'How are we ever to forget that unpleasant chapter if we insist on talking about it? Am I making myself understood?'

'Yes, Mother.'

It was never mentioned again for the rest of my parents' lives.

After sufficient time had passed with me on a stringent diet, Father pulled some strings and got me a job as a nanny. The irony, although unspoken, was lost on no one. I was to care for other people's children, not my own.

However, I like to imagine my sweet little Christopher would have been nothing like my charge, Edmund Crowley-Smythe.

I recall the first day I arrived at their smart Chelsea townhouse. I think it was in late 1942 and the war felt further away than it had before. Edmund had been too young to be evacuated alone at the start of the campaign and Mrs Crowley-Smythe didn't want to leave London, so they had remained.

The townhouse was pristine, with more plants and flowers than Kew Gardens. Both Mr and Mrs Crowley-Smythe worked for the BBC and were awfully busy with it. Jean Crowley-Smythe was keen to return to work and needed someone to care for and tutor Edmund. On our first meeting, he hid behind her legs. 'Oh, come now, Edmund,' she said. 'Don't be shy.'

'I hate her!' he cried.

I wore a tailored cherry-red jacket with a matching beret. I was keen, I remember, to get my life back in order. As soon as the war ended, I would almost certainly read English at Lady Margaret Hall, Oxford. My post with the Crowley-Smythes was to be temporary.

I crouched to speak to Edmund. 'Hello, Edmund. I'm Margot. It's lovely to meet you. I think we're going to have ever such a lovely time.' He promptly delivered a kick to my shin and ran off to hide.

'Margot, I'm terribly sorry. I don't know what's got into him.' I quickly learned, judging from his brattish behaviour, it could well be Satan himself. Every day was a series of battles – to get him to dress or eat or nap. I would have loved nothing more than to resign, but I'd already embarrassed our family enough and Crowley-Smythe was a personal friend of Father's. I was stuck.

During that testing time, Bess and I wrote to each other back and forth. She did indeed track down Reg and they were briefly reunited, but the distance between them, well, came between them.

To be honest, I rather suspect both she and he had met new people and their affections drifted. We were so young, after all. I know you'll balk at this, Felicity, but those first loves, although

317

they do in some ways define us, are little more than blueprints for the relationships we'll build as adults. I know it feels like love, but, from experience, I'd say it's chiefly hormones. Who can say how Rick and I would have panned out if fate had kept us together?

After the war ended, I left London for Oxford as planned. Lady Margaret Hall was quite gorgeous. I have many happy memories of sunny afternoons on the lawn and lavish formal dinners in the hall. A great sisterhood existed between us and I think we all grew up. We were all, in a way, outcasts and misfits – most of the girls had been deemed unfit to be debutantes or marriage material so had been permitted to further their educations. Many of us had been evacuated during the war, so it wasn't the first time we'd been away from home, but it was the first time since Rick and the baby that I felt something like myself again.

I studied hard, eagerly trying, in a misplaced effort, to earn back my parents' respect. When that didn't happen, I decided the only person I ever had to please from that day forth was myself. I would be the best so I knew I was the best.

Inevitably, Bess and I lost touch while I studied and made new friends. That said, in the years and decades that followed I kept a close eye on her. She became a rather remarkable woman. She married none other than Bill Jones and had children young.

Had she asked my opinion, I'd have advised against the union, and you can imagine, knowing what you know, that it didn't last especially long. What happened next was more impressive. She became a primary-school teacher in Llanmarion, worked her way up to headmistress in the sixties – an achievement in itself – before leaving the profession to focus on local politics! The last I saw, she was on the evening news, campaigning for Welsh *devolution – and look how that turned out. Always the proud Welshwoman through and through. I wish her well. I believe she remarried in the seventies, not that it matters.*

As for your grandfather, well, that's a longer, rather more complicated story, one I don't have time to tell now. Leave the diary in the same spot and I shall update at the first opportunity.

Chapter 32

I want to spend the whole weekend with Mum. Even though she's clearly struggling on her crutch, she wants a walk in the woods. She looks so frail, swamped by a coat that used to fit properly. 'It's nice just to get some fresh air,' she says. Her arm is hooked through mine and we take our time, going nowhere in particular.

'Are you in pain?' I ask, scared of the answer.

'To be honest, Fliss, I'm off my face on those pain pills. I'm high as a kite.'

I smile. 'Well, I suppose that's better.'

'If only I could do a poo. I haven't been to the loo in about four days.'

'Oh, that's lovely!' I laugh.

'No one ever said cancer was pretty, did they?' I bristle at the C-word. 'It's cold enough to snow, don't you think?'

It's actually not *that* cold. 'Do you want to go back?'

'Not just yet. I'm getting cabin fever.'

'OK. When we do, I could make hot chocolate and maybe bake some brownies or something?'

We reach the waterfall and the air immediately feels cleaner. I wonder stupidly if it can cleanse Mum of the disease in her bones.

'Fliss, you don't have to babysit me all weekend.'

'I want to!'

'I don't need a babysitter. It's so important you keep your friends around – you're going to need them,' she says matter-of-factly. 'Listen. The one *good* thing that we have is foresight. Nothing is going to creep up on us. Now that everything's out in the open, we can actually make plans. For you, for me, for the future. The absolute last thing I want is my last weeks, months, days – whatever we've got – to be a snotty tissue-fest.'

'I know,' I agree, 'but Danny and Bronwyn aren't going anywhere . . .' *but you are*, is the last part of that sentence that goes unsaid.

'Do you know what I'd really like?' Mum suddenly stops walking.

'I can think of one pretty big thing, yeah.'

She grins. 'Well, aside from the obvious.'

'Go on.'

'I would really, really love it if you danced again.'

Oh man, that's a cheap shot! She knows I can't say no. What kind of monster would refuse a dying wish? 'Oh, Mum, really?'

She takes my gloved hands in hers. 'Oh, come on, Fliss! It used to make you so happy!'

I wince but try to turn it into a smile. 'Yeah, until it didn't any more.'

She shakes her head. 'You had one bad night, just one.'

'Oh, hi, Understatement! It was a total disaster.'

'Life usually is! We all fall down, Fliss. All of us. I've told you I got fired from my first two jobs in TV. I was a runner on

Morecambe and Wise and kept spilling coffee everywhere. It's not about the falling – it's how we pick ourselves up again.' I'm about to argue I'm now two years out of shape and practice, but she carries on. 'And it'd mean the world to me if I could see you dance again.'

I sigh, my head flopping back. 'You know I can't say no, right?'

'Well, you could . . . but you'd be the worst daughter in the world.' She winks theatrically.

'Fine!' Already a plan is hatching in my mind.

'Hi. Is that Danny?' I sit on the bottom step, cradling the big old beige handset and twisting the cord around my wrist.

'Fliss? Hi! What's up?'

'Are you eating?'

'Yeah, but it's just a packet of Wotsits.'

'Oh, OK.' I have a sudden craving for Wotsits. 'You know the crappy old dance studio above the takeaway?'

'I do.'

'Does your dad own that?'

'He does . . . Where is this going?'

'Well. Here's the thing . . .'

On Sunday afternoon I step over a heap of unopened bills to follow Danny up the narrow, leaf-strewn stairs that lead up to the Stepz studio. A second key lets us into a damp-smelling, fusty room. Newspaper over the windows only lets bleak, grey light in and there's literally nothing sadder than a broken disco ball in a bin.

'Yikes,' I say.

'Did something die in here?' Danny says, covering his nose. 'Other than good taste?'

The lights stutter on and I realise, although it needs a good clean, and the sprung floor is covered with boxes of prawn crackers, MSG and ketchup sachets, it's actually a good size studio. The wall opposite the windows is all mirrored, even if one panel is cracked. The barre is still attached and seems able to take my weight. 'Actually, this is OK. I can make it work. Do you think your dad will mind?'

'Fliss, it's been about a year since anyone even asked to see it. He uses it as an extra storeroom. I doubt he'll even notice.'

'Cool.'

Danny performs a (deeply wrong) pas de bourrée before the mirror. 'I'm so excited that you're doing *Chess Club Presents*! It's going to be the shiz.'

I raise an eyebrow. 'I'm not doing it out of choice, believe me. I'm a ballet hostage.'

He executes a passable arabesque. 'What are you going to do?'

'Not a clue. I figure before I attempt an actual dance I should probably train a little so I don't accidentally dislocate my hip or something.'

Danny pauses. 'Don't you think it'd be next lev if we put a pole in here and did pole dancing? Like in *Showgirls*?'

I give him a very firm NO look.

Later I rummage in the back of my wardrobe. I know they're here somewhere. I find a box of old cassettes I should probably bin – although I think there are some pretty cool mixtapes in there somewhere – and some old pleather dance pants and leg warmers.

'Where are they?' I start pulling things out indiscriminately until I find them under my old wellies. They're in a black satin bag, which I take over to my bed. I sit down and open it.

My old ballet slippers. They look more battered than I remember: the pale rose-pink almost grey. The toes are hardened and scuffed from pointe work. Even in my comfy knee boots, my toes flinch, remembering the agony. On the inside, sure enough, is a brown layer of dried blood. I sigh, but a little voice deep, *deep* down asks, *Can you still do it?* I wonder if I can.

I'm so busy inspecting the shoes, it takes me a few minutes to even notice that the diary is back on my pillow.

London, 1952

Enduring the demonic biting and hair-tugging of Edmund Crawley-Smythe brought an unexpected bonus. After I had graduated from Oxford, Jean Crawley-Smythe arranged for me to work as an assistant at the BBC. Predictably I was set to work on some very demanding coffee and tea duties and had to pretend I didn't notice how some of the older executives patted my bottom or brushed against me in the lifts.

I was lucky to work under Charlie Palmer, a lovely, visionary news producer who soon made me a research assistant. It wasn't much, but it was a start. I won't lie, Felicity, it was tough. I had to work twice as hard and speak twice as loud to be heard over the Old Boys Club. I hope things will be different for you.

I can't say things got any easier when I left the BBC and went to the newspaper as a junior reporter. It was largely understood that the women writers didn't have the capacity to report on politics, crime or finance. For many years I wrote wedding announcements and obituaries. Sometimes there's a quiet strength in simply biding your time. When the boys burned out or fell down drunk, I was still there, ready to break the big stories; on spec and on time.

Anyway, I digress. Andrew and I wrote to one another sporadically throughout university – he went to Cambridge on an army scholarship after the war. Quite unexpectedly, in the summer of '52, he called me out of the blue and asked if he could take me to tea.

We met one afternoon at Claridge's – I still vividly remember a Victoria sponge as light as air – and then took a stroll around the Serpentine. The sky was cloudless, cyan blue, and we fed the swans and ducks. He suggested hiring a rowing boat, but I wasn't in the mood. Then he said, 'Margot, I need to talk to you,' his voice shaking.

'I suspected there was something. You've been jittery all through tea. You hardly bothered your scone.'

'Margot, I'm in trouble.'

I remember how pale and fraught his face was. I thought he must be dying. 'Andrew, are you all right? What kind of trouble?'

'The very deep sort, I'm afraid to say.' He explained that one of his university 'friends' had become entangled with a suspected spy ring – accused of colluding with the KGB. 'They can't pin spying on me,' he said, 'but the army are livid. Margot, they want to . . . castrate me.' He whispered the penultimate word, checking no one was listening in.

'I beg your pardon?' I said, aghast.

'It's that, or discharge and jail. Those are my options. It was either admit we were lovers or have them think I'm a defector. What was I supposed to do?'

I stopped walking, the seriousness of his situation sinking in. You have to understand, Felicity, as ridiculous as it seems now, homosexuality was a crime back then. Men were being sent to sanatoriums. 'Andrew, you can't let them do this to you. It's monstrous.'

'I know! There's only one solution I can think of.'

'Which is?'

He paused and took a deep breath. 'If I take a wife, I think I can convince them I'm reformed and it was all a momentary lapse in judgement. A blip.'

My eyes almost fell out of my head. 'Are you seriously suggesting . . . ?'

He got down on one knee right there by the lake's edge. 'Margot Stanford, will you do me the honour of—'

'Oh, get up right now, you twit' I said. 'Of course I'll marry you, but spare me the amateur dramatics.'

He stood up. 'Oh. I got a ring and everything.'

'Let's be having it then.' I held out my hand. He produced a little black velvet box. I'll say this for your grandfather – he had exquisite taste in jewellery. Square-cut diamond, platinum ring. Classic, simple and beautiful.

'Margot, are you sure? I know I'm asking a lot.'

I slid the ring on my finger and admired it with my cherry-red nails. 'No you're not, not in the grand scheme of things. I can help . . . so I will.'

I didn't hesitate. After Christopher, after everything that had happened in Llanmarion, it seemed like a very small favour.

And so we married the following summer. Everyone thought I was marrying a nice, sweet man I'd met in Wales – a childhood sweetheart. The army was satisfied I'd cured him of himself and my parents were delighted their fallen daughter was now an honest woman.

You've no doubt seen the wedding photos. What a beautiful young couple we were. That's the thing with mantelpiece pictures; they're all lies: we all play our parts in public like good little puppets. To the rest of the world we were Mr and Mrs Andrew Hancock, but to him and me, it was something else. A private joke.

That's not to say we weren't happy. We were, blissfully so. Andrew left the army for the civil service and we bought the house in Hampstead village. Imagine living with your best friend. We read Salinger and Nabokov and Bradbury together and discussed them over dinner. We played chess and backgammon in front of a crackling fire. We took a French cookery class. He was very good at it; I made several small fires and huge amounts of mess.

The trick with love is to stop expecting it to look like the cover of a romance novel. I had had that three-ring circus with Rick and it brought nothing but heartache. You see, I think love is like mixing paint: everyone brings something different to a relationship, so you never get the same colour twice. It seems foolish to cherish one shade above others and yet that's what we seem to do.

Down the years, naturally, given our sitation, we had our other loves outside of the marriage – that was part of the deal. For much of the seventies, your grandfather lived in New York with a young photographer called Rodrigo, and I was involved with a married man, not to mention rival editor, for the best part of twenty years.

After Rick, I wasn't sure I'd love again, but it does creep up on you when you least expect, or need, it. I met him (he shall remain nameless) at an awards dinner at the Dorchester in '68. Well, didn't he look a picture in his tuxedo. I remember he was smoking the most ostentatious cigar, puffing out a plume of rich, loamy smoke like a gangster. I was there with Andrew and he was there with his wife, but from the second we clapped eyes on each other, there might as well have been no one else in the ballroom.

Our affair was inevitable. Together we were atomic. Sometimes, Felicity, you just meet someone you are, against all reason, magnetically drawn to. I couldn't resist him and I didn't want to.

We would have exquisitely sordid liaisons in five-star hotels, spend whole weekends in hot tubs, sipping champagne. We'd 'work away' and escape to the countryside or Riviera for gloriously indulgent weekends. We'd sunbathe and drink spritzers on yachts off Cannes or go skiing in St Moritz. I knew he would never leave his wife and children, just as he knew I was committed to Andrew and Julia. They were happy, exhilarating times.

It was definitely, undeniably, love, just not the sort you ever see validated on television. He never did leave his wife – they never do – but he will always be in my life in some capacity. I remain very fond of him, just where he is.

When homosexuality was decriminalised in '67, Andrew and I briefly discussed divorcing, but we didn't see the need. We had such a lovely life, and being married took the pressure of scrutiny off both of us. Julia was still a little girl and it seemed a shame to put her through the hassle of divorce too. And so we stayed married – not a marriage of convenience, I hasten to add. It was a marriage of wonderful friendship and love.

I should explain, as you're no doubt wondering, that Andrew was most definitely your biological grandfather. Few days went by when I didn't think about Christopher. I had my day-to-day life at the newspaper and with Andrew, but I thought all the *time about the alternate existence I'd have had as a lone teenage mother.*

I once reported on a mother-and-baby home in Brighton run by the Salvation Army. Oh, it was a bleak house, quite literally, and yet the unwed mothers didn't seem to regret their choices. They were a hard-faced lot, and they lived in terribly basic conditions, but the love they had for their babies shone through. It could so easily have been me.

People who lived close to the home regarded the girls snottily, 'spoiled fruits', but the mothers were too busy with their babies to pay them much heed. I wondered if my life would have been so very awful, cut off from the Stanford name on the coast with Christopher.

My rumination grew so intense, I decided the only thing for it was to replace one child with another. That the void wouldn't shrink unless I filled it.

I brought it up with Andrew over a splendid Sunday dinner of roast lamb and mint sauce he'd prepared, telling him I wanted a child and asking would he be happy to raise it as his. He took a sip of Merlot and agreed at once. 'I've often thought about having a child,' he said. 'I suppose I'd rather ruled it out, but if you're willing, I'm certainly up for giving it a go!'

'Are you sure?'

'Margot, you have saved my neck on more than one occasion and this is the first time you've ever asked for anything in return. Of course we can have a child! It'll even be fun! Just think . . . you and I, Mummy and Daddy!'

And so it was. I shan't go into details, but Andrew made good on his promise (after a few false starts) . . .

Gross.

. . . *and I soon fell pregnant. This time around it was a very different experience: walking on the Heath with Andrew, feeling the sun on my bump, swimming in the pond. Of course, this time I was an honest woman. Even Mother and Father were thrilled. My previous pregnancy, naturally, was never spoken of. To the rest of the world, I was a first-time mother.*

I adored your mum from the second she was placed in my arms. She was a difficult baby, colic and cradle cap, she screamed and screamed, but I couldn't have cared less. I loved her, and so did Andrew. Becoming a father completely changed him; from that moment on he was more focused than ever before. He endlessly doted on her and created quite the daddy's girl.

I do believe that love is not about the individuals but rather the connection. As much as I loved Julia, and she loved me in return, it was not the same love I would have shared with Christopher. I found very early on, that even while bursting with love for Julia, I still keenly felt the severance from her big brother. I accepted, with deep sorrow, that he was gone and the wound would never heal.

I set about the difficult task of forgetting, or at the very least ignoring, the pain. As I said to you on the landing, Felicity, you train yourself out of feeling. The problem, I suppose, is that by bricking up all that guilt and regret and hurt, I sealed off everything.

I think, from that point, I felt everything less. I could feel everything or nothing. I chose nothing.

I realise I am not always easy to be around. I apologise for some of the things I said to you when you first arrived in Llanmarion. I wholeheartedly disagreed with Julia's decision to keep you in the

331

dark regarding her illness, but felt I had to comply. I found being around you awkward, if I'm honest. I wanted you to be strong, to be ready for what lies ahead.

I set impossible standards for myself and expect others in my life to match them. I am old and calcified, but I promise, for Julia's sake, I shall try my very hardest to adjust.

You know the rest. I think that neatly brings us to the cul-de-sac at the end of Memory Lane. It's funny, but reading it all back now, at such a distance, it's like a story that happened to someone else.

Chapter 33

I close the diary and just stare at it in my lap. I don't want it to be over. But, whether she knows it or not, in fluid, cursive strokes Margot has joined up the girl in the book and the woman in the kitchen.

As gross as it is to think about Margot getting her sexy on in five-star hotels, I'm glad she found love, real love, again. Even if it was with a married dude. I was worried the Rick saga had finished her off. Maybe there's hope for me post-Thom.

I shove the diary into my satchel and go to listen at my bedroom door. The TV is still on, but I think Mum's in bed. I creep downstairs, not sure if I'm feeling brave enough to ask the question that's now stuck to my brain like matted chewing gum. Stalling for time, I carry on past the lounge and into the kitchen. I put the kettle on and rummage at the back of the cupboard for the jar of mint Options.

'Tea?' Margot says, materialising behind me. I bump my head on the cupboard shelf.

'Ow! No, I was looking for the hot chocolate.'

Margot purses her lips. 'Oh, you don't want that instant muck. Let me make you some proper hot chocolate.'

Out of habit and principle I can feel an argument about to launch off my tongue but hold it back. 'OK. Thanks.'

'Pass me that saucepan.' I do as I'm told and she fetches milk. The only light is coming from the lounge, so when she opens the fridge she's illuminated and, just for a second, she looks exactly the same as the girl sitting on the fence in 1941. She sets the milk on a low heat and retrieves a tin of cocoa powder. She pops the lid off with a teaspoon. 'What is it you want to say, Felicity?' she asks, stirring the milk. 'I can tell there's something.'

There is. 'I finished the diary.'

'I assumed as much.'

I bite my lip, thinking about how to word it. 'It's about Grandad. He didn't die of cancer, did he?'

Margot takes her time. She pours the milk into mugs and stirs in cocoa and sugar until all the lumps are gone. She carries the mismatched mugs to the table and sits opposite me. 'No, he didn't,' she says. 'How did you work it out?'

'New York in the seventies.'

'Ah yes.' Margot's face loses its steel and goes slacker than I've seen it. She looks so sad. 'Oh, Felicity, it was the most awful time. He didn't want Julia to know. He . . . we . . . come from a different time. A prouder, more private time, perhaps. It wasn't like it is now with gay chaps all over the television, and he kept that part of himself a secret, even from his own daughter. Especially from her.'

'But he died of AIDS. I mean . . . how did you hide that?'

She blows steam off the top of her mug. 'That was the year your mum was making that documentary in Cape Town. By the time you both got back, he was almost gone. It happened so quickly. One day he found a strange black spot in his armpit and within months . . .

'He made sure she saw him only at home, never on that infernal ward.' For a moment she says nothing, just staring down into her mug. 'In the beginning we bought the best private care money could buy, until I realised a lot of the prim, ignorant, idiot nurses were refusing to treat him. We moved to the AIDS ward at St Mary's, where they at least knew what they were doing.'

'I'm sorry.' I try the hot chocolate and it's at least six million times nicer than the 'instant muck'. Damn. I hate it when she's right.

'I truly hope you never have to witness a plague like that, Felicity.' She rubs her mouth with her hand. Her eyes unmistakably glaze over. 'To see those men, those tall, tanned, Adonises, wither away and shrink until they looked like living corpses. God, that ward. It was like being back at the old asylum during the war. A great long room of dying men all lined up like dominoes waiting to fall. Partners side by side in adjoining beds. So many of them couldn't tell their families. Some of them didn't have a single visitor. I always made sure I brought extra magazines and the like when I visited Andrew.'

I think of Grandad when I was little – some of my earliest memories are us together in the garden in Hampstead. He was such fun, so healthy, so full of life. I wonder if he was already infected, counting down like a silent time bomb.

'Dear Lord, it was cruel, and people were so cruel. All I could do was sit at his side as he faded away, day by day. I remember

335

holding his hand, covered in sarcomas. He looked a hundred years old. Those poor, poor men.'

I can't speak because I'll cry.

'I have never, ever in my life felt so useless. So utterly, utterly powerless.'

I shake my head and swallow the giant cube in my throat. 'You weren't useless,' I say. 'You were there for him. For them.'

Margot nods, saying nothing for a moment. 'Felicity, I can't tell you what to do – you have a mind of your own, as you've demonstrated on more than one occasion – but I am asking you not to tell your mother any of this. I know you'll hardly remember him, but think about what your grandfather wanted and think about how ill your mum is. Whether she really *needs* this information.'

'I won't,' I say, my voice cracking. I quickly swipe the tear off my cheek. 'I won't say anything. I'm . . . I'm so glad I met him before he . . . and I'm glad I remember him too.'

'Thank you,' says Margot, and takes a sip of her hot chocolate. She says no more, but neither can she look me in the eye.

Bronwyn reads the last chapter of the diary on one of the library beanbags. 'Oh wow,' she says. 'It looks like a truce to me.'

I haven't told them the full truth about Grandad and AIDS. I'm not going to tell anyone, even them. 'I know. I feel really bad for being so horrible about her now.'

'Don't,' says Danny. 'She was pretty vile too. She tried to kill your piglet!'

'Valid. The diary kind of makes sense of everything though, don't you think?'

Bronwyn nods. 'It certainly explains why she's a double-hard mofo.'

'Right. I've been thinking about this,' I say. 'It's like after everything she went through, the only way she could survive it all was to shut down or build these fortress walls or whatever. I can't say I blame her. After all that, I'd be a dribbling wreck.' I'm quietly impressed at my amateur psychoanalysis.

'It looks like she's trying to let you in now.' Bronwyn hands me back the diary and I slide it in my bag.

'*Trying* is the operative word. She's still pretty frosty.'

'Frostier than a penguin's asshole,' Danny offers.

'*Ach-a-fi*, Dan!' Bronwyn makes a distasteful face.

The bell clangs, signalling the end of break. 'See you here at lunch, yeah?' Danny asks.

'Sure.' I have RE now, which I dread because Mr Ramsey is old and a bit odd and everyone makes fun of the weird white stuff on his teeth. Gross, but I do feel sorry for him.

I make my way to the classroom and it's even rowdier than usual. 'What's going on?' I ask Dewi, who's waiting in the corridor.

He takes a breath. 'Mr Ramsey is off sick or something, like.'

'Just go in and sit down quietly,' future Mrs Thom Deacon, Miss Crabtree, says over the ruckus. 'I'll find out where the supply teacher is.' She shuffles off in her FLAT SHOES and I briefly imagine pushing her down the stairs.

It doesn't matter how many times I tell myself Thom doesn't like me *like that*, I haven't *quite* got rid of the pins and needles in my heart when I think about him. I shake it off. I've got much bigger things to worry about. A crush is the least of my worries.

We file into the classroom and, without a responsible adult present, it's all a bit *Lord of the Flies*. God, people are immature. Case in point: I'm hardly over the threshold when someone slams into my right shoulder, hurrying to get past me. 'Ow!'

'Oops!' shrieks a loud voice as my satchel slips off my shoulder. I recognise the tone at once. Megan. 'Sorry, love, didn't see you there.' I suspect she did because she then kicks my bag across the floor and the contents spill out.

'Megan, don't be a bitch, yeah?' From the flash of anger in her eyes, I'd say now is not the time for Dewi to step in and be chivalrous.

In my haste to scoop up exposed Tampax before boys learn the secrets of womanhood, I totally forget about the diary. 'Ooh, what's this?' Megan crows. 'Is it your diary?' She snatches it up.

Oh, shitballs. I can't show that I'm bothered or she'll know how precious it is. I play it cool. 'Megan, give it back, please. It's not mine.'

'Oh my God! What does it say?' Rhiannon cackles.

'*The Secret Diary of Lady Felicity Fanny-Fart*,' Megan says in a ludicrously posh accent. 'Dear diary, today I did a fanny fart.'

Some of my classmates laugh. I suppose 'fanny fart' is pretty funny in an alliterative sort of way. Megan starts to flick through the pages and I grit my teeth. it won't take much for the whole thing to fall to pieces. 'Megan, please.' I reach for the book, but she snatches it away.

'Megan,' Dewi tries again. 'Give it back, yeah?'

'God, if you love her so much, why don't you come and get it?' Megan strides across the classroom and I try my very hardest

338

to keep cool. I have no choice but to trail after her. Megan pulls herself onto the teacher's desk and starts to read at random in the same fake accent. '*Tuesday 21st January, 1941. I intended to write yesterday, but I was simply too exhausted.* What's this bollocks then? You writing a little story?'

What else can I do? 'It's my grandma's diary. Please, Megan, give it back. It's really old.'

Wrong thing to say. Knowing how valuable it is, her eyes light up. She's finally found the chink in my armour and, boy, is she gonna slide the knife right in. 'Oh, I better be really careful with it then, hadn't I, like?' She holds it upside down and gives it a shake. The photos and Dear John letter from Rick fall to the floor.

'Megan, stop,' I say forcefully. 'Look, I don't know what I've done to piss you off, but can you not take it out on my grandma?'

'Oh no, is Princess Felicity gonna be in trouble? Better not rip it, had I?' She tears a page out and lets it drift to the classroom floor.

'Megan!' I cry, my voice shrill and whiny. 'Stop it!' I feel so feeble. 'Please! God, what do you want me to say and I'll say it.' Sorry I saw you hooking up in a cave? Sorry for sounding a bit posh? Sorry that Dewi ever spoke to me? Sorry I don't have a sketchy alcoholic mum?

She suggests I perform an intimate act on Dewi. I roll my eyes, but Dewi jumps in *again*. 'Megan, don't be disgusting.'

'Oh, as if you wouldn't,' she scoffs.

'Clearly that's not going to happen.' I hold out my hand again. 'Please can I have it back?'

'Rhiannon, you remember in history when we had to make our letters look all old?'

'Yeah,' Rhiannon says. 'We had to burn the edges.'

'Good idea!' Megan slips a cheap pink cigarette lighter from out of her coat pocket, the sort you buy five-for-a-pound at the market.

'Megan, don't . . .' I say. She will *not* burn that diary.

Dewi goes to snatch it back, but Megan sparks the lighter, holding the book hostage. 'Come any closer and it goes up in flames . . .'

'Please, Megan, you have no idea how much that means to my grandma.'

'Aw, poor little Fliss. Are you going to cry?'

I make one last snatch for it. With a determination in her eyes that suggests she's not just mean, she's a freaking sociopath, Megan starts to burn the bottom corner of the pages.

What I do next is all a bit out-of-body experience. The nearest thing I can lay my hands on is a WORLD'S BEST TEACHER mug with dried coffee stuck to the bottom. The rage is so blinding I hardly see as I pick it up and smash the thing into her fucking face.

Chapter 34

'So let me get this right?' Mr Rees, the head, circles his desk, drumming his spindly Grinch fingers together. There's something a little bit Christopher Lee about him and this is hardly an ideal first meeting. 'You smashed a mug in her face?'

Well, if we're splitting hairs, her nose smashed, the mug is still intact. 'Yes,' seems like the wisest answer. There was a room full of witnesses, so there's no point in lying.

'This is very serious, Felicity. It's assault. You're very lucky I haven't called the police.'

'I'm sorry, Mr Rees. I was just . . . so angry. She was trying to set fire to my grandma's diary . . .'

'Yes, yes, I'm very well aware of that, but, Miss Baker, we do *not* hit people in the face with mugs at this school.'

I have to fight not to burst into hysterical laughter. I can feel excess, unnecessary adrenaline in my blood and it's bubbling up, needing release. 'I know,' I say. 'I've never, *ever* done anything like that before. I suppose it must be everything that's going on at home . . .' If there was *ever* a time to play my CANCER CARD, it's now.

'I'm aware of your home circumstances, but it simply does not excuse . . .' There's a knock at the door and the mousy receptionist enters. Margot looms over her shoulder. Oh crap. 'Ah, Mrs Baker, is it?'

'Hancock. I'm Felicity's grandmother. What has she done?' The temperature drops about twenty degrees as she takes her seat next to me. As ever, she's in her wax jacket, her hair wild.

'I'm afraid to say, Mrs Hancock, Felicity was involved in a very serious assault.'

'I hit a girl called Megan in the face with a mug.'

Margot's hand flies to her mouth. Was it really to cover a smile? 'Felicity, that's awful, just awful. I trust you were in some way provoked?'

'She tried to set fire to your diary.'

Her eyes widen, but she says no more. Mr Rees goes on. 'I'm afraid I have no option but to suspend Felicity until we can establish her suitability to return. I have to warn you, the exclusion may be permanent.'

'What?' I cry. 'It's totally a first offence!'

Mr Rees holds up a hand. 'That will all be taken into account. I shall be in touch. I recommend you spend the time at home studying and reflecting on your actions.'

Margot stands, hauling me up by the sleeve. 'I assume,' she adds coolly, 'the young arsonist is also being dealt with?'

Even Mr Rees wilts in Margot's presence. 'Well . . . yes . . . of course.'

'Good. Felicity – the car.'

Head bowed, I slope out of the head's office. I sheepishly climb into the passenger seat of the Land Rover. Margot slams her door shut. She adjusts the rear-view mirror. The silence is

342

pretty effing loud. 'So,' she finally says, 'this Megan character, did she have it coming?'

'Oh yes. She's been on my case since literally day one and—'

'That's all I need to know. We Hancock girls are no one's victims. A mug though, Felicity? Really?'

'I don't know what happened.'

'Lacks finesse.' She starts the engine. 'Come on. I don't want to leave your mother by herself for too long.'

Mum is none too pleased. 'This is not OK, Fliss. Getting suspended? You've only been there three months! For God's sake!' She looks more alive than she has in months.

'I'm sorry, please don't get worked up.'

'Do *not* treat me like I'm made of glass. I will still whup your ass.'

Margot leans against the kitchen counter, smirking in silence as Mum tears strips off me.

'I said I'm sorry!'

'You will be sorry. If you think this is an extra holiday, you've got another thing coming. I will home-school you to within an inch of your life. I'm going to make Joan Crawford look positively laid back.'

'Who?'

'Lesson one: *Mommie Dearest*.'

We get to work. Discovering that, so far, I've studied Shakespeare, John Steinbeck, Blake, Ted Hughes, Laurie Lee and Hemingway, Mum prescribes Iris Murdoch, Sylvia Plath, Angela Carter and Margaret Atwood to even out the balance. 'Right. You can read these and then write five hundred

343

words about why the contribution of female artists is so often overlooked.'

'How am I going to do that without the Internet?'

'You are permitted to go to the library, and that's it.' Mum pushes herself up, supporting herself on the kitchen table. 'I mean it, Fliss. I'm not having this.'

I suddenly feel such a strong guilt my arms and legs almost spasm. 'I'm sorry. I don't want to stress you out.' I can't look up from my lap I'm so ashamed. 'It was all in the heat of the moment.'

Mum purses her lips and sits back down. 'Look. I'm sure it was, but I don't believe there wasn't some other way you could have dealt with this Megan girl.'

'I know,' I admit. 'I'm sorry.'

Mum seems to soften. 'Oh, well. I guess it means we get to spend more time together.'

I nod, not quite trusting myself to speak.

My suspension lasts for the rest of the week. I like Angela Carter and Margaret Atwood more than Sylvia Plath and Iris Murdoch, but am no closer to understanding why all the authors we do at school are male. Sometimes Margot mutters 'patriarchy' at the evening news, and I think it must be something to do with that.

The following Monday I'm summoned back to Mr Rees's office. This time Mum is feeling well enough to join us, so we all go. His office smells of the Bacon & Egg McMuffin he's clearly had before school. Mrs Evans, as my head of year, is also benevolently present. Her candy-pink nails are the only blob of colour in the head's beige office. Even the dried flowers are wheat-coloured.

'It seems,' Mr Rees begins, 'that Felicity was provoked on this occasion. We also have a statement from a witness who came to me to explain that Megan Jones has singled out and victimised Felicity since she first started.'

My cheeks burn. I feel like the archetypal, Poindexter 'victim' you see in educational videos about bullying. I never thought of myself as a 'victim', but I guess I was. I wonder who the witness was. I'm guessing Thom has spoken up on my behalf.

'It's unfortunate you didn't feel able to report this behaviour to a teacher, Felicity. We could have avoided this incident.'

'Megan was already on her last warning,' Mrs Evans adds. 'This was the final straw. I mean, she could have burned the whole school down. She has been excluded.'

'Permanently?' Mum asks.

'Yes.'

School without Megan? It's almost too good to be true, although the dark goblin of pessimism immediately mutters that she'll probably meet me at the school gates at home time to stab me. I also think about her skanky mum briefly, but find it pretty hard to feel any pity for her. She made her choices. I know it'd be the humanitarian, altruistic thing to reach out and heal her poor broken-home heart or whatever, but Megan Jones is a thrusting megabitch, and this isn't an episode of *Saved by the Bell*; it's my life.

'Am I allowed back?' I ask tentatively. The fact I was told to come to the school in uniform is a good portent, I feel.

'Yes,' Mr Rees says, and I swear I feel iron fists let go of my shoulders. 'Although we will not tolerate any more flighty or violent behaviour. Is that understood?'

'Yes. I promise.'

'This is at least partially my fault,' Mum says. 'There's been very little routine in Fliss's life for the last few years and . . .' She tails off. She looks sickly, clammy.

'Mum? Are you OK?'

'I'm fine,' she says.

'Mrs Baker, would you like some water?' Mrs Evans asks.

'Erm, yes, thank you.'

I don't take my eyes off her. Whatever she says, she looks awful. Once again, I've made her do too much. She takes a sip of water, her hand shaking.

'Perhaps,' Margot says, 'I should get Felicity's mum home.'

'Of course.' Mr Rees stands at once, none too keen to have a dying woman keel over on his brown carpet. 'Felicity, you'll go to lesson two as normal, please.'

I don't need to be in any more trouble, but I also don't want to leave Mum. 'Mum, are you going to be OK?'

Her eyes are glassy. She leans on Margot for support, but tries to stand tall. 'I just need some air. I'll be fine.'

To be fair, the McDonald's smell is pretty off-putting, I could use some air too. 'Are you sure?'

'Felicity, go to your lesson,' Margot says definitely. 'I'll get her home.'

I nod because I know that she will. Whatever else, I trust Margot.

Chapter 35

By Tuesday, Mum has to be admitted to the Ysbyty Cwm Mawr's specialist cancer ward. It's not good. There's a horrible resignation to it, like we're taking a patchy cat to the vet for a final visit.

We're told, by kind, sombre doctors that THIS IS NOT THE END, they simply need to stabilise the calcium levels in her blood. Hospitals, I learned ages ago, are all pretty much the same, only this one has bilingual signposts. Otherwise, it has the same endless linoleum corridors, stark blueish lighting and sad brown visitor armchairs. Even when I'm seventy, I'll never forget my thighs sticking to the vinyl on hot July days.

The worst thing about hospitals is the wailing. At any given time, it seems someone is wailing: either calling for a nurse, crying in pain or just moaning. It's ghostly, like the Disneyland haunted mansion or something. I hate it.

Visiting hours are four till seven. Margot collects me from school and we drive over. I take her books to read and also smuggle in *Chat* and *Bella*, because her guilty pleasure is 'real-life stories' about women who accidentally married serial killers or think they're the reincarnation of Marilyn Monroe. We go every night.

By the fourth night, even Margot is looking exhausted. The new routine is to drive back to the farm, have a late supper and slope off to bed ready to do it all again the next day.

I plonk myself in the Land Rover. Margot climbs into the driver's seat and puts the key in the ignition. She pauses. 'Regular way home,' she asks, 'or shall we go on an adventure?'

'An adventure?'

'Let's turn left and see where we end up.' She turns to me and gives me an uncharacteristic wink.

Uncharacteristic it may be, but I like it. I have to smile. I can't help it. Although I'm aching for bed, I say, 'Adventure it is.'

Margot pulls out of the car park, and, instead of turning right towards the farm, she swings us left into the night.

We drive and drive. With lights on full beam, we snake along winding country lanes, thickly black with no street lights. We pass a disused mine, the skeleton of the lift shaft silhouetted against the pale moon. It's way pretty. We are dwarfed by snow-capped mountains and I'm almost breathless with how beautiful they are and how tiny I feel. How nothingy I am in the bigger picture.

We drive on. I see the city in the distance, a blob of glitter on a black map, busy roads feeding into it like veins, lit with headlights. Planes pass overhead, landing lights flashing. Margot and I don't really talk much, but it's not a scary silence, it's a relaxed one.

We keep going until we run out of Wales. We arrive at a point at the top of a rocky cliff overlooking a curving beach. The sea is gentle, rippling like navy-blue silk. Staying in the car because it's so cold, I stare into it, letting it hypnotise me. I have no idea what time it is. I stopping checking hours ago.

'Where are we?' I say finally.

'Gower Peninsula. South of Swansea.'

'It's beautiful.' At night, the sand looks silver. It's all a bit science fiction, like we're on an alien planet with purple oceans and diamond beaches.

'I didn't know this was where we were going until we got here,' Margot sighs.

We both seem to relax, sinking further into our seats. For a few minutes it feels a bit like we've escaped. I don't want to escape Mum, obviously, but the walls of Llanmarion are shrinking in on me. Farm, school, hospital, farm, school, hospital on repeat are making me crazy. Seeing the beach, seeing out to the horizon, reminds me I'm not in a bubble. There's room to breathe at last.

We sit in quiet for a while, listening to the tide yawn in and out.

'To answer your last question,' Margot says, turning the heaters down, 'I didn't go back to the farm until the late fifties.'

I had completely forgotten there was anything left to know.

'I brought your mother when she was a baby. By then Peter and Jane were long gone, obviously, and it was just Glynis and Ivor and the animals. They doted on Julia. Ivor in particular was so wonderful with her. Between you and me, I rather think Ivor would have taken to fatherhood splendidly.'

'What? You think it was Glynis that didn't want kids?'

'I suspect so, although they were happy enough.' Margot smiles, obviously enjoying rolling back through the years. 'We went back a couple of times, but I stopped when Glynis became ill. She had cancer too. She died in the spring of '66, if I remember rightly.'

'Oh no! What did Ivor do?'

'He ran the farm until the day he died. Which was three and a half years ago.'

I do the sums very quickly. 'That was when you moved here.'

Margot smiles. 'I last saw him about five years ago. I received a letter from him, unusual in itself, asking if I'd pay him a visit. I went at once, abandoning my poor deputy editor. Ivor never changed, the same giant, same giant heart. I arrived at the farm and found it the same as ever. He was very old. He walked with a stick and relied on some farmhands to keep it all in order. By then he wasn't really producing much – about the same as I'm managing.

'I made us a pot of tea and we drank it in the rose garden. He rested his stick against that little bench and sighed this world-weary sigh. "Margot," he said, "I'm too old for all this, like. I'm ready to throw in the towel and go meet my Glynis." I told him he was being a silly old man. "Ah, Margot, I'm tired. I've had enough. I'm off to put my feet up. Now listen," he said, "you're the closest thing to a daughter we ever had, like, and I'm leaving the farm to you."

'Well, how I laughed. The very idea of me having a farm was ridiculous. I'd hardly set foot out of north London in the last thirty years except for holidays. I didn't even go south of the river if I could at all avoid it. He wouldn't hear otherwise. "The farm is yours to do with as you will. Look after it, won't you."

Sure enough, he died about six months later. Just went to sleep one night and never woke up. At first I thought I'd sell the place, to be honest, but I came to have a clear-up after his funeral. Everything was so familiar, so warm, so . . . like home.

I knew at once I could never sell it. I hadn't planned to leave London, especially when your mother was in remission, but, and I know this sounds peculiar, I swear I heard a little voice telling me I was home . . . reassuring me. And it felt right. It felt like the right thing to do. And I think it was. When I left London, I trusted your mother would get better, but even now, with everything that's happening, I *still* think here is the right place to be . . . for both you and me.'

Voices? Like the voices in the woods? Surely not . . . I almost say something, but hold my tongue. 'Was it you who changed the name of the farm?'

She smiles a very slight smile. 'Yes. Keeps the kids away,' she says with a wink. 'Come on. I suppose we should think about driving back, even if tomorrow is Saturday.'

'Just give me a minute.'

She nods and I step out of the car. Despite the calm waters a stiff wind slices across the clifftop and the long, silver grasses seem to bow down. I wrap my arms around me and let the breeze slap me full in the face. I feel it tug and whip at my hair. The air smells super-beachy – salty and briny and piratey. I close my eyes and see candyfloss on Brighton pier, Blackpool Tower, sailors at Portsmouth, Dracula in Whitby and donkey rides on Scarborough beach.

All days with Mum. It's always been just her and me. I feel hot tears blow back to my ears. I just let them roll. I am not ready to lose her. Not even close.

Margot waits in the car until I'm calm enough to get back in.

Chapter 36

There's nothing like a makeover to cheer a girl up. I pull the mirror off the wall in the hallway and sit on my bedroom floor where the light is best. Mum came home two days ago, but she's too ill to really do anything. She can make it to the sofa, but that's about it.

I have nowhere to go (it is Llanmarion) but I find putting on make-up oddly therapeutic. I start with base, as you do. I have two foundations, one for summer, when I have more of a tan, and a cooler one for winter. I'm careful not to cake it on too thick or you get that terrible tidemark around the jawline.

I tidy up my eyebrows with tweezers before using a little primer over my lids. I try to perfect my smoky eye, mixing white, grey and black – blending them over my lid, black extending towards the outer tip of my brow. A little kohl under the eye and liquid liner along the edge of the upper lid.

I glue some false lashes on. I regret it at once – they're too long and look stupidly fake. Maybe if I curl them they'll look better. I do so and add mascara. It's clumpy and a bit 'tarantula lashes'. Christ. I sigh and start on my cheeks.

You have to be so careful with blusher, or you look like a cheap doll hooker. I prefer a very subtle peachy-bronze shade over the cheekbones and then some pale highlighter above the line. Maybe it's the light, but it looks OTT. I vigorously pummel my cheeks with a thick, clean brush to blend, but it doesn't seem to help much.

I've come too far to turn back. Again, to avoid looking like a prozzie, you can choose eyes *or* lips, and with such a heavy eye I need a light lip so pick a pearly 'nude' shade. It's a *too* pale and it looks a bit gothy. I wipe it off and instead choose a dusky pink.

I apply too much, missing my lipline. I swear loudly and rummage in my make-up bag for a lipliner to straighten it up. I take a good look at myself. Am I drunk? I'm so far outside my lips I look like a Page 3 girl.

I look like total shit.

I'm too hot.

I'm sweating.

My left eye is clearly bigger than the right.

I look like the Hamburglar.

Or a raccoon.

Or RuPaul.

I'm boiling.

I want this shit off my face.

I itch all over.

I drag my left hand over my left eye, leaving a horrid coaly smudge over my cheek.

I unwind the pink lipstick all the way and press it hard against my reflection. I write until the whole lipstick is broken off and hurl it across the boxroom.

The big pink letters say CLOWN.

Chapter 37

'How's your mum doing?' Thom asks in the library. We're all there, having morning tea as usual. The stab I used to feel when I saw Thom is now more like pressing on a bruise. My head knows I can't have him, but it doesn't stop me wanting him. I know it's not right, but have you ever tried telling a cloud to stop raining? That doesn't work and neither does telling my tummy not to flip when I think about him. A crush, and I do feel crushed by it.

That said, I love that both of us are chirpily pretending *that* moment never happened. I can sense he's keeping his distance though. If I'm with Danny and Bronwyn, he'll join us; if it's just me, he has work to do. It's fine, I don't want him to be in any trouble, and I brought it on myself, didn't I?

'She's back home. For now.' I squirm. I don't wanna talk about it.

'Will she be home for Christmas?' Danny asks.

'I hope so. Can we talk about something else, please?'

'Sure,' Bronwyn says. 'Every year, Danny and I do Christmas Before Christmas if you wanna join in?'

'What's that?' I ask.

'Does what it says on the tin. We all go away for Christmas so we have our own special one first.'

Danny elaborates. 'I cook a little Christmas dinner and we swap presents and sing Christmas songs. My Mariah is very special.'

'That's one way to describe it,' Bronwyn adds ruefully. She leans in. 'Do you think I should invite Robin this year?' The boy in question is sitting at the other side of the library, reading Terry Pratchett.

'Yes!' Danny and I say in unison.

'In fact,' I say, 'watch this.' I stand.

'Fliss, what are you doing?' Bronwyn hisses.

'Watch.' I weave through the tables and book tree to where Robin is reading. 'Hi, Robin.'

'Fliss.'

I sit in the seat next to him. 'Bronwyn is planning a little pre-Christmas get-together. Would you like to come?'

'Sure,' he says without hesitation. 'When is it?'

'TBC.' I lean in very close. 'PS, if you ever wanted to ask Bronwyn out sometime, she'd almost certainly say yes.'

He looks doubtfully over my shoulder. 'Bronwyn Parry? Really? I thought she hated me. She's always punching me and stuff.'

'Oh, dear, sweet Robin, you have much to learn. She likes you, I promise. Don't tell her I told you.'

'OK!' He looks befuddled, but not repulsed, which I take to be a good thing. Well, that's my good deed for the day done.

I return to our table. 'What did you say to him?' Bronwyn says through gritted teeth.

'Nothing. Just explained the whole Christmas Before Christmas concept. That's all. Relax. He said he'll check if he's free.'

'Oh. OK. Good. Otherwise I'd have to go drown myself in the pool.'

Danny grimaces. 'The piss levels in the pool would kill you before you drowned.'

The bell rings out, signalling what will no doubt be a very long Monday which features double hockey. We return our tea mugs to the pinched-from-the-canteen tray at the centre of the table. 'Fliss, just hang on a sec,' says Thom.

Danny and Bronwyn head off to registration without me and we're left alone.

'I just wanted to check, with everything going on at home, that you're still up for *The Chess Club Presents*?'

Uh, I've hardly thought about it, but I am suddenly determined. 'Yeah. Of course.'

'Are you sure?'

'Yes. I will get something ready, I promise. My mum really wants to see me dance one last time before . . .' An elephantine awkward silence fills the whole library. We both know what words follow: *one last time before she dies*, and he's just dying to ask, *Will she make it to January*? It's so obvious, the words don't need saying aloud.

Even if she doesn't make it to the show, I promised her a dance.

Thom rubs his jaw. 'I also wanted to say something about what happened the other week . . .'

I almost physically fold inwards like shame origami. 'Oh God, do we have to?'

'I want to clear the air, otherwise it'll hang over us, and I don't want that. The library should be a safe space, not an awkward one.'

I take a deep breath. I'd sort of hoped he might suffer a tiny, harmless brain haemorrhage that erased that one memory and nothing else. 'I said I'm sorry.'

'I know.'

'Look.' I meet his gaze, possibly for the first time since the World's Worst-Advised Kiss™. 'I . . . I think, with a little hindsight, that was more about me than you. I obviously thought you were . . . cute.' Oh crapbag, I'm making things worse. 'But . . . but . . . it was me. I don't think I was dealing with things very well. Moving . . . Mum . . . Megan . . . other things beginning with M.'

'I know, that's what I was going to say.'

'Then we're on the same page. I was, like, drowning and I clung to the nearest possible thing. It was you, and I'm sorry.'

He chuckles, again rubbing his stubble. Yep, still hot. Yep, still totally illegal. 'I'm a rubber dinghy.'

I laugh. 'Something like that. I think I channelled all my crazy into you. God, you must think I'm insane.'

He gives my shoulder a deeply professional pat. 'Fliss. Fifty per cent of my job is the Dewey Decimal System and the other fifty per cent is really poorly paid therapist. It's what I'm there for, OK? I will always be there for you lot. Always.'

I nod and smile and I think that is the end of that. I see a day, just around the corner, when I might laugh about my first 'love'.

That weekend I bite the bullet. It's a little like visiting the dentist. You dread it and dread it, but then you actually go and it's never *that* bad. It took every ounce of energy I had (and bribing myself with a visit via the corner shop to get a Kit-Kat-Chunky-shaped reward), but I haul myself to the dance studio.

Danny lets me in. 'Can I watch?'

'Absolutely not! I haven't danced in about a hundred years.'

'Please!'

'Sorry, Danny. This is . . . sort of a big deal for me.'

He feigns a swoon. 'Oh, such a true artist. I'll be in the house. Give me a knock when you're done and we can watch *Powerpuff Girls* or something, yeah?'

'Sure!'

There's no CD player here, only a crap old tape deck, so I've brought the only cassettes I could find – the mixtapes we used to listen to on road trips. I grab the first one that comes to hand and stick it in the slot. It's definitely one of the ones Mum made – the first track is 'Blue Monday'.

I pull off my coat and throw it over the back of a chair. I'm wearing black leggings under a black leotard. They're much too tight – I really did used to be a stick figure. I pull my hair into a messy bun and pull on leg warmers. It's so weird, like travelling back in time.

Using the barre, I stretch and limber up, feeling muscles I'd forgotten existed. I used to be able to hold my leg high above my head, but now my hamstrings angrily protest at the halfway stage.

'Blue Monday' fades to a finish and there's a sad piano chord. A woman howls, reminding me of hospital ward. I stare at the cassette player. I recognise the song, but haven't heard it in a long time. God, what is it? It's Kate Bush, her voice instantly recognisable. Oh, it's 'This Woman's Work'. It's Mum's all-time favourite song.

I stop and listen, really listen, taking in the lyrics, probably for the first time. It's heart-breaking and perfect all at the same time. I listen to the whole song, absorbing the story.

I face myself in the mirror. I didn't even realise my eyes were watering. It's become second nature. I inhale and briskly wipe the tears away. Now I know what I have to do.

First position. I turn my feet out. My hips protest in a way that they never used to. I've let my posture get so slack. Somewhere in Battersea, Madame Nyzda is telling me to imagine a piece of string pulling me ramrod straight from the top of my skull. I tuck my tailbone and stomach in, rolling my shoulders back. 'You should be able to hold a shiny pound coin between those shoulder blades, girls!'

Tendu into fifth position. Even pointing my toes feels alien. Holding the barre, I perform an experimental grand plié: bending my knees and lowering myself almost all the way to the floor. My thighs burn and my knees make a deeply unsexy clicking noise as I come back up through demi-plié. I run through dégagé, working my right leg forward, backward and to the side. I turn and do the same on my left side.

When I can put it off no longer, I hop en pointe into échappé, bobbing from fifth to second position, my legs opening and closing. At once I remember the singular pain in the arch of my feet and toes. It's like my feet are screaming, OH HELL NO, NOT THIS SHIT AGAIN, but I have to admit that in the mirror I look *so* elegant.

I've still got it.

I pirouette a couple of times, finding my centre of balance. I'm ready. I travel across the studio, casually running some steps together: glissade, jeté, coupé, step, jeté again, pas de chat, entrechat quatre, soubresaut, and rest in fifth position.

It's like riding a really super-fancy French bike. I catch my reflection in the mirror and smile at myself. I can do this. I can actually do this.

Chapter 38

Mum is a fighter. People say that about cancer patients a lot: they are 'fighters' and they are 'brave'. It's true though! She is getting sicker and sicker, but I see her clinging on to the dignity and routine she has left. Now me or Margot have to help her around the house. One of us has to walk her to the toilet and make sure she can get in or out of the bath.

Margot does most of it, silently and patiently, guiding her up and down the stairs. 'Mother, I can manage,' Mum will snap, even though she can't. Margot says nothing, remaining at her arm.

For my part, I do my best to be as positive as I possibly can. It's killing me, but I know Mum wants me to be happy. She already said she doesn't want her last few weeks to be snivelly and snotty.

'Do you want me to read to you?' I ask. I've walked her out to the rose garden. It's freezing cold, the ground silver and hard-packed. The paving stones seem to glitter and our breath hangs in the air. I've swaddled Mum in a duffel coat and scarf and blanket. With her head poking out, she looks a little like a turtle.

'I don't think so. It's nice just to be outside.' She closes her eyes. 'Can you hear the stream?'

I strain, but I can't hear it over the twittering birds. 'A little,' I fib.

'I find it very soothing,' she says. 'Are you going to the studio later?'

'Just for an hour or two, if that's OK?'

'Of course it is. All these hours you're putting in – I can't wait to see whatever it is you're cooking up.'

I've been trying to practise every day, either before or after school. I need to get back in shape, reprogram my body. 'If you want, you can come down to the studio and watch. I'm sure Margot will drive us.'

Mum takes my hand. We're both on the dainty bench. 'Felicity. I will be at that show if it kills me. Literally.'

She looks so gaunt, her cheeks so hollow. I wish I could believe that she will be, but I fear the worst. I've set myself a new goal. I just really want her to make it to Christmas. Three weeks to go.

I'm not an idiot. I know she isn't going to get better. What hurts now is that I don't know how much she's suffering. I hate, *hate*, the idea that she's in pain. I hate the notion she's embarrassed or ashamed of needing help to the loo or in the bath.

I don't really believe in God, and I know Mum doesn't, but I've started talking to my bedroom ceiling of a night, speaking to anyone who'll listen. It goes a bit like this: 'Hi, God or Goddess. Listen. I know we don't go to church/synagogue/mosque/ temple (delete as appropriate), but my mum is a good person who spent her life making films that *helped* people. She made films about child soldiers and corrective rape and Romanian orphanages. As I understand it, if you actually exist, you're

362

in the business of rewarding the good. Well, Mum is good. If you only reward people who do things for you, if your love is conditional, I don't think you're all that, really. If you're really as amazing as all these religions say you are, you'll make sure Mum is looked after. And I'll be good too. Deal? Awesome.'

One night, I find Margot sitting at the foot of Mum's bed, just watching her sleep. 'Is she OK?' I ask.

'She's fine,' Margot says in a hushed voice. 'I'm just too tired to plot my next move, even if it is only to the sofa.'

I feel guilty for not helping more. 'If you need a break . . .'

'I don't.' Her eyes flick up, steely blue. She's like a lioness guarding her cub. 'I mean, thank you. I appreciate everything you're doing. And I think taking part in this show is a lovely idea. She's very excited that you're dancing again.'

I nod. After a pause I say, 'Do you believe in heaven?'

She seems to consider it for a second, tucking her wire-wool hair behind her ear. 'No. I think there's a lot to be said for an ending.'

I look at Mum and tell myself the lies that I reckon all of us, all the kids losing parents, and all the parents losing kids, must tell ourselves: it'll be a release, it'll be a relief, she'll be free, she'll be at peace. But maybe, like Margot says, it's just the end, full stop.

I lean over and plant a kiss on Mum's forehead. When she's gone, we'll still be here. That's the hard part, I guess.

The day before Christmas Before Christmas, Danny and I go into town to get our Secret Santa presents. 'I got Sophie,' he moans. 'Like what am I meant to get her? She's so boring.'

'No, she isn't! She loves make-up for one thing. Get her some new brushes. We always need new brushes. Or something from MAC.' I got Bronwyn – a much more difficult prospect. I ended up getting her a book about conspiracy theories, knowing there's a very real chance she'll already have it.

We go to the bookshop café and order their Christmas cappuccinos to go, which are flavoured with ginger and cinnamon. They're heavenly. We share a gingerbread man wearing a little icing scarf and we're so busy deciding who should get the head and who should get the crotch we don't even register Megan's mum until she's right underneath us.

Literally. She's in the doorway of the derelict pet shop, huddled under a sleeping bag. Her sign reads 'hungry and homeless'. A dog – some sort of bull terrier – sits forlornly next to her. 'Any change?' she asks.

I feel a stab of guilt. I haven't thought about Megan since I started back at school, but now wonder where she is.

'No! You're not homeless! You live on the estate,' Danny says. I think if she's desperate enough to sit in a doorway begging, she probably needs the money pretty badly.

But before I can attempt to relieve my guilt with a few coins, Mrs Jones spits about twelve very bad words and we rush away.

The next day we gather at Danny's. They have a hilariously crap white faux tree in the living room covered in pink and purple tinsel which I *think* is meant to be ironic, although I certainly don't say anything. His dad is working in the restaurant and his mum makes herself scarce, only nipping in and out with a plate of mince pies and some bowls of prawn crackers.

It's the three of us, plus Robin and Sophie. I was nervously summoned to Bronwyn's earlier to help her get ready. We raided her wardrobe and she owns, I discovered, a form-fitting velvet dress in pine green. It's a bit Deanna Troi, but at least it's not a hippy smock. We paired it with a simple lace choker and her usual Doc Martens. I French-braided her unruly hair and gave her smoky Shirley Manson eyes, and I must admit she looks like a whole other person. Robin can't take his eyes off her, so I think I can give myself five gold stars.

For the first time in a really long time, I think of Xander back in London and feel a tiny pang of jealousy. Then I feel guilty for thinking about boys when Mum is so ill. I try to shake it off. I sip my hot chocolate. 'Let's do presents!' I announce.

We had stowed our parcels under the tree and now Danny hands them out. I open mine and my Secret Santa has bought me a giant pink tutu. 'Oh, very nice! I shall wear it every day!' I put it on over my leggings and sweater dress. It clashes a treat.

'Gorgeous!' says Danny, wearing his new FCUK hat. Bronwyn, thank God, did *not* have that book and seems chuffed, and Sophie is genuinely pleased with her make-up brushes. They are, I guess, a lot more practical than a tutu.

'So I have a favour to ask,' I say when we're all done opening gifts. 'I need you all to be in my *Chess Club Presents* act.'

'No way,' Bronwyn says immediately. 'I'm strictly there to do the lights.'

'Please . . .' I pretend-whine. 'I really need you all or it won't work.'

'Fliss, I like *really* can't dance,' Robin says.

'You don't have to. I promise. I just need pairs of hands.

Bron, people wouldn't even see your face.'

I tell them what I have planned and they look at me slack-jawed. 'Fliss, we can't do that,' Danny says, his hand covering his mouth.

'I want to. It's . . . what I want to do.'

'I think that would be amazing,' Sophie says, awe in her eyes. 'People would totally freak!'

'So you'll help?' I look at all of them.

Danny and Sophie agree at once. 'I must be effing crazy,' Bronwyn says. 'But yes, if you're crazy enough to go through with this, it's the least I can do.'

Robin rolls his eyes. 'Oh, go on then. But if I so much as see a pair of boy-tights, I quit.'

'No tights, I swear.' I grin. I guess Bronwyn made Robin's mind up. 'Thank you. I owe you one.'

'OH MY GOD!' Danny explodes. 'It's SNOWING!' He wipes condensation off the window and we pile over the settee to see powdery flakes swarming under the orange street lights.

'Do you think it'll settle?' Sophie asks excitedly. 'Snow day!'

It's already dusting the grass verges and the tops of cars. 'I don't know,' Robin says. 'I think it's too wet to settle, like.'

'No!' Danny grabs my arm. 'We must pray to the snow goddess, Frosta. We didn't have a snow day all last winter.'

I laugh. 'Frosta?'

'Yes, she has white hair and a snow leopard and is fabulous.'

'How do we pray to her, exactly?'

'I dunno, I guess we sing Christmas songs.'

'"Let It Snow"? "White Christmas"?' Bronwyn suggests.

Danny shakes his head. 'No! For copyright issues, I think we should go with *O come all ye faithful, joyful and triumphant, o come ye, o come ye to Llanmarion . . .*'

'*O come let us adore her, o come let us adore her, o come let us adore her . . . Frosta, snow goddess,*' I sing.

The others laugh and the snow swirls and dribbles down the wet windowpane. 'Yeah, that ought to do it.'

The next morning, I sit up in bed – my bedroom *freezing* cold – and pull back the curtain to see the whole farm is buried under heaps and heaps of marshmallowy white snow.

Margot pokes her head through my bedroom door. 'No school today, Felicity. Might as well have a lie-in.'

Hark! Frosta has answered our prayers! Amen!

Chapter 39

Because life is a total, utter, ass-munching bitchnipple, Mum has to go back into hospital on Christmas Eve. She's been hanging on by the skin of her teeth, desperate to have one last Christmas at home, but it's not to be.

The snow is long gone. Everything is frosty and crisp and glacier-mint cold, but it won't be a white Christmas this year. When Margot took her some lunch – and right now Mum can only manage soup – she had flopped over in bed and Margot couldn't wake her up. That's when, very calmly, Margot came to the living room, where I was watching *Bedknobs and Broomsticks* while shelling some sprouts into a big bowl, and told me that we needed to call an ambulance.

Credit where credit's due, it arrived about ten minutes later, siren blaring. By this time Mum was awake and telling us we were making a terrible fuss, as if she had little more than a splinter. If only. She's so, so thin now. Her collarbone juts through her skin and her spine is like a stegosaurus.

I held Mum's hand the whole way. She told the paramedic, who in better circumstances I'd have tried my very hardest to marry immediately because he looked a bit like Usher, that she was *fine*, but she had moments where she tuned out of reality. It was so scary; she'd just stop mid-sentence.

Her body is coming apart from the inside. Soon it will get to her mind, and then what?

Merry Christmas, us.

It's her calcium levels again. Now, as the sun sets, she seems a bit brighter, but they are definitely keeping her in overnight. She will wake up on Christmas morning on a cancer ward. At home I was halfway through peeling sprouts she won't be able to eat. Now it'll be a Christmas dinner of blended hospital goo.

But she's alive. There's colour back in her cheeks for now, so none of that stuff matters. Yeah, a farmhouse Christmas would have been lovely, but Mum will still get to see Christmas.

Mum naps while Margot and I wait to speak to the doctor about coming in tomorrow and spending the whole day with her. She shouldn't be alone on Christmas day, surrounded by sick people. In my head, there's still a little-girl version of me, the one who believed in Santa and the Easter Bunny. The little-girl me lives in a Barbie Wendy house and she still, on some level, thinks Mum's going to defy science and magically get better.

I don't have heart to tell Inner Little Me she's deluded, so I just let her believe. She's not doing any harm.

It's after seven by the time we get to talk to the doctor and she tells us we can arrive from eight in the morning. We leave Mum sleeping, but looking, well, alive.

As we reach the Land Rover I'm suddenly starving. 'Are you hungry?' Margot asks.

'Yeah.'

We climb into the car. She pauses. 'Home or an adventure?'

I smile. 'What do you think?'

'Adventure,' she says very seriously.

Off we go again.

We drive and drive until we find a little pub and guesthouse. It has a thatched roof and I can see an open fire flickering through the leaded windows. 'Well, doesn't this look inviting?' Margot says.

'It's way cute. Where are we?'

'Not the foggiest. Shall we see if there's room at the inn?'

'What? Really?'

'Well, what could be more appropriate? Come along, Felicity!' She's already bounding out the car and towards the door, her handbag swinging at her side. I trot to keep up. I'm still wearing the Indoors Outfit – Adidas tracksuit and slipper boots – that I had on when the ambulance came.

We enter the pub and, through a thick cloud of cigarette smoke, I see a handful of locals having a Christmas Eve drink. A couple of grizzled men with nicotine-stained beards stop talking and scan me over like I'm a mince pie. I guess my trackies deter them as they quickly refocus attention on their pints.

A huge open fire crackles and holly wreaths are pinned to sturdy oak beams. Mistletoe dangles over the bar, inviting patrons, no doubt, to kiss the barmaid – an older woman with a mass of dyed black hair and blue eyeshadow. 'Good evening,' Margot says with her usual authority. 'I know it's very short notice and I know it's Christmas Eve, but I wondered if you had any rooms for the night?'

The woman looks a little surprised. 'We do, love. It's a quiet time for us, is Christmas. Two rooms?' She speaks with a down south accent – English down south.

'That would be lovely. And are you serving food?'

'I'm sure our Ken can knock you something up, love.' Her acrylic nails are very long and blood red with tiny Christmas-pudding designs. I wonder, honestly, how she wipes her bum. 'I just need to take a deposit for the rooms, if that's all right.'

'Of course.' Margot reaches into her handbag, a plain brown satchel, and hands over her credit card. The bar is covered in soggy, smelly beer towels.

The landlady goes to scan it, pauses and looks up at Margot. 'Margot Hancock?'

'Yes?'

'You didn't used to be Margot Stanford, did you?'

Margot frowns. 'Well, yes. Yes, I was.'

The woman gasps, her red talons clutching her heart. 'It's me, Doreen Mitchell! Well, I ain't been Mitchell for nearly fifty years, but you know what I mean! Do you remember me?'

Margot shakes her head in disbelief. It's the first time I've seen her thrown. 'Oh my! Of course I remember. Gosh, Doreen . . . I . . . I can't believe it.'

Doreen lifts the hinged part of the bar and comes around to our side to embrace Margot. Margot is awkward, but returns the gesture. 'Look at you! Margot Stanford, you're a sight for sore eyes, let me tell you.'

Margot blinks as if to check she's not hallucinating. 'Goodness, you'll have to give me a minute. I . . . I mean, how are you? What on earth are you doing here? I don't even know where we are.'

'Been one of those days, has it?'

'One of those years.'

'Well, come sit by the fire, pet.' She steers us to a prime spot next to a sumptuous Christmas tree weighed down with glitzy decorations and fairy lights. God, I love the piney smell. 'You're about three miles outside of Pontypridd. And, to answer your other question, I never left, love.'

'After the war?'

'Yeah. Ken was one of the pilots at the hospital. Remember the old asylum? We married in '48. Nearly fifty years, can you Adam and Eve it? It's not always easy, is it? There's days I could happily murder him, truth be told, but I wouldn't trade him in for a younger model. Ain't that right, Derek?' she calls to one of the locals at the bar.

'You're breakin' me heart, Dor.' He grins back.

Margot smiles dreamily and I nudge her.

'Oh, I'm sorry,' Margot says. 'Doreen, this is my granddaughter, Felicity.'

'Oh, I should have guessed. You are alike.' Are we? 'Such a pretty thing. Have you seen your gran back in the day? Stunner, she was.'

I smile. I bet Margot just *loves* 'gran'. 'I've seen pictures. She was a total babe.'

Even Margot's face cracks into a laugh at that.

'Margot Stanford in my pub!' Doreen says. 'Well, I never. Look, what can I get you? And then we've got fifty years to catch up on.'

* * *

Margot and Doreen talk for what feels like hours. She gets a diluted version of what I know. Margot makes no mention of Christopher, or Grandad dying of AIDS, sticking to her stellar career and her decision to come back to Llanmarion. She does explain about Mum and why we're driving aimlessly on Christmas Eve.

Doreen, now a mother of four and grandmother of six herself, goes to prepare our rooms as midnight approaches.

'How weird is that?' I say, leaning close. 'That we'd randomly show up at Doreen's pub. It's like fate or something.'

Margot cradles a goblet-sized brandy. 'I'm not sure I believe in fate. Remember when you asked me about heaven? I don't think I believe in heaven, but I do believe in "goodness".'

'What do you mean?'

'You know when you're running late and you see the bus pull away and you think, That's just so ruddy typical, or when your shopping bag splits open in the street or when it rains on the one day you forget your umbrella?'

'Yeah. It's like that Alanis Morissette song.'

'Who?'

'Never mind.'

'The point I'm making is, we all spend so much time dwelling on the bad – and don't misunderstand me, I think there's a lot of bad in the world too – that we forget to look at the good. We never make a mental note when the bus arrives at the exact same time we do, or when it starts raining *after* we've made it home. Sometimes, I think the universe *is* on our side. Like tonight: the universe wanted

373

Doreen and me to meet again after all these years. And for you to meet her too.'

I nod. If only the universe could look out for Mum.

Margot must be able to read minds. 'Felicity, over the next few weeks, you might have to try especially hard to see the little things – the small kindnesses, the serendipities, the breadcrumbs to get you through the day. You'll need them.'

I nod. 'I'll try. I promise.'

She puts her glass down and fixes me in a stare. Those eyes, she can use them like a bear trap. 'Fliss Baker. You're stronger than you think you are.'

I do not feel strong. I feel like a matchstick girl in a gale. I nod again and finish my hot chocolate.

I wake up in a strange bed and panic, not knowing where I am. I'm suffocated by chintzy wallpaper and a poofy mattress with too many pillows. I remember I'm in the B&B, and that it's Christmas morning, and that Mum is in hospital.

For about two seconds I was worry-free.

There's a bathroom on the landing between the rooms. It's unoccupied so I shower while I can. It's not brilliant, but the pressure is better than on the farm and I feel properly clean for the first time in ages. It's a shame I have to wear the same tracksuit and slippers.

I promised to meet Margot for breakfast at seven, so I head down to the bar. There are only two other B&B guests, but Doreen has set out a little buffet with cereal and fruit and she quickly asks if I want white or brown toast. 'Oh, and Merry Christmas, lovey.'

'Merry Christmas,' I say. Whether fate or the universe, I'm glad we're not at the farm. I join Margot in the window seat. 'Morning! Merry Christmas, Margot!'

'To you too. Did you sleep well?'

'I really did. I think yesterday broke me.'

'It was good to escape.'

I nod as Doreen comes to ask how we'd like our eggs. The craving for bacon is strong, but I've come too far to go back now. I order poached eggs and toast.

I feel something poke against my knee and recoil. 'Shh,' Margot says. 'Take it.'

I look down and see she's passing me a bundle wrapped in a napkin. 'What is it?'

'Your real presents are back at the farm, but I didn't think you should be without something to open on Christmas morning.'

'Oh, thank you! I . . . Yours is back at the farm too.' With Mum so sick, I had to make a present run with Danny. On Mum's instructions, I bought Margot a new pair of swamp-green wellies. Sexy.

'It's nothing,' Margot says. I unwrap the bundle and see it's tiny bottles of shampoo and conditioner, a shower cap, a sewing kit and some sachets of hot chocolate.

'Did you steal these?' I whisper.

Margot gives me a sly smile and a wink as Doreen arrives with our pot of coffee. I hide everything under the table and laugh.

'What's so funny?' Doreen asks.

'Nothing!' Margot and I say in unison.

Chapter 40

By the 27th Mum is ready to come home. I watch as Dr Singh takes Margot off into a little room behind the nurses' station. I don't have to be psychic to tell what they're saying. Margot's head falls forward for a moment, her eyes full of awfulness, before she pulls it high, trying extra-hard to be strong.

It's now a matter of days.

The word 'hospice' has been mentioned.

Meh. The farm is basically a hospice. We came here so she could die in peace. What difference does it make if she's surrounded by other sick people.

Mantra time: *It'll be a release, it'll be a relief, she'll be free, she'll be at peace.*

It doesn't help that when I ask how she is, she's just says, 'I'm fine, don't worry about me.' It's like two squirming ferrets wrestling at the bottom of my tummy. One just wants Mum to live forever, selfishly, to keep me happy. The other knows she's in pain and that death is the ultimate painkiller. All the ferrety tumbling is making me feel nauseous.

I look thinner. Not in a good way. A bit gaunt and haggard if I'm honest.

I see Dr Singh slip Margot some pamphlets. I wonder, is it *Living With Loss*, *How to Explain Death to Your Stroppy Teen* or just a brochure for a local hospice? Margot tucks them in her handbag and leads the way out of the office. 'Are we ready?'

'We are,' Mum says. She hoists herself up, now using two sticks to support herself. She's trying so hard, sinking her teeth into life, and it makes me want to cry. But I can't. I gotta be strong. Maybe this is how it happens – the hardening, the scar tissue around the heart – just like Margot warned it would.

The next day is the first time everyone can rehearse. Stepz looks like a proper dance studio now that I've cleared all the crap into one corner and hidden it under a mildewed dustsheet. 'What the bloody hell are you dressed as?' I ask Danny. 'It's not *Fame*.'

'What? If this is the only time I get to do a dance number I want to do it right.' He's wearing a vest, some very short shorts with leggings underneath and neon pink leg warmers. More *The Kids from Lame* than *Fame*.

'Danny Chung, I love you very much,' I say.

'Mwah!' He blows me a kiss.

'You shouldn't really need to warm up,' I tell them, 'but maybe stretch a little bit or something.'

Bronwyn takes me to one side. 'Look at this,' she says, pulling up her sleeve to reveal a charm bracelet. 'Robin gave it to me on Christmas Eve.'

'Oh, Bronwyn,' I breathe, 'that's lovely.' The charms are so cute – a little alien, a book, a star, a telescope.

'I know! But what do I do next?'

'Don't ask me! It's the blind leading the blind. I tried to make out with a librarian, remember.'

She laughs. 'Do you think I should, like, ask him out or something?'

'Yes. Feminism – why not? I think he's sent you a fairly unequivocal message with the bracelet. Just don't be too full-on.'

'What do you mean?'

'I dunno, don't show up in a wedding dress. Ooh . . . go to the cinema. Easy date . . . you don't even have to talk.'

Her eyes light up. 'Genius. You're an actual genius. *Starship Troopers* is out next week.'

'Nothing says romance like big alien bugs.'

'Oh. You think I should suggest that Jennifer Aniston one?'

'Not unless you want your first date to be your last.'

I explain how the routine will work and play them "This Woman's Work" from start to end. 'I love that song,' Robin says. Sophie is already weeping. 'Sophie, I need you to get through this without crying.'

'It's . . . just . . . so . . . sad.'

'I know. But you'll be fine.'

'Sophie, get it together, babes.' Danny passes her a Handy Andie and rolls his eyes.

We rehearse as much as we can. The problem is that we can only do the 'big finish' once, so have to imagine how much of the song it will take up. The track is only 3.38 long and there's a lot to squish into that time. It's going to be tight and, if I'm honest, Sophie and Bronwyn have two left feet. Robin is the surprise; his lanky frame is oddly graceful, it turns out. I subtly suggest he comes to the front.

I bust out the turkey-and-stuffing sandwiches I made for everyone. We had a very late Christmas dinner yesterday at the farm. Mum even managed a tiny bit of solid food. 'Thank you so much for doing this,' I say as we sit in a circle on the studio floor. This is torture: the sandwiches smell so good and I'm stuck with grated cheese and pickle. 'I think it's gonna look really elegant and cool.'

'I am in total awe,' Danny says. 'I had no idea you could dance like that.'

I shrug. 'I started when I was three.'

'Three?'

'Yeah. It . . . It feels good to be dancing again.'

'It's part of who you are,' Robin says quietly in his low, monotone voice. I don't fancy him, he's not my type, but suddenly understand what it is Bronwyn sees in him.

Chapter 41

New Year's Eve comes and goes, as does New Year's Day. I've always celebrated – last year I watched fireworks explode over Big Ben on a private Thames barge with Marina's ludicrous family – but as NYE is all about bidding farewell to one year and welcoming a new one . . . Well, last year is welcome to burn in hell and, as for the next one, I'm keeping it at arm's length.

This year, I watched pretty much the exact same fireworks on the BBC next to Mum. Bless her, she made us wake her from her snooze on the sofa to see the new year in. It's only fireworks: gunpowder and coloured metal salts. Once you've seen one, you've seen them all. I wouldn't want to be anywhere else. Whatever else happens, Mum saw another year.

By the time school starts back on the 5th, we only have a week to perfect my routine. My friends are the *best* and rehearse with me every evening right after sixth period without a word of complaint. I think they're even enjoying it. Initially they were giggly and self-conscious, but now even Sophie can get through the routine without messing around.

I think it's looking pretty good. On the Friday night we have our dress rehearsal. We do the whole routine, again without the big finish. Thom is watching from the back row, clipboard in hand. I suspect, if we even hinted at the end of the piece, he'd try to stop me.

There's no going back. Unless something awful happens in the next twenty-four hours, Mum is well enough to come along for an hour or two, so I'm going to do it and do it BIG. She deserves it. I want it to be better than any other dance she's seen me do. I want it to mean something.

'Take five,' Thom yells. The other acts are a mixed bunch: Danny is doing 'Seasons of Love' from *Rent* and Sophie is singing 'Nothing Compares 2 U'. Without being a total bitch, it certainly doesn't compare to the Sinéad O'Connor version. There are various other acts: Robin is playing an acoustic Green Day song on his guitar and a group of super-quiet girls who I've never spoken to turn out to be pretty awesome hip-hop dancers, and they've choreographed a piece to Salt–N-Pepa.

I grab a bottle of water from my bag and gulp it down. I don't even realise Thom is hovering behind me. 'Fliss, can I just have a quiet word?'

'Sure.'

He guides me to the corner next to the piano. We're in the church hall. It's bitterly cold; apparently the heating's on the blink but a plumber is coming before the show tomorrow night.

'I think you're very brave doing this, Fliss. The dance is about your mum, isn't it?'

I nod. It's pretty obvious.

'Are you sure you want to do something so personal?'

I take another sip of water. 'I don't think anything is any good unless it's personal. Otherwise you're just swinging your arms and legs around. It has to mean something, right?'

381

Now he nods. 'I think you're right. Well put.'

I feel about ten years old. I also want to collapse on him and let it all out, but I need the pent-up emotion to get me through the dance. Every muscle and sinew is wound tight, ready to spring.

But not yet.

Tomorrow.

I had forgotten how nervous I get. It's a fist around my stomach so tight it hurts. I'm doubled up in a chair in the poky back room that's acting as a dressing room. I feel sick, but I know I have to put some fuel in my body or I'm not gonna get through the routine. Luckily, satsumas are in season and I'm managing to eat them one sad segment at a time.

'Are you OK?' Danny asks. He's already opened the show with his *Rent* number. He was major. I watched him from the wings. Mum and Margot are in the second row, on the aisle in case they have to make a quick getaway. Behind them are Dewi and his dad, Dewi, and behind them are Megan's mates Rhiannon and Cerys, which makes me even more nervous. Who invited them?

'I'm fine,' I lie. I really think this feeling will kill me. Then again, I thought that last time.

'Fliss, we don't have to do the ending, you know? We can just do it like we've rehearsed and leave the end off. It'll be just as powerful or whatever.'

'No,' I say more forcefully than I intend to. 'It has to . . . It has to hurt . . . or it's just . . . nothing.' Danny says no more, but looks deep into my eyes. 'I'm sure. I want to do this.'

He draws me into a big hug. Another thing about Danny Chung: he will never not smell of Jean Paul Gaultier's Le Male. Often you smell him before you see him. 'We're ready when you are,' he says.

They're all wearing very simple black trousers and roll-necks with basic black plimsolls – the type I wore for PE in primary school. I'm wearing, in classic ballet style, a white wrap sweater over a black leotard, white tights and my pointe shoes, tied at the ankle.

My hair, controversially, is loose. Again, somewhere, Madame Nyzda is sensing a disturbance in The Force.

Thom sticks his head into the dressing room. 'OK, Fliss Baker and co. to the wings, please. You're next.'

Oh God, I can't do it. I'm going to go on stage and freeze. I'm going to dance like a dustbin. I'm going to fall down. I'm going to be sick. I'm going to be sick and then fall down in the sick.

'Fliss.' Bronwyn takes my hand and squeezes it too tight. 'You can do this. It's going to be so beautiful. Your mum is going to love it. OK?'

She's not leaving any room for disagreement. 'Thank you. Let's go.'

Dewi's friend Matthew is just finishing his stand-up routine. I get the sense it's not very funny and people are laughing out of politeness. He keeps finishing his lines with, 'Am I right?' Always a sign that you're probably wrong in my book.

'Thank you very much and goodnight!' he announces, and I almost feel the collective relief that his set is over. The applause is grateful to say the least.

Thom takes his microphone centre stage. 'And now for our final act of the night. Ladies and gentlemen, please welcome Fliss Baker to the stage!'

The audience applauds again before falling respectfully silent. I take a moment. I breathe.

I drag my chair into the middle of the space. The legs screech as I pull them over the stage. I sit, knees together, back straight and wait for the music to start.

As Kate starts to sing, I rise off the chair, straight into pointe.

I'm light and delicate, my arms aloft, neck rolling, hair tumbling down my back. My steps gaily follow the piano notes. I spin piqué turns.

Kate Bush's haunting vocals echoes all the way around the hall. Aside from her, you could hear a pin drop.

I spin faster. I whip my head around fast, fixing my eyes on the clock at the back of the church hall so I don't get dizzy. I spin faster and faster – so fast I hear a few 'wows' from the audience – and then I stop.

I just stop. I pretend to be tired, out of breath. I crumple. From the sides of the stage my friends emerge. All in black, balaclavas over their faces, they're shadows. I hardly see them against the black backdrop, but I know they're there. They lurk.

From my folded heap, I start again. Taking a deep breath, I compose myself, pull myself tall into first position, my arms perfectly arched in front of my chest.

Off I go again. I spring into pointe and I jeté close to each of the shadows, almost daring them to chase me.

The shadows lunge at me with their black-gloved hands. At first I spin and leap away. Gracefully, with a smile on my face to begin with, but then they come out of the sidelines: crawling and slithering, prowling closer to me.

I take centre stage and create a (hopefully) perfect arabesque: one leg up parallel to the floor, arms elegantly balanced. As rehearsed, Robin takes hold of the airborne leg and pulls me over. I crash down and Danny catches me just before I face-plant the stage. The audience gasps.

Robin drags me across the floor by my leg, but I wriggle free. I scramble to my feet and attempt to resume my dance.

Now Bronwyn grabs my arm, swings me around and I crash into Sophie who lifts me off the floor. I kick my legs in a perfect circle and land again. I pirouette away, only for Robin to grab me around the waist and hurl me to the floor. I roll and unfurl into a balance.

This is the hard part. Well, second hardest. I bend all the way back and kick into a flip. Danny helps me over and back onto my feet.

All four of them close in on me, surrounding me.

They take hold of me and I fall back into their arms. I give in and they've got me. They lift me aloft, my head tipped back. It's disorienting. They turn me around and I see the audience upside down as I am lowered into the chair which Bronwyn has already turned backwards.

I close my eyes, knowing what's coming next.

I hear a buzz, then another, and then another. A sound like wasps. I feel the electric clippers, from Sophie's mum's salon, scrape against my skull.

The audience gasps louder this time. They mutter and cuss. They can't believe what they're seeing. A voice I recognise says, 'Fliss, no!'

Mum.

Too late now. Three blades mow through my hair and I feel it fall away. I open my eyes. People in the crowd cover their shocked mouths with scandalised hands. My head feels lighter and lighter with every second.

Danny taps me with his knee and that's my cue, telling me it's pretty much all gone.

I kick and push and wriggle, fighting the shadows off. I punch them out of the way and clamber to my feet. The shadows recoil, back away from me, scared. Taking extra care as the stage is now covered in my hair, I kick the chair out of my way, and the shadows flee back into the wings.

I rise en pointe one last time. Fingers splayed, I lift my arms to the light. I tiptoe to the front of the stage as the spotlight settles on me.

I lower my arms and bow my head.

The spotlight fades to nothing and the song ends. In the dark of the stage, I reach up and feel the messy, uneven clumps of hair. They've missed whole patches. My scalp feels like Fuzzy-Felt. I can only imagine how I look. I'm guessing it's nothing like Fliss Baker.

There's a breathless, timeless pause before the audience starts to clap and cheer. The lights come back up and many leap to their feet. Their faces seem to say, *Holy shit, that bald girl is out of her mind!* but they seem impressed at my commitment if nothing else.

Through the crowd, I only see Mum. She rolls her eyes, but she's wearing a smile so broad it divides her face in two. 'I loved it,' she mouths, clapping along.

The others join me for a bow and Danny takes my hand on one side. Bronwyn's on the other.

I look to Margot. She smiles and slowly, deliberately, dips her head.

We take a bow.

Chapter 42

Mum died a fortnight after the show.

She spent her last week in a beautiful hospice called Beaufort House so she could have access to nurses and the really top-notch opiates. 'We can make her comfortable,' they told us. It had expansive lawns and ornamental gardens, dusted with snow, that they wheeled her around. There's a fountain, although it's frozen over at the moment. Icicles hang from the stone dolphins, turning them into swordfish.

It was very quiet. Her last words, perhaps appropriately, were, 'Fuck me, I'm tired.' And then she went to sleep. From the outside it looked painless, peaceful. No moaning and groaning. Thank God. I guess that's the best I could have hoped for in the circumstances – easing her away. Like opening my hands and letting a feather go on the breeze.

They didn't move her until Margot and I had had a chance to say goodbye. I sat at her bedside, alone. Margot felt we should each have our moment. I sat in yet another visitor armchair and held her hand, but it was strangely cool. I think we'd said everything we needed to say. She was right, you know, we knew it was coming. And sure enough, it did. I don't think, in the end, she was angry. She lay under a crochet blanket from the farm, to remind her of home.

It's so weird. Even though she was right there, she wasn't there. Not really. Her laugh; her voice; her patient, forgiving sighs . . . all gone. The body in front of me wasn't her. *She'd* gone. *There's a lot to be said for an ending.*

In the end, I didn't look at the body to say goodbye. I closed my eyes and just let myself feel the love I still had. That I will *always* have. I could feel it glowing like a tiny sun in my chest. I floated it up into my heart and mind, my fingers and toes, feeling its warmth for as long as I could. *Remember this, Fliss.* I committed the love to memory, trapped it, so I won't ever be without it.

She lives on inside me now.

Mum had made arrangements with Margot about her funeral. The service itself was very lovely – tasteful and dignified, with bunches of white peonies tied to the end of each pew. So many of her friends and old colleagues came up from London. There was standing room only at the chapel of rest. Uncle Simon brought Grandma Baker, and Doreen came, now that she and Margot were back in touch. The editor of the *London Courier* was there too, a handsome man with silver hair and an Armani suit. He lingered at Margot's side – close but not too close – all the way through the funeral. I guess it's nice for her that he was there.

I lost track of how many times I was compared to Sinéad O'Connor. I guess it's a compliment. Obviously I had the buzzcut tidied up by Sophie's mum at the first opportunity after the show. She seemed more upset that 'such a pretty girl' had shaved her head than the fact my mum was days away from death.

People did nice readings. Mum once made a film about women's shelters, and an abuse survivor from the documentary came and talked about the impact Mum had had on her life. I cried at that bit. I cried again when we had to say goodbye to the coffin in a sad procession. I was last out, so at least no one saw. Mum wanted to be cremated. 'I don't like the idea of being nibbled by worms,' she'd told Margot. I'm glad there wasn't a weird graveside moment.

Today we're scattering her ashes. In silence, but a nice silence, Margot and I follow the winding paths of the woods. My head is freezing, but Danny bought me some lovely leopard-print earmuffs that totally work with my fur-collar coat.

Eventually, even through the muffs, I hear the rush of the waterfall. Helping each other on the steep bits, we edge down the embankment to the water's edge. 'This is where she said,' says Margot.

I'm carrying the ashes in gloved hands. She – well, her 'earthly remains' – are in a sleek steel urn. 'What do we do?' I ask.

Margot looks wistfully up at the waterfall. 'You just let her go. Your mother scattered your grandfather's ashes at Lake Windermere, you know.'

I stall. 'God, it's like tipping her away or something.'

'That's not her.' Margot is typically brusque.

I nod. 'I know.' I unscrew the lid and, after a pause, sprinkle some of ashes out. They're picked up by the wind and the spray from the waterfall. I shake the rest. They twist and twirl on the breeze, snatched away in a hundred different directions.

It's all very that bit in *Pocahontas*. After a moment, the cloud settles on the water and flows away downstream.

A sob breaks free. Damn. I really wanted to keep it together. Margot's wax-jacketed arm snakes around my shoulder and pulls me upright. 'Let yourself feel it,' she reminds me, and gives my arm a squeeze.

I remember the first time I saw these woods, heard the whispers. I wonder if it was destiny calling. This was where we were *meant* to be, just like Margot said. Mum loved it here.

I listen, really strain, for the voices, hoping more than anything that I'll hear a final message from The Beyond. To hear her voice one last time . . .

It's just water.

I can't *hear* them any more, but I do *feel* that fuzzy pink warmth under my skin again. It's all around me. I don't need to hear her. She's *here*.

Chapter 43

I wasn't ready for how empty I'd feel after all the death admin was done. Now it's like BACK TO NORMAL, EVERYONE! But it isn't normal, not even close. The farm feels huge. Mum's absence is very much there: the dent in the sofa cushion; the pile of Jilly Cooper and Martina Cole novels, spines intact; the Welsh Dragon mug neither Margot nor me will use.

I'm actually quite looking forward to going back to school just to be out of the place, to be honest. I board the bus on the first morning back. As ever, Dewi is the only other passenger to begin with. 'H-hello, Fliss.'

'Hi, Dewi.' I sit in the row in front of him.

'Loving the h-hair. It's very . . .'

'Sinéad O'Connor?'

'I was gonna say GI Jane, but yeah, now you mention it, like.'

'Ha! At least that's a new one. And who doesn't want to look like Demi Moore?' It's already growing back. I have no intention of keeping it *this* short, the sheer amount of eye make-up and earring required to de-butch my head is obscene. That said, I do feel . . . lighter. That hair, now I think about it, was, *old*. I feel free of it.

'I thought your dance was amazing, by the way.'

'Thank you.'

'I . . . I'm sorry I didn't come to the funeral. It . . . It was D-Dad. He said it was a bit much, maybe.'

I frown. 'That's OK. A bit much?'

His big conker eyes fill with sadness. 'Well, you know, it's only a couple of years since we lost Mam to cancer. I think he just thinks it's all bit too soon, like churning up old feelings or something.'

I stiffen in my seat. 'Oh God, Dewi, I'm so sorry. I had no idea.' I had no idea, because I never asked. I suddenly realise that I know almost nothing about a guy I've shared a bus ride with most days for the last five months. 'What . . . ? What type?'

'Breast cancer. It ran in her family.'

I wince. 'That like totally blows.'

'Yeah, cancer can feck right off.' We share in that sentiment for a moment. 'I'm not going to say, "I know what you're going through," because obviously I didn't know your mum at all, but—'

'Thank you,' I say, stopping him before I cry and snot all over his clean jumper.

'I didn't even know your m-m-mam was ill, like,' he goes on. 'It was only when I went to speak to Mrs Evans about Megan that she told me.'

I frown. 'What? Megan? What do you mean?'

'After you went f-full Ripley and hit her in the face with that mug. I told Mrs Evans that she'd been picking on you for weeks.'

Oh my God. I'd . . . Well, I'd just assumed that was Thom. 'Oh, Dewi!' I say, hand on heart. 'I had no idea . . . I thought . . . Well, it doesn't matter now. You saved my ass. You have no idea. I could have been expelled!' I remember the way Rick Sawyer stepped in to save Margot that night in the graveyard. I guess sometimes there really are knights in shining armour, even if we don't see them charging in on their steed.

He's blushing ferociously. It's very sweet. 'It's nothing, like,' he says, looking down. 'It was the r-right thing to do.'

'Well, thank you. I really mean that.'

His hand is holding the bar on the top of my seat. I place mine over the top of his. I'm wearing my gloves, so it's not quite skin to skin, but I still feel a very lovely, toasty heat.

'Fliss . . .' he starts, and I somehow know what's coming next.

'Not yet,' I say, cutting him off.

He nods, understanding. Suddenly he rummages in his rucksack. He thrusts a Curly Wurly in my face. 'I'm still working my way through my selection boxes. Do you want my Curly Wurly?'

I laugh. I can't help it. 'Well, there's an offer I can't refuse! Yes, Dewi, I will gladly accept your Curly Wurly.' I unwrap the chocolate bar. 'But this doesn't mean anything, OK? I just like Curly Wurlys.'

He grins broadly. 'Who doesn't?'

Danny and Bronwyn are waiting for me in the library as we arranged by SMS. All of us got pay-as-you-go mobiles for Christmas. It's so cool. How we managed without them is anyone's guess. Mine has snap-on covers which I can mix and match to coordinate with whatever I'm wearing.

They greet me with big bear hugs. I haven't seen them since the wake, which we held at the pub in town. 'Are you OK?' Bronwyn asks.

'Working on it.'

'There'll be a new OK,' she replies, and I know what she means. Me, Bronwyn and now Dewi: The No-Mum Club.

'We got you something,' Danny says.

'Oh, you shouldn't have.' I take my seat at the table.

'It's not a present like that,' he explains, and hands me a brochure. I look blankly at it like he's just placed a dead kipper in my palm. 'There's a school of ballet and contemporary dance in Swansea.'

'Danny . . .'

'Fliss! You have to! You can't stop now, you're too good. You're denying the world a beautiful gift if you don't dance.'

I roll my eyes. 'OK, I think that's taking it a bit far.'

'We called them,' Bronwyn says, eyes twinkling with definite scampiness. 'They have advanced classes. They said they'd be happy for you to come to a taster session.'

The fact they've gone to such effort makes me feel very loved and Pop-Tart-gooey inside. Do I feel like dancing? Hell no. But should I at least *try*? My duvet is like that snake in the *Jungle Book*, luring me to crawl under it and hibernate until the millennium. I should probably resist its call. 'Guys! This is so lovely! You know what, maybe I will. Keep my feet busy, and stay out of Margot's way.'

Danny frowns. 'Are things not good?'

'Things are . . . I don't know. It's just new. But I've had an idea for a little project that I want to try out first before I do any more dancing.'

'What idea?' Bronwyn asks.

'I don't wanna say until I know more. It might come to nothing. Do you know what time the town library's open until?'

'Six thirty, I think.'

'Cool.'

Danny smiles slyly, taking a sip of his tea. 'Guess where Bronwyn's going tonight?'

My mouth flops open, goldfish style. '*Starship Troopers*?'

'Yep! The seven o'clock showing at the Odeon in Swansea. We're gonna get a Pizza Hut before too!'

I clap my hands together. 'Bronwyn, this is huge! I can't believe you didn't message me!'

'I didn't want to bother you . . .'

'Don't be stupid! I could use the good news! What are you going to wear? Don't get garlic bread, whatever you do!'

'Are you gonna sit in the back row and French him?' Danny asks, and I squeal. We're not there yet, but The New OK is coming along.

I make my way to the public library straight after school. There isn't one in Llanmarion (a little van comes once a week), so I catch a bus into the next town. The library, I'm told, was meant to be a temporary building while they renovated the old one, but it's been here now since 1982. It's a flat-roof block with pebbledash walls and a zigzag disabled ramp leading up to the front door.

The automatic doors open with a screech and I'm greeted by much-too-hot central heating and the smell of slightly baked pages. I love library books. I'd put all my books in plastic covers if I could.

A bank of chunky beige PCs is located at the far end past the reference section. There are five computers but only one is being used, by a teenage boy with a bad proto-moustache a bit like a thin gerbil snoozing on his upper lip. He's looking at pictures of Melinda Messenger. 'Are you allowed to do that?' I ask.

He springs back (thankfully it's still in his pants), grabs his rucksack and flees. I feel a little bad, but giggle to myself.

I pull a notepad, and Margot's diary – slightly charred – and a cocoa-scented pen out of my satchel. I give the mouse a wiggle. A blank blue screen stares back at me. God, I don't even know where to start. I click on Internet Explorer, take a deep breath and begin.

Chapter 44

Bronwyn was so right. It takes a few weeks, but a new normal has settled over the farm, popping up alongside the snowdrops, crocuses and then daffodils. The fields thaw in time for lambing season. I do everything I can to help because, let's face it, who doesn't love little tiny lambs? Some of them need hand-rearing with bottles. I swear I catch Peanut looking on with jealousy a couple of times from his sty. Soon it'll be time for Peanut to make his own babies.

That's pretty weird. I don't wanna think about it. Obviously now he's a GIANT. I couldn't hug him even if I wanted to.

I'm still sad. It goes without saying. But now I am used to the sadness. I can tolerate it. Sometimes I even forget it's there.

I go to a taster dance class, mostly to get Danny and Bronwyn off my case. It's way less stuck-up than Madame Nyzda's school – it's in a brand-new shiny sports centre – although the girls (and guys) are just as talented. Angel, the instructor, a gorgeous, willowy woman who looks a little like Tyra Banks, quickly spots my ballet training. 'Your technique is excellent,' she comments. 'Really strong.'

'Thank you,' I say, having a sip of water as we take a break. I ruffle my hair, which looks pretty cute now in a pixie-ish way.

On my way back in, I stop outside the contemporary dance class in progress in the smaller studio. I watch a pair of girls working on a routine. I can't take my eyes off them. It's so much more dynamic, acrobatic and, I suppose, shocking. It's unpredictable, that's what it is.

At the end of the session, I ask about the contemporary classes. 'Mondays at six,' Angel tells me. 'Sure you don't wanna do advanced ballet though?'

'I think I'd like to try something new.'

'Suit yourself. Either way, you're very welcome; we always need new blood.' She shakes my hand.

I go to the library after school when I need to, beavering away on my little project. I make like a hundred calls on my new mobile, having to buy top-up cards every couple of days sometimes.

But I'm getting there.

I sort everything – the printouts and letters and phone numbers – into a pink plastic wallet for safekeeping. I've done as much as I can. Only one thing left to do.

With the wallet tucked under my arm, I get off the bus and walk down the drive past the old stables and pigsty. The sun is shining and it's warm enough to carry my coat. The Land Rover is parked up so I know Margot is home. I enter through the front door. 'Margot?' I call. There's no response. I yell upstairs but, again, nothing.

I walk through to the kitchen and look out of the back windows. I see her grey head bobbing up and down past the chicken coop.

'Margot,' I call, stepping out of the back door.

'Oh, hello there.' She's pruning the rose bushes. She doesn't look up. 'Don't they look lovely?' She tilts a creamy white rose towards me. 'And what a lovely spring day.'

I didn't really see it. I've hardly been outside and I've come straight from the library. I don't say anything.

'Felicity, what's wrong? I've come to know you well enough to know when you're hiding something. Is it school again? It'd be a shame to have to move you to the private school now, but if that's what it takes . . .'

'It's not school,' I say. 'School is fine. In fact, I'm actually doing quite well again.'

She lets her secateurs swing around her wrist. 'Then why have you been staying so late? I assumed they were detentions and that you were forging my signature on the letters home. I almost admired the effort to conceal it.'

'No. It's not that.' I take a monumentally deep breath and begin. 'Margot, I really hope you're not going to be cross with me.'

'Your tone suggests I almost certainly will be, but go on.'

'I've been late home because I've been at the library using the Internet.' I hand her the pink wallet. 'OK, here goes. Look, I remembered the name of your midwife – Trudy Mayhew – and I did some digging. You know, birth certificates and that. I found out that all adopted babies had to be registered, even if it didn't state the birth parent's names.'

Margot leafs through the documents I've given her. Her hands are shaking, but she says nothing. Oh God, if she's going to be angry, I just want it over with.

'Here's the thing. I had the date, and I knew Trudy's name, and it was enough. She even logged the birth as "Baby Christopher". It was a start. Then I went to a charity . . . they're called Family Detectives . . . and they try to trace people's birth parents.'

Margot finally looks up at me, her face ashen. 'Felicity, what are you trying to say?'

Deep breath. 'Margot, he's looking for you.' I just about keep my voice steady. 'Christopher. Well, he's called Giles, but he tried to trace you about ten years ago. Your family hid you pretty well, and obviously he didn't have the details I had –' Margot's hand flies up to cover her mouth – 'but he wants to be found.'

The pink wallet falls to the paving stones with a slap and the papers scatter. Margot says nothing for a moment before her breathing starts to quiver and shake. Her shoulders crumple inwards. 'My Christopher? You found my Christopher?'

I nod, still not quite sure if she's happy or livid.

And then the first tear escapes her eye. 'Oh, Fliss. I never thought . . . I thought I'd never . . .'

'It's OK,' I say. I take both her hands, because I don't imagine we'll ever be the hugging type. She squeezes them. I look her dead in the eye. 'Just let yourself feel it,' I say.

Margot covers her eyes with her hands and weeps. She rests her head on my shoulder and lets herself cry in the rose garden where no one else will ever know but me.

Acknowledgements

Thank you, as ever, to the whole wonderful team at Hot Key Books and Bonnier Zaffre, especially Emma Matthewson and Jane Harris. Thanks also to Jo Williamson and Sallyanne Sweeney.

Since the conception of *Margot & Me* in 2015 there have been fairly obvious changes in my life, and my family and friends have been wonderful at keeping everything normal. Thank you to old friends who've known me since the start and to new friends, especially the teams at Booktrust, *Glamour* and *Attitude Magazine*, and Stonewall UK.

Thank you Non Pratt and Lisa Williamson for your feedback.

Once again, love to all my readers old and new. I knew you'd be cool, and you were.

Juno x

Juno Dawson

Queen of Teen 2014 Juno Dawson is the multi award-winning author of dark teen thrillers *Hollow Pike*, *Cruel Summer*, *Say Her Name* and *Under My Skin*, written under the name James Dawson. In 2015, she released her first contemporary romance, *All of The Above*. Her first non-fiction book, *Being A Boy*, tackled puberty, sex and relationships, and a follow-up for young LGBT people, *This Book Is Gay*, came out in 2014.

Juno is a regular contributor to *Attitude*, *GT*, *Glamour* and the *Guardian* and has contributed to news items concerning sexuality, identity, literature and education on the BBC's *Woman's Hour*, *Front Row*, *This Morning* and *Newsnight*. She is a School Role Model for the charity Stonewall, and also works with charity First Story to visit schools serving low income communities. Juno's titles have received rave reviews and her books have been translated into more than ten languages.

In 2015, Juno announced her transition to become a woman, having lived thus far as the male author James Dawson. She writes full time and lives in Brighton. Follow Juno on Twitter: @junodawson or on Facebook at Juno Dawson Books.

HAVE YOU READ THESE OTHER BRILLIANT BOOKS BY JUNO DAWSON?

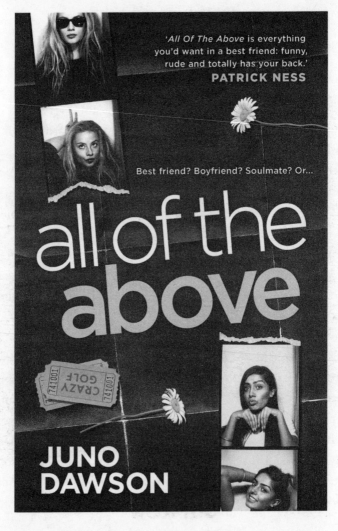

HOT KEY BOOKS

Thank you for choosing a Hot Key book.

If you want to know more about our authors
and what we publish, you can find us online.

You can start at our website

www.hotkeybooks.com

And you can also find us on:

We hope to see you soon!